RAZOR MOUTH

A NOVEL OF **BLOOD** IN THE **SEA**

HOWARD BUTCHER

DEEP
REEF
BOOKS

Deep Reef Books

ISBN 978-1-7379603-0-0

Razormouth: A Novel of Blood in the Sea

©2022 by Howard Butcher

All Rights Reserved

Cover design by Erik Hollander

Bimini Islands map illustration by Tracee Flenard

Deep Reef Books is an imprint of Conservatarian Press
in partnership with
Round Rock Media, LLC

Published in the United States of America

For Sue, Avery, Nolan, Evan,
and
My Students

Bimini Islands
the Bahamas

N
W   E
S

Coral Reefs

Mangroves

East Bimini

Gulf Stream

North Bimini

North Sound

Mangroves

Bailey Town

Lagoon Flats

Bonefish Hole

Alice Town

Harbor

Great Bahama Bank

Coral Reefs

South Bimini

Round Rock

Turtle Rocks

Gorgon Channell

Seabrook's Long Line

SS Sapona

RAZOR MOUTH

A NOVEL OF **BLOOD** IN THE **SEA**

Part One

"The sea, once it casts its spell, holds one in its net of wonder forever."
—Jacques Cousteau

Chapter 1
Bimini

Cael Seabrook took the morning flight from Miami to Bimini in the Bahamas, early summer 1983.

It was his first time flying, his first time leaving the USA, and his first time seeing an ocean from the sky. The world was fresh and new and extraordinary; he felt higher than the airplane he rode in. Like he'd hit the mother of all jackpots.

He was a twenty-eight-year-old ichthyologist flying into the best future he could imagine.

The view through the window didn't seem quite real. He knew this region of the Atlantic from textbooks, classes, charts, and scientific papers, but seeing was believing. A mile beneath the wings of the plane, hazy blue radiance spanned from horizon to horizon. There was no land anywhere—just deep, boundless ocean, liquid brilliance shining back the sun, etched with tiny waves and ribbons of foam.

The Chalks seaplane banked slowly to the left. The propeller engines made a loud *burring* sound. Clouds wisped past the windows and bright sunlight suddenly filled the cabin. Small dots of land, edged with surf, gradually appeared in the east.

He gripped the armrest and angled his face close to the window, determined to get a glimpse of his new life. The small dots of land were the Bimini islands. Only from the sky could you truly appreciate how they sat in the midst of one of the earth's greatest undersea rivers: the Gulf Stream.

The Gulf Stream flowed like a gigantic artery, bigger than the Mississippi River, between Florida and the Bahamas. The current ran six thousand feet deep and stirred the ocean depths, transporting marine life, nutrients, and heat from the Gulf of Mexico to Bimini, up the southeast coast of the U.S., then thousands of miles east across the Atlantic Ocean, where it warmed the western coasts of Scotland and Norway.

The massive underwater river continuously bathed the Bimini islands with a steady supply of pelagic marine life.

It also brought large, deep-water predators right up to the shallows.

Only seven miles long and half a mile wide, North Bimini looked more like a spit of sand than a true island. It was less populated than most college campuses, with fewer than two thousand citizens. But what made Seabrook catch his breath were the incredible colors of the sea. Water so dazzling it hurt his eyes and made him squint. No picture, no postcard could capture what he saw in that moment.

It was as if God had scattered gemstones across the face of the ocean.

The deep water glittered lapis lazuli, the water near the coast radiated topaz, and the wading shallows shimmered blue diamonds. The lagoon and flats to the east and out to the Great Bahama Bank and Cat Cay were shades of turquoise. All of it glowed like a cosmic invitation, an underwater world to go down into and explore—full of extraordinary life.

The Caribbean Sea.

The plane flew closer and he could see the black silhouette of a large manta ray swimming up the shoreline.

"Look down there! What's that *thing* in the water?" gasped a woman seated in front of him. She wore enormous mirror-lensed sunglasses and orange lipstick. She held a motion sickness bag in her hand—at the ready. She threw up again. She sprayed perfume all over to cover the smell. And failed. A smell like rotten fish and flowers filled the cabin.

"That's a devil ray," her husband said.

"I'm not going in the water with *that!*"

"They are harmless," Seabrook said, just loud enough for them to hear.

The plane began to circle the Bimini islands as the pilot waited for clearance to land. The manta ray slipped from view.

The couple argued in lowered voices. She whined, "I don't give a shit. Who's *he*? What the *hell* does he know?"

Seabrook gazed out the window and felt his heart thump faster; he couldn't wait to get to work. Years of hardcore study for his bachelor's and master's degrees (too many all-nighters to count) had paid off. A month earlier he had been accepted to the Ph.D. program at the Rosenstiel School of Marine and Atmospheric Science in southern Florida. He'd won a research assistantship that gave him a full ride. His adviser and boss, Dr. Nixon, a world-renowned shark scientist, had sent him money for the plane tickets and told him to report for work in Bimini. A group of scientists aboard the research vessel *Colombus Islen* were expecting him.

Seabrook had grown up in upstate New York and earned his undergrad and master's degrees at Syracuse University. He didn't look like a scientist or an intellectual, except perhaps in the brightness of his blue eyes. With red hair, white skin that burned easily, and an athletic rough-hewn six-foot-two-inch frame, he looked like a farmhand or maybe a Celtic rugby player. Like he was used to hard labor, dirt, and sweat.

He was, in fact, a rugby player. And his nose had been broken three times in as many years, but he'd never once left the field—not even when the cartilage in his nose felt like shards of broken glass scraping together, or his eyes watered like a squalling baby's. He just wiped the dark blood on his jersey sleeve and played through the pain. Now his nose looked misshapen, like a boxer's. When he ran his finger down the bridge, the cartilage traced left, then right, then a little more right. Permanently crooked. In the future his fiancée would say it was cute, that it gave him character. And she would kiss it.

His ability to grind through pain and adversity had first become evident during high school wrestling. In eleventh and twelfth grade, he'd had corrective braces on his teeth because his right cuspid and lateral incisor had grown in slanted sideways and made it hard to chew food on that side of his mouth.

During most practices and matches, he'd get cross-faced or smashed in the mouth by his opponent. This was before orthodontists issued their athletic clients mouth guards and protective wax. Consequently, the soft tissue inside his lips was pulped, and parts of his inner cheek were cut to ribbons against the sharp steel and wire. Some opponents intentionally hit his mouth to take him off his game. He just gave them a bloody smile—and continued brawling.

The cuts inside his mouth didn't heal all season, and turned into awful canker sores that were gouged and reopened every time he wrestled. He never complained, and won the New York state tournament in the 195-pound weight class during his senior year.

When Syracuse's wrestling program tried to recruit him, he resisted. This made his father angry as hell. He couldn't understand why his son was saying no to big time NCAA Division I sports (rugby was only a club sport) and a potential athletic scholarship, or why he was attracted to a career that paid peanuts.

Old friends told him that becoming a marine biologist was the dumbest idea he'd ever had. They reminded him that he sunburned easily and got seasick when he went on a boat, that it would be a life of endless vomiting. It was true, he had to wear a Dramamine patch or he became violently ill.

Even his rugby buddies, over pitchers of beer, mocked his plan and said he would probably end up unemployed and uselessly overeducated —or, if he was lucky, would get a low-paying job as an adjunct professor at Shithole U in Armpitville. He didn't let any of the naysayers stop him.

Seabrook was stubborn as a pit bull on a bone. He had different priorities. Despite his love of rugby and wrestling, he wanted a life of the mind. As a kid he'd read Jules Verne's *Twenty Thousand Leagues Under the Sea* and religiously watched *The Undersea World of Jacques Cousteau* on TV. As he grew older, his interest in marine science and knowledge had continued and become more serious. Books—like Charles Darwin's *On the Origin of Species* and Aristotle's *Nicomachean Ethics*—had changed him profoundly and also changed his expectations and goals.

He wanted an occupation that had intellectual depth and heft and that brought him to the ocean. Also, perhaps more important, he sensed an energy within himself greater and more enduring than his finite physical body.

As corny and old-fashioned as it sounded, he wanted to follow Socrates's advice and develop his mind and spirit—to pursue knowledge, wisdom, and the improvement of his soul. Marine science and teaching would be his life's work. He couldn't imagine a more beautiful future.

The Chalks seaplane vibrated loudly as it began its final descent. The window gave another perfect view of the islands and how the windward shore declined dramatically into deep blue water, where the Gulf Stream flowed north through the deep ocean trench of the Florida Straits.

Because of Bimini's geographical good fortune, big-game fish cruised very close to land: marlin, tuna, sailfish, wahoo, mako shark, and other species. The fish migrated north from the spawning waters in the Gulf of Mexico and the Caribbean Sea and followed the warm Gulf Stream up to the Atlantic. Many of the fish ran heavier than a thousand pounds.

All that traffic attracted apex predators.

And sharks were not the only things that hunted in Bimini.

The islands' extraordinary empty beaches and world-class fishing put a glamorous mask over an ugly reality: a vicious underworld of drug trafficking.

The island served as a superhighway for illegal smuggling. During Prohibition, from 1920 to 1933, smugglers sneaked rum into the U.S. from Bimini.

The smuggling had continued after Prohibition, but instead of rum it was now drugs. The Miami newspapers and nightly TV news reported that the Bahamas were a key transshipment point for the cocaine traffic coming from Colombia. And the Bimini islands were the very last stop before the United States. A mere forty-eight miles across the Florida Straits. Drug runners used speedboats to run cocaine into South Florida inlets and would return to Bimini with millions of dollars in cash. The round trip took only a few hours in good weather.

And like the giant marlin swimming near shore followed by sharks, the ability to make billions of dollars brought death in its wake: the Dores and Medellín Cartels fighting for territory and terrorizing South Florida and the Bahamas.

Reports of shootings and drug-related torture killings were a staple of the nightly news in Miami. There were so many homicides, the city had become known as the "murder capital of America," and the U.S. Drug Enforcement Administration created a special task force to work with the Miami-Dade Police Department.

Also, the city morgue had to rent a refrigerated truck to store corpses, because the medical examiners couldn't keep up with the number of bodies coming in from the drug war.

But across the Florida Straits, in the Bahamas, crime reports were virtually nonexistent. Bimini had no local news.

Besides, all evidence of criminal activity usually disappeared under the waves.

The Chalks seaplane abruptly landed in the harbor at Alice Town. The amphibian craft bounced, then wallowed down into the water with a dragging, quicksand-sinking feeling. Then the seaplane lowered its wheels and drove up the short ramp onto land like a massive sea beast crawling onto shore.

Once the propellers stopped spinning, the passengers began filing out. Seabrook crouched and ducked his head to fit through the doorway, then stood up straight and stretched to his full six feet two inches.

From the top of the stairs next to the plane, he gazed out over coconut palms and Australian pines at the magnificent clear water of the harbor. Everything looked so different from his life in New York—no crowds, no malls, no traffic, no skyscrapers—it felt like a different planet.

The air seemed to vibrate with damp heat and sunlight.

He paused and took his first sweet breath of the Bahamas.

This was a shark scientist's paradise.

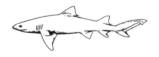

After going through the Customs Office, he was greeted by three scientists waiting to shuttle him to the research ship. One was an attractive young woman with black hair.

As he followed the scientists to the Zodiac boat tied nearby, he had no idea that he'd just met his future fiancée.

Chapter 2
The Torch of Knowledge

The next summer, after two semesters of classes at Rosenstiel, Seabrook returned to Bimini with his fiancée, Aja. They were conducting fieldwork for their respective doctoral dissertations. It was a stunningly beautiful time, like an early honeymoon, with just the two of them in a rental house overlooking a lagoon. They spent every day in the sea doing what they loved, enjoying the tropical island, enjoying each other, and starting a life together.

Their research was focused on different organisms. She studied venomous cone snails in reef habitats and also kept two specimen tanks in their rental house, in order to compare the Indo-Pacific species (*Conus geographus*) to the Caribbean species (*Conus mus*).

Seabrook tracked juvenile lemon sharks (*Negaprion brevirostris*) to discover the activity space parameters, home range, diel activity rhythms, and habitat selection of the subadults of the species in the lagoon and North Sound. He also conducted an age and growth study for which he caught, tagged, and released adult sharks of all kinds in the open ocean.

Their work had gone well for weeks. The ocean and the weather had been mild and sunny. The only concern was that it had not rained on the island for almost two months. The residential cisterns that supplied every house with fresh water were running low. But everyone expected it would rain soon.

A little after midnight, Seabrook drove the Jon Boat, a twelve-foot-long, flat-bottomed skiff made of marine aluminum, across the shallow flats of the North Sound. The sea was calm and glass smooth. He felt tired and was glad his night's work was done. The soft night air, the breath of the ocean rising from the water, made him drowsy.

He drove towards their rented house just north of Bailey Town, a small, quiet Caribbean shantytown with brightly colored houses. Everything looked black in the night except for the dim lights of a couple of the neighboring houses. He steered towards the shore lights and knew his dock would become visible when he got close.

The house served as a research field station and had a small T-shaped plank dock that jutted out into the channel. The channel was narrow and ten feet deep, which allowed medium-size craft to travel up the western shoreline of the lagoon without running aground. The flats were shallow, four feet deep or less, and grew even shallower in the North Sound.

As he drove along, he looked forward to drying his feet. While working, his legs and feet were always waterlogged. They came out of the water-filled rubber boots pruney and white. Letting his feet dry and return to normal was part of his post-tracking ritual. He'd come to think of dry feet as a great luxury.

Seabrook had just spent six hours tracking one juvenile lemon shark he'd previously caught and surgically implanted with an ultrasonic transmitter. It was a young pup, two feet long.

He had waded, thigh deep, in the shallow water of the North

Sound towing the Jon Boat and holding a manual underwater receiver with a hydrophone that detected the ping of the shark's transmitter. He determined the telemetered shark's location by the strength of the signal and key landmarks in the lagoon.

Later, he would use the collective data to plot the range of its travel. He couldn't run the motor to drive the Jon Boat after the tracking started, because the engine noise could interfere with the animal's natural behavior. So he silently dragged the boat after him and walked/waded.

It was hard work towing the boat. The wind and tide always pushed it one way or another. And there was always the risk of stepping on stingrays. Although he wore rubber boots, stingray barbs could stab through. He'd been lucky so far. All the stingrays had raced off without barbing him.

When he stood in the shallow lagoon, listening and following the ping of an implanted transmitter, he concentrated so hard on the small shark he was tracking that sometimes he felt connected to the fish—and also connected to its world. Like there was an invisible thread joining their beings together.

He could picture the shark's distinctive appearance: yellow-brown back, ivory-cream underside, a secondary dorsal fin the same size as the first, and cunning cat-like eyes—vertical pupils set against amber gold.

He knew the tangled maze of tendril-like mangrove roots it swam betwixt and through, the changing tide flowing in or out of the sound, the fluctuating temperature of the water, the cool moon or burning sun, the wind blurring and ruffling the surface of the lagoon, the young shark gliding inches above marine meadows of turtle and manatee grass, eating grunts or silver mojarra and resting motionless, gills pumping, on the sand floor.

Seabrook usually would track an individual shark for six hours, but sometimes as long as twenty-four hours (which he'd done twice this summer). He frequently spent more time with sharks than he did with human beings, including Aja.

When the wind died, swarms of mosquitoes made the night miserable. He rarely saw any other boats on the flats, and never after dark. It was quiet, solitary work. Tonight, as usual, he'd been alone in the shallow water, but he'd collected some good data. Collecting good data made his soul leap for joy—*touching the torch of knowledge*.

Researchers already knew a great deal about the form, function, and anatomy of the lemon shark—its biology and natural history. It was a truly beautiful creature, and knowing about its exquisite design and biology only made it more impressive to Seabrook and added to its mystique.

He knew that lemon sharks' eyes worked very similarly to human eyes with rods and cones for detecting light; he knew about the special sensing organs known as the ampullae of Lorenzini that allowed the shark to navigate and sense the electromagnetic fields around prey, about its diet, how its skeleton was made of calcified cartilage (not bone), the biology of its birthing process, the dermal denticles that were actually small teeth that made its hide incredibly tough, and how pregnant females participated in natal homing (aka philopatry) like salmon returning to their birthplace to drop their pups.

When he compiled, collated, graphed, and analyzed his new data, he would understand something that humankind had been entirely ignorant of before. A new fragment of knowledge already had started to emerge: juvenile lemon sharks never ventured into the open sea.

Remarkably, they remained in very shallow water, even hiding in the mangroves, for the first two or three years of their lives.

Seabrook was beginning to understand the preferred habitat and home range that lemon shark pups required during their most vulnerable stage of life.

The mangroves served as a kind of nursery for juveniles but also for many other species of marine life. As they grew larger, the sharks ventured into deeper and deeper water, until finally they were big enough to swim out in the Gulf Stream.

Why would juvenile lemon sharks keep to the mangrove shallows in this way? What good or benefit could they derive from this behavior?

At least part of the answer seemed obvious. Big predators couldn't swim in a foot and a half of water. Sharks were cannibals, and lemon shark pups probably segregated themselves to stay alive.

Chapter 3
Predator Paradise

Seabrook drove the Jon Boat off the flats into the channel that led down to Alice Town and the harbor. The outboard chugged steadily, and the sea rushed past the aluminum gunwales.

Heavy clouds swept across the sky and the moon, making the night very dark. The tide flowed swiftly in, deepening the channel and lagoon by the minute. You could almost hear the lagoon sigh with relief as the North Sound inhaled fresh, cool ocean into its puke-warm, oxygen-deprived shallows.

As he approached his dock he saw a strange lump on it. Maybe a bag of trash? Also, a cigarette boat he'd never seen before had been tied crookedly to the front side. Like it had been parked in a rush. A high-performance speedboat—the kind used for running drugs to Miami at speeds of up to eighty miles per hour. Roughly thirty feet long, with a black hull and orange highlights. Just like the ones featured in the opening credits of the TV show *Miami Vice*.

What the hell? He felt himself getting angry but also was touched by a peculiar sense of dread. The speedboat was tied off in his normal spot.

Only four people ever used this dock and he knew their vessels by sight: Aja and himself; their landlord Reverend Bastareaud (who kept a small skiff); and occasionally Dr. Nixon when he brought equipment from Miami in an Aquasport boat.

On this evening just two regular vessels were docked: the Whaler Aja and he used, and Bastareaud's skiff.

He sat up straighter and steered the Jon Boat closer.

His eyes went back to the lump on the dock.

It was a man lying facedown.

The feeling of dread grew stronger.

I hope you're just drunk, Seabrook thought. Maybe the guy had had too much Bacardi at the Compleat Angler bar and driven his boat here in a raging stupor. He wouldn't be the first drunk captain on the island this week.

Seabrook angled the Jon Boat to another slip and killed the engine. The aluminum skiff bumped gently off the wood pilings while he grabbed hold and tied her to the dock.

The old wood creaked as he stepped on the planks. Even though he was a large man, he moved with quickness. He walked close to the motionless body.

"Hey buddy? You awake?"

No response. He resisted the urge to nudge him with his foot.

Seabrook spoke louder. "Hey buddy? You awake?"

Still no response. This was real trouble.

He looked around to see if anything else was out of place. He thought he heard a person move and draw a breath. Maybe someone hiding in the tall grass by the shed, or under the dock.

He checked and saw nothing. He stood absolutely still, listening intently, assessing the situation.

Water lapped at the little beach, and dry palm fronds clattered in the night breeze. The tide continued rising, a gentle stirring around the pilings, and creating a barely audible ocean whisper.

Seabrook turned on his flashlight and pointed it at the man for a better look. His heart quickened—there was blood around him; the guy looked dead. Black hair, brown skin, dirty blue T-shirt, and jeans. Late twenties. The corpse lay with one arm dangling in the water. The tidal current tugged gently on the dead man's arm.

Seabrook saw that the hand was missing. The forearm ended in raw meat.

There were teeth marks almost up to the elbow. A shark feeding on carrion. He'd once seen a bull shark cruising in the channel right off the dock. He glanced at the water to see if the scavenger was still around.

Nothing at the surface. It was too dark to see down into the water.

Looking back at the dead man, it seemed evident that the shark hadn't killed him. The dock around his torso was stained with blood, as if he had a serious wound on his underside. The man probably had been stabbed or shot, then died on the dock and dropped his hand into the water. Seabrook didn't want to turn him over and confirm the cause of death, or touch him in any way. He also didn't want to see the corpse's face. He didn't want that memory in his brain.

Who had killed him? Was the murderer still around?

For a moment Seabrook felt paralyzed. Nothing like this had ever happened before, and he didn't know what to do.

Then he saw the bloody footprints going up the dock to the house.

A second man.

Aja! His fiancée and colleague was in the house by herself.

Pointing the flashlight, Seabrook followed the prints at a trot. The old wooden planks of the dock creaked underfoot.

The bloody footprints had been made with medium-size bare feet. Definitely a second man. The dead man on the dock had sneakers on.

At the end of the dock, he ran into the sand-and-gravel backyard and followed the blood to his and Aja's pink Bahamian house. A small, two-bedroom rental home with one bathroom. It was made of concrete to stand up to hurricane weather. A clothesline for drying laundry stretched across one side of the yard.

On Bimini they were isolated from the outside world. There was no telephone or TV inside the house. If a person wanted to make a telephone call from the island, they had to walk to the tiny phone station during normal business hours and hope the system was working that day. Also, the electricity sometimes went out, as the island's power grid broke down frequently. Seabrook and Aja used a backup gas generator in such emergencies—Aja had two saltwater specimen tanks in the living room that needed continuous power for the pumps and halide lights. They also had a large freezer for frozen vegetables and meat. In part of the freezer they kept mackerel and bonito: shark bait for the long line.

The bloody prints led up the back steps to the sliding glass door to the living room. Blood also was smudged on the glass door.

He turned off his flashlight.

Sick fear and adrenaline made him jittery.

He leaned forward and peeked through the glass door.

Aja had the first-aid kit open on the table. She was crouched in front of a Latino man sitting in a chair, naked except for bloody underwear—skinny, with short black hair.

He looked like he'd escaped from hell. Desperate and in pain, shiny with sweat, and bleeding from gunshot wounds. Even without the blood, the man would've looked gruesome, because he had no ears—just two holes encircled with ugly scar tissue. Like he'd been tortured and had his ears cut off. It must have happened some time ago, because the wounds had completely healed. The Earless Man held a black pistol with a silencer, pointed across the room away from Aja. His clothes lay in a red pile on the floor.

She crouched in front of him like an angel ministering to a wounded monster, cleaning and bandaging his shoulder. He'd been shot twice. It looked like she'd already bandaged his leg. She was a certified EMT and knew what she was doing.

She wore her poker face and seemed to be talking in a friendly voice. The man nodded at what she said. She smiled a little.

Everything seemed calm. Like it would be okay—as long as nothing agitated the Earless Man with the gun.

Seabrook felt a pang of affection for her, and at the same time was crazy with fear at the danger she was in.

Aja was everything to him. A small, pretty woman with deep black eyes, she had been on the women's swim team in college. She was also deadly accurate with a Hawaiian sling spear. He'd never met anyone like her. On her mother's side she came from generations of incredible hunters and trappers of arctic big game like walrus, seal, fish, reindeer, and whales. Her mother was a Yup'ik Eskimo who still lived in the traditional way on St. Lawrence Island in the Bering Sea off the coast of Alaska. Her father was Anglo.

On this night Aja was wearing red shorts, flip-flops, and a dark blue T-shirt with the nickname her biologist friends had given her on the back: "Blue Angel." She was wearing no jewelry except the unimpressive engagement ring Seabrook had given her a month earlier; it had a tiny diamond, but it was the best he could do. Her black hair, tied in a French braid, came round her neck down her chest to a point above her heart. The tropical sun had given her a dark tan and pink cheerful cheeks and nose that made her look like she was on vacation.

But she had been misread and underestimated all her life. Although she had a sweet and gentle nature, she could also be hard as nails and cool in a crisis. She was scary smart and had scored one point higher on the GRE tests than Seabrook, hitting the ninety-ninth percentile. Her father was a cop in Nome, Alaska, so guns didn't scare her, and she knew full well what horrors people could be.

To an outsider watching her conversation with the wounded man, Aja could have been casually talking with a friend. But Seabrook could see she was on full alert, waiting for an opportunity. A hint of steel around her eyes and the corners of her mouth.

The man continued talking, and she nodded.

Seabrook had to think. His mind raced, and he could hardly stand still. He wanted to go in and put himself between her and the man with the gun. But wouldn't the man kill her if someone entered the room? Probably yes.

Getting the Bimini police was out of the question. It would take too long, and everyone knew they were a small-time, symbolic force more than anything.

The man kept his finger on the trigger of his gun. He glanced nervously at the doors every few seconds, probably terrified that whoever had nearly killed him would find him and finish the job.

The man suddenly started shaking, and Seabrook thought he was starting to die or have some kind of seizure: maybe from massive blood loss. The man closed his eyes. He began crying. Abruptly, he stood up and barked demands. He was only a few inches taller than Aja. Standing up, he looked even worse. There were old scars on his stomach and back—he'd been stabbed and shot before. The scars were thick and ugly. He had not received proper medical attention for his old wounds.

Seabrook could hear his rough voice, muffled through the glass. The man wanted clothes and water.

Aja made a sympathetic face; her eyes showed concern. She was calming him down again, quietly giving him advice. She stood up and went into the bedroom. In a moment she came back with a pair of her shorts and one of her pink T-shirts. Seabrook's clothes would have been way too big.

The Earless Man put on the clothes without ever setting down the gun. Somehow he looked uglier in her clothes. Like if something putrid and evil wore a lovely white wedding dress.

Aja gave him one of the gallon jugs of fresh water they always kept in the refrigerator.

He drank for a full minute, and water dribbled down his chin. Then he seemed grateful, even apologetic. And he looked like he might start crying again.

She spoke to him in a polite tone and pointed in the direction of the backyard. It sounded like she was talking about Seabrook and asking the Earless Man for permission to do something.

The man nodded yes and started toward the glass door. He walked with a limp, flinching in pain with each step.

Seabrook stepped away and moved around the corner of the house. Then he heard the glass door slide open. Next Aja called him.

"Seabrook? Are you out there?" she said. "It's okay. He's leaving. Come out if you're there." Her voice sounded solid, confident.

She'd had the wherewithal to realize her fiancé might come back from tracking sharks, startle the man, and get shot. She was trying to save his life.

"I'm out here. Don't shoot," he said loudly. He stepped out into the open with his hands up.

The Earless Man said, "I'm not going to kill you—unless you make me."

He pointed the gun at Seabrook and told Aja to get in front of him. She stepped next to Seabrook. Their hands touched and joined for an instant.

Seabrook saw the man's finger was on the trigger.

They were about to die.

He glanced at Aja to say goodbye and could see that she had the same thought. They moved closer together.

"Go down the dock, hands up," the wounded man said. He spoke between short breaths, his voice raspy with pain.

Seabrook and Aja walked slowly down the dock with their hands raised to shoulder height. He let Aja go in front to shield her from the man with the gun. The dock creaked, and the wind stirred the dried palm fronds overhead.

They went down to the dead man at the end.

"Pick him up and put him in the boat," the man said as he limped behind them.

Seabrook grabbed the dead man by the back of his jeans with one hand and around the throat with his forearm. The dead man was small, maybe 150 pounds. He picked the corpse up like it was nothing. The body still felt warm. A wet sound gurgled from the corpse's mouth, and its arms dangled limply.

Sticky blood smeared Seabrook's shirt and bathing suit. He was disgusted and swung around. "Where do you want it?"

"On the boat," the Earless Man said. He pointed to the cigarette boat. "Carry him there . . . but have respect. He was somebody to me."

The cigarette boat looked like an evil rocket: the nose pointed and the hull long and skinny. Its black color made it seem sinister, like a nautical casket, but the highlights and name were in orange: *Allecto*.

Seabrook clambered onboard and tried not to let the dangling arms drag. He stood on the deck of *Allecto*. "Where?"

"In the cabin. Put him on the towels on the floor. Don't touch anything. Come up with your hands up, or I shoot her."

The cabin was dark, and Seabrook had to crouch to get inside. He could barely see. He noticed a square pile in the room. As he stepped closer, he saw that it was large bricks of white powder, stacked eight high, on the floor in the middle of the cabin. It had to be cocaine. It was too dark to count them properly, but there were at least five stacks, left to right, with rows behind. He couldn't tell for sure, because he had no experience with narcotics, but the pile was at least four rows deep, maybe more. If each brick was a kilo, there were a hundred and sixty kilos of cocaine minimum. If it was pure, it was probably worth many millions of dollars—more money than he would ever make in his lifetime. He put the corpse down on the towels in the middle of the floor, right in front of the pile of cocaine.

A cabin door across the room suddenly opened halfway.

A threatening presence.

Silent and still, a woman stared at him.

Sharp eyes that flickered. She was roughly the same height as Aja, but heavier and much older. She wore a necklace and, in the dark, it appeared there were seashells on it. Her head was backlit, so he couldn't see her features clearly, but her face seemed swollen. Middle-aged, maybe much older.

"Salvatore?" She had a Hispanic accent. "Salvatore!" She spoke like she was used to giving orders.

Then her demeanor changed. Her face was in shadow, but she seemed to break into a smile. She did not seem at all troubled by the dead man on the floor or the load of cocaine.

Her eyes continued to flicker. They were somehow familiar and frightening.

She pushed the door open and lurched forward, shambling closer, coming for him.

Yes, she was definitely smiling. Her hands moved quickly and racked the slide of a handgun. She pointed the barrel at him, raising it towards his face, handling the gun like a pro. She didn't seem afraid or nervous at all. Quite the opposite.

Seabrook quickly stepped clear of the gun. As he ran up the steps, he heard her coughing—then realized she was actually laughing. Her voice sounded a thousand years old.

He came up on deck with his hands up and looked to see if she had followed him.

She had not. He heard a door shut below.

The Earless Man had climbed aboard. He was getting ready to start the engine. He told Aja to cast off his lines, then barked at Seabrook to get off.

"Listen to what I say now. It's very important. Do you understand?"

Seabrook stepped off the boat and stood between Aja and the man with the gun.

"Yes," Aja said.

"You're good people. *Say nothing to nobody.* I was never here. Okay?" He seemed to think for a second, breathing heavily. Then he added, "You don't want my life to come into your life."

"Okay," Seabrook said. "We'll say nothing."

"You better not." The Earless Man stared at Seabrook a long moment. Then his voice got quiet. "She doesn't know where we are. If you talk about us, she will find out where we are and come back to kill you and everything you love."

He started the cigarette boat. The twin engines roared like a dozen Hells Angels had just rolled up on Harley-Davidson motorcycles. Smoke filled the air.

Seabrook and Aja covered their ears and watched the drug runner take off down the channel toward Alice Town. The speedboat cut a wake that soon lapped at the beach along the lagoon. The vessel disappeared into the night.

They could hear *Allecto*'s twin engines long after she was gone from sight.

Then the sound faded away, leaving only the murmurings of the rising tide and the wind stirring the treetops.

Chapter 4
Back to Normal?

They took the Earless Man at his word and decided not to report the encounter to the authorities. This made the next move simple: remove every trace of the corpse and the Earless Man from their world. Clean the floor of the house, destroy the bloody clothes and towels, and wash the dock. Seabrook also wanted to burn the clothes he was wearing. They were stained with blood and smelled like the dead man. After that, they would decide whether to leave, or stay in Bimini and finish their summer research. They didn't want to wait until morning, and got straight to work. But as they cleaned, Seabrook and Aja grew angry and upset.

They felt paranoid and unsafe.

"He'd been told we were scientists and doctors," Aja said about the Earless Man. They were both on their knees, cleaning the floor with soap, rags, and water where the man had bled. "He said he couldn't find a doctor. Bimini's medical clinic closes at five p.m. every day. Someone on the island sent him to us."

"The guy seemed scared to death," Seabrook said.

"He was. Someone killed his friend and nearly killed him too. He said he'd been set up. He couldn't see who shot him."

Seabrook shook his head.

"If he doesn't get to a real doctor soon," Aja said, "he may die. Those bullets are still in him."

"Was it a bad drug deal?"

"He didn't say. But someone is looking for him. He said he had to keep moving or he'd be killed."

"He had bricks of cocaine below deck."

"A lot?"

"A whole lot. A hundred and sixty kilos in bricks. Maybe more. It was dark. I couldn't see well and I didn't want him to shoot you, so I hurried back on deck."

Aja nodded and touched his shoulder.

"Right before I came up on deck, a weird woman spoke to me," Seabrook told her.

"What woman?" Aja said.

"There was a woman in the forward cabin."

"Against her will?"

"No. She seemed to be hiding. In the dark she couldn't tell who I was and asked me if I was Salvatore."

"Salvatore? . . . I wonder if that's the Earless Man's name, or maybe his dead friend's name?"

"Probably Earless Man. The dead man was on the floor right in front of me. I think she could see him. But I got a real bad feeling off her."

"What do you mean?"

"Like she enjoyed killing people. And wanted to kill me."

"How could you tell?"

"She pointed a gun at me and smiled. I ran up the stairs before she could shoot. I think she is the woman Earless Man was talking about. Maybe she is some kind of boss."

Aja shook her head sideways. "Jeez. What did she look like?"

"Weird, shaky eyes, kind of bloated face." Seabrook shrugged. "I only saw her for a few seconds and it was dark, but I think she had a necklace with seashells on it. She was crazy in the worst way."

Aja nodded. "I'm glad she didn't shoot you."

Aja and Seabrook thoroughly cleaned the house, then went outside and scrubbed the dock. The bloody footprints came out fairly quickly, but the stain where the dead man had lain was deeply drenched in blood. No matter how much they scoured the planks it seemed like the blood-stains wouldn't come out. They could still see traces of it after working at it for an hour. Eventually they gave up. Seabrook planned to spill fish blood from the bait tub over the spot to camouflage and obliterate any trace of human blood the next day.

They returned to the house. They locked the kitchen door and set a plank of wood on the door runner to jam the glass door in the living room shut. They tried to make themselves feel as safe as possible. It was 3:08 a.m.

They showered together. They soaped and cleaned each other but did not make love. Nothing could take their mind off what had happened. They lay in their bed with their dive knives, the bedroom door locked and the Hawaiian sling spears by their bedsides. The noisy air conditioner rattled though it was set on low. Aja got cold at night and used an extra blanket. She clumped it around her like a nest and cuddled next to Seabrook for his body warmth.

Time went slowly.

Seabrook could not sleep. He stared at the window most of the night and watched the sky outside. His eyes felt sleepy and scratchy.

As a couple, they were used to living with risk. Their work was extremely dangerous. Aja feared, and once had a nightmare, that Seabrook would be eaten by sharks. She knew that sharks were normally harmless, except in specific instances—like when a person was spearfishing or when there was bait in the water.

In her dream, Seabrook had been swimming with an adult lemon shark to revive the fish, when twin tiger sharks, attracted by bait on the long line, glided out of the blue when he wasn't paying attention. The tiger sharks were big females, fifteen feet long, and stalked him from behind, sneaking closer and closer, rising to the surface where he swam. They bit down on his legs, violently tearing from side to side. The shark he was reviving turned on him too. He couldn't fight off three sharks by himself. He died alone in the sea, in a cloud of his own blood, eaten alive.

Because Seabrook usually worked by himself at the long line, the nightmare seemed plausible, and it haunted her. Aja always grew nervous whenever he was gone longer than usual when tagging and releasing sharks.

For his part, Seabrook worried about Aja because the cone snails (*Conus geographus*) in her Indo-Pacific specimen tank might one day crawl onto the upper glass on the inside of the tank or hide in a place where Aja wouldn't notice them in the sand. If she were absent-minded or careless for one small instant and inadvertently brushed against a cone snail while cleaning the tank, it could be fatal.

One sting from the harpoon-like barb would kill Aja almost immediately. Her Indo-Pacific tank contained snails whose venom was among the deadliest in the world. The toxicity was comparable to the venom of king cobras, Brazilian wandering spiders, or Middle East deathstalker scorpions. But in the case of the cone snail, there was no known antivenom to treat victims. Paralysis, agony, and death quickly followed a sting. Sometimes, when Seabrook was out working at sea and had a bad feeling, he would start to worry, and would call Aja on the walkie-talkie to check on her.

As real as the dangers that Seabrook and Aja lived with were, they had chosen their work with their eyes open and both knew how to minimize the risks. And the dangers seemed paltry when compared to the crazy violence of drug cartels.

Aja slept fitfully. Her breathing told him she was nearly awake.

Seabrook kept hearing the Earless Man's warning: "*Say nothing to nobody. You didn't see me.*" And, "*She'll kill you and everything you love.*"

Who the hell *was* she?

Something else also kept him awake: the old woman's eyes. Now that he'd had a little time to think about it, he remembered seeing eyes flicker like that before. It was a decades-old memory but still sharp in his mind. In fourth grade one of his classmates, Rudy Defarge, became seriously ill and missed many weeks of school.

When he finally returned to school, Rudy told everyone that he had been diagnosed with a brain and nervous system disorder called dystonia and said that he'd been given medicine to take for it. Dystonia caused him to have erratic muscle spasms and made his eyes flicker. Looking back on it, Seabrook was surprised Rudy had been so candid and open about his medical condition. He actually seemed kind of proud of it and had talked about his disorder in a lot of detail for a fourth grader. But his symptoms got worse.

After missing more school and seeing different doctors, Rudy came back to school in the late spring. He had a new diagnosis to brag about: a rare form of multiple sclerosis. Despite medicine and treatment, his muscle spasms and flickering eyes still worsened. His eyes became downright scary because they changed even more—all traces of innocence and human warmth disappeared. Instead, they became malefic and hungry.

Seabrook remembered it well because he and Rudy had been placed in the same reading group and taken turns reading aloud a passage in Jack London's *The Call of the Wild*. Whenever it was Seabrook's turn to read, Rudy Defarge stared intensely at him the entire time. His eyes, a light brown color, had pupils dilated to an unnatural degree; and they trembled as if an earthquake or a furnace were rumbling inside him, the eyeballs constantly recalibrating—a fraction of a centimeter up, a fraction of a centimeter down, a fraction of a centimeter back up, or to the left, or to the right—both eyes in unison, again and again and again. The adjustments were small and rapid. It never stopped, not even in his sleep, Rudy said.

Then Rudy started to blurt out vile and nasty things in the middle of class: yelling obscenities and ordering their grandmotherly home-room teacher to give him a blowjob. When she tried to send him to the principal's office, he hissed something much worse, and she fainted.

Her head hit the floor with a loud knock, and Rudy exploded with laughter.

He threatened to hurt children in first and second grade, and menaced them during recess, throwing rocks at them when teachers weren't watching carefully enough. One little girl was nearly blinded by a rock that Rudy threw. That occurred right about the same time that he started walking with a strange spasmodic hitch in his stride—not quite a limp, not quite a stagger. Something in between. But it made your skin crawl to see him coming down the hall like that; it was even worse if he looked your way and you locked eyes with him. They shined with a weird animalistic glee, like he couldn't wait to hurt you.

Students and a few teachers became terrified of him, and the complaints started. The parents of the little girl who was nearly blinded threatened to sue the school district. Things got so bad that Rudy's parents finally disenrolled him from public school. They were going to homeschool him and seek psychiatric help. That was the last time anyone in the fourth grade ever saw him.

Things went completely off the rails for the Defarge family. Seabrook overheard his mother talking to another mom on Parents' Day before spring break. The woman said that Rudy didn't have a brain or nervous system disorder. Something else was happening to him. The doctors were still doing tests.

Then Rudy's baby brother mysteriously died in his crib one night. According to the obituary in the papers, the cause of death was sudden infant death syndrome (SIDS).

Two weeks after that, the newspapers reported that Rudy tragically drowned in the family swimming pool. Two deaths in one family, within one month, whipped the community gossip grapevine into overdrive.

Some older kids on the school bus talked trash about it to scare the younger kids. The story went that Rudy's parents became convinced he wasn't their son anymore, that he'd changed into something else. Something unholy. And they believed he'd sneaked into the nursery in the middle of the night and killed his baby brother.

So, one sunny afternoon, the story went, Rudy's parents pushed him into the deep end of their own swimming pool; they watched their sick, disabled boy sink and drown. Then they claimed that his death was an accident.

Seabrook didn't believe any of the older kids' story—it had been exaggerated and embellished into a campfire monster tale—except for the look of Rudy's face. The old woman's eyes brought it all back.

Her eyes looked exactly like Rudy Defarge's eyes.

Seabrook rolled over in bed.

Was it safe for them to stay in Bimini? Or should they take the next seaplane back to Miami?

He turned the questions over in his mind again and again, trying to get a read on things, but no answers came. A cold knot formed in his stomach. He wished the morning would come. Maybe the daylight would bring clarity, and maybe some solutions.

Chapter 5
Bloodstains

At first light they hopped out of bed and got dressed. The world seemed to have become much more dangerous overnight, and this broke them from their normal routine. They didn't even make the bed. They still felt anxious and paranoid.

"I barely slept," Aja said.

"Me too."

They skipped coffee and cereal and went straight to work cleaning again.

Daylight flooded in through the sliding glass door, and they could see everything much better than the night before.

"I'm going to see if we got all the blood off the tiles in the living room," Aja said.

"I'll check the dock." Seabrook took a bucket of soapy hot water and a brush down to the wooden planks where the dead man had been.

Aja studied the living room floor. Sure enough there were still bloodstains. Two small drops on the tiles near the kitchen door that she had missed the night before. She crouched on one knee. With soapy water and a brush, she scrubbed the stains until they were gone. When she was done, she stood up and looked for other spots that she might have missed.

A new problem presented itself: now all the tiles they had scrubbed in the last twenty-four hours looked too clean compared to the rest. It looked suspicious. The whole floor needed to be cleaned so everything would look even and normal. She would do that later.

She glanced out the sliding glass door to see what Seabrook was up to. He had obviously found more blood too—he was scrubbing the dock. She swore under her breath. *This was not over.*

Seabrook had found blood droplets on some of the pebbles in the backyard and along the path to the dock. He carefully picked out each stone and dropped it in the bucket of soapy water he carried. By the time he got to the dock, he'd collected eighteen. At the dock he threw them, one at a time, into the channel. He threw each stone, sidearm, in a different direction, like he was trying to skip them as far away as he could.

The wood where the dead man had bled on the dock looked darker —although it wasn't obviously stained with blood.

Seabrook began scrubbing furiously. He wanted to erase all evidence of the night before. He wanted everything to be normal again. After scrubbing the heck out of it, he stood up and left the wood to dry.

As he stood there, something shiny in the water caught his attention. It was just next to the dock. Now that the sun had risen, he could see clearly down into the shallow seawater.

He stepped to the edge of the dock and looked down through the moving current. Small silversides darted under the dock as he loomed over them.

Five feet underwater a bunch of bright keys lay on the sand. The image wavered and distorted in the flowing tide.

There was something else bigger and darker next to the keys.

A gun.

He jumped into the lagoon and retrieved the keys and the handgun. The dead man must have dropped them in the water. He climbed back into the Whaler next to the dock and looked around to see if anyone was watching. Nobody was in sight.

He examined what he had found. There were eight keys of various sizes on a ring.

The gun was a nine-millimeter. "Browning Arms Company" was engraved on one side of the black barrel, and "Made in Belgium" on the other side. It had checkered wooden grips and looked beat up and well-used. Seawater drained out of the barrel.

Seabrook shook his head with frustration. *What the hell had they gotten in to?*

He looked up and saw Aja coming down the dock to join him.

Despite the trouble they were facing, she managed to smile at him. For a split second, she reminded him of the first time he'd ever seen her...

Chapter 6
The Blue Angel and Razormouth

Aja was the biggest and best surprise of Seabrook's life. When they first started dating, his emotions alternated between euphoria and disbelief. For years he had resigned himself to a future as a low-paid scientist married to his work. He didn't think any woman would want to share the kind of life he pictured for himself. It turned out he was wrong.

Aja hit him like a tsunami.

They met the summer before, when she picked him up after he'd disembarked from the Chalks seaplane and gone through Bimini's Customs Office. She and two colleagues drove him in a Zodiac boat to the research vessel moored just offshore.

That summer they worked and lived aboard the *Colombus Islen*, University of Miami's famous oceanographic research vessel, as part of three teams of scientists. The ship was anchored by south Bimini in water 150 feet deep, and the trip lasted a month. The research vessel was 170 feet long, with a crew of twelve. Inside there was a wet lab, dry lab, conference room, TV room, and mess hall, and down the gangway there were ten private air-conditioned rooms each outfitted with two bunks and a desk.

Aja spent her days with a team studying nudibranchs—shell-less gastropod mollusks—on shallow reefs, while Seabrook's team tagged sharks in deeper water for an age and growth study. They saw each other only at the end of the day, when everyone returned to the ship to eat and sleep.

The third team studied the green turtle population that nested on the Bimini beaches. Altogether, there were twelve researchers aboard the *Colombus Islen*: scientists, graduate students, and volunteers.

Each team left the mother ship every morning in small boats and spent the day working in different locations around the islands. Two groups used inflatable Zodiac boats, but Seabrook's team used an eighteen-foot Boston Whaler, because sometimes the sharks would bite the boat. Sharp teeth could sink an inflatable vessel, but not the Whaler.

In the evenings everyone sat in the mess room, sunburned and tired, and discussed their findings over dinner. They often held wide-ranging conversations that overlapped from group to group about the day's work and science in general. The conversations were usually animated and fascinating, and often helped along with coconut rum. Each team brought a different area of expertise to the forefront, and it was during these conversations that Seabrook began to pay attention to Aja.

Her team nicknamed her the "Blue Angel" (or BA for short) because her favorite nudibranch—*Glaucus atlanticus*—was commonly called a blue angel. Her team also thought she was a BA or "badass" because she was tough, smart, and pretty. The first time Seabrook ever spoke to Aja, he asked about her interest in the unique nudibranch. She was interested in venomous sea creatures of all kinds, but especially in species that would otherwise be helpless without their venom: cone snails and nudibranchs like the blue angel.

As she started to answer his question, she smiled and her face brightened, and Seabrook thought she was describing herself.

She said the blue angel sea slug looked tiny, delicate, and gorgeous but was in fact deadly venomous and ingeniously camouflaged. The species grew a little over one inch long, lived in open water, and evaded predators with counter-shading camouflage. It floated at the surface

36

using a small air-filled sac in its stomach. It positioned itself upside down so that its blue side faced the sky—so gulls couldn't see it among the waves; and its silver-gray side faced the deep—so fish looking upward couldn't see it either.

It looked like a tiny psychedelic blue and white dragon made of wet feathers, and it fed on the venomous Portuguese man o' war, a predatory jellyfish-like organism hundreds of times larger than the nudibranch. It ingested the venom and stored it in the tips of its feather-like cerata.

Although beautiful and small, it packed a sting as lethal as a Portuguese man o' war's. By the time Aja finished describing the blue angel, Seabrook felt stunned, like she'd zapped him herself.

For the rest of the research cruise, he talked with Aja whenever possible, but she was almost never alone. The lead scientist of her team spent every day working with her and also monopolized her time at dinner.

When she wore a bathing suit, a bikini or one-piece, she looked stunning. Unbeknownst to Aja, Seabrook saw the lead scientist repeatedly and lewdly stare at her crotch whenever she was preoccupied with a task—stepping from the Zodiac up onto the fantail of the *Colombus Islen* or bending over to pick something up—and the horndog wasn't subtle about it. He even elbowed a deckhand so he could look as well. The man was recently divorced and also seemed like he was trying to get Aja drunk every night. Whenever her glass was nearly empty, he aggressively refilled it. He never shared his private supply of rum with anyone else.

Seabrook couldn't tell whether she had any interest in the jerk—Aja had a great poker face. In the beginning he thought the lead scientist would win her, because they seemed quite friendly. Maybe she had a blind spot for prestigious jerks.

But a freak accident changed everything. Seabrook had been building a shark pen: three sides were made of chain-link fence, and the fourth side was the wall of an old rocky pier. The enclosure was intended to hold two mature female sharks for roughly a month. Dr. Nixon, his boss, needed to draw blood samples from the mature female sharks. He wanted to see if the blood chemistry changed when the sharks came into mating season.

Seabrook and another graduate student had worked on the pen most of the morning. As he waded in chest-deep water carrying a length of chain-link fence, he stepped on a rusty underwater spike. It was next to the pier. The spike was as thick as his thumb, about seven inches long, and encrusted with marine growth.

The spike pierced the sole of his sneaker into the bottom of his right foot. It stabbed almost to the bone.

Seabrook gasped. He pulled his foot off the spike before it could go deeper.

He put on his dive mask and looked at it. The spike protruded from a wood beam buried in the sand. Filthy, rusty, and covered in marine growth—if anything could give you gangrene, this was it.

Back on the *Columbus Islen,* he pulled off his sneaker. It came off with a wet sucking sound. He gently turned the bottom of his foot towards him and looked at the wound. It was not bleeding. The marine growth on the old spike had sloughed off deep inside the flesh, near the bone. The wound was packed solid with black junk.

Seabrook cursed.

He limped upstairs from his private quarters. The three teams of researchers were back from the day's work, unloading gear and milling around the mess hall. Seabrook limped past them to the dry lab room and told Dr. Nixon, the lead scientist on the cruise, what had happened. Nixon had him put his foot up on a table so he could take a look. It felt like it was starting to swell up.

Dr. Nixon poked it carefully and made a face. He sighed and leaned back.

"You have two choices," he said. "We fly you back to Miami in a helicopter and get you to a hospital. And your research cruise ends today. Or you let one of us try to clean it out here."

"Let's do it here," Seabrook said immediately. The mere idea of ending the cruise made him feel sick.

"Are you sure? There is no anesthetic, and it is going to hurt like hell."

"I'm not leaving."

"Okay," Dr. Nixon said. "I need a volunteer. Preferably someone who is an EMT."

"I'm an EMT," Aja said. "I'll do it." She stepped forward and took charge. Many of the others gathered around Aja to look at his foot and watch the proceedings. She opened the first-aid box.

"This is deep, Cael. I'll do my best, but we'll have to watch it," Aja said. She'd used his Christian name, Cael, for the first time. Nobody else ever called him that, and he thought it a good sign.

"Healed by a blue angel," he said.

She gave a little smile and opened his wound. She poked into it with the tip of the scalpel. Then pushed deeper.

Then deeper.

And carved the dirty edges. Like scraping and cutting the black off burnt toast.

He suppressed a scream and started to bleed.

With a calm expression, she sliced in a circle, making the hole bigger and cutting out the black marine growth. She glanced up at him, and their eyes met.

Her face was serious, focused, but there was a trace of sympathy and humor in her eyes. Something reassuring and beautiful. Normally, he would break eye contact after a few seconds, but under these circumstances, it was okay to stare.

Looking at Aja made the pain less intense.

Before her, on the table next to his foot, she had several scalpels, a syringe, a bottle of hydrogen peroxide, and some clean paper towels.

When she looked down again at Seabrook's foot, her black hair fell gracefully to one side. He could see the small, fine hairs behind her ear at the top of her neck. Also the tiny beautiful mole by her temple and one below her lip. Her cheeks were pink, but that was normal for her. Later Seabrook would learn that her middle name was Flora, because the day Aja was born, she came into the world with pretty rose-colored cheeks.

She cut deeper into his foot, and Seabrook had to force his leg not to move. She put her left hand on his ankle. His whole leg down to his foot felt hypersensitive and electric. A tidal wave of sensation—gentle touching, skillful poking, sharp stabbing, then carving agony—more than he'd ever felt before, coursed up into him. Somehow Aja's touch was mixed in with all that pain.

"This one is going to hurt." She cut deeper than before, circling around and scraping the black junk out.

He closed his eyes for a second.

Calm and composed, she wiped the blood off his heel with a paper towel.

"I wish I had some rum to give you," Aja said matter-of-factly.

"I could use a whole barrel," he said.

After she finished carving out the marine debris, she picked up the hydrogen peroxide and unscrewed the top. She drew hydrogen peroxide into the syringe.

Somebody behind her said, "This is going to be good."

Aja nosed the tip of the syringe as deeply into Seabrook's foot as she could get it. Then she jammed the peroxide in.

Pain exploded in his foot and jolted up his leg to his pelvis. It felt like Aja had run a red-hot sword all the way up inside his leg. His knee hurt as badly as his foot, and even his hip hurt. More pain than he'd ever felt in his life.

Amazingly, the wound began to whistle like a tea kettle at full boil: *whiiiiiiieeee.*

He could feel it shrieking out. Aja power-squirted the hydrogen peroxide into his foot—*whiiiiiiiieeee*—four more times, until the wound stopped whistling.

Then once more for good measure. Finally, she patted his foot down, drying it with a paper towel.

"It looks pretty good now," she said.

He looked at his foot. The throbbing pain made it feel as big as a sofa, but it was normal size.

"Thanks." He felt lightheaded.

"You're welcome." Gently, Aja put Neosporin in the wound, then wrapped his foot in gauze. She patted his bandaged foot.

"Stay out of the sea for a couple days. Don't get it wet."

"Okay." He couldn't believe how much it hurt. He could only laugh a little now.

"You said you wanted to stay. I'm trying to make that happen," Aja said.

Their eyes met again.

"I'll rebandage it in the morning. Okay?" she said.

"Yes. Thanks again." His foot and leg were still screaming from the ordeal, but his heart was beating with joy. He'd never felt this way before. There was something mysterious and irresistible about her. He'd known Aja for only a week but felt an uncanny sense of recognition. Like a moment of déjà vu. It was the unexplainable feeling that he'd known her for years, but that they'd somehow been separated by circumstances or fate—that he'd been missing her his whole life and didn't know it until now. It didn't make sense, but he couldn't deny the feeling.

For Aja, he'd step on a thousand rusty spikes.

The next day of the scientific cruise, the team studying green sea turtles brought the remains of a dead leatherback to the ship.

They'd found it washed ashore on an empty beach. It had been cut in half by something at the midpoint of its shell.

The back flippers and tail were intact, and there was still meat and organs inside.

The turtle was a pregnant female that had been full of eggs—there were a few still inside the body cavity. The reptile was gigantic, maybe weighing 1,800 pounds when intact and alive. Its shell looked like a boulder-size chunk of obsidian, and its back flippers seemed prehistoric. Like black slate flagstones dusted with snow. The turtle remains so resembled an inanimate mass of dark rock, it was hard to believe that it once could actually swim and float with great agility.

Nobody could figure out what had killed it.

Aja brought Seabrook out to the fantail of the ship. He limped on his bandaged right foot across the deck.

"I thought you'd be interested to see this," she said.

Seabrook glanced at her. He felt flattered that she was seeking his opinion. They were still just acquaintances, and there were other, more accomplished scientists onboard to consult about it.

Later on, he remembered the moment very clearly, because they'd never been alone before, and the evening seemed especially beautiful, despite the fact that he could hardly walk. His wounded foot was swollen, but it wasn't infected. Aja had done an expert job cleaning it.

Through a reef of dark clouds the sun began to sink at the horizon. The waves were coppered by the brilliant sunset and tinted dark purple and gray by the darkening sky overhead. The evening windiness riffled Aja's hair. She crossed her arms and pressed them up against her breasts to keep warm.

"What do you think caused this?" she said.

Seabrook dropped to one knee, taking the weight off his bad foot, to examine the carcass.

Even half the turtle looked massive—maybe eight hundred pounds. He put his hand on the shell. The carapace's ridges ran from the tail towards the head. It felt rubbery. The wound seemed too clean and straight to have been caused by a propeller.

"I don't know," he said. "Something very sharp and incredibly strong."

"Some kind of predator?"

"I doubt it. The cut line is pretty straight. Not perfect though. No jagged marks or tears. I've never heard of something that could fit an 1,800-pound sea turtle in its mouth and bite it cleanly in half. Through a shell like this? It's almost like someone used a surgical saw on it."

"Or a giant guillotine."

"Exactly. Very weird. Frightening if some creature actually did this."

"If it was some kind of animal, it would have to have a freakishly big mouth. And incredible bite power and teeth. I don't know of anything that could do this."

"It's got to be a manmade wound."

"That would be my guess. But what about the eggs? If someone killed her for the eggs, why would they leave any behind?"

"Good question. I don't know. But most of the eggs have been taken. Maybe they missed some."

"If it turns out to be a new species of predator, we should name it Big Mouth," she joked.

"More like Razormouth. Its teeth would have to be sharp as razor blades and the bite power would have to be off the charts."

"Razormouth." Aja nodded. "I like that."

Thus Razormouth, the mythical shark, became a kind of inside joke between them. If something went wrong, if there was an equipment malfunction or unexpected bad weather, they jokingly blamed Razormouth. Or when something remarkable happened, like a flying fish flew into a boat and knocked someone's hat off, it was Razormouth's fault.

It was just lighthearted banter.

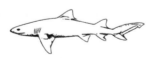

Three days later, Seabrook's foot had healed enough that he could risk going into the sea again. Aja's team loaned her to his team, because she was better at spearfishing than anyone else aboard the *Colombus Islen*, and his team needed to get bait for the long line.

They went spear fishing at Turtle Rocks, hoping to find some big barracuda—the large ones could be cut into ten pieces. They needed enough for thirty hooks.

They set anchor in twenty feet of water. In front of them stood the windward side of Turtle Rocks, like a spine that ran north and south about half a mile long, jutting up out of the sea. Birds nested among the crags and fissures above the waterline where waves smashed against the rocks. Below the waterline, a reef extended from the shallows into the deep. The sky was overcast, and it began to rain.

They back-rolled into the sea and cleared their snorkels.

Wearing wetsuit tops and carrying Hawaiian sling spears, they hunted along a ledge, right at the dividing point between shallow water and the beginning of deep water. Magnificent coral heads marked this part of the reef: giant brain and star coral.

In the shallows to their left, rows and rows of fire coral were lined up like yellow plates leading to a rock barrier. If a swimmer were to try to climb up on the rocky crest of Turtle Rocks, he'd have to scrape over dozens of sharp-edged plates of fire coral. Without a wetsuit, the fire coral would sting and slice a person to hell.

Normally, the reef looked beautiful: countless forms and vivid textures growing everywhere. Green and purple sea fans leaned and gently oscillated with the current. Stoplight parrotfish darted about like watermelon-size Easter eggs, and French angels, elegant in black and white, cruised over the coral city like tuxedoed grooms on the way to a wedding.

The overcast sky made the sea darker and grayer. The colors were almost gone. Also, the rain striking the surface of the ocean sounded like a ghostly waterfall you could hear underwater. The rain clouds made the marine world seem more dangerous, even sinister.

Razormouth

As Seabrook finned downward to thirty feet, looking into crevices and caves for decent baitfish, he wondered if a predator was coming in from the gray-blue deep behind him to feed. He had this concern whenever he went spearfishing.

Aja saw the barracuda first. Sometimes they were easy to spear because they didn't fear people. They came close to look you over, especially if you were wearing something shiny, like jewelry or a watch.

She took a deep breath and finned down towards the 'cuda.

She pulled the spear back, stretching the rubber straps all the way, loading the weapon. She glided closer to the fish, inch by inch. Her arms held the spear motionless, fully poised to strike, and aimed at the barracuda's head.

The silver fish angled to one side and opened its fanged mouth.

She adjusted her aim, following the target. She kicked her fins gently, angling forward, holding the loaded spear . . . holding . . . holding . . . her arm starting to burn . . . then she was in range.

She released the spear.

With a flash of steel, the spear tip went through the barracuda, just behind the eye. The fish died almost instantly. It was nearly four feet long and still looked alive as she finned over to Seabrook.

She showed it to him. They put their heads out of the water to talk, spitting out their snorkels.

"Nice fish," Seabrook said.

"I got him right at the drop-off."

"We should probably head back to the ship."

"I want to show you something first."

"Where?"

"Just over this way."

He nodded. Aja tossed the dead barracuda in the Whaler and led Seabrook through the sea.

He had snorkeled around the Bimini islands many times by this point and knew the wrecks, reefs, and mangroves quite well. So he was surprised and initially dismayed by what Aja showed him.

Someone had dropped anchor on a gorgeous fifteen-foot coral head. It was a giant colony of boulder-brain coral, but now big chunks of it were missing—likely ripped out by a pleasure boat's anchor. At least that's what he thought at first.

He carefully inspected the coral head, and there seemed to be seven places where duffel bag-size chunks of coral were missing. On closer inspection, it didn't seem like the type of damage an anchor would cause. The broken coral would be visible as rubble and debris under the coral head and in the sand around it. This was not the case.

The chunks of missing coral were entirely absent—like they had been removed from the sea. Maybe the damaged areas were some kind of bite marks?

Parrotfish ate chunks of coral, but even the largest were much too small to have caused anything remotely like this damage. Maybe a killer whale-size parrotfish on steroids could do it? But they didn't exist.

Back in the Whaler, they took off their snorkel gear.

"That's new," Aja said. "When I saw that, I couldn't believe it."

"Right. It wasn't there three days ago." He took a drink of fresh water and handed her the water jug.

"I think I should photograph it," Aja said. "Maybe there is some kind of parasite or toxin damaging it. If we get some pictures, we can show them to a coral specialist."

The rain continued to come down. Without their wetsuit tops, they would have started to shiver.

"Yeah. Let's come back and take pictures when it's sunny and visibility is better," Seabrook said. "I'll also measure it. We should show this to Dr. Nixon and see what he thinks. At first, I was almost positive some yacht had damaged it with its anchor ..."

He looked at Aja as he trailed off. Her wetsuit top was unzipped at the throat, and her deep black eyes seemed intense and pleasant at the same time. Raindrops glinted silver against her black hair and over her forehead and cheeks. Even though she was soaking wet, her face looked warm, as if lit by a lovely inner flame. She still had fins on her feet and a dive knife strapped to her right calf. Her legs were naked and tan and shiny in the rain. She still held the Hawaiian sling spear. The dead barracuda lay at her feet in a small pool of blood. Like the sea goddess

Amphitrite, she was simultaneously beautiful and dangerous. She made his heart ache.

"But now you're not so sure," Aja said, finishing his sentence.

"Exactly." He nodded.

Right from the beginning, it seemed like they could sometimes read each other's minds.

Eleven months later they were engaged.

Chapter 7
The Gun and Key Ring

S eabrook came back to the present with an almost jarring abruptness. He was still sitting in the Whaler tied to the dock. Seawater dripped down his face, off his nose, and from the key ring and handgun he had just retrieved from the sea.

Aja continued walking down the dock towards him.

A speedboat full of whooping tourists raced up the channel and back down, filling the air with noise. The wake rocked the Whaler and slammed into the shoreline of the lagoon. It grew quiet again after the tourists cruised south towards the harbor.

"I found more spots to clean," Aja said. She spoke softly and didn't use the word "blood," because voices sometimes carried on the water. A neighbor on a dock might hear what they said. She stood on the dock looking down into the Whaler where Seabrook was sitting.

"Look what I found," Seabrook said in a low voice.

Aja looked at the gun and the key ring. He held them low so the gunwales of the boat hid them from view except from above, where she stood.

"Where?" she said softly.

"In the water next to that." He pointed to where the dead man had lain on the dock the night before. "I think he dropped them near the end." Seabrook pointed to the seafloor where he'd found the things.

Aja looked back at the pistol. "It should still work. But you should rinse it in fresh water first."

"Do you think we should keep this stuff?"

"I don't know," Aja said. She took a deep breath and looked around to make sure no one could hear them. Then she whispered, "I'll bet that gun is linked to a long list of shootings."

"But what if someone comes looking for these? Especially the keys," Seabrook said quietly. "Wouldn't it be smart to be able to give them back?"

Aja thought for a second. "I don't know."

They were torn and uneasy about what to do. In the end, they decided to keep the key ring and gun—at least temporarily.

Seabrook took off his wet T-shirt and wrapped the items inside it. He carried the bunched-up shirt back to the house like dirty laundry.

They rinsed the gun and the keys in the kitchen sink with fresh water. When they were dry, Aja put them in a Ziploc bag.

Next, Seabrook took a shovel and buried them in the sand next to the shed in the backyard. It made him feel guilty, like a criminal with something to hide.

Then they scoured the area for any further bloodstains or evidence that the Earless Man and the dead man on the dock had been there.

Even after they could find nothing and tried to resume normal life again, both of them couldn't help but obsessively glance at the floor in the house or the dock in case they'd missed something. To their dismay, the dark spot where the man had bled and died on the dock could not be removed no matter how much they cleaned it.

Seabrook tried to remember if the wood had always been a little darker in that area but couldn't honestly recall. He hoped that it had.

Nevertheless, the dark patch seemed to be in the shape of a dead man like the chalk outline of a corpse at a murder scene.

It bothered Seabrook and Aja to no end.

It may have been just a coincidence, but seagulls that frequently inspected the wooden planks of the dock for scraps no longer ventured onto the side with the dark stain. Even the local children who liked to play by the water now started to stay away from the strangely marked wood.

The existence of the dark spot represented the end of their beautiful summer. Every time they went to work, they had to go down the dock to get to the Jon Boat or the Whaler and see the spot—an echo of the darkness that had visited them. And of what might return anytime.

But more than that, it crossed Seabrook's mind that the bloodstain was a kind of signal. Like the blood of the Passover lamb the Israelites had marked their doorposts with to protect their firstborn.

Except, in this case, the stain seemed like it might have the opposite power—an invitation to enter, a beacon to darkness.

He dismissed the thought as a silly superstition. Yet he asked himself, *Why wouldn't seabirds and children touch that area of the dock anymore?*

What did they know or feel?

Chapter 8
Reverend Bastareaud

T hat afternoon, on the other side of the island, Reverend Bastareaud, the owner and landlord of Seabrook and Aja's rental house, shouldered the heavy cross once more and dragged it down King's Highway. He was entirely unaware that the Earless Man had been on his property, let alone existed. It was midmorning, and the heat and humidity were already spiking.

Rivulets of sweat poured down his black face and body. The sweat made his forehead and cheeks shiny. His wiry hair stood streaked with gray, and the whites of his eyes were tinged with brown blotches. He wore thick glasses that magnified his eyes. He stood six feet tall and weighed nearly 250 pounds—built like a human bull with thick limbs. His imposing size, wild hair, and magnified eyes gave him a frighteningly intense appearance, especially when he glared at someone. He also had a machete sheathed at the belt of his jeans most days—he said he used it to open coconuts if he got thirsty.

He dragged his cross on the shoulder of the road. The cross was no mere prop. The upright beam was eight feet tall, and the horizontal beam five feet across. It was big enough and solid enough to truly crucify a man. He called the cross God's Love and the machete God's Vengeance.

Several times a week he dragged the cross, in a reenactment of Jesus's bearing his cross to Golgotha to be crucified, all the way to Alice Town, dodging cars and mopeds, and down past the Customs Office where the seaplanes disembarked and boarded their passengers.

Then he turned around and dragged it home—a hard nine-mile round trip. He had screwed wheels to the bottom of the cross so it was easier to drag. Still, it weighed at least a 150 pounds and made his shoulders sore—he used his right shoulder on the way into town and left shoulder on the way home.

He'd built the cross using timber from an old coconut palm he'd cut down at the edge of his neighbor's property. The timber had a dark hue, and he rubbed oil into it to make it shine. He nailed a placard at the top. It read: "Reverend Bastareaud's Ministry of Love."

He'd once had elaborate plans to build a ministry and grow a large flock. He set up a worship area outside his house with pews made of wooden planks set on cinder blocks. But people did not come more than once. After one visit, they called him crazy and noted that he did not follow any specific religious denomination and, moreover, that he didn't even follow scripture. People said he made everything up as he went along, stealing sermons and ideas from several radio evangelists. He answered their complaints by claiming that God talked directly to him, and therefore he did not need to follow scripture to know God's mind.

The whole community, even the drunks and wastrels, rejected Bastareaud as a false prophet. His pews sat empty in the yard outside his house, the wood planks drying and cracking under the blistering sun.

His ministry quickly dwindled to only himself, his wife, and his children. Nobody else ever attended his "services," which he now held in his living room. His captive audience prayed and sang, and he preached to them. He ran the ministry and his family as if their lives and souls were at constant risk. His wife and children did everything he said. They dared not contradict or ever disobey the leader of their "church," lest they be accused of and punished for having the devil inside them.

Occasionally a stranger honked approvingly as he dragged his cross down the road in the sweltering afternoon heat, but people who knew him tried not to interact with him. His fierce appearance and machete were not just for show. He was a violent and unpredictable man, except in matters of business—when he leased one of his rental houses to tourists or sold his giant land crabs to one of the restaurants, he adopted a professional demeanor. But aside from his business dealings, he recognized only divine law as he perceived it, not man's law.

He'd also been married three times, but nobody knew where his first and second wives were. They'd had two children each, and all of them seemed to have vanished from Earth.

Bastareaud had reported to authorities that they had left him, and then had his marriages nullified. He said his ex-wives had moved to Florida. But no one had heard from them since they left. In fact, it had been twenty years since anyone had heard from his first wife and fifteen years since anyone had heard from his second wife. Relatives of Bastareaud's first two wives believed he killed them, but there was no way of proving anything, and none of the authorities ever looked into it.

If his brother weren't a deputy in the Bahamian police department in Nassau, he would have been brought in for questioning about his missing wives and children and also for various other illegal activities. He'd poach giant land crabs off other people's property, openly catch and kill protected sea turtles when females crawled ashore to lay eggs, chase children off his property swinging his machete at them, and drain fresh water from other people's cisterns when his fresh water supply got low. In each instance he'd say God had told him to do it for his ministry.

Aside from his rental properties, Bastareaud made money selling giant land crabs (some people called them white or blue crabs) to restaurants for the famous Bahamian dish "Crabs and Rice." He caught them at night, usually around twenty at a time. On spring and summer nights, especially after the moon started to wane, he'd drive his skiff to the uninhabited beaches and pinewoods of the northernmost tip of North Bimini. The crabs in this wild area grew unusually large, and buyers came a long way to purchase them.

They lived on land but needed to be near the sea, because the females released their eggs in the water. They dug their burrows deep into the sand until they hit brackish water at the bottom, so they could moisten their gills. Their burrows were as wide and deep as badger holes.

Bastareaud carried a sack and a flashlight. He'd walk slowly through the woods next to the beach when he was hunting. When he saw or heard a crab, he'd pretend not to notice it—rushing one would make it run off and disappear into its burrow. The trick was to behave like you didn't even notice it or have any interest in it.

Once you walked close enough, you pointed the flashlight straight at the crab. The light blinded it and made it freeze. If you held the light steady, you could walk up and seize it by the back of the shell. This had to be done quickly, and if you didn't tilt it forward it could pinch you with its claws—the males had one giant claw, sometimes bigger than their carapace (more than a foot long in the North Bimini adults).

When Bastareaud first began hunting crabs, he wore gloves to protect himself, but he'd become so good at grabbing them, he no longer bothered. He caught them one at a time and dropped them into his sack.

After he'd caught enough for one night, he would drive his skiff back through the mangrove labyrinth, using a powerful flashlight to show him the landmarks and channels he knew so well in daylight. Then he'd guide his skiff across the North Sound flats to his dock and carry the full sack to his house.

He'd empty the sack into one of the chain-link cages that looked like dog kennels in his backyard. He collected the giant land crabs over weeks and sold them in bulk. Some buyers came from other islands—a buyer from Andros Island came every few months and bought five hundred at a time.

He had three cages. Each cage was four feet tall, eight feet long, and four feet wide. The floors were solid concrete, because the crabs were excellent at digging holes. Each cage held up to three hundred crabs. There was no way anything could get out of the cages without bolt cutters.

The crabs were easy to take care of. He kept a trough of salt water in each pen, and they ate anything he put in the cage. They were also cannibals, so Bastareaud made sure their food supply never ran out. If he expected buyers to stop by, he'd put fruit and leaves in the cages— wholesome fresh food to impress customers.

If buyers weren't coming, he'd kill one of the many stray dogs with his machete and feed the carcass to the crabs. He just had to be nice to a dog, pet it a few times, and give it a scrap of food. Then the stray dog would happily follow him around the corner of the house, where he would kill it with his machete.

The main thing was to kill one dog at a time. If a second stray dog saw him kill another dog, it would become afraid and wouldn't follow Bastareaud around to the back of his house. You couldn't let them see what was coming—very much like with women and children.

The crabs ate any kind of meat, and once, when he could not find a stray dog, he fed them a lowlife sinner nobody missed. He killed the man like he was one of the stray dogs—even enticing him around the side of the house in a similar way, kindly promising food and water. Then split his skull with the machete.

When tourists saw the crabs for the first time, they were usually scared of them. At full size, with long legs extended, an individual crab looked nearly the size of a soccer ball. The males had a freakishly big claw that looked capable of severing a man's foot at the ankle. The big claw was colored white, so you couldn't miss it.

The carapaces were a pale cream color, and the crustaceans looked at you with alert stalk eyes that seemed to twitch with intelligence. Like nocturnal aliens.

They could run very fast through brush, and their pinch was like the devil's bite.

Bastareaud had three children—Myron, Mookie, and Carmelita—and they were terrified of the crabs.

He made sure of it.

Chapter 9
The Sea Cherubs

"The soul is healed by being with children."—Fyodor Dostoevsky

T
he local kids called Seabrook "Shark Man" (their Bahamian accents made "man" sound like "mon"), because when a shark died on the long line, he'd bring the carcass back to the dock. After measuring and tagging a shark at sea for an age and growth study, he normally released it alive—which usually meant swimming with it until the predator revived and glided off—but despite exhaustive efforts to revive every shark, there were casualties.

Sometimes he would come back from the long line with an enormous fish, like a ten-foot tiger shark and once a thirteen-foot great hammerhead. To the children, these fish were real-life monsters. The stuff of nightmares and legend. They had frightening teeth and enormous gullets, and were described in books and depicted in movies as man-eaters that could smell a drop of human blood from miles away. Each one of the giants could have comfortably eaten two or three of the children on the dock. That Seabrook had caught and (inadvertently) killed the sharks impressed the children immeasurably. In the children's minds, that made him a monster killer.

No matter how much Seabrook advocated for sharks as important apex predators, as misunderstood miracles of evolution that rarely attacked anyone, he could not overcome the farrago of misinformation the children believed or their primal fear of them.

Compared to the big-game fishermen—usually fat, soft-looking millionaires—who caught marlin and tuna from giant powerboats with air-conditioned cabins and state-of-the-art fishing gear, Seabrook seemed more impressive to the local kids because he battled the terrifying sea monsters from a beat-up eighteen-foot open boat. And didn't even use a fishing rod. He caught them using his own back and arms, like Santiago catching the giant marlin in Hemingway's *The Old Man and the Sea*.

Whenever he brought a dead shark to their dock, he'd conduct morphometrics—measuring and recording a series of precise external dimensions of the shark for species identification. After that, he'd perform a necropsy and examine the internal organs and stomach contents. The Bahamian children would gather on the dock, and loved to watch these activities. They would sit patiently, waiting to see what the shark had in its stomach. They always wondered if there would be a human body inside. There never was.

Seabrook performed the necropsies on the floor of the Whaler, and they usually took an hour or so. The children would stand or sit on the dock watching. During the course of the summer, he got to know some of the children very well.

Occasionally, during downtime, he'd play soccer with them, or swing them in a circle by their feet or hands, or launch them off his shoulders into the sea on the ocean side of the island like he was a human catapult. They'd get in line to play with Seabrook, and they'd argue and compete to be on his team when he played soccer with them. Sometimes he had them help with his work.

Reverend Bastareaud's three kids in particular—brothers Myron and Mookie and their little sister, Carmelita—liked to take turns holding the clipboard and writing down the measurements as Seabrook called out the numbers while he collected data for a morphometric analysis of the species.

Myron was twelve, Mookie was eight, and Carmelita was seven.

They were handsome, quiet children, and black as sticks of licorice. They were also very skinny. The boys had short, frizzy hair and Carmelita kept hers in small pigtails. The trio typically wore shorts, and T-shirts, and went barefoot. Carmelita distinguished herself from her brothers by wearing pink clothes and tiny stud earrings. Myron, in manner and disposition, seemed more like their little father than their older brother. He was simultaneously kind to and authoritative with his siblings. And they listened to him.

Curiously, little Mookie always turned his head when you talked to him—so his right ear faced you. It seemed like he was hard of hearing or maybe deaf in his left ear.

They seemed to stay away from Reverend Bastareaud, their father, as much as possible. Like many families in Bailey Town, Bastareaud and his wife let their children run free during summers on the island.

Myron, the twelve-year-old boy, expressed great interest in shark research and science in general. He had a good mind and an aptitude for inductive reasoning. He said he would like to become a scientist. He frequently asked questions that struck at the heart of a theory or natural phenomenon. Once, after sitting on the dock and watching the tide come in, he asked, "Why are there high tides and low tides?"

Seabrook taught him a little about Sir Isaac Newton's law of universal gravitation: the sun and the moon's gravitational attraction caused two big bulges of water on the earth's oceans. The one on the side facing the sun was called a solar tide. The one on the side facing the moon was called a lunar tide; and the moon exerted almost twice as much gravitational pull than the sun. Therefore the lunar tide was bigger.

"How is that possible?" Myron asked. "You said the sun was bigger. Wouldn't it have more gravitational power than the moon?"

"Yes. Except the sun is much farther away than the moon, so its power is lessened."

Myron nodded, absorbing the information. "Ohhh. The sun's power is weaker than the moon because it is farther away from earth."

"That's right."

"Why does the timing of high tide and low tide always change then?"

"Great question. That requires a complicated answer," Seabrook said. "It starts with the fact that the earth is spinning, one full rotation every twenty-four hours. And the moon circles or fully orbits the earth every twenty-seven and a half days, or about a month."

"Is that why the moon gets smaller and smaller for a while, then gets larger and larger in the sky?"

"Exactly. And while all this is happening, the earth is orbiting around the sun, which takes a year to happen. The constant changes in the moon and the sun's positions in relationship to the earth cause the changing tides. Because the earth and the moon and the sun are always moving, this affects the timing of the tides. That's the very simplified version."

"So when I'm sitting on the dock at night near high tide, the moon in the sky is making the sea rise up towards my feet?"

"Yes."

Myron nodded and quietly thought about it for the rest of the morning. From time to time, he cupped his hands over his eyes and peeked up at the sun, then at the current in the lagoon.

Seabrook wanted to help the boy with his growing interest in science. He said if Myron got permission from his father, he could take him out tracking sharks one day.

The boy also took an interest in literature and sometimes read books from the small library that Aja and Seabrook kept in their living room. He and his two siblings were the only children the scientists trusted enough to let into the house.

Over several afternoons the boy read Hemingway's *The Old Man and the Sea* to his little brother and sister or one of the short stories from Ray Bradbury's *The Illustrated Man*. Sometimes he tried to read essays from Stephen Jay Gould's *Hen's Teeth and Horse's Toes*. He enjoyed the titles of the essays but struggled with some of the big words.

Aja or Seabrook would explain the meaning of the words. Myron would listen solemnly, then in a soft voice explain it to his siblings.

Mookie and Carmelita would nod and take it all in. The trio were an unexpected pleasure to have around. They stopped over almost every day to play and help and ask questions.

One day, out of the blue, Myron had a change of heart and said he no longer wished he could become a scientist. He said it wistfully and with a note of resignation, as if he were saying something he didn't quite believe.

"Did you talk to your father about it?" Seabrook said.

At the mention of his father, Myron grew quiet. He stared off into the distance and seemed to shrink into himself.

After a few moments he said, "He said no."

"Would it help if I asked him for you and told him you were good at science?"

"No." Now the boy looked very uncomfortable. After a moment he said, "He will not listen. He says science is the devil's language. God makes the sea rise and fall."

"Maybe God made the sun, moon, and Earth so they would work together."

"No. God makes the sea rise and fall." Myron's voice sounded robotic.

Seabrook was taken aback. Myron's father, Bastareaud, their landlord, seemed reasonable. He'd never given the impression that he disapproved of scientific research, and he certainly had no qualms about taking their rent money. Whenever he'd met with Seabrook, the man had been cheerful and professional and expressed interest in their work. Apparently, he was good at hiding his real views.

"Why did you change your mind?"

"I was stupid. And if I don't listen to my father, it will destroy the ministry and break apart the family. The devil was influencing me before."

"Is that what your father said?"

"Yes."

"How does he know?"

"God tells him."

"God talks to your father?"

"Yes. And if I disagree, that is the devil talking in me."

"The devil talks in you . . . and God talks in him?"

"Yes. Whenever I say something my father doesn't like."

"That's how he wins an argument?"

Myron said yes.

Seabrook felt outrage rising in his chest. What a phony, depraved way for an adult to cow a child.

"Then what happens?"

The boy suddenly looked terrified. He would talk no further on the subject.

He didn't need to say anything. Myron's cheek had an ugly scar that ran up his face to his temple and another on the top of his head shaped like a silver dollar.

His seven-year-old sister, Carmelita, had a crooked forearm. It looked like a boomerang. She told Aja the devil had broken it when she was younger and she had been bad.

"Sometimes I think my father is right," Myron said. "He is harsh for our own sake. He hurts us out of love, to teach us to be good, to watch out for our spiritual development. And sometimes the devil gets in me."

"Do you really believe that?"

Myron nodded. "Sometimes." He took a deep breath. "I didn't used to believe it. When the devil gets in me, my father has to cleanse me. He hurts us because he loves us."

Seabrook's face grew hot. He suddenly worried for the children's safety. He needed to tell the kid the truth. Someone had to do it. "The devil is *not* in you. You are a smart, good kid. So are your brother and sister." A parent telling a child such garbage was vile beyond words. Brainwashing and brutalizing children until they believed they were evil? And these were such good, nice children.

Seabrook suddenly had the urge to kick down the door of Reverend Bastareaud's house and come down on him like a house of bricks, break *his* arm so it looked like a boomerang and he could never hurt a child again. He wanted to save Myron, Mookie, and Carmelita. It was only a matter of time until something horrible happened.

"Science is the devil's language?" Seabrook asked with a bitter laugh.

"That's what he told me," Myron said.

"Science is about knowledge."

The boy just stared at him. A new skepticism had taken hold of him now that his father had worked him over. He seemed different.

"I will take over the ministry when my father retires," he said.

"Are you sure?"

"Yes. That was the devil talking in me before. I don't want to cause you any trouble. I'm sorry, Mr. Seabrook."

Seabrook felt overwhelmed with anger and struggled with what to say. A moment passed. Finally he said, "You don't have anything to apologize for. I don't believe the devil has ever spoken through you. Your father is wrong, and he is cruel to say that. I wish you could see yourself as I see you. You are good."

Myron suddenly seemed like his real self again. He said, "I want you to know that I tried to explain the tides to him. I tried to be brave. I didn't give in right away ..." The boy looked like he was about to start crying.

Seabrook let the conversation die. He felt his heart beating and sadness rising into his face. He wanted to say Myron's father was full of shit, that if anyone was being influenced by the "devil," it was Reverend

Bastareaud. The child was being abused and brainwashed. Seabrook felt awful for him, and wanted to hug him and tell him his father was crazy.

The poor kid said what he said and believed what he believed as a matter of psychological and physical survival. He would have been a very different person with a very different future had he been raised by decent, loving parents. Myron and his siblings were special and deserved so much better.

Seabrook and Aja couldn't help but dote on Bastareaud's children even more and let them into their life. The kids helped feed the cone snails Aja kept in the aquariums (but they were never allowed to reach into the tanks), and they helped Seabrook measure sharks for his morphometric data collection. They absorbed all the encouragement, attention, and gentle conversation the adults could give them.

They were often thirsty and asked for water. It had not rained in Bimini for a month, and the cisterns that stood next to each house on the island were running low. Their father wouldn't let them have water except in the morning and just a sip at night.

Aja gave them as much fresh water as they could drink. Sometimes she told them stories about her childhood on St. Lawrence Island in the Bering Sea. They loved to hear about icebergs, dog sledding, polar bears, and walruses. They'd never seen snow, and her descriptions sounded so enchanting and magical to them that they once asked her whether she'd ever seen Santa Claus's house. She smiled and told them that he lived farther north.

In the late afternoons Seabrook would return from the long line and once in a while he'd bring a shark that had died. If the shark was fresh, and one of the good species to eat, like a blacktip or a lemon, sometimes he'd fix shark nuggets.

He'd cut the fresh white meat into small pieces, dip them in whisked egg yolks, and roll them in flour with salt and pepper. Then fry the shark golden crisp in Crisco. Whenever this happened, Seabrook made enough to put over rice for dinner later; but he always made more than he and Aja needed. These extra pieces he gave to his "assistants" and the handful of other neighborhood children that came around.

Myron, Mookie, and Carmelita once ate three helpings of shark each. Aja took a photograph of them holding paper plates full of golden nuggets. In the picture all three were standing close together on the dock. Their brown eyes looked directly into the camera, and they all had beaming white smiles. The lagoon was behind them, flat and pale green, and the sky a soft blue. It was a beautiful picture. Seabrook had never seen them happier.

Aja taped the photograph of them above the little collection of books in the living room. On the white edge at the top of the picture she wrote "The Sea Cherubs."

Chapter 10
Night Visitor

Seabrook couldn't fall asleep. He had a weird feeling that someone was trying to rob them. That's why he decided to check the Boston Whaler in the middle of the night. He thought he might have forgotten to take the battery and gas tank out of the boat that afternoon. If he left them there, they'd get stolen eventually. It had already happened once that summer.

He slipped out the kitchen door and shut it softly. He didn't want to wake Aja.

Clouds shaped like torn rags stretched across the sky. For some reason he felt nervous. He had the vague idea that it had to do with the dark stain on the dock.

He told himself he was being ridiculous, and walked down the path to the boats. The wood creaked as he stepped on the planks. The lagoon quietly stirred, alive in the darkness. The tide was coming in.

The dock seemed longer at night than in the daylight, and the water looked black as ink.

As he walked down towards the Whaler, he forced himself to ignore the dark patch where the corpse had bled. It unnerved him. Especially at night. But he couldn't help but see it with his peripheral vision. It looked more like a shadow than a stain on the wood.

For an instant it moved.

He froze.

Obviously, it was just an optical illusion caused by the sea moving underneath the wood planks with the running tide. Now he looked straight at it to make sure, and could clearly see motion between the planks. This made the stain on the dock seem alive.

He scolded himself for being so jumpy.

The dark stain seemed to move again. He knew it was nothing and walked straight past it, turned right down the dock, and stepped down into the Boston Whaler tied there.

The sea flowed by. Little waves lapped with small splashes on the pebbly shore.

He sat down on the stern seat and found the heavy square battery underneath, and saw the red plastic gas tank as well. He was right! He had forgotten to remove them.

He pulled the battery forward and began unscrewing the first wingnut connecting the battery cord to the outboard engine.

A small splash sounded. He turned his head to see. Something moved under the dock. He let go of the wingnut and straightened up for a better look.

His eyes saw something big hiding in the water under the dock. A man? A person seemed to be stretched lengthwise facing upward just below the surface. The thief was apparently holding his breath, waiting for Seabrook to leave. *Are you same the son of a bitch who stole my battery a month ago?*

He decided to wait and see how long the man could hold his breath. Then run him off when he came up for air.

But the man did not come up for air.

Seabrook lost track of time as he waited.

The figure floated underwater, facing upward under the dock, for maybe fifteen minutes. Like a corpse encased in a watery coffin.

In the darkness, Seabrook couldn't see him very well, but the man's pale face was right near the surface. The head seemed to bob left and right like he was slowly looking around. For an instant the face seemed to look straight at him.

Could it be another dead man?

Just as Seabrook stood up to leave, it surfaced.

It crept out of the water, moving slowly, pulling itself onto the dock. The matted black hair and clothes were shiny wet.

It crawled across the wood, then rolled over and sat exactly on the dark spot where it had originally bled to death. For it was the same man who had died on the dock the night the Earless Man had intruded on their lives. But it was something other than a man.

The waterlogged corpse turned and gazed at Seabrook. Salt water dripped out of its hair and down its face and at the corners of its mouth.

Cold fear turned over in Seabrook's stomach. Somehow, the dead drug runner had come back. He wore the same clothes, had the same hand bitten off by a shark, but now there was a new, more gruesome wound. A shark had bitten him across the torso. Seabrook could see into his lungs and ribs.

The corpse's eyes were black stones.

"Give me back the keys. And the gun," it said.

"I buried them."

"You stole from ... *us*," it said.

"I'll dig them up for you," Seabrook said.

It laughed with wet lungs. "You don't have time."

"It'll just take fifteen minutes."

It shook its head from side to side. "No time!" The far-off sound of a drug runner's speedboat began to approach. It was coming up the channel towards the dock. The boat engine grew louder and louder.

The thing on the dock grinned and said, "How fast can you run?"

The speedboat got closer and was now visible racing over the water. Above the angry growl of the engine, Seabrook could hear the old woman's drawn-out, coughing laugh.

He woke up with a jolt. Mouth dry and dripping with sweat. The air conditioner was on full blast, but it didn't make a difference.

The nightmare had been so vivid, it seemed real. He felt feverish and had a headache. He went to the bathroom and took three aspirin and chased them with a glass of water. He lay back on his side of the bed, frustrated. Now, more than ever, he wanted to get rid of the dark stain on the dock. And the key ring and the gun too.

He stared at the ceiling.

After thinking a little while, he decided he would take action. Dig up the keys and gun, drive out into the deep ocean, and throw them overboard. Maybe he would do it the next time he went to check the long line.

He would talk it over with Aja in the morning.

He couldn't get comfortable for the rest of the night. He tried sleeping on his back, then his left side, then his right side, but couldn't fall back asleep. Near dawn, Aja startled him.

She gasped loudly in her sleep—he'd never heard her do that before. Then she began making distressed sounds as if she were being attacked: muttered unintelligible words.

"Aja, Aja," he said, trying to gently wake her. "It's okay. It's just a dream."

She sat up and touched her forehead with both hands. "Oh my God," she sighed, shaking her head. "That's the worst...the worst... nightmare...I've ever had."

"What happened?"

Aja reached over to the bedside table for her glass of water. She drank a few gulps, set the glass down, and sat still. She seemed stunned.

"The dead man on the dock," she said in a half-awake voice. "He wanted his gun and keys back."

Seabrook couldn't believe what he was hearing. A jolt of fear spurred him.

"What did you say?"

"The dead man. He came back for his gun..."

Aja's voice was emotional. She was still in the throes of the nightmare, and her eyes were still closed.

"And..." she said. "It was so awful."

"It was just a dream," he said, trying to comfort her. "It doesn't matter. It wasn't real."

"But I've never dreamed anything like that before. You..." She stopped talking.

"What is it?"

"You...The dead man from the dock...he killed you. But it was not just that. How he did it...I screamed and screamed...but he wouldn't stop."

"What?"

"I'm not going to say. It was too horrible. Too awful."

Aja lay back down. A few minutes later she began to breathe deeply and slowly. Then she drifted off to sleep.

Thankfully, in the morning, she did not remember the dream at all.

Chapter 11
Aja's Reef Tanks

Two one-hundred-gallon aquariums sat on stands against the wall in the living room. Each was sixty inches long, twenty-one inches deep, and eighteen inches front to back: large rectangles of shimmering light.

Soft purring pumps circulated and filtered the seawater in an endless cycle. The surface water in both tanks continuously roiled and rippled like a current in a miniature sea and, under the intense metal halide lights, made glitter lines in the tank and on the walls of the living room.

Cone snails with gorgeous shells moved slowly about the rubble of the tiny reefs or hid in the sand. The aquariums looked like museum dioramas, glowing works of art, except that they were alive: mini reef ecosystems. The tanks were distinctly different. One housed Caribbean species (*Conus mus*); and the other, Indo-Pacific species (*Conus geographus*).

Aja's dissertation focused on the metabolism and growth rates of Caribbean cone snails, particularly as they related to the metabolism and growth rates of cone snails in the Indo-Pacific. Her research was made possible by piggybacking on the well-funded shark research that

Seabrook was conducting. Everything—the house, the boats, the fuel, the food, the travel expenses, all the shark tracking and tagging equipment—was paid for by Dr. Nixon via a National Science Foundation grant. This enabled her to do her own fieldwork as well.

She'd brought the two aquariums from the Miami lab, and frequently used one of Dr. Nixon's boats to observe a group of cone snails living under the wing of a sunken plane, a Curtiss C-46 Commando aircraft that drug runners had crashed into the sea three years earlier. The plane sat on the seafloor with coral and sponges growing up from its wings and fuselage.

One time, Aja had entered the cockpit with scuba gear and sat in the pilot's chair just for fun. When she looked out the front windshield, she saw dozens of blue striped grunts staring back at her. She felt, for a funny moment, like she was being observed by a crowd of schoolchildren viewing an exotic creature in a public aquarium.

A population of cone snails thrived under the plane's wings and the small reef growing over the wreck. She photographed and studied their movements, eating habits, and interactions with one another.

She liked sharks and helped Seabrook with his work if needed, but her focus was on cone snails, and most of her time was spent studying them. It was a very nice arrangement, because it also allowed her to live with her fiancé in the Caribbean.

She had caught a variety of marine organisms for the Caribbean tank: local cone snails and a pair of striped bumblebee shrimp. Half a dozen tiny sergeant major damselfish schooled in the Caribbean tank as well. They made a small cloud of silver, black, and yellow colors that moved about endlessly. One pearly jawfish had made a tunnel in the sand and hovered over its den like a genie emerging from a lamp—always ready to dart down into the sand if spooked. The Sea Cherubs loved to press their faces against the glass and watch the jawfish during feeding time. It seemed to look back at them with its large goggle eyes.

"He's watching me again!" Carmelita would say with a laugh.

In contrast, the Indo-Pacific tank seemed empty and lifeless. It did not have cleaner shrimp or a miniature school of sergeant major damselfish, because Aja didn't want to mix Atlantic and Pacific species. The environments needed to be as close to the real thing as possible. She had no access to Indo-Pacific species except the cone snails, which she'd brought over from the Miami lab.

During the day, the Pacific cone snails usually buried themselves in the sandy bottom, but at night, after the lights went off, they came out of the sand like zombies and hunted for food in the darkness. They had stunningly beautiful shells but were among the most venomous creatures in the world.

When undergraduate college students asked why the Indo-Pacific species' venom was so deadly compared to the much milder venom of Atlantic and Caribbean species, Aja explained it in terms of a military arms race.

The Indo-Pacific Ocean was roughly three and a half billion years old, and there was no evidence that it had ever been anything but an ocean. Whereas the Atlantic Ocean and Caribbean Sea were babies by comparison—only three hundred million years old. So species in the older Indo-Pacific Ocean had had billions of years longer to develop and also longer exposure to sunlight—a known mutagen. And mutation was a good way to get species to evolve. This was one plausible explanation for why there was such high diversity in tropical areas (such as rain forests and coral reefs), wherein UV radiation was high.

The only wrinkle in the sunlight theory was that the deep sea competes with and perhaps exceeds the biodiversity found in the tropical areas worldwide. And of course UV radiation does not penetrate into the deep sea.

So perhaps something else was promoting rapid diversification: environmental stability. Tropical seas have roughly the same temperatures year-round, so organisms can really develop a specialized anatomy or physiology. Species that live in highly variable and unpredictable areas (such as New England) cannot specialize. They need to remain generalized so that they're prepared for anything. This ability to specialize in stable, unchanging habitats (the tropics and the deep sea) seemed to explain the promotion of diversification and speciation.

All of which was to say that, although they lived in gorgeous shells, the cone snails in Aja's Indo-Pacific species tank could kill a man with their venom in a matter of seconds.

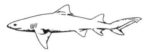

Aja's research included the observation and comparison of Indo-Pacific cone snail behavior with Caribbean cone snail behavior—feeding rates, growth rates, and diet preferences. She kept a notebook and checked the two tanks at least a dozen times a day, frequently with extended observations.

She diligently maintained the tanks in order to keep the environments as close to the natural habitats as possible. She programmed the timer on the lights to go on and off to match a normal day and night cycle in the sea. She monitored the temperature, salinity, and PH levels, and perhaps most important did weekly water changes so the tank water was always fresh and had the same level of trace elements as natural seawater.

On the morning after her nightmare, she dumped two buckets of old seawater from her specimen tanks off the dock. Bent on one knee, she lowered one bucket at a time so they filled with fresh seawater.

She heard the children coming down the dock before she could see them. They liked to help take care of the cone snail tanks and often visited around midmorning.

The children came running down the dock, their voices boisterous with excitement. They said they'd made a scientific discovery, that they'd found a new kind of creature that nobody had ever seen before. They wanted to name the new creature.

"It will be called the flipper fish!" Mookie shouted excitedly.

"Come look!" Carmelita pulled on Aja's arm. "You have to see it!"

"It's over on the ocean side," Myron said.

"What do you think it is?" Aja asked.

"Something pretending to be a turtle," Myron said. "Like an octopus turtle."

"That way enemies will think it has a turtle beak and will leave it alone," Mookie said.

"They won't want to get bitten," Carmelita said with evident delight.

Aja laughed at the idea. The Sea Cherubs laughed with her, and Mookie imitated a turtle biting with his hands.

"Okay," Aja said. "Show it to me when I'm done this."

After she topped up the hundred-gallon aquariums with buckets of fresh seawater, she followed the children to the ocean side of the island.

They walked across the field where they sometimes played Wiffle ball and soccer, then went up a narrow trail over a small sand hill covered in dune grass. At the top of the ridge the wind gusted stronger, and the blue water of the Gulf Stream stretched out and glittered in the distance.

As usual, they had the beach all to themselves. Tourists never came this far up from the hotels in Alice Town. Aja and the kids walked down the dune and across the hot white sand—made up of billions of pulverized shells and skeletons of ancient sea life—to the smooth, wet sand where the surf rolled up. The coolness felt good on their bare feet. They went to the right, towards the north end of the island.

The children left small, perfect footprints in front of Aja as she followed them. They walked for a quarter of a mile. When Aja looked back she saw that the waves, fizzing and white, had erased any sign they had come this way. A couple of seagulls followed them down the beach.

The children led Aja along the surf line to a spot where bits of driftwood lay strewn near large rocks that formed a tide pool. A crescent-shaped edge of turtle shell leaned against a branch of driftwood. It was wedged in the cleft of a boulder. It looked about four feet long and was bent like an archery bow. A pair of big, dark gray turtle flippers moved to and fro with the flow of the surf.

The Sea Cherubs were right. It looked like a reptilian sea anemone with two paddle-like tentacles.

"See?" Myron pointed at it.

Aja moved closer. The two flippers were jutting out from the edge of a carapace. She reached into the tide pool, touched it, and then tugged on the shell. It came free with little effort—it was not a new species.

It was part of a dead leatherback sea turtle. Except for the edge of the shell with the flippers, everything else was gone, including ninety percent of the shell. The whole rest of the animal had been sheared off.

No head. No tail.

It was understandable that the children thought it was a new species of sea creature. Aja told them it was the remains of a sea turtle, but they still were excited about it. They insisted they show it to Seabrook.

The Sea Cherubs took turns carrying it and they wanted to present it to him jointly, since they'd made the discovery together.

"Thank you," he said.

Crouching on his knees, he examined the remains of the turtle on the dock. Aja and the Sea Cherubs watched him.

"Do you think she was a pregnant female?" Seabrook asked. He was thinking of the enormous leatherback sea turtle that they'd examined on the research cruise the previous summer. That turtle had been a pregnant female still carrying eggs.

"We found her on a stretch of beach where turtles are known to crawl ashore to lay eggs. The time of year is right for it," Aja said.

"The cut marks are clean and almost straight." He ran his fingers along the edge where the shell had been severed.

"Like the leatherback we looked at on the *Colombus Islen* last summer?"

"Yes, very similar." He looked at Aja and shrugged. Back in Miami, they had consulted colleagues who studied sea turtles about the wound on the massive leatherback turtle they'd looked at on the research ship. Nobody had seen anything like it and didn't have a clue as to the cause. The best guess was the propeller of a cruise ship.

"Do you think it's a coincidence?" Aja asked.

"I really don't know. What do you think?" Seabrook said, turning to the Sea Cherubs, who had been listening to everything.

The Bahamian children looked at one another a moment, then whispered like a committee in deliberation. Then they broke out in quiet laughter at something one of them said. Heads nodded yes. They reached a consensus.

Myron stepped forward. "We think there is a sea monster that hunts pregnant mothers. It likes to eat fat bellies full of babies."

Carmelita nodded in agreement.

Mookie, with a giant smile, swept his arms down over an imaginary swollen belly to pantomime being pregnant. He capered and wiggled, flapping his elbows like chicken wings. With his tiny torso and thin arms and legs, he looked very funny.

They all laughed.

Mookie loved the attention.

Up on the path that led to the dock, Bastareaud stood watching. Seabrook and Aja were preoccupied with the remains of the sea turtle and joking with his children. The man wore his machete. His fingers gripped the handle like he wanted to unsheathe the blade. He stared at them a long moment.

Aja felt eyes on her. She turned and looked.

By that time nobody was there.

Chapter 12
Rainbow of the Sea

Seabrook's and Aja's lives were completely entwined with the sea. Every waking moment, and oftentimes while they dreamed at night, the ocean rolled endlessly through their conscious and unconscious minds. Even on land, if they tried to quit her for a day, they still breathed and sensed the salt breath and briny whisper.

On it, half in it, or deep in the Caribbean Sea, its colors engulfed them like air engulfs a flying bird. They wallowed in blue, they played in blue, they worked in blue, and they felt their lives most intensely in blue.

But to call this sea blue would be to paint with too crude a brush—for, in truth, the sea they knew and loved and depended on had such a spectrum of extraordinary oceanic hues that it was more accurate to call it a blue rainbow. A sister to the conventional rainbow of the air, but instead of having red to violet bands of refracted light, this watery relative was entirely composed of distinct tints of marine color: some gilded and electric, others mystical, others dark and opaque, and others celestial and crystalline.

But the sea was much more than divine scenery or a neutral arbiter of a day's events. At her worst she was an outrageous and titanic destroyer, and sometimes, when at her best, a sparkling, soft-spoken friend. She presented different faces that could change with quicksilver speed, by turns whimsical, solemn, or cheerful, or grandly magisterial, or evasively mysterious, and even violent and deadly. She could cast daydream spells and stir profound emotion and deep thought in her mortal acquaintances. After all, her cathedral depths have been calling to human souls since the beginning of time.

And each shade of blue held a strange hint of mortality, partially derived from its very impermanence, forever at the mercy of the sun's angle and the inevitable onset of night.

Even as the rising sun emblazoned and enlivened the deep with opalescent light, the setting sun diminished and snuffed the blue fire from the heart of her depths.

When Seabrook and Aja said they lived in Bimini, they really meant that they lived in a blue rainbow of liquid light.

Chapter 13
The Long Line

The day after he examined the remains of the leatherback sea turtle, Seabrook loaded the Boston Whaler for a trip to the long line: gasoline, a battery, a large plastic bait tub full of frozen mackerel, his tagging kit, a Hawaiian sling, a walkie-talkie, and a gallon jug of fresh water. Then he did his daily sun protection ritual, because he would burn horribly without it. He wiped his face, nose, ears, neck, forearms, and lower legs with sunblock lotion. He pulled on a T-shirt and swimming trunks that extended nearly to his knees. Last, he stuck a Dramamine patch behind his ear to prevent seasickness.

Then he dug up the key ring and gun from next to the shed and discreetly put them in the Whaler. They were going overboard into the deep sea. Aja had agreed.

He looked at the dark spot on the dock for a few seconds and wondered if he should try to scrub it clean again. He looked down into the water under the dock where the corpse had been hiding in his nightmare. The space looked perfectly normal in the sunlight. Just small fish flitting about in the aquamarine seawater.

It amazed him how anxiety and stress could cause such horrible thoughts.

But why had he and Aja had such similar dreams?

He started the outboard, cast off the lines, and drove the Whaler down the channel towards Alice Town. When he got to the smooth water of the harbor, he slowed down a little, going easy, so as not to make a wake and disturb the twenty or so sailboats at anchor.

He turned the throttle on full as he approached the mouth of the harbor. As the Boston Whaler accelerated, it lifted out of the water, the hull skimming on a plane over the surface of the sea. He turned left to avoid the sand shoal and drove out towards open water. The boat bounced and cut across the waves with a watery ripping sound. The air felt cool, and amazingly he could see down to the sea floor thirty feet below.

On his left stood South Bimini island. Trochoidal waves battered and rinsed the rocky coastline where a retaining wall of boulders stood. Coconut palms stood crookedly in the wind.

A Viking Sport Fisherman yacht raced past, leaving a deep V-shaped wake that rocked the Whaler hard. Two girls in tiny sorbet-colored bikinis waved at him from the flying bridge. The yacht accelerated and soon disappeared into the blue distance.

It normally took him forty minutes to get to the long line during fair weather if he went directly there. But today he took a detour. He turned right and headed out to the deep water of the Gulf Stream.

Twenty minutes later he put the outboard in neutral. He'd reached water that was thousands of feet deep. He took the key ring and Browning nine-millimeter out of the plastic bags. He threw them into the sea and watched them sink. The keys glittered as they sank and small bubbles floated out of the gun.

Maybe now he and Aja could put the drug runners out of their minds.

He motored back the way he came. Soon he saw Round Rock, a small dais-like rock platform, rising up out of the sea on the left, and up ahead in the distance, the western point of Turtle Rocks, which marked a reef system. He and Aja knew the Bimini islands and the water around them like it was their own backyard: every sunken wreck, every plane wreck, every reef, and every hidden passage through the mangroves.

He headed east to the Great Bahama Bank—flat, shallow seas that stretched for miles. The banks were submerged limestone platforms that had been dry land during the Ice Age and were amazingly level, like a vast underwater parking lot.

This was his favorite part of the day, gliding and bouncing over the turquoise sea with the wind in his face. He could see the seafloor as vividly as if he were looking through clear aquamarine glass: small coral growths, dark patches of turtle grass, spotted eagle rays like black kites hunting juvenile queen conchs, and occasionally a pod of wild dolphins.

All of it was lit up by shifting lances of sunlight that hit the white seafloor patterned as radiant hexagonal prisms, endlessly stretching and contracting under the hull of the Whaler. The extraordinary sparkling glow made it seem like he was motoring on the skin-like surface of something dynamically alive and sublime. It was easy to stare down and lose himself in the beautiful depths.

He wondered whether the line would be intact. At the end of the first week of setting the long line, he had found one of the steel leaders cut. He studied the leader and couldn't figure out what had happened. No shark could have done it, not a bull shark or even a white shark. The steel was too thick and strong: 920-pound-test stainless steel forty-nine-strand cable. It was flexible and kink-resistant. Maybe bolt cutters could do it.

But why would vandals take only one hook, and leave the remaining twenty-nine hooks? It didn't make sense. He had replaced the severed steel leader and missing hook with a new rig. He forgot all about it until it happened again three weeks later. Of course Aja blamed Razormouth when he told her about it. And they laughed it off.

The giant orange buoy marking the south end of his long line came gradually into view. It bobbed gently in the waves ahead. Half a mile long and marked with a giant orange buoy at each end, the long line ran horizontally across the flat seafloor with thirty hooks spaced evenly apart.

Each shark hook dangled at the end of a steel leader and floated in the water column three feet above the seafloor with a small buoy-like float. The long line was necessary for the age and growth study Seabrook was conducting.

Most sharks were measured, tagged, and released alive—so that when they were recaptured in the future, the fisherman would see the tag and follow the tag's instructions: report the length and location of the shark. That way Seabrook could calculate the rate of growth and age, based on the difference in length between one capture and the next.

He had baited the hooks with the mackerel from the freezer they brought over on the cruise ship from Miami at the beginning of summer.

The oily fish on thirty baited hooks put a strong scent in the water, and if the current was running in the right direction, attracted very big sharks from the depths of the Gulf Stream.

Whatever sharks he caught were measured, injected with tetracycline hydrochloride, tagged at the base of the dorsal fin, and then released. The tetracycline hydrochloride injection was intramuscular; it would become incorporated into the shark's vertebral column and be used as a time marker in the age and growth study in the event of future recapture.

Releasing a shark was easier said than done. They frequently seemed dead and needed to be revived. It usually required getting into the sea and swimming around with the shark, and driving ocean water through its gills until the predator was revived. He would hold the shark's left pectoral fin in his left hand and put his right arm across its back—almost affectionately, like he was on a movie date with Aja.

Once Seabrook swam forward and gathered a little momentum, the shark's extraordinary aerodynamic shape made lifting even the largest and heaviest shark manageable.

Initially, the shark would be lifeless and somewhat rigid. After a few minutes of swimming, he would feel energy start to animate its body. The tail would begin to wave left and right, subtly at first, then stronger and stronger, until the fish was able to swim on its own.

Sometimes, if he was very lucky, there was a moment he felt in the center of his being: a convergence that lasted just seconds—when the shark had come fully back to life and was swimming powerfully again. And Seabrook would still be swimming with it, still holding the fins, still connected with the fish. A mesmerizing primal moment, like riding a real-life phoenix risen from the ashes—a kind of wild flight, razor-edged with precariousness, the blue universe rushing past, beyond human language.

Then he would let go.

Chapter 14
Tiger Shark

Seabrook could see a shadow in the sea twenty yards away. It was big enough to be mistaken for a large patch of turtle grass on the seafloor or, perhaps, the beginnings of a reef. As he motored closer, the shadow morphed into a very large shark, maybe too big for one man in an eighteen-foot Boston Whaler. A big shark in a fighting mood could capsize a small boat.

As he moved even closer, the contours of the shadow became clear enough to identify the species: *Galeocerdo cuvier*, a massive tiger shark. It looked like a torpedo with fins but with the bulk and power of a small diesel pickup truck. It lay motionless on the white sand bottom, except for the opening and closing of its mouth, ventilating its gills.

He put the motor in neutral and carefully pulled in the line hooked to its lower jaw. The long line was rigged for small to medium-sized sharks, not giants. The rope was frayed and almost broken—the shark had nearly broken free. Any serious run by the great fish would snap the line. Anxiously, Seabrook continued pulling in the rope, as gently as possible, until he could feel the shark on the other end.

Suddenly the shark began to swim, rising off the seafloor, growing bigger and bigger, and more formidable, fanning its tail from side to side. The long line allowed it to move back and forth in a semi-circle by the side of the Whaler.

That's when he got his first true look at it.

She was absolutely magnificent, a beautiful female. She moved through the glowing water with sinuous sweeps of her tail, and the sun played across her dark gray back. Somehow the bait, a large barracuda's head, was dangling from the corner of her mouth, still attached to the hook—a gruesome trophy that stared with dead, hollow eyes. The tiger shark tried to swim away and pulled the frayed line taut, almost snapping free. Seabrook nearly stopped breathing.

Then she felt the pull of the hook and settled down in the sand again. Her breaking the line seemed inevitable.

If Seabrook could catch her, it would be one of the highlights of the summer.

Tiger sharks were one of his favorite species. They were a true apex predator and the most feared shark in the Caribbean and French Polynesia. The species ranked second only to the white shark (*Carcharodon carcharias*) in confirmed unprovoked attacks on humans and boats. They were deservedly famous for their voracious and undiscriminating appetite. Items found in the stomachs of tiger sharks included all types of marine reptiles, various marine mammals, grass, carrion, dogs, birds, cows and horses (presumably from local slaughterhouses), fish, conchs, sharks, cephalopods, billfish, and an amazing variety of typically inedible junk, including nails, wood, tools, tar paper, and an unopened can of salmon.

Seabrook put on his mask, snorkel, and fins to evaluate her condition—she was far too long and heavy to bring into the boat. The moment he saw her underwater, he suspected she was pregnant. Her belly was swollen to an enormous size. Either she'd eaten something like a whole manatee or she was approaching the full term of pregnancy.

Afraid she would snap the frayed line if he tried to pull her to the surface again, he swam down to her. He brought a tail rope. Normally, he didn't tail-rope sharks until he pulled them to the surface, because sometimes they thrashed and snapped their jaws to get free. It could get dangerous.

He wanted to catch this shark so badly, he was willing to take risks he normally wouldn't. He sneaked up and discreetly tail-roped her underwater, gently tightened the noose, and quickly got out of the sea.

When he started pulling in the tail rope, the shark exploded to life. She thrashed and churned the waves for a couple of minutes. Then she did something he'd never seen before: somehow she pushed off the bottom with her tail and for a crazy moment stood up out of the water. (The sea was only ten feet deep and later, when he measured her, he learned she was seventeen feet long, almost the same length as the boat.) Her head was broad and blunt, her jaws enormous, and at the height of her effort, she seemed to stand taller than Seabrook in the Whaler. Yet she was horribly disfigured. One side of her mouth had teeth missing and bulged out with hideous scar tissue, like lumpy pink cauliflower. It looked as if she'd bitten a spinning propeller years before and shredded half her mouth.

She came towards Seabrook—all power, teeth, and attitude—like she might come across the boat. He moved back in fear. Then she crashed sideways into the sea with an enormous splash.

Seabrook pulled the tail rope tight and tied it to the stern cleat. Then he tied the line hooked to her mouth to the forward cleat. She slammed her tail into the side of the Whaler, making the boat lurch and shudder.

After a few moments she grew calmer and, finally, idle alongside the boat.

He immediately used the walkie-talkie to call Aja. He told her he might have caught a pregnant tiger shark. While he took measurements, tagged her, and prepped her for release, Aja raced out to meet him in the Jon Boat and brought her Nikonos underwater camera. She took the short cut across the flats, because the Jon Boat was excellent in shallow water.

The tiger shark measured seventeen feet, one inch in length and six and a half feet in girth. She was by far the largest shark Seabrook had caught so far that summer.

Aja arrived just as he was finishing measuring.

"I think she's released some pups already," he said as Aja tied up alongside the Whaler.

"Why do you think so?" she asked. She unpacked her camera from its bag.

"There are fetal membranes hanging out of her vent."

Nobody had ever seen a tiger shark give birth. If she were to give birth, it might begin to answer important questions: where and when do tiger sharks give birth? How large are the babies at birth? Where do the babies live? The information would give the world a better sense of the species' natural history and needs. *Touching the torch of knowledge.*

Seabrook and Aja recognized the moment and its possible significance. They were over the moon with excitement but forced themselves to stay calm.

If they witnessed the birthing process, they could possibly publish a paper on the reproduction of tiger sharks in peer-reviewed scientific journals such as the *Bulletin of Marine Science*. If their photographs turned out well, their story and photos could possibly be accepted by *National Geographic*.

They both went into the sea and inspected the shark. Sure enough, fetal membranes protruded from her vent, indicating she may have already released some pups. Tiger sharks were ovoviviparous; they hatched from a thin egg case while still in the mother and were then born live.

When Seabrook first touched the pregnant tiger shark near her vent, she violently slammed her tail against the Whaler. After a moment she relaxed and suddenly gave birth to a baby. Seabrook gently caught the pup in the palms of his upturned hands. The first baby measured thirty-two inches in length. It came out fully formed with striking blue eyes, unlike adults of the species.

For a moment the pup seemed stunned, then suddenly wriggled to life and swam off. Once the birthing started, the babies came out one after the other. The babies had vivid stripes on their sides, and their eyes seemed disproportionately large, like cartoon characters. The pregnant tiger shark gave birth to eleven pups, then seemed finished. Perhaps they were a little premature and she was giving birth only as a result of the stress from being captured. Seabrook could feel many more babies inside—tiger sharks have as many as eighty pups at a time. All of the babies that were born swam off, but one. Seabrook kept the dead one as a specimen.

Even though she was still very much pregnant, Seabrook untied the shark's tail and removed the hook from her mouth. She had been in the water the entire time and did not need to be revived.

Underwater, they watched the giant shark go free. For an eerie moment she glanced at Seabrook with one of her flat, dark eyes, and he wondered what she was thinking. Then she swam off into the hazy blue distance, her giant body gliding through the sea.

She didn't seem in a rush and didn't seem particularly bothered—just cruised away in a sort of nonchalant, business-like manner.

Seabrook and Aja climbed back into the boats. They were silent a moment as the experience sank in.

"Did you get all that?" he asked.

"Yes," said Aja. "I think I got some great shots. That was amazing!" She had been snapping pictures the whole time.

She pulled off her mask and gave a big smile.

"That was incredible," Seabrook said. They wanted to talk about everything they'd observed, but Seabrook needed to follow the big female tiger shark before she disappeared from sight—he could still see her swimming near the surface twenty yards away. "I've got to follow her. We'll talk tonight."

Razormouth

With their faces and hair still dripping seawater, they kissed goodbye.

Aja drove off in the Jon Boat.

Chapter 15
The Gorgon Channel

Seabrook followed the seventeen-foot-long tiger shark, keeping the Boston Whaler's engine slow. He wanted to test a theory he had been developing about how the long line attracted open ocean predators. He'd caught, over the course of two summers, several very large sharks. The top three all happened to be females, and by an odd coincidence, each had been distinct in its appearance: hoary, disfigured, and scarred by age and many battles. Like old female lions after years of dangerous hunts and lethal fights with enemies.

Earlier in the summer he'd caught a twelve-foot female bull shark. She had terrible crescent-shaped bite scars across her back, and the top of her tail fin had been lopped off. Seabrook told Aja about the bull shark the day he caught her. He described the fish as being ugly, somewhat like a Gorgon. He told Aja how he'd followed the Gorgon bull shark across the shallow water of the Great Bahama Bank to see where she would go. The shark swam straight for Turtle Rocks and exited the shallow water through a channel in the middle of the reef.

The reef stood as a barrier between the shallows of the Great Bahama Bank, where the long line was set, and the deep blue of the Gulf Stream. The Gorgon bull shark went through to the deep side.

Seabrook thought that perhaps she'd also come through the channel following the bait scent of the long line into the shallows during the previous night—that the channel was a two-way thoroughfare for hungry Gorgons.

The previous summer, Seabrook had caught a twenty-foot great hammerhead shark. The fish was also a female, and Seabrook swam with her for almost an hour before she revived. She was the largest shark he'd caught in three months, and she also had a gruesome appearance. Her mouth was so studded with stingray barbs, it looked like she had a kind of shark goatee made of porcupine quills. Seabrook followed the Gorgon hammerhead after he released her, and sure enough, she also swam directly through the channel in the middle of Turtle Rocks to get to deep water.

Now Seabrook followed the enormous tiger shark that had just given birth to some of her pups. He wanted to see if she would also use the channel. In a way, she was more hideous than the previous Gorgon sharks. Her scarred mouth, missing teeth, and pink cauliflower-like scar tissue made her mouth look like a monster's maw. From the surface you couldn't see it, and she appeared intact—beautiful and enormous. With each tail stroke the surface stirred a little, and every now and then she rose close to the surface and her dorsal poked up and left a tiny wake.

The shark cruised slowly through the clear aquamarine water. The depth fluctuated from about eight feet to about twenty feet. The Gorgon tiger shark stayed about two feet under the surface, and she was very easy to follow. She didn't seem to care that she was being followed.

Seabrook motored slowly right behind her, trying not to get too close but making sure not to lose her. He didn't want to flank her and drive her one way or another. He just wanted to cruise slowly and let her lead the way. After fifteen minutes he saw the rocky ridge of Turtle Rocks up ahead. The rocks, which represented the crest of the reef, appeared as a dark line, about a half-mile long, on the horizon: a thin rock outcropping, barren except for the many seabirds nesting on it. The birds were active, taking off, landing, and circling the sky above. In the distance they looked like fleas circling above the thin strip of rock.

The Gorgon tiger shark started swimming faster as they approached Turtle Rocks. The rock ridge at the top of the reef had a gap in the middle. It was deep and wide enough for big marine life to swim through. The shark went through the channel, and Seabrook followed.

The shallow turquoise sea of the Great Bahama Bank suddenly gave way to deep water. Ocean waves rocked the boat, and a current pulled the Whaler sideways. The reef started in the shallows, roughly six feet deep, but quickly dropped away to one hundred feet, then eventually thousands of feet deep, and then after that was the Gulf Stream.

The shark stayed near the surface, swimming towards the Gulf Stream.

Seabrook felt incredibly satisfied. He had personally documented three large female sharks using the channel to cross from shallow water to deep ocean. He suspected they came through the channel at night after he baited the long line, following the scent of food.

He worked with sharks every day and had a great respect for them; he knew they were very dangerous at certain times. Even with all his expertise, or perhaps because of it, Seabrook wouldn't ever want to swim in the Gorgon Channel at night. He believed big sharks traveled through it from deep water, smelling blood and oil from the bait on the long line, and headed into the shallows. At such times the Gorgons were in full hunting mode and expected meat.

He continued watching the tiger shark, waiting for her to go under the surface and disappear into the deep. But strangely, she suddenly turned back and started swimming directly towards him!

She accelerated aggressively, breaking the surface of the water with her dorsal fin and back. Why was she suddenly so agitated? Had he followed her too long? Maybe she was trying to drive him away?

A cold feeling crawled up his back. He turned the boat to get out of her way. She was swimming as if she was going to attack the Whaler and, given that she was almost as big as the boat, he feared she would flip it over. She seemed to raise herself up out of the waves.

Then he saw why.

Another fish was in the water right below her—much bigger and lighter colored. A blast of white light suddenly flashed in the sea. Like underwater lightning. Seabrook blinked several times, and it was hard to see for a second.

The next moment he saw that the other fish had come up under the tiger shark, with a tremendous uprising of water, splashing, and foam.

The tiger shark's entire back and tail abruptly burst upward out of the water—flailing from side to side, all seventeen feet—as if she was being lifted from underneath.

Then she sank back under, and the water clouded red with blood.

The tiger shark continued to thrash and lamely swam in a circle, but the cloud of blood grew darker and larger around her. It was hard to see where the other fish had gone.

Seabrook killed the engine, threw out the anchor, and put on his mask and snorkel. Despite being afraid, he had to risk getting in the water to find out what was happening. He jumped overboard. He kept one hand on the side of the boat, ready to clamber back onboard if he was in danger. His eyes widened, and he took a big breath at what he saw.

Over the years, he had seen with his own eyes, or studied photographs and drawings, or read descriptions of every known species of shark identified by man—but he did not recognize what he now saw swimming thirty feet away. Nothing like it was contained in any scientific literature he'd seen, and nothing even remotely similar was recognized in the shark bible, Leonard J.V. Compagno's FAO species catalogue *Sharks of the World* that described all species of sharks worldwide. This creature looked vastly different and moved differently than any species he knew about.

It was as large as a basking shark, thirty-five feet or longer, but its head and neck seemed disproportionately huge—like an anaconda's head, swollen and distended, and the neck looking as if the anaconda was almost choking, trying to swallow prey (a large boar or an alligator) too big for it to eat.

Its pectoral fins were incredibly broad and long, like a hang glider with extra-wide wings.

He saw a normal-looking eye on the side of the head where sharks normally have eyes. Yet on the back of its head there seemed to be another strange feature: two concentric circles, as big as dinner plates, with an oval rise in the middle. He at first mistook the feature for some kind of giant blowhole because of the location. Then he thought he saw a large pupil looking back at him—a possible third eye on the back of its head that stared up towards the surface. He couldn't see the face or the mouth. Just the broadness of its head and the thickness of its neck from the gill flaps forward.

Yes! The thing on the back of the head seemed to be watching him.

The hide of the animal had freakishly large dermal denticles—as if its skin were made of bristling two-inch-long shark teeth that all pointed towards its tail. The overall effect was that the hide looked thick and incredibly tough, like armor.

The color of the back was gunmetal blue and marked with small whitish patterns, some resembling irregular wood shavings and others dots, flecks, scribbles, and right-angles, like a kind of foreign alphabet. As the shark moved farther away, the marks made it look as if the fish had been sprinkled with slushy snow melting.

Aside from the eye on the back of the head, the strangest thing was how it moved—undulating its body from side to side, in a creepy way, more like an underwater snake than a shark. It did not have external claspers (male reproductive organs) and thus appeared to be a female of its species.

Perhaps it was an illusion or simply foolish anthropomorphizing on Seabrook's part, but the fish gave the impression of brute arrogance, of an animal that feared absolutely nothing.

Electrified with excitement, he stared motionless at the other-worldly fish.

It disappeared in two seconds.

The devastated tiger shark, a magnificent seventeen-foot-long female, had been dwarfed by the new predator. She sank right in front of Seabrook, twitching and convulsing as she died, dropping lower into the blue depths.

The carcass settled on the sand roughly fifty feet below and was no longer really recognizable as a shark. Now she looked small and squalid, like trash thrown overboard by a tourist. The majesty and power that had emanated from the tiger shark just minutes earlier had been torn away.

She had been one of the most impressive sharks Seabrook had ever seen, and the stark difference between life and death would have been difficult for him to fully appreciate except for the fact that he had seen the shark alive and free, and he also had seen the moment when her grace, beauty, and power ended. She had been completely disemboweled.

Her swollen belly was gone. All her babies were gone. Her giant liver was gone.

Instead, there was a pony-size bite mark where her abdomen used to be.

Seabrook watched to see if the new shark would come back to continue feeding on the dead tiger shark. He looked at the open water where the strange predator had merged into blue.

No sign of it.

He waited longer.

After ten minutes a stocky bull shark casually cruised in from the deeper water and commenced eating the carcass, then another.

Seabrook climbed out of the water into the Whaler. He wanted to retrieve the dead tiger shark to examine the bite marks on it, but it was too dangerous. The bull sharks would guard their meal.

He went straight to the plastic toolbox tagging kit. He took out the small hardback notebook wherein he recorded the data on every shark he caught, tagged, and released. He shook the seawater off his right hand so it wouldn't drip on the paper excessively.

He flipped to the back pages and with a pencil drew a sketch of the mysterious shark he'd just seen while the details were fresh in his mind.

He also wrote notes on what he'd seen: the tiger shark's behavior, the flash of light, the eye on the back of its head, the sheer size of the bite cavity, the spooky way the giant shark had moved, and more. His hands were almost shaking, he was so excited.

Above the drawing and the notes he wrote the question: "Razor-mouth is real?"

Chapter 16
Baby Clara and the Day Visitors

C armelita carried the piece of mackerel sideways across her small hand. The fish was oily and had a strong smell. It felt cold and wet on her palm, because Aja had taken it from the freezer in the house. She'd cut it in half and given Carmelita the part with the head. The fish's eyes were clouded white with frost.

Myron and Mookie followed their seven-year-old sister down the dock. The Sea Cherubs took turns feeding Clara, the baby nurse shark that Aja and Seabrook kept in a pen between the dock and the beach.

Seabrook had caught the baby nurse shark (*Ginglymostoma cirratum*) on the long line. The fish was eleven inches long and somehow had hooked itself on a large shark hook. Extracting the hook from such a tiny mouth made a terrible wound in the baby shark's cheek, and it seemed likely she would die from it. So Seabrook brought the nurse shark back in a bait tub of seawater to try to save it.

Aja loved the little shark immediately. Its rounded fins gave it a softer appearance than sharks with triangular shaped fins. Its small eyes made it seem sleepy, and the little nasal barbels on either side of its mouth made it reminiscent of a cute catfish. It was vulnerable and sweet-looking.

Aja stitched its wound closed to help it heal. Then she and

Seabrook built a small enclosure with PVC posts and chicken wire fencing in the shallow lagoon between the dock and the shoreline. They intended to feed the baby, let her heal, and when she was bigger and stronger, release her.

Clara quickly became part of their improvised Bimini family: Seabrook and Aja were Dad and Mom, the Sea Cherubs were the children, and Clara, the baby nurse shark, was the family pet.

Sometimes Aja went swimming in the pen with the little shark. If she brought a piece of mackerel, Clara would take it from her hand. When Aja swam about the pen with her mask and snorkel, Clara would follow her like a pet dog begging for treats.

Over time, the little shark became quite tame and seemed almost affectionate. Sometimes she would react to a human's presence by swimming near the surface. And when Aja or Seabrook went into the pen with her, Clara always approached them, hoping for food. If they stood up in the shallow water, Clara would settle at their feet, or even between their feet. As if she wanted to stay close to them and catch any scraps they might drop down to her.

One day Aja enticed Clara into her arms and gently turned her over so she was belly up. In this position, the baby shark entered a state of tonic immobility and seemed to fall asleep. Aja stroked the baby shark's tummy, then fed her a small piece of mackerel. After three days of tummy rubs and mackerel treats, Clara would swim up and turn belly up just at the sight of Aja wading into the pen. She would do this behavior only for Aja—Seabrook tried but baby Clara just acted confused.

On the small table next to Seabrook and Aja's bed stood a framed photograph of Aja holding Clara like a human baby and kissing her on the head.

Aja had named the shark Clara after one of her heroes, Clara Barton, the famous Civil War nurse who founded the American Red Cross. They were both females and were both nurses of a sort.

"There she is! Near the side!" Mookie shouted.

"Right there!" Myron said, pointing.

Carmelita saw Clara resting on the bottom just next to the fence.

The children were so busy paying attention to the baby shark that they accidentally stepped onto the strangely dark stain on the dock—it made them feel weird and uneasy. They had avoided it for days and quickly walked away from it.

Carmelita had angled her arm back to throw the mackerel to Clara when a loud engine caught her attention.

A great long speedboat came rumbling up the channel. Going really slow. Two Latino men sat onboard. They were behaving strangely. Everyone always drove up the channel looking forward, watching the water in front of their boat. These men were facing the shoreline and idled the engines long enough to drift and stare at each dock along the channel between Alice Town and Bailey Town. As if they were searching for something.

Looking at the men gave Carmelita a scared feeling. They were two docks away, pointing and talking. Not in English.

"Feed her! Clara is hungry," Mookie said.

Carmelita looked back at the baby nurse shark and threw the mackerel into the pen. The dead fish splashed and sank just to the right of the resting nurse shark. Clara noticed it immediately. She stirred, moved her head, then turned and inhaled the piece of mackerel in one impressive gulp.

It never failed—whenever Clara ate, the Sea Cherubs cheered.

"Boy, she sucked the fish in like a good baby!" Myron said.

Clara swam about for a few minutes, energetic and excited, inspecting the area for more food. She splashed near the surface; her tiny dorsal fin briefly jutted out of the water, then went back under.

The children watched her and pointed. After finding nothing, the baby shark eventually settled back in the sand in almost the exact same spot.

The great long speedboat cruised up to the dock in front of them. Its engine rumbled and chugged like a huge monster at rest, snoring.

Carmelita looked at the men. She was suddenly afraid and wanted to run away. One had a thick gold necklace with sharp fangs on it—like the teeth of a mountain lion. When the men looked at her, she turned to run. Before she could move, the man with the necklace asked a question.

"Who owns this dock?"

Myron stood up straight and confident. "Reverend Bastareaud," he said.

"Do you live in the pink house?" the smaller man asked. He had jumpy eyes and looked around constantly.

The Sea Cherubs were afraid to answer. They didn't want these men to know where they lived.

"Is that your house?" the man with the necklace said, pointing to the house that Seabrook and Aja lived in.

"Reverend Bastareaud owns it. He rents it out. We live across the way," Myron said, being intentionally vague.

"Who does he rent it to?" the smaller one asked. He seemed hyper and kept moving his head as he looked around. Short little jerks like a chicken looking for something to peck on the ground.

"Why do you ask?" Myron said.

"Because we might want to rent it. Come here for a vacation. We might want to do business with your father," the smaller one said. Carmelita could tell he was lying. He seemed weird and twitchy, like people who snorted the white powder or drank too much coffee.

"Shark Man rents it!" Mookie shouted defiantly. "He catches sharks that could eat you up!"

The man wearing the necklace with fangs smiled. "Is Shark Man a scientist?"

"Yes," Myron said. "But if you want to rent, you need to speak to Reverend Bastareaud. He owns it. It belongs to the ministry."

"Is that the reverend's boat?" the shorter man asked, pointing at the Jon Boat that belonged to Seabrook and Aja.

The men were asking too many questions. Myron was about to tell his siblings it was time to leave the dock.

"No," Mookie said. "*That* is the reverend's boat." He pointed to the skiff his father used for catching crabs on the uninhabited shoreline along the tip of North Bimini.

"Why do you ask about the boats?" Myron said.

The men ignored the question. The smaller man put the speedboat in gear, and the engine grew much louder. They motored slowly up the channel to the next dock, then the next one, then the next.

The Sea Cherubs watched them go. A little quantity of oil from the engine spread a rainbow on the water behind the boat's stern. There were only three more docks for the men to look at. Then there was wild shoreline, and farther north the mangroves started.

Moments later, the men turned around in the channel and raced back past Bastareaud's dock.

They went fast, and their heavy wake slammed against the pilings as they went south towards the harbor.

Chapter 17
Dr. Nixon

"The most important scientific revolutions all include, as their only common feature, the dethronement of human arrogance from one pedestal after another of previous convictions about our centrality in the cosmos." —Stephen Jay Gould

A day later, Dr. Nixon, Seabrook's boss and mentor, drove his favorite research boat from Miami to Bimini to review the tracking data Seabrook had collected and also to deliver equipment. Small-boned, just shy of six feet tall, the man had sparse gray hair and a dark tan. There was a hollowness around his eyes and a shuffle in his gait that suggested a man used up before his time—he'd burned the candle at both ends his entire adult life. Nonetheless, he was always busy with one project or another. He was a genuine workaholic, and gaunt from skipping meals.

He usually wore a green patrol cap like Fidel Castro. He'd once been married, but his wife divorced him after a year. He worked around the clock and sometimes called Seabrook in the middle of the night with instructions or to discuss research, oblivious to anything but his own agenda.

Razormouth

Dr. Nixon was a world-famous shark expert. He was the primary reason Seabrook had chosen the Rosenstiel School of Marine and Atmospheric Science instead of Woods Hole Oceanographic Institution to pursue his doctoral thesis. Dr. Nixon was well-funded by grants from the National Science Foundation. He was also widely published in scientific journals as well as the less serious (but more important for fundraising) popular science magazines such as *Discover*, *Natural History*, and *National Geographic*. He had enough grant money to conduct shark research on lemon sharks simultaneously in Bimini and the Florida Keys, and on schooling hammerheads in the Sea of Cortez. He visited Bimini several times each summer to check how the work was coming along. Any publications that came out of Seabrook's work would feature Dr. Nixon's name as the lead researcher regardless of the fact that Seabrook did all the heavy lifting. In exchange, Seabrook would earn a Ph.D., get published, and accrue zero student loan debt.

Dr. Nixon usually flew to Bimini on a Chalks seaplane, but when he was delivering equipment, he drove an Aquasport 29 Tournament Master. The boat was almost new and outfitted with twin 350- and 260-horsepower MerCruiser engines. It was a great, fun fishing boat. Seabrook and Aja had once used the Aquasport to spend a long weekend diving in Cat Cay. It had a small galley and a decent-size stateroom for overnights. It was the flagship vessel in the little fleet of boats that Dr. Nixon's graduate students had at their disposal.

Dr. Nixon brought four new rechargeable batteries for the underwater receivers they used to track juvenile lemon sharks—two to replace a pair of batteries that wouldn't charge anymore and two spares. Plus, he brought two extra receivers in case any of the ones already in use had to be replaced.

The receivers were critical pieces of equipment. Seabrook couldn't manually track all the sharks in the lagoon simultaneously, and the receivers helped record the behavior (albeit in a less detailed way than manual tracking) of all the sharks.

The receivers were the size of traffic cones and could detect an ultrasonic transmitter signal inside a shark from two hundred yards.

Seabrook had buried a dozen separate receivers at key underwater locations in the North Sound of the lagoon. They recorded data twenty-four hours a day and were battery-operated. Seabrook retrieved the receivers every two weeks and downloaded the recorded data and recharged their batteries. He had recently collected all twelve, and they sat on the living room floor being recharged. Later he would rebury them underwater in the lagoon.

It took Dr. Nixon forty minutes to read all the new data Seabrook had downloaded onto his computer from the receivers, and another thirty minutes to review the data from Seabrook's manual tracking. He stared at the monitor on the small computer, checking the numbers on each tracked shark, clicking on one range profile after another. Occasionally, he scratched the side of his head or cleared his throat. He seemed pleased by the results. At the end he said, "Good work. You've been busy. At this rate, I think you'll be done this part of the research in a month. We've almost got enough here for your dissertation and to publish. I think the finish line is near."

Seabrook already knew this, but it felt good to hear Dr. Nixon say it. He needed to track one more batch of juvenile lemon sharks to increase his sample size. This meant he had to catch new pups and surgically implant ultrasonic transmitters in each of them, then track each of them for multiple six-hour increments.

But first he had to catch the pups that he'd already tracked, surgically extract the transmitters from them, and release them.

Dr. Nixon got up from the desk and walked across the living room to look into Aja's specimen tanks. The pumps made a low humming sound, and the halide lights made the saltwater tanks flicker with bright light. The halide lights would have made the room as hot as an oven without the air conditioner running.

"These are fascinating," he said. Nixon gazed at the cone snails that Aja had collected locally. They were in the hundred-gallon tank on the right. Although elasmobranchs (sharks and rays) were his field of expertise, he knew enough about cone snails to be impressed. "They have such pretty shells. These Caribbean specimens can sting you but are not fatal unless you are allergic to their venom."

"That's correct," Aja said. "These I collected here in Bimini."

Then Dr. Nixon moved to the hundred-gallon tank on the left that housed the Indo-Pacific specimens. He watched a cone snail, *Conus geographus*, as it moved across the bottom of the tank. The snail's shell was gorgeous, six inches in length, colored pink and overlaid with a fine chocolate-colored mesh pattern. It looked like a French pastry. A small silverside fish swam near it—food Aja had put into the tank. The snail extended its proboscis and then, with lightning quickness, speared the fish with its venomous harpoon. The fish died instantly. The snail retracted the venomous harpoon and quickly devoured the whole fish with its proboscis. It took several minutes, but Dr. Nixon watched the whole process.

"Really amazing. Aren't these usually nocturnal hunters?" he asked.

"Yes," Aja said. "That one has not eaten in a while."

"How many do you have in here?"

"Three."

"And they're very different from the Caribbean species?"

"In some ways. I'll send you my paper when I'm done writing my dissertation," Aja said.

"I'd like that. Please do."

After it swallowed the fish, the Pacific cone snail buried itself under the sand. Dr. Nixon watched it disappear. "It's ironic that something so deadly could have such a beautiful shell. I read somewhere that one drop of *Conus geographus* venom is enough to kill more than twenty men, that it is one of the most venomous animals in the world."

"Some people call it the cigarette snail," Aja said. "If one envenoms you, you only have time to smoke one cigarette before you die."

Dr. Nixon crossed the room and sat down on the sofa. "Tell me, have you found any more damage on the coral heads at Turtle Rocks? Like you found last summer?"

"Yes," Aja said. "We've found new ones every month this summer." Seabrook nodded.

"Are they the same size?"

"They look the same in every way," Seabrook said.

Dr. Nixon paused a moment. He glanced across the room at Aja's aquariums and watched the little pearly white jawfish emerge from its tunnel in the Caribbean specimen tank. It hovered in the water column like a three-inch-tall ghost. This brought a faint smile to his face. "I've checked around with colleagues at Rosenstiel and Woods Hole. I don't think those missing chunks of coral are caused by parasites or some kind of pathogen. I think they might be bite marks."

"We've also found the remains of another leatherback sea turtle. Its shell had been cut or bitten through in very much the same way as the one from last summer," Seabrook said.

"The power needed to bite such a large sea turtle cleanly in half would be stunning," Aja said.

"Right. Think of the bite power required to take bites out of a fifteen-foot coral head. Honestly, I think we may be on the verge of discovering a new species of shark or other big predator," Dr. Nixon said. "Something with amazing power and teeth."

"We've also had something bite through or cut the steel leaders on the long line," Seabrook said.

"Really? How many times?"

"Three separate times this summer. Just individual hooks," Seabrook said. "I've also seen something ..."

Aja looked at Seabrook and gave a knowing smile. He had already told her about seeing Razormouth. She knew he was planning to tell Dr. Nixon.

"I think I've seen it," Seabrook said.

"What?" Dr. Nixon said. He stood up.

"I think I saw it. Two days ago."

"Where?"

"Off Turtle Rocks. I'd just released a pregnant tiger shark from the long line and was following her to see if she used the Gorgon Channel."

"The Gorgon what?" Dr. Nixon said.

"It's a channel that I think big sharks use to swim from the Gulf Stream into the shallows of the Bahama Bank—it is an opening in the center of the reef system at Turtle Rocks. The sharks might be picking up the scent of thirty baited hooks through the channel and heading towards the long line. I've followed big females through it three times. They were older, scarred, and ugly."

"Like Gorgons," Aja said.

Dr. Nixon nodded.

Seabrook told him the whole story about the pregnant tiger shark and the enormous predator that had disemboweled it. He told every detail. Then he showed the sketch he'd made.

"Fantastic!" Dr. Nixon grew excited. "Imagine—a distinctly new species. And not one that is merely a slightly different version of an existing genotype, like megalodon and white sharks. Or another sixgill shark that is very similar to known sixgills. This sounds like an entirely new species without any known precursor. With unique and novel biological traits and a truly specialized natural history. You say there was a flash of light?"

"I think so," Seabrook said. "Right before it attacked the tiger shark."

"Perhaps to stun or disorient its prey," Aja said.

"Where on its body did the light come from?" Dr. Nixon said.

"I have no idea. It happened so suddenly, I almost doubt I saw it," Seabrook said.

"If it is responsible for killing the turtles and now a pregnant tiger shark, maybe it selects pregnant animals as a primary food source," Dr. Nixon said.

"Maybe it eats coral heads also, like a parrotfish," Seabrook said.

"If it prefers pregnant prey, how would it know if something was pregnant? Wouldn't it have to have some kind of echolocation ultrasound ability or other sense?" Aja said.

"Maybe ..." Dr. Nixon said.

"This is all sheer speculation," Seabrook said. "We're getting way ahead of ourselves here."

"I know. We're just brainstorming. But you *saw* it," Dr. Nixon said. "It is real. Whatever it is."

"We have to catch one," Aja said.

"That's right," Dr. Nixon said. "A new species needs a specimen that is collected and stuck in a museum."

"A type specimen," Seabrook said.

"Yes," Dr. Nixon said. "To establish a new species, you must have a type specimen. This is exciting. If you pull it off, and it is in fact as extraordinary as it seems, this could change the trajectory of your careers."

Seabrook nodded. He glanced at Aja and could tell she was thrilled by the prospect. Their futures suddenly seemed very bright.

Dr. Nixon had to return to Miami and wanted to get going before it got too late. He hated crossing the Florida Straits in the dark. But before he left in the Aquasport, he showed them three odd-looking shark tags.

Each was the size of a hot dog and had a short antenna at one end. Wiring, hardware, and a battery were visible inside the waterproof casings. "I have a present for you," he said after he set them on the kitchen table.

"What are these?" Seabrook said.

"These are the future. These will revolutionize and accelerate our ability to track wildlife. They are prototype satellite tracking tags that we've been given to test. Soon there will be no more need to use ultrasonic transmitters and receivers or to manually track sharks. Just tag a shark along its dorsal fin with one of these, and every time its fin pokes out of the water into the air, the tag will send data to a satellite in orbit. This is brand-new, state-of-the-art technology."

"How do you retrieve the data?" Seabrook asked.

"You just check the manual satellite receiver; the location of the shark will pop up when you select the tag number. We will know wherever the tagged shark goes. These tags report data to the satellite in real time."

"Where is the manual receiver?" Aja said.

"Here." Dr. Nixon opened a plastic case the size of a lunch box. Inside it was something that looked like a large calculator: the satellite receiver. He showed them how to turn it on, and they took a reading from one of the tags in the room—they were already reporting data. The screen showed their coordinates on Earth, and there was an outline of North Bimini with a red dot where they were standing.

"The batteries last about two years," Dr. Nixon said. "The engineers want us to field-test this prototype. They want to find out whether they are truly waterproof, especially at great depths. Will sharks just scrape them off? Will they malfunction? Things like that. Identify the bugs."

"I suddenly feel like I've been tracking sharks with Stone Age equipment. My God, I wish you had given me these one year ago," Seabrook said. "My work would have been so much easier."

"Science and technology march forever onwards," Dr. Nixon said. He smiled.

"So how do you want to test these?" Aja said.

"I want you to tag three midsize lemon sharks on the long line. We are going to start collecting data on the post-juvenile home range of *Negaprion brevirostris*. Once lemon sharks are big enough to leave the lagoon, where do they go? How far do they range? Do they ever return to the lagoon? Et cetera."

"Do the tags report depth or temperature?"

"No. Not yet. The engineers tell me that capability is coming in a few years. These are crude prototypes. They just give location."

Dr. Nixon looked at his watch. "I have to get going. Call me immediately if you catch a type specimen of the new shark."

He shook their hands and went out through the sliding glass door of the living room.

Seabrook and Aja followed him outside to see him off. They walked down the worn path to their dock.

Just before Dr. Nixon climbed aboard the Aquasport, he turned and faced them. Seabrook noticed he was standing on the stained spot where he and Aja had scrubbed so hard to get the blood of the dead man out of the planks of wood. It made him uneasy, and he remembered the horrible nightmare. A surprising and terrible impulse rose in his throat.

Seabrook almost blurted out, "We have to leave Bimini! It's not safe here!" But he kept his mouth shut. Their research on juvenile lemon sharks was only one month from completion, and they were on the verge of discovering a new species of shark. It would be insane to leave when they were so close to such extraordinary accomplishments.

Nonetheless, the Earless Man's visit haunted him. He thought he had put it behind him, but apparently he hadn't. Seabrook feared the man might come back, or worse, others might come looking for him.

"Good luck!" Dr. Nixon called and waved.

They waved back. A minute later Dr. Nixon shoved off in the Aquasport. He drove down the channel towards Alice Town.

"Are you okay?" Aja asked.

"Yes. Why?" Seabrook said.

"You look a little sick."

"I'm just tired."

Seabrook thought, *We have to finish the fieldwork and try to catch Razormouth. Just four more weeks and we're done. Afterward we'll leave Bimini and resume our normal lives as graduate students at Rosenstiel.*

Finish the job and all will be well.

Chapter 18
Pelon, the Hairless One

The orders always came straight from Concha, the much-feared matriarch of the Dores Cartel. Pelon needed to go with a crew of sicarios (hitmen) to the Bimini islands in the Bahamas and find fifty million in cash that someone had stolen. She wanted him to personally do the job and make an example of whoever had taken the cartel's money. The Dores Cartel was famous for brazen acts of violence. Concha wanted him to create a public spectacle that would make international news: horrify and intimidate her enemies and "shock the conscience of the public!" she said with a dry laugh.

The only unusual thing about the job was that Pelon was supposed to start by chopping Salvatore Dores, the Earless Man, because he had stolen or lost the money—unless he returned every single penny. Salvatore was Concha's grown son and a pilot. He flew small planes so low over the sea, they did not appear on U.S. radar, and he had the skill to land on the sketchiest landing strips imaginable, in remote areas of the Florida Everglades. He'd personally delivered or supervised thousands of shipments of cocaine to the Miami market—hundreds of tons of cocaine in five-hundred-kilo installments.

Salvatore had worked for the Dores Cartel since its inception. He had been their best smuggler, a legend in the Caribbean and Miami narco businesses, until recently "retiring" to be with his sick father. In truth, the South Florida Drug Task Force (CENTAC 26) had completely shut him down. They'd made it impossible for Salvatore to fly loads into the Everglades anymore—now the Dores Cartel smuggled the cocaine shipments hidden in legitimate commercial cargo. Therefore, Salvatore's pilot skills were no longer needed. Still, he was Concha's own son, and she had never sent Pelon to kill a relative before.

He shrugged at the thought. It didn't matter; he always followed orders and did exactly what the boss told him. Nothing more and nothing less. It was his personal professional code.

During the early days of her rise to power, before she was infamous and feared, Concha Guadalupe Dores had recruited Pelon as her top enforcer and sicario when she toured a slaughterhouse in Antioquia, Colombia, and saw the man's talent and potential. She knew the security guard of the meat plant and was visiting in order to see the equipment inside. She wanted to buy rending equipment that her crew could use in the Tumaco chophouse, a human slaughter house she was building for her enemies.

But Pelon caught her eye more than the equipment. He looked freakish, and the security guard was clearly scared of him—there was a rumor that Pelon had butchered a coworker, along with the coworker's wife and little boy, because the man had threatened him. Supposedly, he'd dismembered the family, starting with the child, then the wife, and finally the man, but first tied them up and made each one watch their loved ones die horribly until it was their turn. Reports were that he processed them like common steers and mixed the human meat in with the beef. There was no way to be sure of the truth. But the coworker and his family were never seen again. This story intrigued Concha. She wanted people to fear the Dores Cartel.

Pelon also stood out from the other young men working in the plant because he was larger and taller than everyone else. He had dead looking eyes that didn't quite match in color: the right one was damaged and discolored from street fighting. He also had weirdly dark red skin.

And even stranger, he did not have a single hair anywhere on his body —no eyebrows, no eyelashes, no pubic hair, no hair anywhere—she confirmed this herself. His red skin and utter hairlessness were due to a horrible work accident.

One year earlier Pelon had come to work after being beaten and robbed by street thugs. He had two broken ribs and a concussion, and could hardly walk straight. At the time, he was working in another part of the meat factory, operating a scalding vat, immersing dead bled hogs in a mixture of burning hot water and chemicals. The scalding tank softened the hog's skin and loosened the hair follicles, then scraped off the hair with rotating rubber paddles. Whatever hair remained was burned off with gas flames at the next station.

One big sow arrived at Pelon's station, thrashing and kicking on the chain hoist, somehow still alive despite being stunned with an electric shock and having its throat cut with a long knife—this meant the animal hadn't been killed or bled properly. When he submerged the dying sow in the putrid water of the scalding tank, the animal screamed and tried to crawl out.

Pelon stepped on the hog's face and pushed the sow down, but his balance was bad because of his concussion. He slipped and fell in the vat with her. The water temperature was set at 150-degrees Fahrenheit, but after many hogs, it usually dropped much lower, into the 130-degree range. Fortunately, Pelon had scalded eighteen hogs in quick succession. So the scalding vat wasn't quite hot enough to kill him.

The hog and Pelon both screamed, and it was impossible to tell which sound came from the man. He tried to climb out, but the shrieking sow thrashed and pushed him back under. The rotating rubber paddles started spinning and scraping his skin and hair. Pelon's and the hog's squirming bodies tumbled about in the scalding tank, and Pelon nearly drowned.

Finally, he moved clear of the dying hog, and the paddles stopped rotating. He crawled gasping from the vat.

His eyes were closed, and he lay on the concrete floor in a sick pool of hog drippings and filth from the scalding tank. Steam rose from his clothes and skin. His whole body had been scalded raw.

A few moments later he stood up and, amazingly, went straight back to work scalding hogs. He finished his shift and didn't even take a coffee break or change his clothes. But the scalding vat had permanently changed the color of his skin and destroyed all the hair follicles on his body. For several weeks afterward, blistered dead skin peeled from his body like a snake shedding.

Pelon, "the Hairless One," was the emptiest human being Concha Dores had ever met—he could kill anything or anyone in the most horrific manner without batting an eye. Screams, tears, begging, and bribes were feeble jokes to him. As Concha came to learn, Pelon took people apart as calmly and casually as if he were taking apart a child's puzzle. She never saw him angry, upset, lustful, or excited—never saw him show emotion of any kind. He never even smiled.

He could have lived big; he could have gone crazy with the money he earned, but he didn't want drugs, fancy cars, mansions, sex of any kind, or to have a spouse. He did not know how to enjoy himself or react to success. He had grown up in abysmal poverty, always hungry, forced to go door to door as a boy, begging for food at night and doing whatever was necessary to survive in the worst neighborhoods in Colombia.

He never went to school and was almost illiterate—he barely knew how to read street signs and could only crudely sign his name on documents. Everything he knew and understood about the world, he'd learned on the streets, and it was ugly, brutal, and vicious. His only human connection was his blind father. Now the old man lived in a small cottage in Pelon's compound. Aside from his father, Pelon cared only about having money saved up so that he would never go hungry again. And he liked doing his job well.

But he was loyal, and above all, professional.

On the day Concha Dores first saw him, Pelon was working in a beef slaughterhouse. She watched him operate the tail cutter, the belly ripper, and the hide puller. He was training a new employee and went through all the stations, beginning with the killing room. He stabbed the long, thin knife just above the breastbone of a steer, driving the blade up toward its head, cutting the carotid artery and jugular vein in one motion. Blood sprayed out in a geyser as he moved the steer to the bleeding station.

Pelon was an expert at butchering with pneumatic equipment: severing cattle legs with a pincer-like hock cutter, skinning cows with a cattle dehider, opening chest cavities with a brisket saw—but without puncturing or spilling the viscera (an important skill if you wanted to prolong a man's death), or at the end, using the splitting saw to halve a beef carcass down the backbone.

When one of the animals occasionally came to his station still alive because it hadn't been stunned or killed properly, it didn't matter to him. He skinned them and cut them apart all the same. He could turn a live steer into a pile of supermarket meat in thirty minutes. Impressed by his work, Concha talked to Pelon during a break.

"Do you know who I am?" she asked. Her bodyguards stood by her side and looked respectfully at him. They too were impressed with his skills and speed.

Pelon nodded. "Concha Dores, the Queen of Narco-Trafficking."

"Could you do this to a man?" She pointed to a skinned slab of meat hanging from a hook.

Pelon glanced at the beef carcass. "Easy," he said in a soft voice.

He looked at her strange eyes. They flickered slightly. He'd never seen such a thing before.

"No problem?" Concha said, double-checking. She had a good feeling about him.

He shook his head no. "It's all the same to me: steer, hog, man, woman, little girl, baby boy." He shrugged. "I kill them all, one piece at a time. Then I get my paycheck."

One of her bodyguards suppressed a laugh and nodded at him.

"I need a killer like you," Concha said. "Work for me. I'll make you rich."

At the age of nineteen, Pelon took over all the killing and torture for the Dores Cartel. He established two chophouses, one in Tumaco and the other in Buenaventura. And unlike low-level killers who used crude machetes, knives, and saws, Pelon had professional chophouses equipped with modern slaughterhouse cutters, saws, and grinders.

Concha Dores gave him his own crew and a secure house in the Colombian port city of Tumaco. He was in charge of terrorizing and intimidating all rivals and building the Dores Cartel's reputation for shocking violence and ruthlessness.

He personally tortured, killed, and dismembered hundreds of people for Concha: rival cartel members, informants, police officers, judges, politicians, and anyone else she wanted slaughtered. He also trained many underlings to do the work for him. They usually killed at night, and the screams of their victims filled the dark streets and poor neighborhoods where they lived like kings and queens.

Concha sometimes came to the chophouses to watch him work; it excited her, and she always held a party and needed cocaine and boys afterward. Sometimes the boss wanted the dismembered bodies scattered in the street to send a message to enemies in the Medellín Cartel, or for the media, but mostly she'd have him dump the remains straight into the Pacific Ocean.

Once, when he dumped a torso into the ocean, a big shark surfaced and began eating the body, one bite at a time. This fascinated Pelon. He stood on the boat and watched the feeding predator until there was nothing left. He felt that the shark had appeared to him for a reason, as a kind of kindred spirit. The next week, he had a large tattoo of a great white shark jaw put around his right eye—the eye that was damaged and discolored from street fights. He wanted his victims to know he was going to kill them one bite at a time.

He butchered anyone Concha told him to, including grandparents and small children, and the cartel grew richer and richer selling cocaine on the streets of the USA, sometimes grossing eighty million dollars a month.

The Dores Cartel grew so powerful, it controlled most of western Colombia and, most important, the ports of Tumaco and Buenaventura, which gave it access to the smuggling routes through Central America and up through the Bahamas and into Miami. The Dores crew operated a fleet of planes and boats, and became known as the bloodiest and most violent cartel operating between Colombia and Miami.

They were extremely well-armed, and police and prosecutors

wouldn't enter the slum neighborhoods where they worked. It was better and easier to accept bribe money and look the other way.

Also, everyone feared Pelon, the Hairless One, and his chophouses.

Chapter 19
The Invisible Natures

"I easily believe that in the universe the invisible Natures are more numerous than the visible ones. But who will clarify for us the family of all these natures, the ranks and relationships and criteria and functions of each of them? What do they do? In what places do they dwell?" —Samuel Taylor Coleridge

Razormouth was no longer a joke. Seabrook and Aja talked about it almost every day. When Seabrook came back from working on the long line, Aja would ask him, "See anything?" And "anything" really meant Razormouth.

And when Aja came back from studying cone snails on the airplane wreck, Seabrook would ask her, "See anything?" And again they were talking about Razormouth.

Their individual research necessarily remained their primary focus —however, the existence of Razormouth now competed for their attention. It struck their imaginations with a touch of monomania, reigniting the powerful allure and serving as the instantiation of the very aspects and ideas that had originally drawn them to the field of marine biology: the mysterious nature of the sea, the limits of mankind's knowledge, the wonder of science, and the thrill of discovery. Based on Seabrook's encounter, they suspected that Razormouth represented a unique new species with a remarkable physiology and life history.

On several occasions, Aja asked Seabrook to redescribe the unknown shark in as much detail as he could recall. From these descriptions, she drew a rendition of Razormouth on the blackboard that had been provided with the rental house—normally they left messages on the blackboard for each other and listed items they needed to pick up from Brown's Grocery Store. However, Aja used the full length of the blackboard to draw Razormouth as correctly and precisely as possible.

Now they lived with the portrait. They saw it on the wall all day, every day, whether eating a meal at the kitchen table or working on Aja's cone snail aquariums in the living room. Discovering the new shark and identifying it for science grew more and more important.

Some couples might set for themselves the goal of one day buying a nice small house wherein they could raise a family, or save enough money to retire early. Not Seabrook and Aja.

They wanted to bring a remarkable new species to the world and to spend their lives working in the sea. However, they conceived of a future where they would do much more than simply "discover" a new species and provide a type specimen to a museum. They intended to conduct scientific inquiries into its biology, morphology, evolutionary status, and—assuming their speculations weren't way off base—the implications of finding a distinct new species with no known predecessors or known fossil record.

If the creature turned out to be as strange as Seabrook's first impression, would it support Darwin's theory on the origin of life? Or would it fit into the unexplainable and apparently spontaneous appearance of abundant life associated with an event like the Cambrian explosion?

A type specimen of the coelacanth (*Latimeria chalumnae*) believed extinct for sixty-five million years was caught in 1938 and contradicted the accepted evolutionary timeline for the species. Its features were discovered to be unlike those of any other living fish: a heart shaped like sausage casings; unusual paired lobe fins (perhaps precursors of primitive legs) that interestingly also moved in a tetrapodal pattern. The way a trotting bear would move. Instead of a typical backbone, the fish had a notochord, a hollow oil-filled tube, and was protected by armor-like cosmoid scales. Paleontologists placed the coelacanth in the Lazarus taxon because it was believed to have gone extinct during the late Cretaceous period, when its existence disappeared from the fossil record—yet it was rediscovered as a living fish millions of years later. Back from the dead like the biblical Lazarus. Coelacanths are big fish that grow to around six feet in length, but Razormouth looked closer to thirty-five feet in length.

How could such large animals exist and remain entirely unknown to mankind? Were they somehow invisible until they decided to venture forth from the pelagic ether into the collective human psyche? And how many more creatures were still "invisible" to humanity? Was the number finite or infinite?

The occurrence of seemingly hidden creatures was not unprecedented. In addition to the coelacanth, Razormouth reminded Seabrook and Aja of the spade tooth whale. Nobody had ever seen one alive or even the carcass of one. In fact, they were known to exist only because a fragment of jawbone washed ashore in New Zealand in the 1800s, then a piece of skull washed ashore in the 1900s. One theory to explain why no one had ever seen one postulated that spade tooth whales had evolved their breath-holding ability to such an advanced degree that they spent most of their lives hidden in the deep, maybe surfacing only once or twice a day for a single breath. Like Razormouth, spade tooth whales were large, mysterious animals unknown to mankind.

Over the years of study and arduous fieldwork, Seabrook and Aja had asked themselves many times: how could humanity expect to dissect, catalog, and accurately comprehend such formidable and astonishing secret creatures? Doing so sometimes seemed a futile Sisyphean task. Life was too short to carry the torch of knowledge far—yet pursuing truth and wisdom and the improvement of one's soul was still the best way to live. That's why they had become scientists and teachers, despite the daunting nature of the work.

Chapter 20
A Child Crying

Seabrook woke up to the sound of children's voices. The noises came from outside the window. At first he thought he was dreaming. One voice was faint at first, like a whispered conversation, but the other child was crying—and not just crying. It was the awful sound of a devastated soul, anguished and inconsolable.

The sound wrenched his heart and made Seabrook feel sick. Was it some of the neighborhood kids coming over? Not likely. It was too early. The voices grew louder.

He quietly got up and went to the window. It was just getting light outside. He couldn't see anyone. The yard was empty.

He looked toward the shed where he kept the batteries and gas for the boats. No one was there or on the trail down to the dock. Maybe the voices were coming from the other side of the house?

He felt relieved when the crying suddenly stopped. Sometimes the kids were very rough with one another. Maybe they had sorted out the trouble. After all, it wasn't his job to police the neighborhood—he was a foreigner visiting the Bahamas and knew his place. He went back to bed.

Then the children's voices were back outside. They sounded familiar—possibly the Sea Cherubs? One was crying again.

Seabrook sat up and put his feet on the floor. Aja lay behind him, still trying to sleep. She was facing the opposite wall, curled up under the blankets. It sounded like the children were heading down to the dock. When he looked out the window again, he saw nothing.

Seabrook checked his watch. It was only six fifteen a.m.—the children had never come over so early. Where were the parents?

The voices grew fainter, and Seabrook couldn't hear them anymore.

What was going on? Why was the child crying?

Did they need his help?

Chapter 21
Inflection Point

"We're used to having everything handed to us, to pulling ourselves up by other men's bootstraps, to having our food chewed for us. Well, and when the great hour struck, everyone showed what he was made of ..."
—Fyodor Dostoevsky

Part of him didn't want to know why the child was crying, because the answer might force him to get involved. Another part of him was deeply worried about it. Maybe it was Myron, Mookie, or Carmelita in trouble? All the local kids he knew were generally very tough and rarely cried, let alone wailed like the sound he'd heard. They walked around barefoot, playing, roughhousing, and exploring all day on the wild beaches, splintery docks, and unsupervised yards. They were independent and uncoddled. Like Bahamian Huckleberry Finns. So crying could mean something serious.

Seabrook felt agitated and conflicted. He had become increasingly restless and troubled of late, but it had been simmering under the surface, and he had been ignoring it. His research and life with Aja had taken precedence—and rightly so. But now matters seemed to be reaching a critical mass, and he needed to take their measure, review how they'd come to this moment, and see what should be done. For they had everything to lose!

He and Aja had carefully planned a simple, straightforward life. And they felt extremely lucky—maybe even blessed. The single fact that they had found each other and fallen in love seemed a miracle—prior to their meeting, both of them had thought they'd never get married. They didn't plan to have children, and they didn't like to pry into other people's business. They were serious people who pursued their goals with clarity and discipline. Their lives were about science and the pursuit of knowledge, wisdom, and the improvement of their souls. As the philosopher Socrates prescribed.

Earning a Ph.D. would be the culmination of decades of tremendous work and sacrifice. Marine science was a calling both of them felt right down to the marrow of their bones.

As a child, Aja had been obsessed with trumpetfish (*Aulostomus maculatus*), and wrote a book report about their natural history in third grade. Then her curiosity about the northern lights (aurora borealis) in the Alaskan skies of her childhood led to a fascination with astronomy. In high school she thought she wanted to study planetary science and eventually become an astronomer. This goal lasted until freshman year at MIT. After going to the beach at Cape Cod during fall break, she suddenly knew that she should study marine science. The ocean convinced her.

Ever since Seabrook could remember, he had been fanatical about sharks—even before Hollywood popularized and demonized them with *Jaws* and all the schlocky rip-offs that followed.

In second grade, his homeroom teacher had the students in the class draw pictures of themselves as grown-ups, in some kind of profession. With Magic Markers he prophetically drew a picture of himself scuba diving with a bright yellow tiger shark.

As he grew older, his enthusiasm for being a shark scientist grew. He read every book and article published on the subject.

As a graduate student, he continued to read voraciously. Every weekend, he went to the University of Miami Richter Library and read any new scientific paper on elasmobranchs (sharks and rays) published anywhere worldwide. Then he copied them for his personal library.

He had painstakingly collected and collated every single scientific paper on elasmobranchs ever published. He had built the world's only complete collection of everything known about them. Most shark scientists focused on a specific area of study. Not Seabrook.

He needed to know *everything*. He took no short cuts despite the Herculean academic load before him.

Even as an undergraduate at Syracuse University, despite the temptation to specialize and take marine biology courses his first year, he chose to study all the sciences. He had the view and the instinct to build his career on a solid and broad foundation. He did not want any gaps in his education—blind spots could sink his career like an Achilles heel.

Therefore, he took hard classes in inorganic chemistry, organic chemistry, physics, basic biology, and also advanced math, computer science, and both Spanish and French. He took advanced English classes and learned how to write properly, because he knew that one day his ability to get research money would depend on his ability to write excellent research proposals.

His last two years as an undergraduate, he continued to resist the temptation to specialize (a self-destructive shortcut in his view) and instead continued to build as broad and strong a scientific foundation as possible. He studied all aspects of biology and took courses in ecology, cell biology, developmental biology, physiology, evolution, comparative anatomy, botany, genetics, microbiology, parasitology in all groups of organisms (bacteria, fungi, protists, plants, invertebrates, vertebrates). So after four years, he graduated summa cum laude with a B.A. in biology.

The next step, in graduate school, he switched his focus from biology to marine science—but in the broadest possible sense, not just fish or reefs, where his real interests lay. He took classes on plankton and marine production, marine invertebrates, marine vertebrates, marine physiology, marine ecology, marine food webs, marine bacteria, marine fungi, and marine protists.

Then, in order to understand the world in which marine organisms lived—which was obviously vastly different than terrestrial environments—Seabrook took courses in oceanography: chemistry of seawater, geology of the ocean floor, and the physics of waves, currents, and tides. In the end he earned his master's degree in biology with summa cum laude honors.

He approached his education in a methodical, ambitious, and relentless manner so that he could build a successful career and life out of it. Failure was not an option, and many times along the way he'd felt mentally exhausted and pushed to the limit—but he always pressed on.

His high school wrestling coach taught him many valuable lessons, but most of all about the absolute importance of mental toughness. He extrapolated that strength to the rest of his life and relied on it all the time. During high school, every day on the way to practice, he passed a large plaque over the entrance to the wrestling room. It read:

"This building is dedicated to the development of a more rugged and self-reliant American."

He'd read the credo hundreds of times, and it had well and truly sunk in. During brutal two-hour practices when their nationally ranked wrestling team had been pushed hard over the limit and were sweating, bleeding, shaking with exhaustion, and gasping for air, the coach used to say, "Pain is just weakness leaving the body" before making the team drill even harder.

Likewise, each step of the way, in his academic career, Seabrook worked furiously to be at the top of his class. This made it possible to earn scholarships with which to pay for an otherwise very long and extremely expensive education.

Now as a Ph.D. candidate, after eleven years of ferocious study, he was approaching his end game. He had finally started to specialize and become an ichthyologist and focus on sharks.

Even during Seabrook's time as a graduate student, other established scientists began to realize he was brilliant and driven, a scientist's scientist in the making. He had a breadth of knowledge and a fierce intellectual curiosity that never rested, and he possessed an encyclopedic knowledge of everything he had read.

His scientific heroes were thinkers like Galileo, Newton, Darwin, Tesla, Lyell, Gould, Compagno, the great French anatomist Georges Cuvier, and many others. Nothing was more important to him than to seize and carry forward *the torch of knowledge*. Even just a few inches—but hopefully much further: to do work that was solid and unassailable and that others could build on after he was gone.

Aja felt the same way and had followed a remarkably similar academic path, although she had earned her master's degree at the more famous Woods Hole Oceanographic Institute rather than Syracuse. A deep and serious education was something profound they shared, and it brought them closer together.

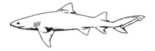

As he lay in bed, unable to sleep, Seabrook's uneasy feeling morphed into a terrible realization. Somehow, out of the blue, everything he and Aja had planned and had been working so hard to accomplish was being threatened. Last week the Earless Man and now a sobbing neighborhood child were problems that had dropped out of the sky on them with the weight of an existential crisis. And had the power to end their research, and possibly even get them killed. Would all the years of meticulous planning and unbelievably hard work all be for naught?

Maybe they should leave Bimini immediately?

But what about their life plans? What would they do instead?

He remembered the sound of the child's pain. It sank into him, a cold, aching feeling like chilblains over his heart. Questions he'd never let himself dwell on before rudely asserted themselves in his mind and demanded clear answers:

Why were Myron and his siblings so skinny? How exactly had Myron's face and head gotten scarred?

How had little Carmelita broken her arm, and why had it healed crookedly? Hadn't she seen a doctor? If not, why not?

Carmelita had explained, "The devil broke it when I was younger and bad."

How exactly had Mookie gone deaf in his left ear?

Seabrook shook his head. What did any of this have to do with science? Nothing.

What did any of it really have to do with him? Or Aja? It was unclear.

Should they just leave it alone? What was the price of getting involved? *Maybe everything.*

But could he live with himself if he didn't? This was the bigger question. Seabrook put his face in his hands and rubbed his closed eyes.

Perhaps there was a perfectly benign explanation for the Sea Cherubs' injuries and their fear of their father. After all, Seabrook didn't know the man and maybe was judging him unfairly. Sure, Bastareaud was rough with his children, but was it truly bad enough that Seabrook should inject himself into the situation? Who was he to say anything? He shook his head. This line of thinking felt all wrong: false and timid.

He needed to make the right move. He reviewed the facts again. He knew that whatever he and Aja decided to do was going to be a possible inflection point that could ruin their lives if they made the wrong decision.

It was often dangerous and foolish to interfere in family dynamics—even if an evil parent was emotionally and physically abusing his children. There was no Bahamian child protective services to call—Aja had looked into it. If the police talked to the children, would the kids be too afraid to tell the truth? Would it just make matters worse?

Also, he and Aja were in a weak position. They were able to work in Bimini only because the Bahamian Ministry of Fisheries had granted them and Dr. Nixon a special permit to conduct biological research in these waters. It was normally illegal to long-line for sharks or other big game. It was normally illegal to put equipment like underwater receivers for ultrasonic transmitters in the North Sound. In fact, some local bonefishing guides believed the receivers spooked the bonefish in the flats and therefore interfered with their livelihoods. They had already complained to the Ministry of Fisheries. The scientific permit that allowed Seabrook and Aja to do research was already on thin ice, and their relationship with some of the locals was already awkward. If they stepped on the wrong toes, their permit could easily be revoked, their ability to conduct research halted.

Still, there had to be something he could and should do. Nothing in the world upset and enraged Seabrook more than children being abused. He could hardly restrain himself when he saw an adult berating and humiliating a child in a grocery store, let alone mentally or physically abusing one. His feelings were intense. He didn't think he could turn his back on the current situation.

He took a deep breath and tried to cool off—he needed to reason this out. He could easily justify doing nothing and just look the other way, but the idea sickened a place deep within him. Unconscious living, empty platitudes, and chicken-shit rationalizations had always made him want to vomit.

As he weighed everything out, he felt something stirring inside himself that was not based in intellect. Unlike many of his scientist colleagues, Seabrook was not an atheist, but at the same time he did not go to church. In fact, some of the very worst people he'd ever met called themselves Christians and went to church every Sunday. So he fully understood why most of his colleagues were atheists. Most of his own experiences with organized religion had been repulsive.

Curiously, despite this fact, he felt something spiritual in his own life. He never told anyone about it except Aja, but sometimes he felt sort of guided. The impression of being guided, in the form of a quiet persistent feeling, a gentle murmur, was present inside him now. The feeling was unexplainable yet familiar, and often came to him and was most noticeable when he had important decisions to make.

Years before, when he'd first contemplated and weighed the relative legitimacy or falseness of "the quiet voice" (was it just his imagination? Or some sort of wish fulfillment?), he reassured himself that the experience of it was not without precedent. He recalled that in Plato's *Apology*, Socrates, while on trial for his life, famously described an inner oracle, or voice, that he consulted and trusted. So Seabrook had learned to trust and heed his feelings. And now the quiet murmur pointed him towards helping the children.

But what about the Earless Man? Had they truly seen the last of him? What about the people trying to kill him? The Earless Man's words spooked Seabrook: *"You don't want my life to come into your life."* And, *"She'll kill you and everything you love."* They sounded like lines from a cliché Hollywood villain, but they weren't. This was as real as it could get. He pictured the weird woman in the speedboat the day the Earless Man had visited them. He remembered her face in shadow, backlit, her awful smile, and the feeling of malevolence coming from her—and her eyes, which seemed to say that she would *enjoy* killing him. A powerful and obvious reason to leave Bimini.

But Seabrook had to live with himself. If something terrible happened to Bastareaud's children, and he did nothing to stop it, his inaction would haunt him for the rest of his life. The feeling—strange, but as sure as the tides—murmured within him presently: *Help the children.*

Despite his expertise about the marine world, Seabrook was very much aware of his incredible ignorance about most things, and had an inkling of the great limitations constraining all humans when trying to understand the world, the universe, and their place in it. He therefore accepted, with a sense of genuine humility, that there were forces at play in his life that he could not always see or understand. He remembered Nobel Prize-winning physicist Werner Heisenberg's famous quote: "The first gulp from the glass of natural sciences will turn you into an atheist, but at the bottom of the glass God is waiting for you."

So he tried to maintain an open mind, an agnostic viewpoint, but fervently wanted the truth, to live rightly, and to have a good life in the classical sense. That is why, in addition to his scientific heroes, he quietly read ancient books: those by Homer, Plato, Aristotle, and Thucydides; the Greek tragedians Sophocles, Euripides, and Aeschylus; and the King James Bible, Chaucer, and Shakespeare, among others. In addition to science, he wanted to understand the human condition, but even more important, he believed in the old-fashioned ideas of wisdom, character, truth, and grace.

All these thoughts flickered through his mind in mere seconds. He felt a final decision rising to the surface. In spite of the Earless Man's warnings, it didn't feel right to leave Bimini. In spite of the legitimate risk that his intervention on behalf of the children could backfire and destroy everything, something inside him—he did not know for sure what, but maybe intuition? Maybe his own innate sense of right and wrong? Or perhaps simple decency? His soul? Or perhaps God?—nudged him to stay and help Myron, Mookie, and Carmelita.

He sat up on the bed and pushed the sheet off. Now he needed to talk with Aja.

He would wait for her to wake up.

Seabrook stood up and quietly left the bedroom. He pulled on a T-shirt he'd left to dry on the clothesline outside, then went down to the dock.

The sky and clouds were tinted brassy gold. The mangrove thickets across the lagoon were black silhouettes hunkered low, foregrounded against the brilliance of the rising sun. The tide rushed out, seawater flowing quietly around the pilings. The turtle grass on the other side of the channel bent and waved underwater. The lagoon looked calm, pale green and liquid silver. A shimmering, beautiful morning.

Then he saw that one of the boats was missing. The Jon Boat.

Someone—probably the children—must have unlocked the padlock on the shed where he kept the batteries and gas tanks for their two research vessels. *Dammitt!* Whoever it was had stolen critical equipment.

Seabrook used the shallow-water craft to track sharks in the North Sound because it was the only vessel that could do it. Aja also used it to study the cone snails that lived by the sunken Curtiss C-46 Commando airplane when he went to the long line in their other boat, the Boston Whaler.

Without the Jon Boat, tracking juvenile lemon sharks would come to a halt.

A seagull circled overhead. Another stood at the water's edge and made a repetitive cry that sounded like a complaint: *huoh-huoh-huoh-huoh.* Then the gull flew over the channel.

Seabrook looked across the shallow lagoon to the blue sea in the offing beyond, then up and down the channel as far as he could see. No sign of the missing vessel.

He went back into the house. Aja came out of the bathroom. She still had sleep in her eyes. She gave him a kiss.

"What's wrong? Who was crying?" she asked.

He kissed her back.

"I don't know. But they took the Jon Boat. I'm going out in the Whaler to see if I can find it."

"What about the local authorities?"

"I don't want to get the kids in trouble. What if they had a good reason to take the Jon Boat? What if they were running ..."

Aja understood perfectly. "Bastareaud."

Seabrook nodded. "I couldn't sleep much last night. I've had this growing feeling that something bad is happening to the children. And I guess I'm still worried about the Earless Man and what he said too." He explained his concerns and the great risks he saw.

Aja nodded. "I was going to bring it up too."

This didn't surprise him. They were often in sync. "What do you think?"

She pulled out a chair and sat down at the kitchen table. He took the seat opposite her.

"In the last couple of days, the children have suddenly started opening up to me," Aja said. Her face grew serious as she talked. "They tell me things ... sometimes unintentionally. Bastareaud is a vicious man. He abuses them physically and mentally—can you imagine telling a child that Satan is talking through him? And he beats them. Half starves them."

Seabrook nodded. He knew all this.

Then Aja told him some things he hadn't heard before. She said, "Their father doesn't let them have water during the day, especially since we've has this long dry spell. Their cistern is almost empty, apparently. Myron, Mookie, and Carmelita come over here every afternoon and ask me for cups of water. They are always hungry. They complain about stomachaches—I think it's stress, fear, and hunger. Every Sunday he has his version of a "church service," where he makes them sing and pray for four or five hours straight, and he alone preaches to them. He isolates them, abuses them, and controls them. Textbook brainwashing techniques. There are no other people present besides his wife, and she is under his thumb also. It's a cult, and they've been stuck in this environment with this crazy man since they were babies. And they believe the garbage he tells them. His voice is in their heads. And they believe what the lunatic says."

Seabrook shook his head in disgust.

"We have to help them," Aja said.

"I agree."

He got up and went to the bathroom cabinet. He stuck a Dramamine patch on his neck behind his left ear.

"I am going to report him for child abuse," he said.

"Do you think that will help?"

"I really don't know. But we should start with the local authorities."

"Okay," Aja said with resignation. She looked like she had mixed feelings about it.

"What else can we do?"

"I don't know." Aja started making coffee. "I just wish I had a better impression of the police here."

"Maybe it will help to have an official complaint on record."

"I hope so," Aja said. "Or maybe he'll evict us from his rental house."

"He can't. The rent has been paid in advance for the whole summer."

They kissed goodbye, and she wished him luck as he left.

Seabrook drove the Boston Whaler all the way down the channel to the harbor at Alice Town. He took his time, carefully looking at each inlet and dock along the way in case the Jon Boat had been abandoned or parked. No sign of it.

For twenty-five minutes he steered the Whaler between and around the sailboats moored in the harbor—mostly single-mast vessels from the U.S. that were thirty to fifty feet long. He drove slowly so as not to create a wake. Then made a second pass by the docks of the Big Game Club, the Blue Water Marina, then the dock near the ramp where the Chalks seaplanes drove on to land. Still no sign of the Jon Boat.

Next he drove out of the mouth of the harbor and cut left to avoid the shoal. Once clear of the sand bank, he drove towards the Gulf Stream and open water. The sea grew deeper and darker blue. A few fishing yachts cruised in the distance. Seabrook looked in all directions. He didn't see the Jon Boat anywhere.

He put the engine in neutral. The boat rocked up and down, riding over the waves, as he thought of what to do next. Then his mind was made up for him.

Out on the horizon, piles of dark blue and gray clouds filled the sky. The thunderheads flickered with lightning. A tropical storm was heading their way. Seabrook had seen quite a few tropical storms moving over the sea, and this one looked strong.

The wind picked up and felt good. The ocean started growing rougher, waves growing taller in the wind, the surface scalloped and cresting white.

He turned the Whaler around and headed back to Alice Town.

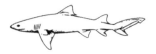

The Bimini Police Station was a small one-level building sandwiched between rows of palm trees on either side. The station was made of cinder blocks painted yellow. Two official vehicles were parked in the front: one police car and one golf cart. A large official seal had been painted on the wall. It read "Royal Bahamas Police" and had a crown over it and a red ribbon underneath with the words "Courage, Integrity, Loyalty."

Seabrook pushed through the twin glass doors at the entranceway.

One constable was on duty. The man looked fifteen years old and was dressed in a blue uniform that looked too large for him. He sat leaning back in a chair with his feet up on a desk. He got up and came to the front counter.

Seabrook said good morning, and the officer asked how he could help him.

"I'm here to make an official complaint. I want to report child abuse," Seabrook said.

The constable listened to Seabrook's description of Bastareaud's children and their injuries. He seemed to write something down but also seemed distracted and disinterested. Then the officer asked

Seabrook his real name—the island was so small, the man knew exactly who he was, but he'd heard only the nickname "Shark Man."

Once Seabrook gave him his name and address on the island, the officer said, "Did you witness Mr. Bastareaud beating his children?"

"No. I've seen the wounds on their bodies. The fear in their eyes."

The constable frowned and pulled back from the counter a little. As if he wasn't going to do anything.

"Do you know the man?" Seabrook said.

"Yes," the constable said.

"I'm telling the truth, and you know it."

The constable looked him in the eyes and seemed inclined to believe him. Finally he said, "We'll check on the family."

"Thank you."

Seabrook did not report the missing Jon Boat because he suspected the kids had taken it and he did not want to get them in trouble. He wanted the authorities to stop Bastareaud from abusing his children. That was all.

He left the police station and walked down to the concrete wharf where he'd tied off the Whaler. He walked past the restaurants and little stores that were on the way. The red-faced American captain of a yacht stepped out of the liquor store right in front of Seabrook. The man carried a case of Bacardi Gold rum and looked up at the racing storm clouds. "I guess I'm stuck on the island till this squall blows out," he said cheerfully, then glanced at Seabrook. "But I've got supplies!"

Seabrook just nodded.

The tropical storm had moved closer. The sky had darkened, and the wind was coming in strong gusts, hurling waves and spindrift at the coast.

To the citizens of Bimini, the storm was more than welcome. The islands badly needed the rain. There hadn't been any precipitation in a month, and the days had been scorching hot.

Seabrook also hoped the storm would hit Bimini full-on—sometimes they went another way and missed the islands. The cistern next to the house needed to be replenished. Still, the storm would make it harder to get the Jon Boat back. If whoever had taken it got caught in the rough seas of a tropical storm, they'd sink. The Jon Boat was not made for the open ocean and certainly not a tropical storm. But there was nothing Seabrook could do about it. He looked up at the dark sky and thought he might as well enjoy the cooling rain—even if it would make recovering the Jon Boat harder.

He got into the Whaler and headed for home, glad to be safely inside the harbor.

Chapter 22
Rain

The storm moved swiftly, and drops started to strike Seabrook's head and shoulders like the cool, wet fingers of a ghost tapping him. By the time he drove the Whaler up to their dock at Bailey Town, the rain was coming down in a deluge. He loved it, and sat on the dock to enjoy the scene. Just watching, and feeling the storm.

Gusting rain pounded and slushed the lagoon. The surface simmered and steamed under the torrent. Raindrops thrummed the wood planks on the dock. Everything was soaked and dripping. It felt incredibly nice, like his skin was absorbing the fresh water. After ten minutes in the rain shower, he stood up.

Soaking wet, he strolled up to their house. The storm filled the scenery with drama. Blustery wind made the coconut palms bend and the fronds wave. Every now and then the wind made a soft whistling sound as it hit the corner of the shed or one of the trees just right.

As he came off the trail from the dock into their backyard, he stopped when he saw Aja.

She was standing in the backyard where it was most private. She too had come outside to enjoy the weather. The gutter over her head gushed fresh rainwater, sluicing to the cistern next to the house. The full gutter gurgled and rattled, water overflowing and pouring down in a mini waterfall.

Aja stepped under the waterfall. They always had very short showers in the house—a quick soak, then they'd turn off the water. Lather up with shampoo, then briefly turn on the water to rinse—then quickly turn it off again. They used as little house water as possible because fresh water was in limited supply. But today was different.

Warm rain poured from the sky.

The rainwater showered from the overfull gutter onto Aja's head and shoulders, splattering on the grass at her feet.

She slipped her bikini down to her ankles, stepping out of it one foot at a time.

Then she untied her top and dropped it in the grass as well.

Naked in the storm, she began shampooing her hair. Her tan lines stood out like gorgeous stripes. Her bottom looked almost white.

Aja's whole body glistened wet, and she leaned forward, methodically wringing suds from her black hair. Rain and soap trickled and splashed down her shoulders, over her breasts, and between her legs.

She saw her fiancé and waved.

For a moment Seabrook's breath was gone. The sea goddess *Amphitrite was standing before him*. His bride-to-be was the most beautiful vision he'd ever seen; an image and moment he would remember for the rest of his life.

"It's amazing!" Aja called. She pointed at the sky with both hands.

Seabrook joined her. He took off his clothes, and they showered in the thunderstorm together. Then they made love next to the overflowing gutter. Miraculous warm rainwater, an indescribable luxury, washed over them.

They embraced and ran their hands over each other. They got on the ground. She hooked her legs around his waist. Then he was inside her.

Sensations and feelings and images blurred together: slippery hot nakedness, gusting wind, flattened grass, small seashells around them, palm trees bent in the wind. The storm churned the sky and lashed the lagoon, turning it greenish gray.

Sand stuck to their elbows, knees, and bottoms. Their hearts raced to the end.

Afterward, they slowly moved back under the overflowing gutter and rinsed off.

The loveliest dream made real.

Chapter 23
Maintenance

Pelon, the Hairless One, personally oversaw the maintenance, packing, and loading of equipment onto the seaplane the Dores Cartel was taking to Bimini: a Grumman SA-16 Albatross that enabled the drug runners to land anywhere in calm waters. He'd meet Vuelta and the other *sicarios* on a boat near the islands, switch from the seaplane to the boat, and approach Bimini by sea, pretending to be a tourist on vacation.

The Dores Cartel had a customized, portable version of the regular cutters and saws they used in their Colombian chophouses—a small-scale moveable slaughterhouse. But the equipment hadn't been used in some time, and he always checked that everything worked properly and that all the blades were clean and still sharp, so there'd be no screw-ups once it was time for blade to meet bone. Details mattered. Precision mattered. He was a professional and very methodical about his preparations and work.

They needed the equipment because shooting Concha's enemies wasn't good enough. She always demanded that the assassinations be gruesome and cruel to terrify the public and intimidate her enemies. They always killed as many people as possible—not just the target. They wanted TV stories and big headlines in the papers. In fact,

Concha Dores kept a scrapbook of all the news stories that highlighted the cartel's atrocities and hellish brutality.

Pelon examined the equipment, lubricated the parts, and ran each machine for a few minutes. He made adjustments as needed.

Although the saw on the carcass splitter looked good, he couldn't remember the last time he'd replaced it. So he changed it out to be sure —a standard fifty-inch saw blade.

Next he greased the dehider. There were three fittings: one on the blade, one on the camshaft, and one on the ball-bearing shaft.

Lastly, he took care of his favorite tool: the portable pneumatic hock cutter. It looked like a big claw. He greased the blades and the clevis. The tool had surgical-grade stainless steel pincers that were obsidian-sharp, and it also had a pistol grip that made it really easy to use. The hock cutter turned people into pieces incredibly fast: three-quarters of a second for the jaws to close and three-quarters of a second to open when biting through something substantial, like a beef leg.

Human legs were faster.

Less meat, less bone.

Chapter 24
The Fisherman's Hut

The tropical storm made terrifying noises. Storm waves pounded the beach in a steady rhythm: a foaming roar, followed by a long, receding hiss—again and again. The roof of the old shed creaked and shook like it might tear off and blow away in the wind. Rain made the rusted sheet metal violently shake and rattle. The pine trees outside, swaying in the storm, creaked and moaned, and every now and then, one of the coconut palms would drop a coconut that thumped across the ground.

It sounded like the giant land crabs had found them and were moving about and trying to dig through the ceiling to get at them—at least to Mookie. The Bahamian boy's eyes grew wide as he imagined the big crabs clawing through the edge of the roof to eat him. He was only eight and deathly afraid of the crabs because of how his father had terrorized him and his siblings with them. He also suffered terrible nightmares and was scared of the dark. He knew all too well that the crabs crawled out of their deep, wet sand holes at night, hunting for things to eat. The two boys huddled in the corner.

"Don't be scared," Myron said. "It's just rain." He was only twelve, but to his brother he sometimes seemed like a grown man because he was so confident.

"Are you sure?" Mookie asked.

"Yes. We are safe here."

Mookie nodded, then softly repeated, "We are safe."

"I wish I had shoes on. So I could step on them," Mookie said. He looked at his bare feet.

"We'll be okay," Myron said.

The tiny shed, an old fisherman's hut, was tucked away among the pine trees in the woods near the very northern point of North Bimini. The beach was only two hundred yards away. It was an uninhabited part of the island.

"When the rain stops, we'll make a little fire and eat something," Myron said. Since the storm had started one day earlier, they hadn't eaten anything except the candy bars their mother had given them. They had two cans of beans, a can opener, two gallons of fresh water, matches, and a half-full plastic gas tank they'd taken from the Jon Boat. Their mother had given them the provisions and told them where to go. They had run away from their father. Their mother had told them their father wasn't safe to be around. They knew it was true. They saw what he'd done to Carmelita.

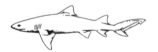

A day earlier, before they ran away from home, their mother had woken them early in the morning. It was still dark out. She made the "quiet" sign with her finger upright across her lips. She looked scared and exhausted.

Their father had just finished cleansing Carmelita of the devil again and had finally gone to bed—they could tell because the shouting and banging had stopped. And they couldn't hear Carmelita crying and begging anymore.

They sneaked out of the house and went around the back where their father kept the crab pens. They saw Carmelita, their little sister, lying on the floor of the pen that contained the most crabs. Myron and Mookie ran to the cage. They put their faces close to the chain-link walls of the cage to get a good look at their poor sister.

Mookie started crying—out of pity for Carmelita and fear of the crabs. He didn't want her to die. He wanted to take her with them, but their mother came up behind them and shooed them along—they had to be long gone before their father woke up.

Their last glimpse of their seven-year-old sister made them terrified and deeply upset. Her body looked broken. Three of her fingers were crooked, and her good arm wasn't good anymore. With swollen eyes and a lumpy face, she seemed lifeless. Her cheeks were streaked from crying. But she wasn't crying anymore.

She was very still. Too still.

She didn't seem to be breathing.

The crabs would decide. That's what their father always said. Sometimes when he was mad, he'd lock them in the cage and say they did something wrong. Then, if they didn't pray hard enough and do what God said—and only their dad knew what God thought—he'd leave them in the pen with the crabs until the devil left them. So far they'd always prayed hard enough that he released them.

Some of the giant land crabs were colored a sick yellow-white like a dead fish belly, and some were colored corpse blue. They clung to the side of the pen with long, spidery legs, more than two hundred pairs of eyes silently watching the girl. Claws opening and closing, mandibles smacking like they were chewing air. Waiting.

As the boys walked past, one of the largest crabs started climbing down a chain-link side toward their sister.

Mookie burst into tears, unbearable sadness rising up in his chest. He chest started to convulse, and he wailed. Myron covered his mouth.

"Shh, shh, shh. Dad will hear."

"But, but ... the crab ... is climbing down to her."

Myron looked for a second. Both boys knew what it meant.

The crabs would decide.

They ate only the dead.

Ten minutes later, Myron and Mookie decided to take the Jon Boat—somehow Myron felt the scientists would understand and forgive them. They knew Seabrook kept the keys to the small storage shed under an old sun-bleached conch shell. Myron unlocked the door. Mookie carried the heavy boat battery, and Myron carried the plastic gas tank down the dock. Mookie sobbed loudly for a minute, then suppressed it so they wouldn't get caught.

Just before sunrise, they drove the Jon Boat across the North Sound and entered the mangrove swamp.

They slowly steered through the thickets—they'd done this trip several times before when their father had taken them to the northern tip of the island to hunt the giant land crabs. Still, they got lost for an hour in the maze-like mangroves, coming to three dead ends in a row. Just when it seemed like they would never find their way through the mangroves, they found it.

The channel opened up and widened, the thick branches and leaves seemed to part, and they gradually came clear of the maze.

They motored into Bonefish Hole. It was clear and deep, like a big swimming pool. Then they drove the Jon Boat out of the enclosed safety and calm waters of Bonefish Hole. They passed entirely from the calm, shallow waters of the North Sound through the protective barrier of mangroves and into deep water.

The ocean.

Waves suddenly rocked the boat in a scary way. They turned left and followed the beach.

The flimsy Jon Boat swung left and right and bounced through the rough water. The boys kept close to the land and looked for a good spot to drive up onto the beach. They were following the directions their mother had given them when she woke them up and told them to run for their lives. She said they should hide until she came for them.

They could tell she was very upset. One side of her face bulged out swollen, and her eye was bloodshot where their father had punched the devil out of her. She hugged her boys, tears on her cheeks, for a long time. She was shaking and made a small hiccuping sound, because she didn't want to ever let go of them. That's what she said to them.

They drove the boat along the northern beach looking for the signs their mother had told them about. First they saw the spot where the woods looked thickest. Then they saw the big white rock. Waves shredded into foaming rags against it, rinsing and washing around the crags. Their mother had said it would look like the molar tooth of a giant.

Myron drove the Jon Boat up on the sand as best as he could, trying to beach it. He didn't do a very good job, because as soon as they got what they needed (the two water jugs, cans of beans, can opener, gas tank) out of the boat, the waves pulled it off the sand. It was lighter without the boys and their provisions. The sea quickly lifted the vessel off the wet sand and swept the Jon Boat back out to deeper water. It bounced and turned as it floated over the green waves. The boys watched it drift out to sea, too afraid to swim out and retrieve it.

Myron felt guilty and ashamed of himself for taking the boat. Even though his mother had told him to do it. He knew stealing was wrong.

Then Myron and Mookie went into the pinewoods to find the old fisherman's hut—their mother had said that her grandfather had built it and used to live in it many years ago. Very few people ever went to the northern tip of the island, and fewer knew about the old shed, because it was partially hidden amongst the pine trees by the beach.

Once they found it, they went inside. The rain started soon after. The boys lay down on the sand floor of the hut and tried to fall asleep.

Chapter 25
After the Storm

The rain didn't stop for three days, but on the second day someone reported that the Jon Boat had washed up on North Bimini's western shore. The battery and the gas tank were gone, but the vessel was intact and still seaworthy. Oddly, the thieves had not stolen the outboard engine.

Seabrook stuck a Dramamine patch on his neck and readied the Whaler. He drove the boat through the rain, down the channel to Alice Town, and out the mouth of the harbor. He drove to the right, up the coast of North Bimini, to get it. Although the rain continued unabated, the gusting wind had eased off, so the waves were down to two feet. The sky was overcast and gray. The sea undulated and splashed milky green along the coast. The beaches were littered with flotsam and jetsam: driftwood, sea foam, buoys, sargassum weed, and the odd Styrofoam cup blown in by the storm.

He eventually spotted the Jon Boat up on a beach, clear of the waves. He drove the Whaler's bow, scraping onto the sand near it. Then he ran and quickly tied a rope to the nose of the Jon Boat, and connected it to a ring on the stern of the Whaler.

Waves repeatedly rolled up and withdrew. When the waves came in, the Whaler floated, and when the sea swept back, it dropped motionless on the wet sand.

He splashed through the water and hopped into the Whaler, which was now floating, started the Evinrude outboard, and carefully dragged the Jon Boat off the beach.

He slowly towed it back to the dock, squinting into the spitting rain and wind. The whole way back he wondered who had taken the Jon Boat. Was it Myron and his brother Mookie and his sister Carmelita? If it was them—and he had a hunch that it was—were they safe? He had a feeling they were in grave danger, probably hiding somewhere on the island with their mother. If they had stolen the Jon Boat, it was pretty obvious they were still on Bimini somewhere; otherwise the boat wouldn't have washed ashore as it had. Seabrook hoped the police were taking action to help the children and their mother.

Back at the dock, he tied the Jon Boat in its normal spot. When he walked up the planks of the dock, Reverend Bastareaud greeted him. He had his arms folded and looked at the Jon Boat. "I'm glad you found your property," he said.

"Thanks," Seabrook said.

"Whoever stole it should be punished to the fullest extent," he said as Seabrook walked past him. It seemed like the man had more to say and wanted to talk, but Seabrook just nodded at him.

Bastareaud stayed down on the dock in the pouring rain and stared at the North Sound. Seabrook could have sworn the man was talking to himself.

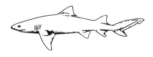

Early the next morning, when the tropical storm had blown itself out, the rain and wind gradually died down. The storm sounds—creaking, hissing, sighing, rustling, dripping noises—slowed and finally stopped. Myron watched the morning light grow brighter under the crack of the front door, and it matched the hopefulness that was growing in his chest. Maybe they would survive. Maybe their mother would rescue them.

Mookie lay in the sand next to him with one leg extended across Myron's legs, hugging his big brother. The little boy had cried on and off all night, burying his face in his big brother's neck.

Myron had comforted Mookie until he fell into a fitful asleep. He was used to it. He had been taking care of and protecting his little brother for years. When Mookie was very little, he used to get terrible ear infections. At the time, he was so young that he hadn't started talking in sentences yet and couldn't say what was wrong. Instead, he used to cry because he was in so much pain. He would point to his ears, trying to communicate. When Myron figured out what his little brother was trying to say, he told his parents. But they did nothing to help. His mother wanted to help, but she couldn't cross her husband.

Their father, Bastareaud, never took them to see a doctor. He and God would provide all the healing and medicine they would ever need, he said. Myron began to worry that the untreated infections would permanently damage Mookie's eardrums and make him deaf for life. But more than that, he feared the violence of his father. The man would scream at them and beat them if they ever disturbed or disobeyed him.

One afternoon, Mookie had tears running down his face and begged Myron for help. He kept pointing to his ears and couldn't stop crying—he looked so miserable, it made Myron's heart want to break. Then, out of nowhere, his father strode up behind Mookie and forcefully clapped both his ears.

The boy screamed and dropped to his knees.

Then his father seized both ears and roughly jerked the two-year-old left and right, like he meant to tear off the appendages.

"Shut up!" Bastareaud bellowed. "Shut up! Sissy boy! Or I will give you something real to cry about!"

Mookie gasped like it was his last breath, a long, ragged exhale. His father let go of his ears, and the boy fell to the floor, lifeless. He lay on the ground and looked dead.

After a long moment, Mookie's chest started rising and falling as he started to breathe once more. Yellow pus and blood leaked out of both ears.

"Praise the Lord! I healed him!" Bastareaud declared. "The evil disease is over. Praise the Lord!"

But it wasn't true. Mookie kept having ear infections, and he turned stone deaf in his left ear.

The next week, their father locked him in one of the crab cages for crying loudly and waking him. That night Myron lay in bed, sick with worry. He could hear his brother wailing outside—his ear infections raging. He knew Mookie was bathed in sweat and delirious with fever. Being alone in the dark, with the agony in his ears and the fear of being eaten by the crabs, made the sick little boy bawl louder than ever.

In the middle of the night, their mother rushed into Myron's bedroom.

"Myron," she said. "You need to help your brother before your father wakes up again."

Just looking at her made Myron more upset and afraid. She was frazzled and bloody, like she'd been hit by a car. Then he had a strong premonition that somebody might die that night. It took everything he had to stay strong and follow her directions—when all he wanted to do was run away with his brother and sister and mother. Find some island where they had no ministry, no crabs, and no reverend to cleanse them anymore. If he could find some safe place, he would never return.

His mother bent her knees and kneeled next to his bed. She was eye to eye with him. Her face was shiny with tears and sweat and blood. Her right eye was red and nearly swollen shut. She made a face as if all her insides were twisting in knots. It made Myron feel awfully sick and sad to see her like that.

"Listen," she whispered. She thrust a bottle of milk into his hand. It smelled like there was rum mixed in. "Give Mookie this. It will calm him. Stay with him. Help him. Please ... help him be quiet. Or your father will ... your father . . . will make him. Please ..." she begged.

Myron nodded and stood up. His mother kissed him on the head before he left.

He slipped outside, gently shutting the screen door in the kitchen behind him so that it did not make a sound. He walked in the darkness into the backyard where the crab cages stood, and saw Mookie in the first cage. He was crying hysterically.

"Little brother, I am here. You must calm down and be quiet. I will protect you from the crabs," Myron said.

Mookie made a wordless sound that indicated he understood. He seemed relieved to have his brother with him. He had his back to the cage wall so he could see all the crabs and they couldn't sneak up on him.

"Little brother, I will sit with you and keep you safe. You must be quiet now, okay?"

Mookie nodded. Myron sat down and pressed against the crab cage so the brothers were touching through the chain-link fence, back to back.

Little Mookie calmed down by degrees, until he was only whimpering. Then he begged to get out of the cage. He turned and pointed to the door.

"I can't do it," Myron said. "I'm not allowed. It would be worse for us if I break our father's rules."

Mookie began sobbing again. Myron whispered, "Shush, shush," and stuck the nipple of the bottle through the links of the cage. Mookie turned his head, then started drinking. He did not stop until the bottle was empty.

Being comforted by his big brother and the soothing effect of milk and rum ended the hysterics. Exhaustion took over. He quietly sobbed and had the hiccups for a short time, but finally fell asleep.

Myron sat with Mookie all night long. He also fetched a long stick. Unbeknownst to his little brother, whenever one of the crabs crawled over to see if Mookie's flesh was ready to eat, Myron poked it away. Fear of the crabs getting his brother made him stay awake until his father finally let Mookie out of the cage around lunchtime the next day.

Ever since that night, Myron had protected his little brother and sister as much as he could. That night also marked the beginning of Mookie's habit of always angling his head slightly to the left so that his right ear, the good one, pointed to whomever he was listening to.

Still in the fisherman's hut, Myron didn't want to move, even though the light under the crack of the door told him the sun had fully risen— Mookie needed to sleep. The problem was that Myron needed to go tinkle in the sea and couldn't hold it much longer.

Mookie's eyes suddenly fluttered open. "What's wrong?"

"I need to tinkle."

"Me too."

The boys slowly got up, sleep still in their eyes.

Myron opened the door to the hut. The ocean glowed brilliant blue, and the beach was painfully bright.

The sand outside was wet and crusty from the rain, and the ground was littered with leaves and coconuts that the storm had blown down from the trees. The boys went down to the water's edge and peed in the surf.

Then they walked down the empty beach exploring and looking for dry driftwood so they could make a fire. All the driftwood was wet, but some pieces were soggy and heavy. Those ones were no good. The good pieces of wood were wet only on the outside. Mookie was still terrified of the giant land crabs and stayed very close to Myron.

Myron said, "Don't worry. They only come out at night. We won't see any." He knew the crabs were nocturnal and would hide in their large badger-like holes until the sun went down. Mookie kept grabbing hold of Myron's elbow to stay close to him.

They each picked up several small pieces of driftwood and carried them along.

As they made their way down the beach, they stepped around piles of sargassum weed and stranded jellyfish that had washed up in the high winds the night before. The jellyfish looked like small rubber puddles glistening along the edge of the high-water line.

"Look," Myron said. He pointed down the beach. In the distance it looked like an old brown shoe on the sand.

"What is that?" Mookie said.

"That's a slipper lobster," Myron said.

They walked up to it. It looked more like a large brown bug, nearly a foot long, than a lobster. Unlike spiny lobsters, it did not have long antennae.

Myron picked it up. It was still alive and snapped its tail. It must have washed ashore in the early morning.

"We can eat this," Myron said.

They carried the slipper lobster and driftwood up to higher ground near the fisherman's shed. They set the pieces of driftwood on dead leaves and palm fronds, making a small pyramid with them. Myron splashed the little pyramid with the gasoline they'd stolen from the Jon Boat.

He struck a match and started a fire. The flames briefly whooshed high with the gas fumes, then dropped lower and almost went out. But the leaves and palm fronds crackled and burned. Small embers glowed. Then the driftwood caught fire. Thin smoke rose into the air.

The two boys ran down the beach and collected more driftwood. They fed the flames until the fire was strong. Once it was going nicely, Myron dropped the slipper lobster into the flames. It snapped its tail several times as it died. It would make a good meal.

While they made the fire and cooked the lobster, Mookie kept looking around, terrified of the giant land crabs. He thought they might sneak up and attack him.

Myron said, "Do you think we should make our campsite crab-proof?"

"Yes," Mookie said, nodding his head earnestly.

"You stay here by the fire," Myron said.

Mookie almost burst into tears. "Don't leave me!" he shouted. He stumbled to his feet.

"You will be safe here by the fire. The crabs are scared of the fire and won't come near you."

"No," Mookie said, starting to cry. "Don't leave me here."

"Mookie, you will be safe here," Myron said firmly. "I'm going to catch some crabs from their holes. I will kill them and put their bodies near our shed so the others will stay away. They will see their dead friends and run away like babies. Don't you want me to make our campsite safe?"

Mookie nodded yes and wiped the tears from his eyes.

"You don't want to put your arm in one of their holes to help me catch them, do you?"

"No," Mookie said.

"Okay," Myron said. "You stay here and I will take care of everything."

Mookie sat down in the sand next to the fire and watched his brother walk into the woods where there were many giant land crab holes in the ground. Since it was daytime, all the crabs were hiding at the bottoms of their dens.

Earlier, Myron had noticed several crabs that had died overnight in the storm. He didn't know why, and he hadn't pointed them out to his younger brother because he was already so scared of them.

He walked up to the dead crabs and picked two up. Bugs had started to swarm over them. He went down to the waves and rinsed them off.

Then he carried them up to Mookie, saying, "Look what I killed."

Mookie stared at the crabs Myron held, one in each hand. He looked skeptical, as if he wasn't sure they were truly dead.

Myron held the crabs up high in triumph, hamming it up, trying to get his brother to laugh. "Now we will place these weaklings around the camp! And all the crabs will KNOW we are CRAB KILLERS and they will stay AWAY."

Mookie smiled and nodded. "Yes. They will run to their mamas."

Myron said, "That's right. They will run to their mamas and suck their thumbs like little babies, they will be so afraid of us!"

Finally, Mookie laughed.

Myron placed the dead crabs on either side of the shed. Now his brother would be less afraid.

With a long stick he dragged the slipper lobster out of the fire and let it cool. They took sips from the gallon jug of fresh water their mother had given them.

After it was cool enough to touch, they tore the shell off the lobster. It had turned completely black, like the lobster was made of coal. The shell felt soft and peeled off like wet paper. The meat inside was pure white and delicious.

The boys ate hunks of lobster meat with their fingers and sipped water. As they took their meal, the waves rolled up below them. They looked up and down the beach in case someone should appear. No sign of human beings anywhere. They were completely alone, and they both quietly wondered when their mother would come and get them.

Once they'd eaten all the lobster, they put out the fire with wet sand so nobody would see the smoke. Then they went back into the shed to avoid the heat of the afternoon.

Before entering, little Mookie stood and regarded with great satisfaction the dead land crabs that stood as warnings, on either side of the shed, to all other crabs. In broad daylight, with a belly full of lobster and his big brother nearby to keep him safe, everything seemed so much better than yesterday. He felt less anxious and suddenly incredibly tired.

Inside, they set the two cans of beans, the can opener, and the two gallon jugs of water their mother had given them in the back corner. The can opener was rusty, but it would do the job. They planned to eat one can of beans for dinner and the other for breakfast the next day. They set the gallon jugs of fresh water next to the beans. They'd already drank one jug down to about the three-quarters line.

They shut the shed door and lay down for a nap. Both boys quickly nodded off.

Chapter 26
Vandalized

Seabrook wanted to check the twelve receivers he'd hidden in the shallow water of the North Sound. They might have been damaged by the storm. He drove the Jon Boat over flat, calm water early in the morning while it was still relatively cool. As usual, he saw no other vessels.

The receivers were spread out and hidden at key locations in order to cover as broad an area as possible, so that he could record the activities of the baby lemon sharks he was tracking. The cone-shaped receivers were camouflaged light brown, partially buried, and hidden out of the way in case bonefishermen ran their boats nearby. He didn't want the equipment tampered with or accidently hit by boats. All summer, the receivers had been working perfectly. None of them had leaked or been disturbed.

He put the outboard in neutral as he came to the spot where the first receiver was hidden. It was nestled at the foot of mangroves. He climbed out of the Jon Boat into the thigh-deep water. When he tried to pick the first cone-shaped receiver out of the sand, the top lifted off.

"What the hell?" He brought it out of the water, in two pieces. Seawater poured out of the broken base as he lifted it out of the sea. He set the top and the base in the Jon Boat. The receiver had been busted open and the interior flooded. Maybe someone had accidently run over it with an outboard engine and broken it.

He climbed back into the Jon Boat and motored to the next receiver. As soon as he touched it, he could tell it was also damaged. It was broken in exactly the same manner as the first receiver.

Seabrook's heart beat faster. This couldn't be a coincidence. He put the second broken receiver in the Jon Boat and motored to the third one.

By the end, he found that all twelve receivers had been smashed open. Someone had broken open their seals, flooded them with seawater, and knocked them over. He put each of the broken receivers in the Jon Boat—someone had done a real job on them. The tops had either been hit so hard that they cracked apart, or they had been chopped with something like a machete. The damage was beyond his ability to repair it.

All twelve receivers destroyed.

Two weeks of data lost.

Rage filled his mind like a red mist. He cussed out loud. How would he finish the research now?

He couldn't collect the final data points until they could get the receivers overhauled or replaced in Miami. As he considered the situation, Seabrook realized that someone had been secretly watching him all summer; that at least some of the times when he had thought he was alone on the water, someone else had been there as well—someone he could not see, perhaps a person with binoculars—spying on him. The thought made him feel paranoid, and he looked around to see if anyone was watching him at that moment. He saw nobody in any direction.

But he didn't trust he was alone. How could he? He had believed that no one but Aja and himself knew where all the receivers were hidden; he'd been dead wrong.

Next he thought about who could have done it. Who was aware enough of their day-to-day activities to be able to watch them and figure out where he'd put all the receivers? Their landlord, Bastareaud was the only person who came to mind.

Sometimes he'd seen the man motoring across the sound on his way to harvest the giant land crabs he sold to restaurants. Sometimes, Bastareaud lingered on his dock, tinkering with his boat engine. But the man owned the dock and the property, and had every right to be there. Still, it had to be him. It gave Seabrook a cold feeling to think of it.

Lately, he'd also noticed that Bastareaud had taken to carrying his machete all the time, and he seemed cagier and surlier than before.

When he added it all up, things seemed clear. There was an obvious timeline of events. Seabrook had reported Bastareaud for child abuse. Now, three days later, his research equipment had been destroyed. Coincidence?

Not likely.

Seabrook shook his head in frustration. The island police must have told the man who had lodged the complaint. No good deed goes unpunished.

As soon as he got back to the house, he would warn Aja about Bastareaud, then call Dr. Nixon and have him collect the broken receivers so they could be repaired in Miami. In the meantime, Seabrook would continue to manually track the sharks.

Finish the job and all will be well.

Chapter 27
Crab Hunter

At midday Myron woke up. He'd had a terrible dream that a ghost was chasing him. He sat up and thought he heard a man shout outside. He woke up Mookie, pushing on his shoulder until his eyes opened. He put his upright forefinger across his lips and whispered, "Shh, shh, shh."

Mookie nodded, and his eyes grew fearful.

They cautiously ventured out of the shed. The boys froze after walking two yards. In the distance they saw the small figure of a man coming through the woods down at the edge of the beach. Mookie went back inside and took one of the gallon jugs of water. Then the boys shut the door to make it look like they hadn't been there at all. Quietly and discreetly, they sneaked into the woods towards the mangrove fringes and the upper edge of the North Sound.

Crouching, they hid behind a pine tree.

They caught another glimpse of the man. He was still walking along but had changed his direction so he was now moving towards them, heading inland away from the beach. But he didn't look their way. He seemed to be watching for something on the ground in front of him. Finally, they could see him well enough to know he was their father. They recognized his walk and the machete he carried in his right hand.

Mookie started crying. He didn't want to be cleansed by his father. He didn't want to be locked in the cage with the crabs.

"Shh, shh, shh," Myron said. "He'll hear us." It was probably already too late. Myron had watched his father hunting crabs many times. The man knew how to pretend he hadn't seen a crab and wasn't focused on it—while the whole time he actually walked along moving "accidentally" and "randomly" closer and closer to what he wanted to catch. They watched him coming towards them a moment longer, then Myron couldn't stand it any longer.

"Let's go," he whispered, and took Mookie by the hand. They left the water jug on the ground by the tree.

The two brothers sneaked off, crouched over, scrambling towards the brush and brambles of the mangrove woods that fringed the North Sound.

They heard their father start to run. Heavy footfalls chasing after them. The large man crashed through the pine woods. *He had seen them all along!*

They saw him coming straight for them, machete in his hand. His eyes were wild, like when he would punch the devil out of their mother.

Mookie cried, "No!"

The boys ran as fast as they could. Sprinted terrified through the brush. Stray branches scratched and whipped their skin.

They could see the mangrove thickets standing in seawater ahead. If they could just get into the water, it would be easier to hide and harder for their father to follow them.

"Stop, evil boys!" their father shouted.

The boys pushed branches apart, dropped onto their knees, and crawled into the mangroves. Their knees and hands turned wet. Sand and leaves stuck to their shins. They slipped downward over sand, logs, twigs, and leaves into the murky water among the mangrove roots.

"Myron and Mookie! It's me, your father!"

The boys crawled on their bellies, like alligators, farther away from the dry land, away from their father's voice. Only their heads protruded from the swampy water.

Mosquitoes buzzed in their ears. The water got deeper, and now they could stand without showing their bodies. The water came up to Mookie's chest. Dense branches and leaves stood between them and their father and covered their heads from view with a leafy green canopy.

They scuttled sideways away from where they had entered the thicket and worked underneath the strongest branches they could see. The water was even deeper now, up to Mookie's chin. He kicked his legs underwater and grabbed onto his big brother's shoulder so he wouldn't drown. He made small desperate squeaking sounds. Myron whispered, "Be quiet," and hugged his brother so the little boy wouldn't sink.

"Myron! And Mookie! It's your father! Come out here! Right now!" the man boomed. He was very close, pacing around the mangrove thickets by the edge of the water.

Mookie closed his eyes and clung to Myron's arm with both hands. Stabilizing himself.

"I am worried about your souls." Their father suddenly used his nice voice, showing concern. "The devil is in you. You will burn in hell unless you let me help you. *Please let me help you.*"

The boys didn't fall for it this time. They stayed motionless. If they moved, he might hear them.

"Myron! Mookie! Listen to your father! I love you. Let me save you from the devil!"

Now he seemed to move away from where they were hiding.

"I see you!" he suddenly screamed and began furiously chopping through branches of the mangroves. "I'll teach you a lesson you'll never forget! The crabs will decide! *The crabs will decide!*"

Birds flew up in the sky, alarmed by the loud ruckus. Mookie nearly screamed, but Myron covered his mouth. Their father was chopping nowhere near them, which meant he didn't know where they were.

They listened intently to the sounds of the man hacking away at branches. He stopped after a while and muttered, "I'll find you. *The crabs will decide.*"

Next, the man crashed through some branches like a crazy person. It sounded like he was turning and looking in every direction, looking for signs of his boys. He suddenly stopped moving again.

Moments passed.

No more human noises. Just the sound of life in the mangrove forest. A mangrove cuckoo gave its guttural call: *ahrr, ahrr, ahrr.*

Then quiet.

Their father made no noise for what seemed a long time, maybe twenty-five minutes. Could he be gone? Or was he listening?

Waiting for them to come out of hiding?

Or waiting for them to make a noise that would give them away?

Again a mangrove cuckoo cried *ahrr, ahrr, ahrr!*

Quiet again. The boys began to wonder and hope.

"Honor your father!" the man suddenly roared from very near. He'd sneaked closer and begun searching through the mangroves again.

Chopping with his machete.

He whispered in a dry voice, *"The crabs will decide."*

The two boys hugged each other as tightly as they could.

And hardly dared to breathe.

Chapter 28
The Searchers

The next morning, farther south, Seabrook and Aja resumed work before sunrise. It was time to surgically remove the ultrasonic transmitters from the six lemon shark pups that had been tracked to conclusion, roughly eight days each.

They drove the Jon Boat out to the North Sound at four thirty a.m. After anchoring the aluminum boat in three and half feet of water, they set out a gill net right where they knew the pups would swim—the sharks moved westward over the flats at sunset and back eastward at sunrise. They seemed to use the sun as an orientation cue and were predictable in their travel patterns. The sky was dark, and the water was thigh deep and as black as octopus ink.

Seabrook and Aja set the monofilament gill net perpendicular to the shoreline right up to the water's edge. Then they sat in the boat in the predawn darkness and listened for splashes, waiting for the sun to rise over the mangroves.

On most mornings, a quiet stillness hovered over the North Sound and noises traveled far. Once a shark became entangled in the gill net, it violently thrashed to get free; you could hear the splashing from a long distance across the water.

Aja wore a light blue hoodie sweatshirt, because it would get chilly after her legs and bathing suit bottom got wet and the morning breeze picked up. Her cheeks were rosy in the cool morning air, and the palms of her hands and fingers were pink from handling the rough gill net in the sea.

Seabrook wore a black rugby jersey with his favorite team's name stenciled on the left breast: New Zealand All Blacks, with a white fern above the name. He wore dark blue bathing trunks, and rubber boots to protect his feet.

While they waited for sharks, they sipped hot coffee from a thermos. The sky brightened very gradually, and the surface of the lagoon was smooth and dark; it reflected the changing light and mangrove thickets like a mirror.

The dawn was usually stunning after a storm, and this morning was no exception. The eastern horizon gradually lit up in lilac and pink that grew more luminous by the second. To the west, gray storm clouds hovered and drifted as the tail end of the tropical storm receded from the area.

They sat still and looked at the heartbreakingly beautiful sea and sky. They did not talk.

For a moment they held hands.

The first splash occurred twenty minutes after they set the gill net, and the second splash five minutes later. The sounds prodded them into action.

Seabrook and Aja took turns wading out to the gill net to retrieve the tangled sharks. Each was roughly two feet long and had a mouth full of very sharp teeth. A shark had to be handled carefully, one hand clasping its back in front of the dorsal fin and the other hand clasping the base of the tail. This was necessary so as not to injure them, but also to avoid injury to oneself. If you held one by just the tail, it would turn and bite. They were muscular, lithe, and quick.

Even little lemon sharks could rend flesh with their teeth.

Once they retrieved a shark, they carried it to a nearby enclosure. All the juvenile lemon sharks were placed in a fifteen-foot-wide circular pen made with PVC poles and chicken wire fencing. The pen stood in the lagoon in three feet of water. The sharks swam slowly in a disorganized circular pattern.

While Seabrook and Aja worked, another skiff motored into the lagoon and headed their way. It stopped about 250 yards in the distance. It looked like a bonefishing guide had brought a client out for a day of fishing on the flats.

They noticed the boat, and kept working. They caught five baby lemon sharks with transmitters. The sixth one never turned up. Later, when Seabrook listened for it with the hydrophone, he heard nothing. It may have been killed by a predator: a man with a fishing rod, or perhaps a bigger shark. Or possibly, it had swum to a different site.

Next they needed to surgically remove the ultrasonic transmitters from each captured shark. This required careful and extended concentration. Each pup would need to be anesthetized, cut open, and sutured shut after the transmitter was removed. Seabrook and Aja had to go back to the house to prepare themselves: eat something, take off their cold-weather clothes, apply sunblock lotion, and collect the surgical equipment. This break would also allow the lemon sharks to settle down from the stress of capture. But today was different.

The boat that had come onto the flats earlier had moved closer to them. The morning sun glittered brightly on the water and made it difficult to see the individuals on the boat as anything more than two silhouettes. But even without binoculars, it was clear that they were not fishing. Nobody cast a rod.

"What do those guys want?" Seabrook said out loud.

The two figures on the boat seemed motionless.

"They're clearly not fishing," Aja said.

"If they don't leave soon, I don't want to go back to the house and leave these sharks trapped in the pen unguarded. I'll wait here and you go."

"Let's see if they leave first."

Seabrook and Aja collected the gill net, rolling it up like a great long carpet, and picked out any sponges and coral tangled in the monofilament. This took another hour. Then they set it in the bow of the Jon Boat.

The two figures on the boat still hadn't moved. They sat on their skiff and seemed to be staring straight at Seabrook and Aja.

"Do you recognize the boat?" Seabrook said.

"Maybe, but I'm not sure because of the glare," Aja said. "I think it's a red one I've seen before." The sun had risen high in the sky. It got so bright during summer days that sometimes it was hard to see—especially without sunglasses. And if you weren't careful, the glare gave you a blinding headache.

They studied the people watching them a moment longer.

Suddenly the boat's engine started, and the two figures motored south towards the harbor.

After Seabrook and Aja came back from the house, they began surgically removing the transmitters from each shark. Seabrook caught the first pup with a scoop net. He quickly placed the wriggling shark in a small tub of tricaine methanesulfonate anesthetic until it went to sleep. Then he placed it on a wet towel (soaked with seawater) on the bow of the Jon Boat.

Aja inserted a PVC hose into its mouth with a plastic funnel at the other end. She began dunking the funnel into the lagoon so that fresh seawater flowed through the patient's gills. Seabrook wrapped the wet towel over the shark's head to keep it moist and protect it from the sun.

They traded duties and took turns performing the surgery. Aja went first. She used a sterilized scalpel to make a small incision in the shark's abdomen. Wearing surgical gloves, she gently located the transmitter inside the shark and carefully extracted it with her fingertips. Afterward, she stitched the incision shut with an absorbable suture material, making eight perfect square knots.

When Aja was finished putting in the sutures, Seabrook took the shark to the pen, and held it gently underwater, and walked it so that the sea flowed through its gills. The shark quickly revived and swam on its own. Then Seabrook released it.

Back at the Jon Boat, Aja sterilized the surgical tools in isopropanol in preparation for the next patient. They did all five sharks, one after the other, in this way.

When Seabrook began stitching up the fifth shark, a boat came into view. It headed towards them.

It was now late afternoon, and the sun had moved to the west.

"Look," Aja said. She was now wearing polarized sunglasses.

Seabrook glanced over his shoulder. There were two men, like earlier in the day, on a red bonefishing skiff. The boat did not keep its distance. This time it came right up to them.

Seabrook was down to the last two stitches. The shark's head was covered with the wet towel.

The boat stopped fifteen feet from them. Two Latino men were onboard. The taller one was a little less than six feet tall. Maybe twenty years old. He had a scraggily, thin beard and a soft-looking body. The shorter one was much older, was skinny, and moved with a nervous tick. He seemed to be the boss. He reminded Seabrook of an insect, because he was so twitchy—maybe a cokehead. His eyes darted everywhere as if he was paranoid. They both wore jeans and light-colored, short-sleeved, collared shirts open at the neck.

"Good afternoon," the bigger man said with a Colombian accent. He was wearing a gold chain necklace with fangs on it.

"How can we help you?" Seabrook said as he tied a square knot on a stitch. He didn't look up, because he didn't wear sunglasses while performing surgery on sharks. He saw detail better without them. His eyes would hurt if he looked up into the glare, so he looked at the shark under the wet towel in front of him.

"We have a serious problem," the cokehead said.

"Our friend visited you. We need to ask you about that," the man with the necklace said.

Seabrook looked at Aja as if to say *here we go*. She put on her game face and nodded almost imperceptibly.

"I don't know what you're talking about," he said.

"I know you remember him. He had no ears," the cokehead said. "What did he say? Where did he go?"

"We're the wrong people. I have no idea what you're talking about," Seabrook said. He finished the seventh stitch and started on the eighth and last. Aja funneled seawater into the shark's mouth, irrigating its gills. The shark started to revive. Seabrook held it down and felt its muscles contract, trying to get free. Then it relaxed again. They had to finish or the shark could die.

The bigger man climbed off the boat with a splash and aggressively walked through the thigh-deep water. He now had a gun in his hand. "Don't be stupid. Our man is missing, and we need to find him pronto. What did he say to you?"

"I'm sorry we can't help," Seabrook said. He finished the last stitch on the baby shark.

Aja took the wet towel off the shark's head. Seabrook was about to put the fish in the water.

The man pointed his handgun at them, a black nine-millimeter.

They froze.

Aja put her hands up. Seabrook put his hands up as well.

The shark lay on the bow of the Jon Boat in front of him.

"What the hell is that?" said the man with the gun. "Baby Jaws?" He waved his gun, so Seabrook and Aja moved back.

Then he grabbed the shark by the tail and shouted to the cokehead on the skiff, "Look, *patron*. Baby Jaws!" He raised the small shark up high to show his boss. Its tawny yellow skin glistened in the sunlight. Its eyes seemed alert.

The shark pup suddenly turned and bit the man's hand. It jerked its head, the muscles along its side flexed, and its teeth ripped the flesh from the man's pinkie.

The man screamed and dropped the shark into the water. Then he dropped his nine-millimeter. He brought his injured hand slowly up before his eyes. A shocked expression came over his face.

His little finger had been completely defleshed.

It was now a skeletal pinkie covered in blood.

The cokehead's chest heaved like he was forcing himself not to laugh, but he picked up a shotgun. It had a pistol grip, and he racked a shell into the chamber. He raised the barrel and pointed it at Seabrook and Aja. He was still on the skiff, looking down at them.

The wounded man bent over and looked in the water for the rest of his finger, but could not see it. Maybe the shark had swallowed it before swimming off? He stooped and picked up his wet gun. Then he waded back to his boat.

The cokehead said, "You people lie. I know you helped our man. That's the only reason I don't kill you. People are looking for him and the money he took. You should help us find him before the cartel gets him."

"He was wounded," Aja said. "He pointed a gun at me and made me bandage him and give him water. That is all. He said nothing."

"We know nothing about him, or his business, or any money," Seabrook said.

The nine-fingered man climbed back into the red skiff. Both men in the boat stared at Aja, then Seabrook, for a long moment—trying to decide whether they were lying and whether to kill them. After a moment, the cokehead started the engine, and the red skiff drove off.

Seabrook and Aja felt overwhelming relief. They had told the truth and that had been good enough. The men looking for the Earless Man had accepted what they said. Perhaps that was finally the end of it.

Chapter 29
Long Night

The night seemed endless, as if the sun would never rise again. Maybe "the end of days" that Myron and Mookie had learned about in their father's church had arrived. They hid in the seawater under the mangroves the entire time. Wet and dirty and bitten by mosquitoes, Mookie clung to his older brother Myron for dear life, and he shivered for hours even though the weather was warm and humid. He also spoke, just once, to whisper that he was thirsty.

Fear of their father kept the boys motionless even though a fish occasionally nipped at their bare toes. Spiders lived in the mangroves and covered some of the low branches with their webs. Several times, spider silk got stuck on Myron's face and hair, and he had to carefully wipe it away, one-handed, without dropping Mookie.

Also, the stilt-like underwater mangrove roots that elevated the trees above the waterline, teemed with life after sunset, and the boys wondered what strange marine organisms came out in the darkness, gliding, scuttling, and undulating in the flowing liquid underworld. Sometimes Myron felt like he was dreaming as the weird creatures moved around and occasionally poked their feet and legs. He imagined needlefish, spiny lobsters, eels, stingrays, turtles, snails, trunkfish, and baby sharks. Even though it scared them to be surrounded by nameless and invisible sea beasts, it was still better than being caught by their father.

When the sun began to rise, Myron saw that Mookie's face looked gray. He knew he'd better get his younger brother some fresh water and a place to get warm as soon as possible.

Nevertheless, Myron and Mookie stayed put until long after the sun had risen. It was too dangerous to move at dawn. In silence they watched the reflection of the morning sky on the water grow brighter. Myron knew how patient and cunning a hunter their father was—and expected he was waiting silently in the woods for them to come out of the mangrove swamp and walk on dry ground through the pinewoods towards the old shed on the ocean side. Then he'd catch them in the open.

Therefore, when Myron felt safe enough for them to move, they didn't return the way that they'd come. Instead, Myron led Mookie along the edge of the shallow North Sound. They moved through a muck of floating leaves, seeds, plant tendrils, and bits of manatee grass, their actions concealed under the outstretched foliage of the mangroves. The boys sneaked away from where they'd last heard their father's voice.

They waded and paddled in the shallow seawater like sea turtles on their bellies, going as silently as serpents, always staying chin deep in the water.

They stopped every few minutes and stayed absolutely still.

They listened intently for any sign that their father was lurking in the brambles on higher ground—they knew that he'd have to move along the shore to follow and catch them, and this would cause bushes to rustle and twigs to break under the big man's weight. Birds would spook into flight at the sight of the intruder. But they heard no such sounds. Gradually, they started to believe that their father, the Reverend Bastareaud, might be gone.

After they waded and scampered for twenty minutes, Myron and Mookie crawled ashore. Muddy sand, leaf litter, sea foam, and briny twigs covered them from toes to chin. They looked like creatures whelped from the mangrove swamp, not regular human beings. The filthy boys crouched in silence, again listening for any inkling that their father was near. Humidity made the air swelter. A small lizard did push-ups, then darted from sight. Except for the insistent hum of insects and whistle of birds in the mangroves, the place was silent. No human noise whatsoever.

Soon a large insect buzzed nearby, a black Jeff. The four-inch wasp landed on some leaves in front of them, its abdomen shiny black, its wings flickering red, and its waving antennae orange. The boys' mother had taught them that the black Jeff was a good bug, that it hunted spiders. Myron thought it a good omen. The boys stood up and walked out of the mangroves towards higher ground. They entered the pinewoods and could hear waves hitting the beach on the ocean side far off.

They proceeded cautiously, stopping every few minutes to listen. They heard no threats and continued on until they found the gallon jug of fresh water that Myron had left on the ground when they'd run from their dad the day before. It had been knocked over. The lid had been unscrewed. Their father had found it and poured out the water.

Myron picked it up. There were still a few mouthfuls inside. He took one, then let Mookie have the rest. Mookie swallowed twice and threw down the empty jug. He was still thirsty. He looked ready to cry.

"Be strong," Myron said.

Mookie nodded. His face looked less sickly now that the sun was beginning to warm him. The muddy sand, leaves, and gunk began to dry and crust on them.

"Let's keep going and see if he found what we hid in the shack," Myron said.

They cautiously walked back to their shed. The dead crabs that Myron had placed around the shack to scare off live crabs were gone. They had been pulled apart, probably by other crabs during the night, and eaten. Little bits and pieces lay scattered across the white sand, and ants had gathered to devour the remnants.

Myron saw his father's large footprints in the sand around the shed and leading into it. Their last gallon jug of fresh water had been emptied and thrown against the wall. Their cans of beans were gone, and their gas tank and matches too.

"He took everything," Mookie said.

"Yes," Myron agreed. He went to the corner of the shed and picked up the empty jug. There was a thin puddle of fresh water still inside. Maybe two tablespoons' worth.

"Drink this," Myron said. He handed the jug to his little brother.

"Thank you," Mookie said. He raised the jug to his mouth and drank it all.

Afterward, they walked down to the ocean and waded into the small waves. They sat down in the glowing blue water and washed the mangrove swamp off. They rubbed their arms and legs and dunked their heads underwater. When they stood up, they looked like themselves again.

They walked out of the waves and up to the big white rock their mother had told them about—she'd said it looked like the molar tooth of a giant, and she was right. The giant rock felt somehow connected to their mother, and the boys went to it mainly because they wanted to be with her.

"That's mom's rock," Mookie said.

"Yes. Let's rest on it."

They climbed up to the dry part and sat down to dry off. Its warmth soaked into their bodies like their mother's love. It felt good and made them sleepy. They stretched out flat on the uneven surface. It was very uncomfortable, but they still fell asleep. Two hours later, the tide had risen enough to splash them and wake them. They were still exhausted.

They sat up and rubbed sleep from their eyes.

"I'm thirsty and hungry," Mookie said.

"Me too," Myron said. "But don't think about it. That will make it worse."

Looking up and down the empty beach made the brothers afraid. They had no water and no food, and their father would come back to hunt them again. He didn't give up easily, and he knew about the old fisherman's shed. So they had to abandon it.

"When will Mom come?" Mookie said.

"As soon as she can," Myron said. He wondered whether his mother and Carmelita were still alive. Or had their father cleansed them to death already? That would explain why nobody had come to pick them up.

He did not share his terrible thoughts with Mookie. It would not help anything.

Chapter 30
The Fort

Myron had hunted crabs with his father several times before and knew his habits and strategies. He knew the man would come back at night, when he could use the darkness to sneak up on them. And he probably would not come back until very late at night when he thought they'd be sleeping—he would want to surprise them and catch them quickly, so they could not run back into the mangrove marsh.

Myron led Mookie through the pinewoods. They walked to the spot on the mangrove side of the land where their father normally landed his skiff when he hunted crabs.

"What are we doing?" Mookie said.

"We are looking for a special tree," Myron said. The pine forest was littered with pine needles, and the ground was harder and didn't leave clear footprints like the soft white sand at the beach did. Myron looked up at the pine trees, his eyes lingering on the big ones that had plenty of branches.

"Later tonight, we are going to climb a tree and sleep up in the air. Father will hunt us, but he won't look for us up in the trees. I don't think he can track us through the pinewoods. We don't leave footprints in this place." Myron wanted to pick a tree near the spot where

Bastareaud normally landed his skiff, because then they would hear his boat engine. This would tell them when he arrived and when he left. When it was safe and when it was dangerous.

"Can the crabs climb trees?" Mookie asked.

"No," Myron said. He'd never seen a crab climb a tree before.

"What do we do until tonight when we climb the tree?"

"We need to find a spot along the beach to hide but where we can still see the big white rock. Mom said she would come and get us and to stay near the big white rock. Maybe she will come today."

The boys found a shady spot behind a coconut palm that had a clear view of the shoreline and the rocky outcropping where the white boulder stood amidst foaming waves. They took branches of palm leaves and constructed a sort of tiny fort with leafy walls on four sides. Inside the fort, they were hemmed into a small space and completely hidden from anyone who might be walking on the beach or coming through the woods behind them.

But Myron knew they'd left footprints in the sand—this troubled him, but he didn't know how to fix it. Someone who came up close could see where they'd been walking. He didn't expect anyone to look for them during the day—except maybe their mother. When it started getting dark, they'd go to the pinewoods and find the big tree he'd chosen to hide in for the night.

The boys crept inside and sat down in their little fort. It felt safer than being out in the open. The rhythmic sound of the waves seemed to make their eyelids heavy. Mookie lay down on the warm sand and quickly fell asleep next to his brother.

Myron tried to force his eyes to stay open so he could stand guard, but it was no use. He'd been awake all through the previous night when they were hiding in the mangrove marsh. His eye closed and his chin dropped to his chest. He drifted off to sleep while sitting upright against the trunk of the palm tree.

Chapter 31
Missing Cherubs

I t was the fourth day in a row that the Sea Cherubs hadn't visited.
Seabrook and Aja's concern for the children grew stronger with
each passing morning. They hadn't seen Myron, Mookie, and
Carmelita since the night they heard the child crying outside their
house, right before the Jon Boat had been stolen. Their absence was
very unusual and impossible to miss. The children had visited almost
every day all summer long and were a regular part of Seabrook and
Aja's lives. They usually helped Aja with the water changes on her
aquariums, liked to read the books in Aja's library, and hovered about
the dock when Seabrook went to check the long line—waiting to see if
he brought a shark back for morphometric measurements. But most of
all, the Sea Cherubs loved to see Clara, the baby nurse shark, and had
never, until now, missed a chance to feed her.

Aja went with Seabrook to the Bimini Police Station in Alice Town.
They rode downtown in the Whaler so they could pick up some
groceries at Brown's Grocery Store on the way back. They tied off at
the dock near the Big Game Club and walked to King's Highway, the
main street. Together they pushed through the glass doors of police
headquarters. The same young Bahamian officer wearing a too-large

uniform came up to the counter. However, this time there were two other officers present. They were sitting at desks farther back in the room.

"How can I help you?" the young constable said.

"Good morning. We want to follow up on the report I made last week about Bastareaud's children," Seabrook said. "We still haven't seen them."

"We are worried. Have you looked into it yet?" Aja asked.

"Yes," the officer said. "We sent a man. His wife and children have gone to Miami for a few weeks."

One of the policemen at a desk wore a different, more official-looking uniform. He was also older and wore black-rimmed glasses. He raised his head from his paperwork and looked towards Seabrook and Aja.

"That's what he told you?" Seabrook said. "Do you think it's true? I'm concerned something has happened to them. They come and play at the dock all the time. And they never said anything about going to Miami."

"Could you please make sure they are alright? Verify his story," Aja said.

"Is this an official complaint?" the young constable said.

"Yes. We have reason to believe they are in danger. Their father is violent and now they are missing," Seabrook said.

The older, more official-looking officer stood up from his desk and walked up to the counter. He wore a gold-colored metal name clip that read, "Superintendent Poitier." "Hello, I am the commanding officer and superintendent of the police station. Who are you complaining about?"

"Mr. Bastareaud," Seabrook said.

The man nodded slightly.

Everyone looked at the commanding officer. The two other policemen were much younger and clearly subordinate to him.

"How do you know Mr. Bastareaud?" Superintendent Poitier asked.

"We are his tenants. We live in one of his rental houses."

"Are you the scientists?"

"Yes," Aja said.

"I see." After a moment he added, "We could look into it a little more."

"Thank you," Aja said.

Chapter 32
The Sea Turtle and the Shark

I n the late afternoon, the sound of an engine woke Myron and Mookie. A fishing boat was motoring close to the shore. The boys stood up and watched the vessel cruise southward down the coast. Watching it leave reminded Myron how alone and abandoned they were. But at least the brothers had each other.

As the sun sank close to the horizon and the sky grew darker with the coming night, a sea turtle suddenly appeared in the waves near the shore. Myron believed it had to be a large female that had come to the beach to lay her eggs. Her head poked out of the water like a small tree stump. She was easy to spot because the water was crystal clear and the sea floor was pure white sand. Any large animal looked like a dark silhouette as it swam into the shallows.

Myron and Mookie watched the turtle paddle closer to the beach—they knew their father would have poached it, if he'd been there. Normally, Bastareaud let turtles crawl onto the beach, where they were helpless. Then he cut off their heads with his machete and took the turtle meat and eggs home for food. He ignored the laws against killing turtles.

The boys suddenly saw a very large fish glide swiftly into the shallows. It looked like the black shadow of a giant shark, or maybe a small whale. The shadow swam quickly towards the turtle—and as it got very close, they could see it had a weird way of swimming: its tail rolled left and right like a snake zigzagging across the ground. Its dorsal fin rose out of the water, and the boys could hear a soft hissing sound as it cut through the waves.

"Look at that!" Myron said.

"That's a big fish," Mookie said.

The boys had seen several very large sharks that had died on the long line or been killed by other sharks: the biggest was a fifteen-foot-long hammerhead that was so wide and thick, it filled the entire Boston Whaler. Seabrook had found it lifeless and could not revive it despite swimming with it for an hour, so he brought the great shark to the dock to measure for a morphometric study. That incredible beast looked like a baby compared to the shadow before them.

The shadow glided up to the turtle, and they saw its massive head break the surface. It grabbed the sea turtle's shell in its mouth. The sea turtle disappeared for a moment. Then half of the turtle popped up and bobbed in the waves. Blood colored the water around it.

The shadow swam in a circle, then came back to the surface and grabbed the remains of the turtle. After a minute, the shadow swam out of the shallows to deeper water and, in the darkening blue sea, eventually vanished.

"I think that's Razormouth," Mookie said.

"We have to tell Seabrook and Aja."

They watched the sea for any other sign of it, but nothing happened.

It was time to leave the fort and get ready for the night. They walked across the beach and headed up into the pinewoods.

Eventually they made their way to the chosen tree: a tall pine with a thick trunk. It was close to where their father usually put his skiff on the lagoon side of the island when he went crabbing at night. Myron was content to sit by their chosen tree for a while before climbing up, but Mookie was worried about the giant land crabs. They came out of the burrows at night like vampires.

The sun had completely set when the boys started up the tree, but the sky still glowed with red light in the western sky. Myron helped Mookie scamper onto his shoulders so he could reach the first branch. Once Mookie took hold of the lowest branch, he quickly climbed up the tree.

Still down on the ground, Myron inspected the earth around the tree and, in the dimming twilight, couldn't see any footprints—there was no trace that they'd come this way. This made him feel good.

Branch after branch, Myron climbed upward to Mookie. The brothers positioned themselves about three-quarters of the way up, where there were still plenty of branches to hide amongst. Their hands and feet were sticky and smelled of pinesap. The bark was scratchy, and little bits of it stuck to their bodies. It even got in the crooks of their elbows. They sat close together on two solid branches while holding on to higher branches and the tree trunk to steady themselves.

"Get as good a position as you can. We will be here all night," Myron said.

They were high enough that they could see both sides of the island: the shallow North Sound lagoon and the deep Caribbean Sea on the other side.

The boys watched the moon rise over the ocean. It made the black waves glint with silver.

Down on the ground, Mookie knew the crabs were waking up. They were crawling out of their deep, wet holes and searching for things to eat.

Chapter 33
Wind

Myron and Mookie passed the time watching massive swells roll across the moonlit sea. It somehow reminded Mookie of their mother—when he would watch, eyes level with the ironing board, as she unrolled a big sheet for a tablecloth, spread out in waves of fabric, smoothly pushed along, rolling and spreading, until swept off the world of the board with a hot iron pushed by the woman who was a goddess to him.

Up in the tree, the boys constantly listened for the frightening sound of their father's outboard engine. A fair wind made the tree move and the branches wave. The breeze felt nice and helped them stay alert. It also made the clouds move quickly across the sky and hid the moon for long stretches of time.

In the beginning, being in the tree was good, but the boys quickly grew tired of it. They had to shift their weight frequently, because their arms turned numb clinging to branches and their butts began to ache from sitting for hours on such hard, narrow perches. At times, they each rested their heads against the trunk and closed their eyes in a kind of half sleep. But they could never truly fall asleep.

They felt hungry, but even more than that, very thirsty. Their throats and mouths were parched. They could not even spit. As the hours ticked past, they fantasized about drinking all sorts of refreshments: tall glasses of fresh water, cold milk, orange juice, and even chocolate milkshakes.

It was hard to judge time, but it felt very late when the distant sound of a boat engine first reached their ears. It was the distinctive *chug chug chug* of their father's old outboard. The sound grew stronger, then fainter, and then stronger again, as the skiff made its way through the mangrove maze and sudden gusts of wind briefly snatched the sound away.

Soon they heard their father pull up on the sand bank between two mangroves where he always landed. The engine went silent.

"He's here," Mookie whispered.

"Shh, shh. Don't talk," Myron said.

The dim light of their father's flashlight waved back and forth as he made his way from the mangroves to the pinewoods. He seemed to be heading straight for their particular tree. For one heart-stopping moment, Bastareaud's flashlight seemed to linger on the ground around their tree.

The boys held their breath.

Then the flashlight moved on in the direction of the old fisherman's shed. Then it went out. There was total darkness below.

"Stay calm. Stay silent. We will wait him out. He will never find us up here," Myron whispered to Mookie.

Chapter 34
Devils

The next morning, Bastareaud left the mangrove swamp empty-handed. His sons had evaded him again. Blind rage tore through him like a kicked-over hornet's nest. He drove his skiff through labyrinthine mangrove passages and channels that did not look passable to the uneducated, then across the North Sound towards his property. With a rictus grin and crazy eyes, he marinated in his failure and in his boys' outrageous disobedience—IT WOULD NOT STAND!

He would eventually catch Myron and Mookie, and the cleansing would last days: he'd bust a dozen hard switches on their backs—maybe two dozen, stripe them up good, then lock them separately in dark rooms for a few days of fasting, repentance, and prayer. When he was done forcing the devil out of them, he'd lock them in a crab cage for the final mortification.

Bastareaud was so enraged, he could barely sit still. How had his infernal boys known where to go? Did Seabrook and Aja have anything to do with it? He fantasized about burying his machete in Seabrook's head and taking Aja. Punishing her and making her repent—once he broke her, anything was possible. She could learn to serve him. She

189

already liked his children. Maybe she could become their mother. Besides, he was feeling ready for a new wife.

His mind drifted back to Myron and Mookie. They were excellent at hiding, but at least now he knew roughly where they were. He'd seen their fresh footprints in the white sand on the beach. He planned to resume hunting them later, in the afternoon. He'd made sure they had no food and no water. Once they were dying of thirst, he'd offer them water to come out of hiding. Thirsty dogs and children were easy to sucker. And women too.

After a time, he pulled up alongside his dock and tied his skiff near the scientists' boats. Fortunately, they were not anywhere to be seen— he hated them. Their lies and ungodly beliefs had confused his children and were a threat to the ministry. As he walked up the dock, he fantasized some more about killing Seabrook and taking Aja for his new wife.

A few locals saw Bastareaud walking towards his house. He was a big man, but when he was angry he seemed even bigger and more dangerous. Today, he was muttering to himself and had a murderous look in his eyes. They got out of his way.

Bastareaud slapped himself on the side of the head, deep in thought, reviewing everything that had gone wrong. His wife had run off. His daughter, Carmelita, was missing—he didn't know whether she was hiding with his sons or had gone with his wife. On top of everything else, he knew the scientists had reported him to the police! That would be the biggest mistake of their lives. He would make them pay— ruin their work and drive them from the island for good. He wished he could kill them, but he couldn't figure a way to get away with it. And he'd done nothing at all to deserve their attacks! He was just following the voice of God, which he heard in his head. Doing HIS will.

His special relationship with God was a gift. It was the source of his power. It also enabled him to recognize the three devils pretending to be men who walked across his yard and up to his house later in the afternoon. They didn't fool him for a second.

He saw them through the kitchen window and got ready. He waited and watched them approach his front door. The most powerful devil was a bald man whose skin was burnt purplish red from being so near the flames of eternal damnation—a dead giveaway. He also had a shark jaw tattooed around his right eye and was carrying a large black suitcase with the name Jarvis Products in bold white letters on it. Pretending to be some kind of businessman.

Bastareaud was raring to fight, even before they knocked. He slammed open the front door and immediately hacked off one of the lesser devil's arms with one good swing from his machete. The devil screamed, and his severed arm dangled like a broken tree limb, the hand still grasping the handle of the front door. Then it flopped to the stoop.

When he stepped out to attack the others, something touched his head. There was an explosion of light.

When he awoke, the devils had tied him up in his own kitchen. The devil with only one arm had some kind of tourniquet on his stump.

Bastareaud roared at them with righteous indignation. He overpowered them with his preacher voice and vanquished them from his house by calling on God the Father, Jesus, and the Holy Spirit. And they left, but their demonic spirits remained and caused him many terrible hallucinations.

In his hallucinations he was still tied up. The demonic spirits asked him many questions about fifty million dollars. They believed he had given the money to his wife and children and told them to run and hide. Were they in Miami? Fort Lauderdale? Key Biscayne? Or were they still in the Bahamas? They asked questions like this again and again. They wanted an address. A phone number.

Then everything changed.

The bald demonic spirit with the skin like scalded meat placed his black suitcase with the Jarvis Products lettering on the kitchen table. He unsnapped the latches and opened it.

The bald demon's eyes seemed to float above the opened case, gazing downward at its contents; they were empty black holes that moved like normal eyes but weren't normal at all. Up close, he could see that they were slightly different colors, and they were too dead for human eyes. Like a tree that had been struck by lightning and burnt to a black stump—you couldn't call that a tree anymore. And there were no eyelashes or eyebrows. And the weird shark jaw tattoo around his right eye seemed to move, like it might snap shut.

Bastareaud wondered: *Can the demon really see with those unnatural eyes, or does he just sense the world around him through his horrible skin?* Now the demon spirit began setting out tools on the kitchen table and looking for an electrical outlet on the wall nearby. One tool looked vaguely like a big steel claw with a pistol handle, but Bastareaud got only a quick glimpse of it.

He suddenly felt nervous—the demon spirit's eyes frightened him— and he couldn't remember what he said from one moment to the next. So he told everything—he was an open book, a servant of God, and had no reason to lie to the devil spirits. They asked, "Where exactly in the mangroves are your children hiding with the money?"

He told them the names of his kids and how to find them on the northernmost tip of Bimini. He told them their ages and that they were bad and disobedient. And that they had no water or food and could be easily lured into the open. Giving up his kids was easy.

Then he told them that God's fury would strike them down if their demonic spirits didn't leave. "I vanquish you!" he screamed.

The demon with one arm laughed and called him "*loco, loco.*"

Bastareaud felt lightheaded and closed his eyes. He had a terrible nightmare.

The bald demon grew an exoskeleton and transformed into his true form: the Emperor of the Crabs. He and the lesser crabs gathered close over him. Their legs clicked on the kitchen floor; their mandibles made nibbling sounds.

With his giant silver claw, the Emperor of the Crabs cut off Bastareaud's feet and hands.

Part Two

For the moon never beams, without bringing me dreams
Of the beautiful Annabel Lee;
And the stars never rise, but I feel the bright eyes
Of the beautiful Annabel Lee;
And so, all the night-tide, I lie down by the side
Of my darling—my darling—my life and my bride,
In her sepulchre there by the sea—
In her tomb by the sounding sea.
—Edgar Allan Poe

Chapter 35
Aja's Birthday

I
n the early evening, Seabrook took Aja out to dinner and dancing to celebrate her twenty-sixth birthday. They walked south down King's Highway, one of two paved roads on North Bimini. It was a pleasant forty-minute stroll past homes, cottages, and shops. Bahamian children played outside in some of the yards, and the occasional local zoomed by on a moped. The slanting sunlight backlit the tall coconut palms. Their fronds trembled in the warm sea breeze that blew continuously across the island.

North Bimini was only half a mile wide at the widest and two hundred yards wide at the narrowest. You could always smell and see the ocean. White coral sand and seashells were omnipresent. Some people decorated their yards with conch shells.

As they walked along, the occasional mangy dog trotted out for a few pats and some of the local kids who knew them said hi.

Holding hands, Seabrook and Aja strolled past Brown's Grocery Store, the telephone station (the only phone service on the island), and a food shack where a heavy local woman sold sweet Bahamian bread.

After walking for half an hour, they entered the downtown area in Alice Town and turned right through a break in the stone wall that bordered part of King's Highway. They strode up a path and concrete stairs to their favorite restaurant.

The Blue Water Restaurant sat on the high point of the island next to the Queen's Highway, the only other paved road, and looked out over the windward ocean side of North Bimini. The restaurant had big glass picture windows, and Seabrook and Aja always took a table next to one because the view was magnificent. Overhead fans whispered at the ceiling. You could see the waves coming in from far off—big, lazy swells— and the clear aquamarine shallows changing to cobalt blue as you looked out towards the Gulf Stream.

Aja ordered conch fritters and a bottle of Beck's beer. Seabrook asked for a bowl of conch chowder, the club sandwich, and a Beck's beer as well. This was their favorite meal at their favorite restaurant, and they felt spoiled with luxury. It always gave them a much-needed respite. They normally spent many hours a day in the sea, were always sticky with brine afterward, always sandy on shore, and constantly in the harsh tropical sun. Some days, they could not escape the sun no matter what they did. It scorched down on them from the sky, and if they lowered their eyes to avoid it, they saw it mirroring off the water at them. It made their eyes ache, made the Jon Boat burning hot to sit on, and it slowly fried their skin all day.

Most nights they slept with the dried ocean still in their hair and on their bodies. The cistern next to the house held a limited supply of fresh water, so they didn't always shower. They figured that most of the time they were clean enough to skip it because they'd bathed in the sea.

Day in and day out, they wore nothing but bathing suits, T-shirts, and sometimes shorts at night. They had nothing else to wear. Aja didn't have a single dress, and Seabrook didn't have a single pair of long pants, because they weren't needed. They usually went barefoot and had grown tough pads on the bottoms of their feet. The sea and sand were with them all day, every day, in every part of their lives. Even when they made love, they tasted and smelled like the sea and felt the sand.

On a normal day in their rental house (before the Sea Cherubs disappeared and the Earless Man visited), after working underwater or in the North Sound for many hours and documenting collected data and notes, they'd often unwind after dinner—unless Seabrook was night tracking. The timers on the halide lights of Aja's aquariums would switch off in an imitation of the onset of night, and the Sea Cherubs would have gone home hours before. Silence and peace arrived in the late afternoon.

In the evenings the island cooled off, and they liked to sit on the sofa near the large sliding glass door with a fine view of the lagoon. They always opened the sliding door to let the sea air in. The breeze normally filled the house and gently disturbed the curtains. During these golden moments, they sipped a little rum with lime and read together. Sometimes they read different books about natural history or scientific journals quietly on their own. Other times they read a famous novel jointly and took turns reading to each other.

When they read a book together, they preferred novels that had a good story and that neither had read but had always meant to. *Return of the Native* by Thomas Hardy and *1984* by George Orwell were the last two choices they co-read and enjoyed very much. For the person being read to, it was lovely and peaceful to hear the other's intimate voice and imagine the narrative while looking at the lagoon.

Sometimes they would read poetry collections: Emily Dickinson, Robert Frost, James Dickey, and Mary Oliver were favorites. One night Aja would read to Seabrook, then the next night he would read to her. Back and forth, they would continue reading the text out loud until the novel or poetry collection ended.

There was no TV, telephone, or other distraction. They had each other, their work in the sea, and the company of great scientists and writers. It was a simple and beautiful life. And they loved every minute of it—even in spite of the Earless Man and Bastareaud. And the dark stain on the dock.

Aja's birthday was a special day and a cause for celebration. That's why they had deviated from their usual nightly routine and come in to town. They'd showered with fresh water, used soap and shampoo, and put on dry, clean clothes for the first time that week. Seabrook had even used shaving cream to make his face extra smooth.

The beer bottles came ice cold with drops of condensation on them. The waiter set down tall, cold glasses to pour the beer into. It was an incredible luxury to be served delicious food in a clean, pleasant place with such a stunning view.

For dessert the waiter brought out a small chocolate cake made with lemon frosting that Seabrook had specially requested days earlier. After Aja blew out the candles, Seabrook gave her two presents: a light red sundress with spaghetti straps, and a necklace made with tiny seashells with a large cone shell in the middle. The cone shell looked like it was made of pink and cream-colored marble. It had geometric shapes patterned across the back and in the edges of its whorls and spire. Seabrook had collected each shell, and every one was exquisite.

"The necklace matches the dress," Aja said happily.

"I thought you should have at least one dress."

"It's very nice."

"I picked the shells off the beach. The seamstress who made the dress helped me turn the shells into a necklace."

"Where did you find this cone shell?" She held the shell up to her face and studied it. Her eyes seemed to darken, and her lips parted ever so slightly in an expression Seabrook knew well—when she saw or felt something that moved her.

"I have never, ever seen one like this!" She got up and came over to Seabrook and kissed him. "Thank you for the dress and the necklace. This is gorgeous!"

He stood up and hugged her tight. "You are welcome!"

Then they sat down to eat the cake. She looked across the table and he could tell his gifts had touched her.

"Shark Mon," she said in her best Bahamian accent. "You are the *best* ever."

"Well you *are* the Blue Angel," he said with deep feeling. "And I love you."

Their hands touched across the table.

Through the giant window overlooking the ocean, Seabrook suddenly saw two speedboats appear at the horizon. They looked like drug runner boats coming from Miami. He shook off the sudden uneasy feeling. It was probably nothing but tourists with speedboats.

"What's wrong?" Aja sensed the sudden change in him.

"I was just noticing those speedboats coming our way."

"And it reminded you of the Earless Man and his friends."

"For a minute." He made a dismissive expression. "Probably just rich tourists joyriding from Miami."

They looked out at the sea. The speedboats grew larger as they watched.

Aja changed the subject. "Where did you find this cone shell?" she asked again. "I hope you didn't pick it up alive."

"Of course not. I found it by the *Sapona*." The SS *Sapona* was a 282-foot-long concrete cargo ship built in 1924 and used by its last owner to smuggle rum during Prohibition. The ship had run aground near Turtle Rocks in 1926 during a hurricane. However, she did not sink out of sight because she was wrecked in shallow water. Most of her, roughly forty feet up to the bow, still stood above the waterline. During World War II, Navy pilots used the wreck for target practice. The hull and deck of the ship were shot full of holes by the fifty-millimeter gun rounds and bombs of Navy fighter planes. Time, weather, and target practice had viciously aged the great ship, leaving it decrepit, pockmarked, and haunted.

Covered in rust and encrusted with marine algae, the *Sapona* could be seen on the horizon at a great distance like a ghost ship, still visible long after its natural life. Her sides had great gaps between large structural supports where divers and snorkelers could enter. The sea around the wreck was nearly twenty feet deep, and the ship had become an artificial reef for all kinds of marine life below the waterline.

Sometimes, Seabrook and Aja went to the *Sapona* after snorkeling at Turtle Rocks. You could snorkel inside the cavernous cargo hold of the ship. The deck above shaded swimmers inside the wreck from the sun. It was a pleasant place to snorkel, because inside the currents were minimized and sometimes the sea life behaved as if it were night, even as the sun made the undersea glow outside the interior of the wreck. You could look at the marine life growing throughout the engine room and on the boilers and bulkheads. Nocturnal orange cup coral extended their brilliant fiery polyps in the middle of the day, and yellow spotted stingrays seemed to congregate inside.

There was also an enormous green moray eel that lived in a small chamber below a rusted steel ladder next to the engine room. You could climb twenty feet up the rungs of the ladder, out of the sea, and gain access to the upper deck.

During the day, the eel lurked in its den below, but by night it ranged around the wreck looking for spiny lobsters. The eel was an adult male that Seabrook had named Lennie Small after the famous character in John Steinbeck's *Of Mice and Men*, because despite his formidable appearance, he was normally harmless.

Lennie the eel would sometimes swim out of his lair and let Aja handle him, gliding about her shoulders and arms like a silky green, seven-foot sea scarf. A scarf with teeth and opaque blue eyes, filmy as if the eel were going blind with cataracts.

If you climbed up the ladder above Lennie's den, you'd find the deck unsafe in the extreme. The flooring had already collapsed into gaping holes in many places, and rusted rebar pointed every which way like disorderly spear tips waiting to impale anyone who fell. Still, Seabrook and Aja sometimes carefully made their way across the deck and climbed up onto the bow.

From the bow it felt like they were standing on a cliff. They could stretch out their arms in the wind and look at the sea far below and all around them. Then they would jump and fall thirty-five feet through the air—like flying—then hit the water with a thunderous splash. Seabrook's feet sometimes touched bottom when he plunged into the twenty-foot sea.

"By the *Sapona*? Why didn't you tell me about it before?"

"I wanted the necklace to be a surprise. If I told you about the cone shell and where I found it, you might have figured out what I was up to."

"Okay. Tell me now."

"It was just an empty shell when I found it."

"Where was it?"

"Outside the wreck just before the point where the stern breaks off."

"On Lennie's side?"

"Yes." As they talked, Seabrook saw the speedboats veer south, as if they were going to enter the harbor at Alice Town.

Chapter 36
An Ancient and Unbreakable Law

"Where we are, there's daggers in men's smiles." —William Shakespeare

After dinner, they walked outside the restaurant to watch the sunset. They stood facing the ocean and held hands. The wind picked up, ruffling their hair and clothes. The waves gently rolled in, collapsing with soft thunder on the beach, and sea birds patrolled the hissing foam. Hovering, landing, gliding with muted cries. The planet spun on its axis, and the sun gradually sank, inch by inch, below the line between ocean and sky, leaving a pink and yellow afterglow in the high atmosphere. This was their island life.

They strolled down the path and made a right into town. They walked to the Compleat Angler bar and hotel. The historical building, built like an old English country house, sat in the heart of Alice Town. A stone wall with a small wooden archway set it apart from the rest of the pink, blue, and yellow buildings in the downtown area. It stood elevated, an imposing edifice, three stories tall, made of rock and wood pillars pirated from the wreck of the *Sapona*. Its balconies overlooked King's Highway, and live bands performed in the second bar many nights.

As they went up the steps to the entrance, the reggae music from a local cover band met their ears. They went inside and ordered two Planter's Punches from the bartender. The place was half full. Several groups of fishermen were telling stories and laughing raucously. An old gray dog was sleeping in one corner. Another crowd of tourists clogged the dance floor in front of the band. Several locals were dancing among them. Except for the locals, the accents were all American, and everyone seemed friendly and buzzed with rum.

Seabrook and Aja took a small table. They sipped their drinks and reveled in the indoor air conditioning. The wall behind them had a black and white picture of Ernest Hemingway and the artist Henry Strater standing next to what looked like a one-thousand-pound marlin. It had been half eaten by sharks, and only the spine connected the mid-section to the tail. Every wall of the Compleat Angler—covered with countless photographs of fishermen with monster-sized fish, infamous politicians, musicians like Jimmy Buffett performing, and Hemingway memorabilia such as letters and newspaper clippings—provided a kind of debaucherous scrapbook history of Bimini. One photograph even showed a happy fisherman weighing his girlfriend on the big-game scale at the dock. She hung upside down like a tuna, topless, and was grinning from ear to ear.

In the adjoining room a different atmosphere prevailed. It had a stone fireplace, shelves with old books, and walls decorated with good illustrations of scenes from *The Old Man and the Sea*. You could quietly read in this room during the afternoons. On the second floor there were rooms for rent. Hemingway had lived there.

The band began to play Bob Marley's "Three Little Birds."

"Let's dance," Aja said. Seabrook nodded. It was one of their favorite songs.

He took her by the hand, and they went out on the dance floor. The whole crowd shuffled and bobbed to the bass and steel drums' chugging rhythm. The music and lyrics felt infectious, and they had a great time. They stayed on the floor and danced for the rest of the set. The band ended with a reggae-infused cover of Eric Clapton's "Wonderful Tonight."

Seabrook and Aja slow-danced until the last note. Everyone on the dance floor erupted in wild applause as the band members set their instruments down for a break.

Seabrook and Aja returned to their table and finished their Planter's Punch cocktails.

"Want another?" Seabrook asked.

"Definitely," Aja said.

More people had entered the Compleat Angler while Seabrook and Aja were dancing. A large group of fishermen were pressing up to the bar to order drinks. Seabrook squeezed in on the end. He had to wait a couple of minutes to get the busy bartender's attention.

When he came back with two fresh drinks, a strange thin man was sitting at the table with Aja. He looked out of place. Not a fisherman, not a tourist. He had no drink. Medium-size, maybe thirty years old, maybe Colombian. Well-dressed, with a short-sleeved collared shirt and tan slacks. He had wavy black hair, strangely long arms, and a wide, humorless smile.

"You must be with this beautiful woman," the man said as Seabrook sat down. Definitely a Colombian accent.

"Yes, I am." Seabrook gave Aja her Planter's Punch. One glance told him she knew something was wrong. It pissed Seabrook off that this jerk had sat down with his fiancée. He was about to tell the guy to leave their table.

"I just need three minutes of your time," the strange man said.

"Who are you?" Seabrook said, biting back his anger.

"Vuelta." He was not a partier. There was something hard and businesslike in his demeanor.

"Are you in Bimini to fish?" Aja asked. It was obvious he was not a fisherman. She was trying to get a read on the guy.

Vuelta shook his head no. "I just help," he said. He reached one long arm out and raked a handful of salty peanuts from the dish on the table. His hands looked soft, but two of the fingers on his right hand were crooked—they had been badly broken and hadn't healed straight. His face was angular and sharp-nosed. It reminded Seabrook of a barracuda's face.

Aja glanced at Seabrook and spoke with her eyes. This was a bad man. He looked like he could cut his mother's throat and smile while doing it. Perhaps he thought they wanted to buy cocaine. Plenty of people came to the Bahamas to party.

"My boss does the fishing," Vuelta said. "Not me. I just help land the fish. If a shark tries to steal my boss's fish, I kill it." He paused and ate the handful of peanuts. "You must know the number one law of the sea, *si*? ... Eat or be eaten? It is an ancient and unbreakable law." The man chuckled, and his face broke into an awful smile. "And it's a *hungry, deep sea* ... a very hungry sea. You are shark scientists, no? You must understand this better than anyone."

"Why do you think we are scientists?" Seabrook asked.

Vuelta looked across the room. "A certain man ... who was *very* motivated to tell me the truth ... told me there are shark scientists working on the islands. I look around this place. I see fat, rich fishermen. I see sunburned drunks. I hear exaggerated talk of the big fish everyone caught. I see foolish, half-naked college students on vacation. But you two are different. You talk differently and you have bright eyes, like you know things. You aren't drunk, and anyone can see you are a couple. So I think you must be the scientists."

Vuelta stood up and gently pushed his chair back. On cue a bald man at the bar walked over to the table. He stood next to Vuelta.

Seabrook hadn't noticed him before. The bald man was roughly six feet tall and had wide shoulders. He had strangely dark eyes that didn't match in color and strikingly discolored skin. Like the sun had broiled him into corned beef. He had a waxy complexion—and no hair whatsoever—no eyebrows, or even eyelashes. The jaws of a great white shark had been tattooed around his right eye. His savage appearance made it deeply unnerving to look at him; and it had to do with his face, especially his eyes—because they were so intense. He seemed somehow absent from his body. But not drunk or high.

Seabrook got to his feet. He felt violence coming.

"Am I right?" Vuelta said. "Are you scientists? He told me it was a big man and a small, beautiful woman."

"What man told you this?"

"A man with no ears."

Seabrook looked at Aja. Fear passed between them like a cold draft.

"We are graduate students working towards our Ph.D.s," Aja said. "Just doing fieldwork, collecting data for our research."

"See? You talk differently. More precisely. I also went to a university."

"What's this about?" Seabrook said.

"You must know Latin if you are a scientist. Another law that is unbreakable: *Lex Talionis*."

"The law of retribution," Aja said.

"Very good," Vuelta said. "So we have another question."

"What?"

"Not me. Him." He gestured to the bald man standing next to him.

The bald man stepped closer to Seabrook, looking at his face, then into his eyes. Suddenly, the man seemed mildly curious, like he was judging Seabrook's suitability for some purpose. Three awkward seconds passed. Then in a quiet, reasonable-sounding voice he said something in Spanish. He had the tone and manner of a librarian. He was still staring at Seabrook's eyes.

"What is he saying?" Seabrook asked.

"He says you have beautiful blue eyes," Vuelta replied.

"What?" Seabrook couldn't help but laugh. "You're barking up the wrong tree."

The bald, tattooed man said something more. He spoke very softly, almost in a whisper. It sounded like a question.

"Now he wants to know, can he have them?" Vuelta said.

Seabrook immediately stepped between the men and Aja, protecting her and getting a better angle to hit either man. He clenched his hands into fists, keyed to go.

But nothing happened. It seemed like these men played by different rules or had something else in mind—usually threats in a bar preceded a fistfight. These men had no interest in fighting. Something about that put Seabrook more on edge. What did they want? What were they going to do? He couldn't see their angle.

The bald man seemed almost indifferent to the confrontation, not threatening. As if he was looking straight through and beyond the people in front of him and at some far-off object.

"Well?" Vuelta said. "Can he have your beautiful blue eyes?"

Seabrook noticed something the color of dried blood on the collar of the bald man's shirt. One small maroon drop. The shark jaws tattooed around his eye seemed to move a little when the man slowly blinked.

Seabrook ignored the question and stepped a little closer, primed.

Vuelta grinned, then looked at Aja. He looked at her body and naked legs. Then he looked back at Seabrook and shook his head sideways. "You don't understand. This is a special kindness we offer you ... because you are regular people ... and made a stupid mistake. If you want to avoid the worst, return the money."

"What money?"

Vuelta stopped smiling.

The bald man shifted his feet, suddenly energized by Seabrook's question. Just like that, a decision had been made. Now he ran his eyes over Seabrook in a brazen and aggressive way. As if he was a tailor visually estimating the length of his limbs, fitting him for a new suit. Getting ready to cut the cloth. Then he looked around the room, at all the customers and the bartender. After two seconds, he shook his head no at Vuelta.

What did it mean?

Seabrook said, "Anytime, asshole."

"Return what is not yours," Vuelta said. His voice was now intense, and he enunciated every syllable with a low snarl. "*Every fucking dollar*. A man will be here in Hemingway's old room upstairs. You have until eight o'clock tomorrow morning."

The bald man leaned in. He spoke in broken English, "Remember ... *you* ... said *anytime*." His voice was eerily calm.

Vuelta said, "I showed you respect. I gave you a way out. But you give me bullshit. Worst mistake of your life." He shrugged and smiled. "So stupid."

He went to the door and strolled out into the dark. The bald man with red skin followed.

Two other men that Seabrook and Aja hadn't even noticed followed them out. They were short men with black hair. Everybody got the hell out of their way as they walked across the crowded floor. Despite their average size, people sensed they were dangerous.

One was exceedingly ugly. His long face had hard, striking features, like they had been engraved on dense whalebone into a kind of ghoulish scrimshaw. His eyes sat deep in their sockets, and his forehead had a pronounced ridge above the eyebrows.

The other man had thick laborer's arms and a box-shaped chest. His neck was matted with wiry hair, and his mouth had a cruel twist in the corner.

Altogether they made Seabrook remember a pack of wild dogs that had terrorized the woods near his house as a boy. The whole neighborhood changed because of them. Mothers wouldn't let children go outside to play. Adults went out only in pairs or with a gun. Seabrook suffered many nightmares about the wild dogs at the time.

The neighborhood's worst fears were confirmed when one afternoon the wild dogs dragged two teenagers into the woods and ate them.

A hungry, deep sea.

Seabrook and Aja stayed at their table. He watched the door. They ignored their drinks and tried to make sense of what had just happened.

"There were four of them," Seabrook said. "I didn't even see the last two until they left."

"What money?" Aja said.

"I have no idea. Probably something to do with the Earless Man."

"They were the cartel men that guy talked about."

"What did Vuelta say to you when I was up at the bar getting drinks?"

"He just sat down and said, 'You look like a scientist.'"

"Just like that."

"Just like that."

"The Earless Man must have given him a description of us," Seabrook said. "Small black-haired woman with a big white guy with red hair. I don't think there is anyone who looks like us on Bimini."

"He said the Earless Man was *highly motivated* to tell the truth. What did that mean?"

"The bald man had a drop of blood on his collar. They tortured him."

This comment dropped them into an uneasy silence.

Aja broke it a moment later. "They were evil." Her face had paled from the encounter. Her expression was grave. The intensity of her observation alarmed Seabrook. He had never heard Aja call anyone evil before. She did not throw the word around lightly.

"We should leave the island," she said matter-of-factly.

"Let's catch the next flight out tomorrow."

"I'll go to the airport in the morning and get us tickets."

"I'll call Dr. Nixon first thing and tell him what's going on."

"Do you think he'll want us to leave Bimini?"

"Yes. He won't want us to be in danger. And we sure don't have any money for them."

The band started playing again. They didn't feel festive anymore. Or like dancing. They didn't even finish their drinks and, after a few moments, decided to walk home.

Seabrook paid the bar tab, and they left the Compleat Angler. They turned left and walked up King's Highway towards their house in Bailey Town.

Chapter 37
Bait

At seven thirty the next morning, Seabrook tried to call Dr. Nixon. He went to the island's telephone station to tell his boss their lives were in danger and that they were leaving Bimini, temporarily abandoning the research station. He went into one of the little booths and made a collect call to Miami. He and Aja had decided overnight that they should leave the island for a few weeks and let things blow over. They weren't sure what to do about the Sea Cherubs, and toyed with the idea of visiting the police again. Seabrook sat in the old wooden booth and listened to the telephone ringing at Dr. Nixon's house. Before anyone could pick up at the other end, a local operator came on and told him the phone line had gone down. Seabrook cursed quietly—he really needed Dr. Nixon to know what was going on. He'd have to try calling again later.

Next he went out in the Boston Whaler to check the long line and free any hooked sharks. He stopped briefly at the fuel dock in the harbor and filled the three twelve-gallon portable plastic fuel tanks in the boat. He paid, as per usual, using the credit card Dr. Nixon had given him for the purpose. Seabrook put the receipt in the tagging kit. He had to keep records for Dr. Nixon's report to the National Science Foundation, which was funding their research.

Then Seabrook drove out to sea. It was 8:41 a.m.

The Whaler was lifted by two-foot waves and bounced in the troughs, spraying white foam out from the hull. The sea rushed under the hull like blue glass and churned out behind the stern, spreading a white wake. He pushed the tiller, steering left, after angling past Round Rock.

He straightened the tiller and headed straight east towards the long line out on the waters of the Great Bahama Bank. The sea grew shallower and greenish blue. He needed to tag and release any sharks he'd caught overnight.

He had a lot on his mind: the Sea Cherubs were still missing, and the men who had approached him and Aja at the Compleat Angler the night before had his hackles up. They were much worse than the two men they'd already encountered in the North Sound. These new men were magnitudes of order more dangerous. They had to be cartel soldiers. He also needed to finish his research somehow—after they came back from Florida. And even though he hadn't seen Bastareaud recently, the man was becoming more truculent by the day—always carrying his machete, always glaring at Seabrook and Aja. Seabrook had a hunch the man had killed his children. He didn't believe they were in Miami for one second, but he didn't know what else he could do to help, beyond complaining to the island police.

As he drove the Whaler across the waves, he felt anxious about leaving Aja alone at the house. Much more anxious than normal. Before, when he'd told her he didn't feel right leaving her in the house alone and that she should come with him, Aja insisted she'd be fine and for him to go. Vuelta said they had until eight a.m. to return missing money—which they'd never seen or taken. Aja said that by the time the cartel made good on their threat, Seabrook and Aja would be long gone to Miami. Despite her confidence, he nearly turned back anyway —twice.

A deep disquiet settled over him as he looked at the blue horizon. He counterbalanced his uneasiness with the fact that he would be back more quickly than usual and that if he didn't go, any sharks hooked on the long line would die. He was merely doing the responsible thing, the ethical thing. Also, he wasn't baiting the long line, which took a lot of time; just tagging and releasing sharks—because he and Aja were planning to fly out of Bimini that afternoon if possible.

He drove the Whaler as fast as the sea would allow him. Forty minutes after leaving the dock, he saw the large red buoy that marked the south end of the long line. He pointed the Whaler's nose straight at it.

A few minutes later, he came up to the large buoy. He hooked its rope with the gaff and pulled the line in. Salt water wet his hands.

He was all alone on the turquoise waters of Great Bahama Bank—as usual. No other vessels were anywhere to be seen.

The buoy line was attached to the main line. The main line ran horizontal across the seafloor. He pulled the main line up and gaffed onto it. Now the Whaler was hooked by the gaff to the main line, and he slowly started motoring along the half-mile length of the long line to check the hooks. There were thirty hooks, and the sea was only fifteen feet deep, so he could see the bottom very clearly.

The first hook had nothing. As usual, the bait had been eaten by swimming crabs, so the hook was shiny silver and clean.

He motored forward. The hooks were spaced roughly ninety feet apart. The second hook also had been picked clean.

And the third.

And the fourth.

The fifth hook was loaded. Seabrook could see a large shark resting at the bottom of the water. He put the engine in neutral and pulled the main line in enough to cleat it at the bow and stern. He pulled the individual hook line toward the surface, expecting the shark to start swimming.

The shark rose off the bottom, hanging heavy on the line. It did not come to life, and he knew it was dead by the rigid way it was coming up through the sea.

When he brought it to the surface, he saw that it was a partially eaten bull shark (*Carcharhinus leucas*). He tied the hook line off on the forward cleat, then roped the shark behind the pectoral fins with the stern line and pulled the carcass upward, leaning back hard, putting his full weight into the effort.

The dead bull shark came up over the gunwale into the Whaler. It made a wet scraping sound as it slid down and thumped against the fiberglass side. A female.

The shark rolled belly up and he could see that she had been disemboweled. Her pectoral fins were facing up, like two large petals of an enormous sea flower—white underneath.

A weird feeling came over Seabrook—a sensation like déjà vu. The bite wound looked very much like the bite Razormouth had taken from the pregnant tiger shark on the deep side of the Gorgon Channel. All the organs were missing, and the caudal fin was attached to the rest of the body by the spine only. Seabrook wished he'd been able to inspect the bite wound on the pregnant tiger shark, but it had been too dangerous. Other sharks had started to feed on it. Therefore, his observations weren't supported by careful analysis but by casual observation only.

Still, his gut told him this was Razormouth's work.

With a twinge of excitement, Seabrook quickly looked into the sea for any sign of Razormouth. If he could catch it, then he'd have the "type specimen" required to establish a new species. It might still be around, feeding on the sharks hooked on the long line. It was such an enormous fish, it would be easy to see against the white sand seafloor. He looked in every direction but saw no sign of the big predator in the waves around him.

He turned his attention back to the remains of the bull shark. It was a mature female. He measured her: nine and a half feet long. Then he began unhooking the shark and remarkably found another smaller shark, a Caribbean reef shark (*Carcharhinus perezi*) inside the bull shark. He brought the four-foot-long reef shark out of the bull shark's gaping mouth; it was mostly intact. The bull shark had obviously found the reef shark on the hook and swallowed it whole.

Then Seabrook began to unhook the smaller shark and amazingly found a one-foot-long sharpnose shark (*Rhizoprionodon porosus*) inside its mouth.

Incredible.

Three sharks on one hook—each one bigger than the last—like Russian nesting dolls. And the biggest shark, the female bull shark, possibly pregnant, looked to have been killed by none other than Razormouth.

Excited, Seabrook turned on the walkie-talkie. "Aja, Aja. Seabrook on the long line. You're not going to believe what I found. Come back," he said into the receiver.

No response.

"Aja, Aja. Seabrook on the long line. Come back," he said again.

No response.

He tried two more times, but Aja didn't answer. He figured she was outside doing a water change on her reef tanks. He would tell her about the three sharks on one hook when he got back.

He put the walkie-talkie back inside the tagging kit. Then he dug the record book out of the kit and began writing notes in the back. He wanted to get each detail down. He remeasured each shark to be precise, then resumed writing notes. He was so absorbed that he didn't register the sound of a large speedboat approaching until it was close.

The speedboat came up behind him, splashing through the waves as it decelerated. When he turned to see who it was, he knew instantly that he was in serious trouble. The wild dogs had come for him—or at least some of them. He did not see the bald man with corned beef-colored skin. The ugly man, the one with a neck matted with wiry hair from the night before at the Compleat Angler, was pointing an M16 rifle at him.

The speedboat pulled alongside the Whaler.

The ugly man aimed the M16 rifle straight at Seabrook's chest. His finger was on the trigger, and he didn't move or say anything. He just waited for orders.

Vuelta, the man who had done all the talking at the Compleat Angler, quickly came out on deck with a third man. Vuelta said something in Spanish and gestured towards Seabrook. The third man had also been at the bar the night before: the one with the box-like chest and big arms. He picked up a plastic bait tub from the deck of the speedboat. It looked heavy as he hoisted it up and stepped onto the Whaler.

The man set the big plastic bait tub right at Seabrook's feet. Vuelta passed him an M16. Then the man sat at the bow of the Whaler and pointed his rifle at Seabrook's face.

Seabrook sat down on the cross-plank seat by the outboard.

"Open it," Vuelta said.

"What is it?" A feeling of dread came over Seabrook. He suddenly remembered the dead man in his dream asking, "*How fast can you run?*"

"Bait. For your hooks."

"No thanks. I don't bait the hooks until the end of the day. The sharks feed more at night," Seabrook said. He looked straight down the barrel of the gun pointed at him.

"Open it and bait the line," Vuelta said forcefully.

Seabrook saw the man's finger on the trigger of his M16. He was not used to someone pointing a gun at him. For a split second he thought about diving into the sea—but they would kill him for sure if he did that.

Seabrook pried the plastic lid off the bait tub and set it down.

The tub was full of blood and meat. His eyes widened. He had studied human anatomy as an undergraduate and quickly understood what he was looking at.

Detached human flesh.

Sections of legs and arms. Wads of cut muscle.

A foot. A ridge of spine. A piece of torso. Part of a lung.

Intestines.

All of it in a soup of thickening, congealing blood.

Seabrook moved back, recoiling from the horror. The sight of body parts wasn't the only thing that sickened him.

The smell hit his nose. Decay hadn't really started, so whoever was in the bait tub had been murdered recently. But the metallic scent of blood mixed with rancid vomit, emptied bowels, urine, and sweat made him gag.

He turned his head away, tried to inhale fresh sea air.

"Bait the hooks," Vuelta said.

His stomach seemed to drop, and he suddenly felt lightheaded. As if his blood had turned to water. His mind scrambled with thoughts and questions, and he knew that he was in shock. Still, he did as he was told.

He silently prayed that Aja was safe and was glad he hadn't gotten ahold of her with the walkie-talkie. Knowing her, she would have come straight out to see the three sharks on one hook. He didn't want her in this situation. Part of him suspected that the cartel men were framing him and going to kill him. Once he put the body parts on the long line, they could anonymously report Seabrook to the local police. Claim he had murdered the person and tried to get rid of the evidence by feeding it to the sharks. How could he ever explain why the long line was baited with human flesh?

Blood and viscera did not normally bother him, but this was different. Nausea, horror, and fear cascaded over him in alternating waves when he put his hand into the bait tub. He picked up a piece of meat that might have been part of someone's hamstring. He couldn't tell if the dismembered body was female or male, but it seemed like the flesh of a young adult. Human blood, clotted and thickening, splashed on the Whaler. He grabbed the hook that had previously had the three sharks on it and pushed the meat down over the barb. The hook easily pierced through the flesh. Then he cast the baited hook into the sea.

"Next one," Vuelta said.

Seabrook put the Whaler into gear. The outboard chugged louder, and with his gaff holding to the main line, he drove slowly forward to the next hook. Then he put the engine in neutral and retrieved the hook from the sea. It came up clean and shiny in the sun.

"Bait it," Vuelta said.

He put a piece of calf onto the hook. Black hairs were standing up from the skin. Probably a man's leg. He threw the baited hook into the sea. It sank under the surface.

The hooks speared into the pieces of human flesh as if they were cuts of tuna or beefsteak.

The speedboat cruised right next to the Whaler. The cartel men were different than any human beings Seabrook had ever observed. At first glance, they looked like unremarkable thugs, but if you studied their faces, they were distinct. They had been deeply marked by their lives and wore it in their faces: eerie dumb eyes and hard, empty expressions; a sense that there were no boundaries. Like their souls had been stamped out and extinguished—if they'd ever had them in the first place. There were three of them: Vuelta and the ugly long-faced man who was holding an M16, casually at the ready. The third man, barrel-chested, and the strongest, was sitting on the bow of the Whaler and had been pointing his M16 at Seabrook the entire time.

Seabrook didn't know what was stranger about them: their casual viciousness or their absolute indifference to it. Their behavior seemed unnatural. They did not seem to hate him, but they would torture and kill him with no more compunction than required to blow their noses.

In benighted silence they watched him work. There was no talking, no joking, and zero interest in what Seabrook was doing—as long as he did what he was told. This was obviously business as usual for these men. Just a job.

He noticed that the limbs of the corpse had been cleanly severed. Several times, as the boat rocked with the waves and shook the bait tub, the sections of limbs and intestines seemed alive and swimming in the blood. But when he lifted them out of the blood, they were dead and motionless. The wounds on the limbs were even and straight, like a skillful butcher had made them—probably not the work of these men. He thought of the weird hairless man with corned beef-colored skin and a shark jaw tattoo. It came to Seabrook that they delivered victims to him. They all worked for him.

"Why are you doing this?" Seabrook said.

"*Estupido*. You had a chance last night," Vuelta said. "Now you shut up. You just listen and follow."

One hook after another, Seabrook baited the half-mile-long line. He did the work as if it were any other day—except today he baited twenty-five hooks with a dismembered human body. Luckily, the rest of the hooks had no sharks on them.

The worst were the organs. The intestines, liver, and stomach weren't firm like muscle tissue and didn't want to stay on the hooks in the same way. But Seabrook made it work by double- and triple-hooking the grisly mush.

By the last hook, his hands and forearms were grotesquely red and sticky with splashes of blood and little bits of meat. He put a piece of thigh muscle, purplish red, on the final hook. When he was done, there was still plenty of meat in the tub. He noticed that most of the body had been in the tub, but not all of it. There were no severed hands, and some of the torso seemed to be missing.

A human head lay on its side in the congealing blood amongst viscera that oozed around the tub with the rise and fall of the waves.

"Pick up the head," Vuelta said.

Seabrook picked the head up with both hands. Wet and warm. Sickening.

"Look at him," Vuelta said.

Seabrook turned the head so he could see the face. The ears were gone.

They had dismembered the Earless Man.

The mouth hung open, and the lips were swollen. Teeth were missing and broken off. Both eyes had been burned out. He'd been horribly tortured before they cut him up. The blackened eye sockets reminded Seabrook how the hairless man had said to him, "*You have beautiful blue eyes,*" then later asked, "*Can I have them?*" This was what he'd had in mind.

"He doesn't look so good now, eh?" Vuelta said.

Seabrook wanted to throw the head overboard. He also felt bad for the Earless Man. What a horrible end.

Is this going to happen to me and Aja too? Seabrook thought. *Please let Aja be safe!*

The speedboat moved right up next to the Boston Whaler. The strong man sitting at the bow of the Whaler with the M16 stood up and pulled a plastic trash bag out of his pocket. He opened it so Seabrook could see inside it.

"Put the head in that," Vuelta said.

Seabrook dropped the head into the trash bag. It slid to the bottom with a soft, wet thump.

The ugly man climbed onto the speedboat with the bulging trash bag.

"You and your woman were the last people he saw before we got him. He told us this many times."

"What do you want from us?" Seabrook asked. His voice came out strange, wretched and laced with dismay. *They were after Aja too.*

"You have twenty-four hours to return the fifty million dollars you stole from his boat." Vuelta nodded towards the trash bag.

"Or what?" Seabrook asked.

"Or tomorrow you bait the hooks with pieces of your woman. Then it will be your turn to scream."

"Where is she?"

"We took her this morning after you left the house," Vuelta said. "She is now with the man you met last night."

A crazy nauseous feeling spread through Seabrook's chest.

"I don't have the money. I've never seen it. I don't know anything about it!" Seabrook shouted.

"You have twenty-four hours," Vuelta said. The speedboat began to pull away.

"Where do I meet you if I find the money?" Seabrook yelled to be heard.

The speedboat's engine grew louder.

"We will have a man waiting at the Compleat Angler!" Vuelta shouted.

The speedboat suddenly accelerated and drove back towards Bimini, cutting a wake across the turquoise sea.

Seabrook opened the tagging kit and pulled out the walkie-talkie. He called Aja.

No answer.

He tried again and again.

"Please pick up," he whispered.

Still no response. After ten attempts, he sat down heavily on the cross bench.

In the distance, Vuelta's speedboat disappeared into the blue horizon.

Chapter 38
Gone

Seabrook emptied the bait tub over the gunwale into the sea. Blood clouded the water, and the leftover human flesh sank. He rinsed the blood out of the tub, then submerged and filled it a quarter of the way with water. He poured seawater over the blood-spattered deck. He poured until the crimson rinsed away; it would wash out the back when he pulled the drain plug once the boat was moving and on a plane over the waves.

Next, he sank the tub in the sea.

He jumped overboard and, underwater, scrubbed his forearms and hands, trying furiously to get the human blood off. He would be zero help to Aja if he got pulled over by the Bimini authorities or the U.S. Coast Guard with the remains of a dead man onboard.

Even though he was in a near panic, he also knew that panic would ruin any chance to save Aja. He had to stay cool and think—but it wasn't easy. He pulled himself back onboard the Whaler.

For a few seconds, he was utterly overwhelmed. The boat rocked in the waves, and he couldn't think. His body shook, and deep grief seized him. It felt like the best part of him, the most important part, all the beauty, tenderness, and goodness in his life—Aja—was being torn away. In that moment he felt utterly doomed, like something (no matter how horrific, how devastating, how unthinkable) was going to happen to them.

And he couldn't stop it.

As if the universe had declared open season on them.

He would not have been surprised if the sky itself fell and crushed him or the sea suddenly swallowed him up. He'd never seen fifty million dollars in his life and couldn't see any reason to hope he could find the money. Still, after a few seconds more, he made himself press on anyway.

He would think. And he would fight.

He started the outboard, put it in gear, and raced the Whaler back to the house. He saw the ghostly profile of the SS *Sapona* in the distance, Turtle Rocks on the left, and, after half an hour of motoring, Round Rock up ahead with South Bimini island visible behind it. He pulled the tiller towards him and turned right to go around Round Rock.

The ocean turned darker blue and choppier as he got closer to the Gulf Stream's deeper water. He did not slow down like he normally would. The hull of the Whaler rose up and slammed down between waves, spraying seawater that foamed and churned as he pressed on.

He went full throttle the whole way. If he got back quickly, maybe he could see the boat that had kidnapped Aja. For all he knew, Vuelta had lied about when they grabbed her, and they were actually seizing her right now. If that were the case, then they'd probably drive out the mouth of the harbor at Alice Town. Maybe he could catch the name of the boat.

He stared at each ship coming out of Bimini's harbor and passing his way—the agonizing fact was that Aja could be held captive below deck on any one of them. She very well might be cruising right past him. The idea made him crazy. He wanted to stop every vessel and search it.

He stared at the name on the stern of each boat: *Sea Breeze II, The Elsie, Monkey Business, Fat City.* All of them looked like fishing yachts owned by wealthy businessmen. None of them were drug runner speedboats like the one Vuelta drove.

Nevertheless, Seabrook looked to see whether the people onboard each yacht looked like cartel people. If he were to see something, he wasn't sure what he'd do. Maybe try to board? But all he saw were pleasure boaters having a good time.

He considered where the cartel could take Aja. Just keep her below deck on a boat? Take her to a nearby island like Cat Cay? Into a house on North Bimini? Or perhaps into a house on South Bimini? Or as far away as Florida? Or perhaps they went north across the sound, then threaded their way through the mangrove maze to come out into the ocean through Bonefish Hole. This last idea he eliminated, because the North Sound was too shallow for most boats and the cartel would have to know the way through the mangrove maze. Only locals knew how to get through the narrow and winding channels that serpentined, dead-ended, and eventually went through the mangroves.

Seabrook grew increasingly upset.

There was no sign of cartel speedboats, and it seemed like Vuelta had told the truth. They had snatched Aja hours ago, just after Seabrook left the house to go to the long line in the early morning. This gave them a head start of several hours.

Given the elapsed time, they could have taken her all the way to Miami by now.

He was too late to save Aja.

After tying off the Whaler, Seabrook ran up the dock. His bare feet raced across the small stones and dry grass in the backyard. The sliding glass door was partially open—strangers had been here. Aja always locked it before she left.

He went up the concrete steps and slid the door open.

"Aja!" he called, just in case, miracle of miracles, she was home.

No answer.

The John Boat was tied at the dock, and everything inside the house seemed in order. No obvious signs of a struggle. Nothing missing —except Aja.

He shouted her name inside the house. He called her name again and ran into each room, then checked the bathroom. He even looked in the bathtub. The place seemed eerily quiet: just the humming of the pumps circulating seawater in Aja's two cone snail aquariums.

No trace of her anywhere inside. He went outside and walked around the house and yard, yelling her name like a madman.

Still no response. The yard was empty, and there wasn't any traffic on the road.

Then he grew quiet. If he was going to be any help, he had to think.

The Jon Boat was still tied at the end of the dock, so she hadn't gone out to work.

There was no obvious sign of struggle. No blood. They'd taken her alive. And she hadn't speared one of them—he almost smiled at the thought, because he knew she would have wanted to fight.

He went back down the dock. He paused when he saw Clara resting in her pen. She saw him and swam up near the surface, her baby dorsal fin slicing the surface of the water.

"Clara," he said to the shark.

She circled at the surface of her pen as if Aja and the Sea Cherubs were about to feed her.

"I'll try to get her back," he promised the shark. "And the Sea Cherubs."

His heart ached at the thought. How could he fight back? What could he do?

He had to think.

Aja would have thought of him. She would have wanted to leave him a message or some clue ... unless they'd caught her by surprise and she'd had no time. Or she hadn't had a clue to offer him.

He went back into the house and tried to piece together how the cartel had taken her. Then he noticed that the plastic buckets she used to do water changes on the aquariums were sitting on the floor by one of the tanks. A cone snail was moving slowly across the sand inside the Caribbean specimen tank.

Seabrook wiped his hand along the inside of one bucket. It was still wet. Aja must have just finished doing an aquarium water change when the cartel arrived. He wondered if she had seen them arrive and had time to prepare or make a note?

He knew Aja would have wanted to leave him a message. What was it?

Chapter 39
A Friendly Voice on the Beach

Myron and Mookie heard the sound of their father's outboard start up and slowly leave. It was almost morning; they had spent the night in the pine tree. As the sound grew distant, the boys were tempted to climb down. Myron decided they should wait a little longer and let daylight come. Maybe the sounds of their father's leaving was a trick, and he was going to circle back and try to catch them after they came out of their hiding place.

After sitting in the tree for another hour, the boys slowly climbed down the branches. Their bones were sore from sitting so long, and their mouths felt dry as sandpaper, they were so thirsty. On top of that, they were both exhausted.

Myron and Mookie shuffled and stumbled, half delirious, out from the pinewoods and went back towards their small fort behind the palm tree. When they crawled in, they instantly knew their father had found it. He had gone inside and ruined it. His giant footprints were all around everywhere, and the sand looked rained on—except that it was not rain. Their father had urinated and pooped right in the center of the small space.

Mookie started to cry. But his mouth was so dry that it came out as a croaking bird sound, and his eyes could not make tears because he was so dehydrated.

"Let's make a new fort in the pinewoods," Myron said.

They had to search hard for a good spot. They focused on an area where they wouldn't leave clear footprints.

Eventually they found a dead pine tree that had fallen over. Part of the trunk was lying on the ground, but another part was resting roughly three feet off the ground.

Myron crawled under the log first. It was dry and well-hidden by brush on three sides. Dry pine needles covered the sandy earth under the log, and the ground was mildly inclined and pretty flat. A decent sleeping spot.

The boys collected branches from near the top of the dead pine tree and used them as a natural-looking barrier to hide the opening under the log. Then they crawled into their new fort, pulled the branches over their entranceway, and lay down on the pine needle-covered ground.

Their great thirst kept them awake for a while, but exhaustion eventually swept them off to sleep.

They woke up because they heard their names being called.

"Myron! Mookie!" the voice shouted. It had a Spanish accent. "We're here to rescue you! Come on out! You are safe!" Initially, the voice sounded fairly close, as if it was coming from the direction of the old fisherman's shed.

"Mom sent help," Mookie said in a hushed, cracking voice. His lips were flaky and chapped.

"Maybe. Maybe not," Myron croaked back. "Let's listen."

"Myron! Mookie!" the voice shouted again. "We're here to rescue you! Come out! You are safe!"

Then the voice started to sound smaller and farther away, like the man was walking away from them down the beach. "Come out! You're safe!"

It went on like this for half an hour. Then the man's voice grew distinctly louder. He was walking into the pinewoods in their direction now.

"I brought water and food! I know you are thirsty!" the voice called.

Myron peeked out through the dead branches and saw a man holding a plastic bottle of water in each hand. His throat gulped involuntarily at the sight of it. The man had a mean face, but his voice sounded friendly. His hair was black, and he looked sort of Cuban or South American.

"Your mother sent me! We don't have much time!" he yelled. "We are here to pick you up! Your father will come back soon. Let's get out of here now! While we can!" The bottles of water shined blue in the sunlight.

Mookie was suddenly beside himself with thirst and crawled forward to go get the water. One of the smaller branches cracked loudly under his elbows. Then Myron got ahold of his leg and pulled him back.

That's when they saw the other two men. A prickly feeling crawled up Myron's back like a spider with needle legs when he realized what he was looking at: a trap. One man was trying to draw them into the open with his friendly voice and water bottles. Then the other two would catch them.

But why? Who were these men, and what did they want?

How did they know their names?

One man looked like he was part dog. His face was hunched up, and he had tangled hair that ran down his neck. The other man had a big, round chest and muscular arms. Neither of them held water bottles or spoke. Instead, they held billy clubs in their hands, and their eyes darted around as they searched the area. They were sneaking along, looking behind every tree. They walked slowly and carefully, trying to be as silent as possible, but they weren't good at it.

Myron could hear them walking if he listened carefully. The hunters had heard Mookie break the small tree branch, and now they were walking towards their fort.

"They are trying to catch us," Myron whispered. "Be silent."

"What do you want me to tell your mother? She's very worried about you!" the leader yelled in a voice that pretended to be worried.

The boys lay their heads on the ground and prayed they would not be found.

Then it became quiet for a few minutes. Seagulls cried and bickered down on the beach, but there were no other sounds. Myron couldn't tell what the men were doing: coming closer or moving away? He was afraid to move his head and look.

Suddenly, the friendly voice was very close and made Myron want to jump out of his skin.

"Well, if nothing else, let me give you this nice cool water! Then I can tell your mother that I saw you, and that you are okay," the boss yelled. "Don't you want your mother to know you're okay?"

Myron and Mookie did not react.

After ten more minutes of this, Myron had the feeling that the bad men were moving away from their fort. He slowly raised his head. He could see all three men talking in whispers. They seemed angry, and turned to go back to the beach.

As the two silent men turned to go back with their boss, Myron could see that each had a long knife with a handle grip hanging off the side of his belt. They also had plastic zip ties protruding from their pockets.

Chapter 40
Aja

Aja, three hours earlier, saw the men coming for her. Two walked swiftly up the dock with guns. She immediately tried to run out the side door of the kitchen but saw another man, Vuelta from the Compleat Angler the night before, with a handgun blocking the way to King's Highway. She slammed the door shut and locked it.

Aja was trapped. Her heart raced. Her throat felt dry.

Through the sliding glass door she could see the men now coming up the path from their dock. She considered spearing one of them with her Hawaiian sling. Bad idea. That would probably just antagonize them.

She had two minutes at the most to leave Seabrook some kind of message.

Think! Think!

Vuelta and his men picked the lock on the kitchen door. When they pushed the door open, Aja had just set down the chalk she'd used on the black board. She wore a bikini underneath shorts and a T-shirt. She had been getting ready to go out in the Jon Boat and study the cone snails on the airplane reef. The right side of her shorts bulged very slightly—she'd slipped one of the satellite tracking tags into her pocket. Maybe Seabrook could track her? It was the best move she could think of.

"You are coming with us," Vuelta said.

"Why? What do you want?"

"Fifty million dollars. Do you know where it is?"

"No. I've never seen money like that in my life. This is some kind of mistake. You've got the wrong people."

"What happens to you depends on what your boyfriend does. If he does the right thing, maybe you will be safe."

A wave of gloom swept over Aja. There was no way on earth Seabrook could produce fifty million dollars. One man pointed his gun at her; the other looked like he wanted to hurt her with his fists.

Vuelta told her to turn around and put her hands behind her back, and she did. Moments later, he jerked a zip tie around Aja's wrists so tightly that it hurt. Vuelta and the two other men walked her quickly down the dock.

She started shaking. She felt it most in the knees. They came to their speedboat, which was tied off at the end of the dock.

Suddenly, someone pulled a black bag over her head. She screamed. They were going to rape or hurt her horribly.

Her knees started shaking more, and her heart seemed to flutter. How could she get out of this?

A man picked her up and threw her over his shoulder. As if she was nothing and they could do whatever they wanted to her.

She wanted to stay cool and detached, but suddenly lost control. She screamed again and again and again. Like her lungs would burst.

There was a jarring bump, and it felt like the man was carrying her aboard the speedboat. He moved quickly and squeezed her legs hard, as if he was angry she was screaming. Then it felt like he was carrying her down a short stairway below deck.

She was dumped hard to the floor. The boat's engine started up, and the boat started moving. The motion was smooth. They were obviously going down the channel towards the harbor at Alice Town.

Again, she screamed for help. Then something hard smashed her in the face. A fist? A boot? A baseball bat?

Flashing light waltzed behind her eyelids. The worst headache she'd ever felt began to pulse inside her skull. Whoever had hit her could have killed her, the force was so great. The blow had been delivered with murderous intent. If she hadn't fallen to her side with the force of it, she'd probably have a fractured skull.

Groggily, she sat up and wondered, had it even been a punch? Or had someone tried to kick her head off? Never in her life had she been handled with such viciousness. It told her that they would kill her, rape her, or torture her without a second's hesitation. If she screamed again, they might kill her just for that. She thought she could feel the slight weight of the satellite tracking tag she'd put in her pocket before they snatched her. But she couldn't touch it, and she couldn't be sure. It could have fallen out when she was being carried.

Her head throbbed and felt woozy as the boat moved along. There weren't any waves because the boat didn't bounce or sway at all. Determined to survive, she listened to the boat sounds and tried to track time. She counted in her head: one, two, three, four, five, six ... until the boat stopped. She'd counted up to 914. They couldn't have traveled far.

The boat hadn't bounced and rocked as it would have in the open ocean. No. They had stayed in calmer waters and never even left the harbor. Could they have merely taken her from North Bimini island to South Bimini island on the other side of Alice Town harbor?

The boat was tied up, and the engine was switched off.

Rough hands seized her and lifted her up by her shoulders. Then the hands were on her throat, squeezing. She couldn't breathe, and her larynx felt as if it would break.

"Don't make a sound or I'll cut out your tongue. Nod if you hear me."

Aja nodded. They took her off the boat. She heard the sound of water—not rough waves but gentler, like an inlet. They hadn't traveled far. They had to be somewhere on South Bimini island.

Next they walked her up a dock onto land. Then one of them threw her over his shoulder and carried her for ten minutes. He took her inside some kind of structure. Maybe a house. A door shut, and she heard it lock.

The place reeked of blood. As an EMT and as a biologist, she had worked with blood many times and it had a distinctive metallic scent. The place smelled worse than anything she'd ever encountered before. Like a filthy slaughterhouse.

They seemed to go from one room into another room. She was set down roughly on a hard floor. The black bag was suddenly lifted off her head.

She could now see. Three other people were sitting on the floor next to her—a pregnant white woman and also the two men who had questioned her and Seabrook in the North Sound. The one who'd had his finger defleshed by the little lemon shark now had the stump of his pinkie bandaged. The smaller one, the cokehead, was dripping sweat, like he was going through withdrawal. He seemed ready to jump out of his skin.

All of them were sitting in a row with their backs to the wall facing the only doorway in or out. The men's faces were bruised and bloodied. They were too afraid to speak—they didn't want their tongues cut out. It seemed like they were in a kid's bedroom in someone's vacation home. Aja had the terrible thought that she would probably die in this house.

Everyone had their wrists zip-tied behind their backs, and their ankles zip-tied together as well.

The man who had taken the black sack off Aja's head now zip-tied her ankles together. She felt helpless—she couldn't run now. She probably couldn't even walk. Her head hurt and she felt terrifically tired.

The horror of the situation was overwhelming—blood and death in the next room. She wanted to escape from this place, if not physically, then maybe mentally. But she could barely keep her eyes open. Her body wanted to shut down, go to sleep. Maybe the blow to her head was making her drowsy. Her mind began to drift as she fought to stay conscious. Where was Seabrook? Little by little, she lapsed into vivid memories ...

She was snorkeling with him at Turtle Rocks on the deep ocean side.

The sea was amazingly clear, with visibility to a hundred feet. They held hands as they finned along the surface, gazing down at the intricate architecture of the reef below: velvet-textured hillocks, yellow blades of fire coral, secret alcoves, porticos of sponge columns, shell-shucked octopus refuse, craggy obelisks rising tower-like to the surface, and bowl-shaped satin valleys.

Flickers and flashes of electric color animated the scene as magnificent tropical fish moved about like so many swimming sapphires, gold pieces, and rubies. The limpid water sparkled with sunlight that lanced downwards into gorgeous blue depths.

Next to a butte-shaped colony of brain coral, Aja and Seabrook encountered half a dozen reef squid. They were less than a foot long. She'd never seen the species before. The cephalopods hovered in the water column and allowed the humans to swim close.

The squid stared at them with large eyes, unblinking and intelligent-looking. The six of them seemed unaffected by the sea currents. They hovered in a manner that looked effortless with undulating fins that ran the length of their bodies.

Their elongated bodies glowed incandescent and were dotted with bright flecks and marks of rose, blue, and gold pigment. They changed colors as if blushing with sweet embarrassment: from a regal gold-blue complexion to passionate bright maroon red.

Like shy lovers seeing each other naked for the first time ...

A loud voice brought Aja out of her memory. She remembered that her hands were painfully zip-tied behind her back and that she was sitting on the floor in a dark room: a child's bedroom with stuffed animals on the bed. Three other prisoners were with her: two men and a pregnant woman. Colombian men talked loudly in Spanish in the other room, but one voice was soft and calm and sounded reasonable. She had no idea how much time had passed.

The bald man with the shark jaw tattoo from the Compleat Angler suddenly came to the doorway and looked at each of his captives. His eyes lingered on each person for a few seconds. His stare was frightening. He was making judgments about his victims. What order? What method? Who first? Then he said something quickly and softly that Aja couldn't understand. He turned and went into the other room. Aja closed her eyes, wishing the headache would go away. Mercifully, she escaped into her memories again:

The squid hovered like flying cylinders in front of them. Then Seabrook swam a little ahead, and the cephalopods darted away like a squadron of UFOs.

He waved her on towards a drop-off, where the seafloor disappeared downward like the steep slope of a mountainside.

Two French angelfish colored creamy white, banana yellow, and black chocolate swam by a spire of coral at the edge of the drop-off. The species was well known for mating for life. These two were large, fully mature fish, whose Frisbee-shaped bodies were one and a half feet tall.

Both fish suddenly glided into the vast open blue area above the drop-off. They circled and followed each other, above the deep, exposed to any predators and unsafe.

But free.

Focused on nothing but each other, like two gorgeous kites in a clear blue sky ...

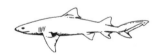

Two men came into the room, and Aja woke up. The men hoisted the man with nine fingers to his feet. He stared at his captors stoically, not saying a word. Then he grew visibly paler and started sweating, because he had a clear view into the living room. He could see what awaited him. The cartel men dragged him off.

Aja closed her eyes again. Maybe if she could rest a little, the exhaustion and grogginess she felt would let go of her. She drifted ...

Seabrook took her hand, and they swam to the shallower part of the reef. He tugged on her arm as if he wanted to show her something. He must have noticed an interesting fish or invertebrate.

He dived down ten feet to the mouth of a small cave. He peeked inside. Then he turned his face upward and waved at Aja, beckoning her to join him. He must have found something really good, because he seemed excited.

Aja inhaled, then snorkeled down next to him. He pointed into the small cave.

He kicked his fins and edged deeper under the overhanging ledge.

Aja followed him. As she pulled even with him, he pointed to a mollusk sitting in the sand: a Triton's trumpet sea snail, or at least the shell of one. The shell was resting with its opening facing up. The shell's mantle sat nearly level, with dramatic markings like a jaguar's pelt on its smooth surface.

Seabrook gestured towards the shell, urging her to move closer to it.

Aja gently kicked her fins and glided another foot closer. Suddenly, she saw a twinkle of gold on the mantle of the shell.

Again, Seabrook pointed at the shell, seemingly focused on the small golden object.

All at once, Aja recognized what she was looking at: a gold ring with a tiny diamond.

An engagement ring.

She picked up the ring, pinching it between her index finger and thumb, then turned to look at Seabrook.

He was already facing her. He held up a small underwater tablet they sometimes used to communicate with when scuba diving. They would write messages on the tablet and shared them with each other. Today, the tablet had a message written in Seabrook's handwriting:

"I love you from the bottom of the sea and the bottom of my heart.

Will you marry me?

Please say yes!"

Aja's eyes watered in her mask. She suddenly needed to breathe, and went to the surface grasping the engagement ring tightly.

She spit out the snorkel and inhaled fresh air.

As she pushed her mask up on her forehead, Seabrook surfaced next to her and spit out his snorkel.

"What do you think?" he said.

"Yes," Aja said. "From the bottom of the sea and the bottom of my heart—yes!"

A loud sound woke her. She sat up straight and looked around the room. The pregnant woman and remaining man were still sitting on the floor next to her. She remembered that the nine-fingered man had been taken. Her mind felt less cloudy; maybe the shock was wearing off, or her instinct to survive was kicking in. Either way, her head hurt less and she was coming back to herself.

She could not see into the living room from where she sat, but she could hear very clearly. Sounds to lacerate the soul.

A heavy thump like a suitcase being thrown on a table.

Someone said something unintelligible. Then it was quiet a moment.

Someone grunted as if in pain.

A man's soothing voice spoke. It had the calm, helpful tone of a librarian. It had to be the bald man with the shark jaw tattoo. Someone called him Pelon.

"*Donde está el dinero?*" Pelon said. *Where's the money?*

"*No lo sé,*" the nine-fingered man said. *I don't know.*

A loud metallic *clip.*

Horrible gasping, followed by rapid breathing.

Someone threw something into the room where Aja and the others were sitting. It slid to a stop on the linoleum floor: a man's severed foot, still wearing a shoe. Blood seeped from the raw end.

Aja pushed back and raised her knees up. To get farther away from it—farther away from everything. It was suddenly hard to breathe.

An animal groan and agonized breathing filled the other room.

Again Pelon's gentle voice said, "*Donde está el dinero?*"

"*No lo sé!*" the nine-fingered man gasped.

Another metallic *clip.* Gasping sounds.

Now a piece of leg slid across the floor. Ankle to midshin, bleeding from both ends.

Crazy panic rose in Aja like a white fever. Her limbs felt numb, and her heart seemed to flutter like it was beating too fast. She looked around the room, trying to figure a way to escape. They were definitely in a child's bedroom. A queen-size box spring and mattress sat on an old frame with wheels at the end of each leg. The floor was covered in linoleum tiles. Stuffed animals—teddy bear, parrot, and a Raggedy Ann doll—were sitting on the bed against the pillows. Posters of horses and unicorns decorated the walls.

There were no windows. No closet. Nothing she could use as a weapon.

The only way out was by going through the room where they were cutting the nine-fingered man into pieces. The stench of blood filled the air even more strongly than before.

Voices interrupted her thoughts. The kind, patient voice said, "*Donde está el dinero?*"

"*No lo sé,*" the nine-fingered man sobbed.

Clip.

A severed hand bounced into the room, the one with four fingers.

The cartel men were trying to terrorize their hostages, and it was working.

The sound of gas being turned on. The whoosh of ignition. A blowtorch?

Again the kind, infinitely patient voice said, *"Donde está el dinero?"*

"No lo sé," the nine-fingered man said, agony in his voice.

People were moving. A sudden banging sound like a person frantically trying to break free. Deep moaning sounds.

The smell of burning meat floated in the air.

Aja couldn't believe the victim hadn't screamed. He groaned and gasped as they dismembered and burned him, but he couldn't or wouldn't scream. Maybe he was in shock, or just tough as hell and didn't want to give his killers the satisfaction. Aja didn't know how he could hold it in.

Again she looked desperately around the room for any weapon, or even a sharp edge with which to cut the zip ties binding her wrists and ankles. She thought that maybe she could cut the zip ties by scraping them on the bed frame.

But how would she do it with the door to the killing room open? They would hear her efforts. She kept looking but found nothing visible.

The killers now moved quickly and professionally. They didn't ask the victim any more questions. Pelon commenced taking him apart fast: *clip, clip, clip, clip.*

The man struggled and grunted. The horrific sounds seemed to go on forever, and Aja lost track of time. Had she been there twenty minutes? Two hours? Or two days? She couldn't say.

Again the hissing, rushing sound of a blowtorch. The horrible thrashing sound started again, followed by a low inhuman, bestial sound.

Aja looked at the pregnant woman sitting next to her. She'd been quietly crying. She had brunette hair and looked very young—maybe eighteen. Next to her, and nearest to the door, sat the partner of the nine-fingered man. He looked sick. He could see into the living room.

A new sound started: the shrill buzz of a power saw. It lasted less than a minute.

The nine-fingered man must have finally died.

The cutting and burning sounds stopped. The killers threw something heavy, like a torso, on the floor in the living room. Then another. Had they cut his body in half?

Aja closed her eyes, choking back her feelings of terror.

She forced herself not to scream.

Chapter 41
Searching

Seabrook searched everywhere in the house, looking for a clue from Aja. He found nothing that could be even remotely interpreted as a message for him. He rifled through their dresser drawers, the kitchen drawers, the books in the library. He carefully read the list of needed groceries on the blackboard. He looked beneath and behind her aquariums, in the bathroom drawer, underneath the sink, in the bathtub, under the bar of soap, in and on top of the refrigerator. He checked in the freezer among the frozen bait and their frozen food. He walked around the outside of the house and examined the cistern. Nothing anywhere.

Maybe she hadn't gotten a chance to leave a message?

He knew he was losing precious time and had to do something.

The fact that a cartel man was waiting for the money at the Compleat Angler kept popping into his mind. That was his only link to Aja.

How could he return missing money he didn't have? His best guess was that Bastareaud had sneaked aboard the Earless Man's speedboat and stolen the money. Maybe the crazy woman had been asleep while the speedboat got robbed. Bastareaud might be sitting on the cash at that very instant.

Seabrook decided to go to the landlord's house with the half-baked idea that he might get the money and confront the man about abusing his children and wife. Kill two birds with one stone. He expected violence, but it didn't matter at this point. He'd do whatever it would take to save Aja.

He grabbed his Hawaiian sling spear on the way out the door. Quickly, he jogged across the backyard, then across the road. He went to the ocean side of Bimini, where Bastareaud lived. Then he ran along the edge of the soccer field and went down a path to his landlord's house. As he approached the front door he saw dried blood on the stoop. *The killers had already gotten to him.*

He stepped carefully around the blood on the stoop. He rapped his knuckles on the front door. It was open and ajar.

"Hello? Is there anyone home?" he shouted.

No response.

Seabrook expected that the place had become a crime scene and didn't want to enter. He was worried that he could get falsely implicated in whatever horrors existed inside. He elbowed the front door back so it swung more open. He looked in but couldn't see much. Then he pushed the door wide open with the blunt end of the spear he was carrying. He didn't want to use his fingertips and leave prints.

There was blood all over the place. He didn't need to go any closer to guess that Bastareaud was dead. He saw the man's machete on the living room table. On the kitchen floor, in the blood, lay severed black hands and feet. Flies were buzzing over the scene.

If Bastareaud had stolen the money, he had surely confessed and returned it. But Seabrook couldn't be sure he'd stolen the money. Still, he could hope. Then the cartel would be more inclined to let Aja go.

But the cartel killed bystanders too.

He turned and left the property.

Chapter 42
Claws

"Though thou exalt thyself as the eagle, and though thou set thy nest among the stars, thence will I bring thee down, saith the LORD."
—*Obadiah* 1.4

Just outside, around the back of the house, Reverend Bastareaud woke up because something was hurting his ankles.

A chewing, gnawing sensation. His shins felt on fire.

He kicked out with both legs to make the pain stop. Several things scuttled back from his ankles.

His eyelids fluttered open, then closed. He felt very weak. It was difficult to focus or think straight.

He cracked his eyes open again, but his vision was blurry around the edges. He didn't know where he was or how he got to this place. Somehow he was naked. He looked around for his shirt and shorts but saw nothing except the hard concrete floor he was sitting on.

He heard a clicking noise.

Dozens of clicking noises, close by.

The pain in his right ankle flared up again. He kicked his legs to make it stop. Something fell off his leg and scurried away.

He forced his eyes to open wider, and saw hundreds of small eyes looking at him. The eyes moved on little stalks that protruded up from just under the carapaces of the land crabs—shells colored rotten yellow or baby blue. Long, hard, spidery legs.

And he saw claws.

The land crabs were clinging to the side of a chain-link fence that he had built. The crab that he'd kicked away scuttled forward toward his raw ankle again, its large claw open wide. Its pincers and mandibles were oddly red-colored. He'd caught thousands of crabs over the years, and none of them had ever had red claws or mouths.

He tried to stomp it with his heel. Then he saw that he had no heel.

His feet were gone. His lower legs showed exposed muscle and bone. Someone had skinned them; then he remembered the devil with the bald head: the Emperor of the Crabs. It was him!

Bastareaud could see his own shinbones, pinkish white, with red calf muscle on either side. Like two long uncooked rib bones for the crabs.

Now he saw that many crabs had gathered next to his legs, and more were climbing down the chain-link walls towards him.

The crabs around his legs looked different than normal. Their mouths and claws were also smudged with red, like a harlot's lipstick.

His blood! They'd been eating him while he was unconscious.

His eyes grew wide with the realization: *The crabs will decide!*

The devil spirits had put him in his own crab cage.

He could not stand up without feet. He could not open the door of the pen without hands. Silver pipe brackets were clamped at the end of each of his stumps so he couldn't bleed out.

The crabs suddenly became more active. They scuttled up to his legs. They aggressively climbed down the walls. Dozens of them.

Bastareaud did the only thing he could.

He screamed for God's mercy.

Chapter 43
Clue

"Ye shall know them by their fruits." —Matthew 7:16

Seabrook went back to their rental house. He sat at the kitchen table in a funk of despair, looking at the room. Aja's little touches were everywhere: traces of tenderness, peace, elegance, and erudition. The beautifully cared-for reef tanks that sparkled with light and excellent water quality and healthy sea life; the well-organized little library with the photo of the Sea Cherubs pinned over it; the photo on the bedside table of Aja kissing Clara, the baby nurse shark. Two large conch shells that Aja used as decoration, one on the kitchen table like an oversized paperweight, the other on the kitchen counter in the corner—they were not dead, broken things, crumbling and bleached white, but rather exquisitely colorful, unblemished, and eye-catching, their mantles as glorious as a rose-colored dawn.

At the foot of the kitchen table stood her two plastic crates full of files, stacked one on top of the other. They contained pertinent research papers: records and detailed accounts of her ongoing data collection in the sea; also, her observations (with diagrams and drawings) and hypotheses regarding the cone snail behavior in the two specimen tanks. It was her thesis work: the purest distillation of her academic

248

knowledge in practice, her accumulated research, and her intellectual life and essence refined and recorded on paper. Although Aja was physically absent, he still felt and could almost see her like a ghost present in the room with him. Would he be haunted like this for the rest of his life?

He stared at the beautiful wind catcher Aja had made of fishing line, sand dollars, and twigs. The sand dollars were the flat, skeletal remains of burrowing sea urchins. She had found them on the seafloor among other detritus near the sunken wreck of the Curtiss C-46 Commando airplane while doing her research on a cone snail colony under the plane's wing. They had beautiful markings that resembled the pressed leaves of a weeping willow tree. The wind catcher dangled from the ceiling in the corner of the room. It turned slowly with the stir of air. He half wondered, had Aja's ghost touched it, or had the slowly spinning fan made it move?

For how could she be gone? It seemed impossible. He glanced at the kitchen door, and part of him expected she might walk into the house, like on any other day. And she would simply explain that she'd just gone for a walk down the beach and then sweetly upbraid him for worrying. But time continued to tick by, and she didn't walk into the house.

The distant sound of a police siren suddenly became audible. He'd never heard one in Bimini before.

Stubbornly, his mind went back to the notion that Aja could still be alive and that she must have left a clue. He knew her, and he knew she would have done something to communicate—if she could.

The siren grew louder and louder. The police were obviously driving up King's Highway in a rush. He wondered if someone had gone into Bastareaud's house and discovered the carnage.

He pushed the siren noise from his mind and glanced at the elaborate drawing of Razormouth that Aja had put on their blackboard. She'd spent a lot of time making it just right. She was so thorough when asking him questions about each feature of the strange shark, he'd felt like he was being interviewed by a forensic sketch artist trying to get an accurate image of a suspect for the police.

Then it hit him. Something about the drawing of Razormouth was slightly different. A very small change he couldn't pin down at first.

The skin on his neck tingled.

His eyes quickly scanned Aja's drawing, and he suddenly found the detail that had not been there before. Of course!

She had drawn a small, almost unnoticeable tag at the base of Razormouth's dorsal fin—it resembled the new prototype satellite tags that Dr. Nixon had asked them to field-test when he last visited.

Now the police siren seemed right outside the house.

He ignored the shrill sound and jumped to his feet—he suddenly knew what Aja's clue meant: she'd taken one of the satellite tags with her so he could find her.

He went to the box with the tags in it to see if he was correct. If he was right, one would be missing. He began opening the box.

He was interrupted by a heavy knock on the door. Seabrook turned from what he was doing.

"Who is it?"

"Police!" a man's voice yelled.

The door opened and two Bahamian officers entered the room. They wore blue trousers, blue short-sleeve shirts, and vests that said "police" in large white lettering across the chest. They also wore ball caps with large gold stars on them.

Seabrook put his hands in the air. Through the sliding glass door he could see a police patrol boat pulling alongside the dock.

The officers had their guns drawn. They looked excited and aggressive.

Through the open kitchen door, red and blue lights flashed from the police car parked outside the house.

A third officer entered: Superintendent Poitier, the commanding officer of the Bimini Police Department. Seabrook recognized him from the station. He was the same man that he and Aja had spoken to about Bastareaud's domestic violence. He wore black frame glasses and a different uniform than the others. Dark blue trousers, a light blue collared shirt with gold buttons, and a patch with badge number 318 above his right breast pocket.

Superintendent Poitier said in an official voice, "Mr. Seabrook, you are being detained for questioning on suspicion of murder. Please put your hands behind your back."

As they put handcuffs on him and started to lead him out of the house, he turned and stared at the box of satellite tags on the kitchen table—he had to know if one was missing. *Dammit!*

How could he help Aja now?

Chapter 44
Two Bottles of Water

Myron and Mookie lay in their hideout a long time after the men left in a speedboat. They were too afraid to move, and gradually fell asleep again. It was shady and cool under the log, and the boys slept for hours.

When they finally cautiously emerged like foxes from a den, it was late afternoon. Neither of them had ever been so thirsty. Myron's throat was dry, and his tongue felt swollen. He could barely talk. Mookie looked even worse. His lips had dried so much that there were tiny cracks at the corners of his mouth. The cracks bled and stained his teeth red.

Then Myron touched his own mouth, and he realized his lips were also dried and cracked. He tasted a hint of blood.

The boys walked slowly down to the beach. They paused every now and then to listen and watch for any sign of trouble or threat. They saw no trace of the men who were hunting them.

When they got to the old fisherman's shed, they peeked inside and were surprised: two plastic water bottles sat in the sand in the center of the room.

A gift for them. Clear blue and shiny, the plastic bottles sparkled with temptation. Like fresh water from God's kitchen table.

Mookie stepped forward, but Myron extended his arm and blocked him.

"Wait," he said. "I don't trust it," his dried-out voice rasped.

Myron got on his knees and looked carefully at the bottles. The seals were broken. It looked as if the caps had been unscrewed, then screwed back on. "Maybe they poisoned it or put drugs in it."

Mookie's eyes widened with desire and despair. He stared intensely at the water bottles, almost hypnotized. "But—"

"Let's go," Myron interrupted. "Maybe our mother will come back for us today."

They tore themselves away from the sight of the water bottles and shuffled off with hanging heads. Myron wished they'd never seen them —it was impossible to forget they were there, and he couldn't be one hundred percent sure they were poisoned. This tortured his mind. *Maybe they were okay to drink?* When he felt on the verge of running back and guzzling the water down, he reminded himself of the men who had hunted them. They were evil. They would never give good water to people they wanted to catch—unless it was a trap.

To Myron it felt like they were moving through a slow-motion dream. They walked in the hazy sunshine across the hot white sand down to the water, then waded into the waves. The glowing turquoise sea felt amazing and refreshing. Myron found himself wishing that his body could somehow absorb the cool seawater through his skin. A wave splashed his face, and the salt stung the cuts on his lips.

Mookie had grown weak. He seemed barely able to stand against the jostle of the waves, and Myron worried for the first time that his brother might die of dehydration.

He reached out and took Mookie by the hand. Together, they ambled up onto the beach. Mookie seemed to be sleepwalking and silently followed his brother's lead.

They made their way to the huge white rock that looked like the molar of a giant. Their mother's rock. They climbed onto the highest part and sat waiting for her.

They would wait until it got too hot.

Then they would go hide under the fallen tree.

Chapter 45
Bimini Police Station

The Bahamian police put Seabrook in the back seat of the police cruiser. They drove him down King's Highway to the station in Alice Town, running the siren and lights the whole way—it seemed as if they wanted to make a show of his arrest.

At the station, they locked him in one of two holding cells. Three desks stood in the main room, and one small office room contained another desk for the commanding officer. Aside from Seabrook in the cell and the commanding officer sitting in his office with the door shut, the station was empty. Seabrook could see him on the telephone through his office window. Soon the man ended his conversation and set the phone down on its cradle. The commanding officer came out of his office and walked up to the bars of Seabrook's cell.

"Mr. Seabrook," he said. "Right now my officers are searching the crime scene where Mr. Bastareaud was murdered and searching your house and boats, going through all your belongings, looking for any shred of evidence to connect you to the crime. Is there anything you wish to say before they come back?" The man was holding a note pad.

"I haven't killed anyone. You have to release me. There is nothing to find." Seabrook spoke in a respectful tone, because he knew this man could control whether he was released quickly or not. He was glad that he had not entered Bastareaud's home, had not seen his manner of death. It strengthened his ability to convincingly deny any involvement with the crime.

"I know you and Mr. Bastareaud were in conflict," the commanding officer said.

"I think he was in conflict with many people," Seabrook said. "Ask his wife and children. In fact, ask all his wives and children. I have nothing to do with whatever happened to him."

"Where were you earlier this morning?"

"I was out at sea, doing research, tagging sharks. We have a permit from the Bahamian Ministry of Fisheries. We are studying marine life, not murdering people."

"Did anyone see you doing research today?"

Seabrook thought of what to say. Then it came to him. "I bought gas from the fuel dock on the way out to sea. I used a credit card to pay. They will have a record of it, and I have a receipt."

The commanding officer stared at Seabrook for several seconds, judging him and weighing his words. "We will wait to see what my officers find. If this is a mistake, you will have my apology."

Seabrook remained seated on the cot in the cell. He didn't think about lawyers, or contacting the American Embassy, or Dr. Nixon. He focused solely on getting released as quickly as possible. He thought about how to accomplish that alone. In a normal situation, he would have gotten a lawyer and spilled his guts, told everything: the Earless Man, the cartel hunting him, the dismembered body used as bait on the long line, Aja's abduction. But he had no confidence that the island police could help. They were a tiny undermanned force, not exactly the NYPD.

If he told the island police the truth, they'd probably keep him locked up for days or weeks until they checked out his whole story, and then maybe prosecute him for the dead man used as bait on the long line. He might never get free, and Aja would be dead by tomorrow morning. So he kept his mouth shut.

He had to get back home and see if his hunch was right: that Aja had one of the satellite tags. Then maybe he could find her.

He did not think the Bahamian Police could connect him to Bastareaud's death—*unless someone had seen him go to the man's house and reported it.* This possibility worried him more and more as time went by. He didn't think anyone had seen him.

He really hoped he was right.

The clock on the wall of the station house indicated 3:35 p.m. The day was passing quickly, and his chances of saving Aja were diminishing with every passing second.

Anxiously and helplessly, he waited.

Chapter 46
Concha Dores

"Hate is a bottomless cup; I will pour and pour." —Euripides

Two men came in and pulled their next victim to his feet: the nine-fingered man's cokehead partner. The man stared blankly at his tormentors. He did not struggle and did not fight. He seemed oddly at peace with his terrible end. As if he'd known all along that this would happen to him one day—and this was that day. The cartel men were butchering the men first and waiting to kill the pregnant woman and Aja last.

People began talking in the other room, and suddenly someone new seemed to have entered the house and interrupted the killing.

The voice of an older woman asked questions and gave orders. The voice sounded grating and raspy, as if she had smoked unfiltered cigarettes for decades. It also had a masculine deepness. The other male voices sounded subordinate to her.

Aja heard the name Concha. She knew Concha Dores was the head of the Dores Cartel; everyone in South Florida knew the name. Could she be in the next room?

There was a moment of tense silence.

Pelon, the hairless man with the shark jaw tattoo, abruptly walked into the hostage room, and a short, heavy woman followed. Pelon was wearing rubber gloves and a butcher's apron flecked with blood. Concha had on black trousers and a black blouse. A necklace with seashells hung around her neck. Her head was square; her face looked bloated and fleshy. Her hands were rough like a bricklayer's. Her eyes twitched, and her lipstick was uneven. It was impossible to tell her real age. Aja suspected she was in her early forties but had lived so hard, she looked sixty.

Despite her age and small size, there was something imposing and fierce in her demeanor. She looked smart, with a kind of animal cunning, but also warped and unpredictable. Aja had the notion that this was the same woman Seabrook had seen below deck in the speedboat the day the Earless Man visited them.

Concha saw the pregnant woman, and a sneer broke out on her face. She became volcanically angry, and her arms suddenly shook. She went over and bent down to the woman and grabbed her by the chin. One of her fingernails cut the woman's cheek. The tiny comma-shaped cut turned red with blood.

"I did everything you asked," the pregnant woman pleaded in a sad voice. "I called him and told him I was with my parents. I also called my parents and told them I delayed my trip. What do you want from me?!"

"*Te maldigo y sufriras!*" *I curse you, and you will suffer!* Concha snorted and spit in the woman's face. She stooped closer and looked into the captive woman's eyes. For a second it seemed as if she might bite her face.

Concha jammed the woman's head hard against the cinder block wall. As if she were trying to crack her skull. Then she let go of her face. She turned and took a breath, shaking off some of her rage.

Aja said, "I didn't take your money. We never saw any money."

Now Concha briefly turned towards her, staring for a couple of seconds as if trying to figure out who had spoken to her. Aja felt the crazy woman's eyes settle on her. She had never seen such horrible eyes. Worse than a rapid animal's. The pupils flickered.

Pelon said, "Scientist."

"I didn't take your money," Aja said again. "I have nothing to do with any of this."

"So?" Concha said in a dry voice.

"Then why am I here?"

The woman looked at Aja from head to toe. She nodded as if the answer were obvious.

"But I have done nothing to you," Aja said.

Concha made a strange expression and began to yawn. Like a constrictor snake that slowly opens its mouth to rehinge its jaws after swallowing prey whole. Aja could see yellow teeth and a swollen-looking tongue inside. The Queen of Cocaine patted her lips, then waved a gold-plated .45 and made the pregnant woman and Aja scoot along the wall, closer to the door. She wanted them to see what was in store for them. "*La juventud y la belleza mueren hoy,*" she said. *Youth and beauty die today.*

The pregnant woman started crying harder.

Concha Dores produced a strange cigarette from a little case in her pocket. She held a lighter up to it and inhaled. It was not tobacco. Maybe stuffed with cocaine?

Pelon patiently waited for his boss by the doorway. She exhaled smoke and walked up to him. "*Listo,*" she said. *Ready.* Then they left the room.

Everything got worse. Aja could now partially see into the living room: it was a human slaughterhouse. Blood everywhere. A torso and other pieces of human meat scattered on the floorboards. The man they'd seized moments earlier lay tied down on a table. Pelon picked up his hock cutters and put the pincers on either side of the man's ankle. Aja looked away.

Concha's voice grated, "*Donde está el dinero?*" *Where's the money?*

Then the woman let out a laugh like a hacking cough. As if she'd heard a great joke.

"*No lo sé,*" the man insisted. "*No lo sé! No lo sé! Por favor!*" *I don't know! I don't know! I don't know! Pleaaaase!*

A loud metallic *clip*. The victim screamed like his throat would burst.

Aja recoiled. Then a powerful spasm—of fright, and moral revulsion, and pity—rose shuddering out of the center of her being. It made her hands shake and her shoulders jerk back. Tears filled her eyes. Then she looked at the pregnant woman next to her. Aja began sobbing uncontrollably.

"Do you have anything sharp?" she whispered through her tears. The pregnant woman shook her head no.

In the other room, Concha Dores shouted, "*Donde está mi maldito el dinero!?*" *Where's my fucking money!?* Again the old hag laughed.

"*No lo sé,*" the man groaned.

Another loud *clip* and more terrible screams.

In the moment of silence that followed, a new sound filled the air. The poor man was begging, his voice plaintive and sobbing. Almost child-like. "*Por favor, por favor, por favor ... sólo dispárame.*"

Please, please, please ... just shoot me.

Aja had to escape. She could feel the weight of the satellite tag in her pocket, but she didn't have enough time for Seabrook to find her. It was time to make a move. Sitting still would guarantee her death. Again she searched the room with her eyes, looking for any kind of weapon or way to get away. She looked for something small and pointy, like a Bic pen. Perhaps if she couldn't cut the plastic ties, she could take the pointy, thin part of the cap and jam it into the locking mechanism of the zip ties. Breaking the locking mechanism might free her. She'd rather die fighting than tied helpless to a table. But she couldn't see anything that would help her.

No pens. No pencils. Nothing sharp that she could see, except maybe the bedframe edge—but that probably wasn't good enough.

And there was no way out except through the kill room.

She continued to study the place for a way to escape. Could the posters of the unicorns and horses be hiding a window? Not likely.

The walls were made of cinder blocks painted white; the ceiling looked ten feet up, white plaster.

What about the floor? She ran her eyes slowly across the linoleum tiles, looking for a seam, maybe a removable section, like an access to a crawl space under the house.

She saw nothing irregular in the open area of the floor, or where she sat, or in the corners of the room.

There was another *clip* from the other room, and the victim shrieked, high and keening at first. Then the voice trailed off to a hoarse, raspy sound like a wild animal dying in a trap.

Chapter 47
Poitier

S uperintendent Poitier, the commanding officer of the Bimini police, was a competent man with thirty-one years' experience in law enforcement. He'd worked mainly in the northern islands such as Abaco and the Berry Islands, but served the bulk of his career (two decades), as district commander in Freeport, Great Bahamas, before transferring to Bimini.

He'd started out as an entry-level constable and risen through the ranks. He'd seen plenty of crime scenes, and very little shocked him anymore. Yet he had never seen the aftermath of such gruesome violence as this.

His officers had gone to Bastareaud's house to inquire about the well-being and whereabouts of his wife and children, and found the worst crime scene he'd ever come across. Actually, he surmised there were three crime scenes: one at the front door, because blood had pooled on the stoop and sprayed the front door. The kitchen was the second location and seemed like the primary scene, because of the volume of blood and the human remains there. The third crime scene was the crab pen.

At first, his officers thought Bastareaud had killed his own family, because of all the blood and the complaint against him, but they could not find the remains of children or the mother. Just the hands and feet of an adult black male.

After searching inside the house, his men went outside and around to the backyard, where they found Bastareaud horribly mutilated in one of his crab pens. The crabs were eating him, and the officers had to push the crustaceans off as they pulled him outside the pen and laid him gasping on the ground. Shockingly, the man was still alive.

The officers asked who had done this to him, hoping to get a lead while the man was still conscious. Bastareaud slowly turned his head to the nearest constable and deliriously muttered, "The red devil." He was barely alive, and lasted only twelve minutes more. He died before medical help could arrive.

When Superintendent Poitier arrived at the scene, he looked for a potential murder weapon, specifically something sharp and strong enough to cut through bone. The only thing he found were a few kitchen knives still in their block and Bastareaud's machete. The kitchen knives were clean and sharp, but seemed like they hadn't been used recently. His men collected them as evidence just in case. The machete had some blood on it but had been found outside by the front door. They collected it as well.

Poitier didn't know anyone on the island he considered capable of such a crime—but how well does one really know another person? The layers of deception that some people hid behind could be astonishing. He'd been surprised many times by how depraved and vicious human beings could be—even individuals that seemed mild-mannered and good-natured. He also knew that Seabrook had a serious problem with Reverend Bastareaud, and he did have red hair. Could he be the "red devil" Bastareaud had mentioned before his death?

It made more sense than anything else, but it still didn't add up.

The Americans seemed genuinely concerned about the reverend's children, and they had brought their concern to law enforcement. Why would they take matters into their own hands after involving the authorities? Plenty of people disliked Bastareaud, and there had been numerous complaints and rumors about him for many years. Whoever had killed him had tortured him first and was one sick son of a bitch.

Seabrook seemed capable of violence, but not like that. Still, he needed to rule him out as a suspect and interview his girlfriend.

As he continued to think about the nature of the killing and about who could have done such a thing, he had a growing hunch that it was related to the cocaine traffickers. The Dores and Medellín Cartels reveled in outrageous violence. But why would they have tortured Bastareaud? To his knowledge, the cartels had not been active in Bimini for a couple of months, and the reverend had nothing to do with the drug trade—at least as far as he knew.

After thinking it over, he decided to call his DEA contact in Miami and see if he'd heard anything. His contact was on the CENTAC 26 task force that worked with the Miami-Dade Police Department to fight the drug war in south Florida. The man would ask questions that he would have to answer if he wanted help. He'd have to tell him about Reverend Bastareaud.

Superintendent Poitier hated to report violence in Bimini, because someone in the Miami Police Department always tipped off the U.S. press. They always seemed hot to take the spotlight off the latest shootout on Miami's streets. Last time he called, there had been a machine-gun massacre on Miami's Palmetto Expressway in broad daylight, but the press still came to Bimini to cover a single drug-related killing.

Like ants swarming roadkill, TV crews and newspaper reporters would be on the islands within hours—it was a short flight by helicopter. The negative press would hurt Bimini tourism and make him and his men look bad.

But it was still the right call.

He had to get a handle on what was happening to his beloved island.

Chapter 48
Next

She was running out of time. They had butchered the last man. Now only Aja and the pregnant woman sat waiting.

Aja looked back at the floor, specifically the area under and by the bed. There seemed to be an almost imperceptible raised edge next to the underside of the bed frame. She studied it and followed it with her eyes. Yes, the barely noticeable edge extended along two full tiles.

She hardly dared to hope.

Aja pretended to be lightheaded, and fell over on her side towards the bed. Lying sideways with one ear pressed against the floor, she could see the flat plane of the floor all the way to the spot next to the bed. Perfectly smooth. But there was definitely a seam—invisible to anyone not scrutinizing the floor closely.

It had to be a crawl space under the house.

Loud footsteps walked up next to her face. Two cartel men were staring down at her.

Aja pretended to have fainted and hoped they would just leave her on the floor.

Suddenly the two men seized the pregnant woman by her arms. She cried out as they wrenched her to her feet. They dragged her into the other room. She saw very clearly the horror awaiting and began screaming.

"My baby! My baby! Please!" she cried. She had a Midwestern accent. Then her voice was gagged by something.

There were some other sounds. Brief talking.

"*La juventud y la belleza mueren hoy!*" Concha said in a voice triumphant with glee. *Youth and beauty die today!* There were no questions for this victim. The killing started immediately: a loud metallic *clip.*

A muffled scream came into the room. The sound shook Aja's soul.

Concha Dores's hideous barking laugh filled the room like Satanic joy. She was having the time of her life.

Aja had to escape right now, or she would be next. She had been flexible and athletic her whole life, and hoped it would help her now. She rolled onto her back and raised her bottom up in the air as if she were trying to do a backward somersault. Then she brought her bound wrists from the small of her back over her bottom and down to the back of her knees. She sat up, leaned forward, and extended her arms as far forward as they would go. She bent her knees to shorten her legs and brought her bound wrists over her heels and feet. Now her hands were in front of her, and she could use them better.

Her fingers tingled and felt somewhat numb. The zip tie around her wrists was very tight and had cut off her circulation significantly. The zip tie on her ankles wasn't as bad.

A sound like a power saw buzzing erupted in the next room, and the pregnant woman screamed through her gag.

Aja crawled with bound ankles and wrists to the seam on the

floor by the edge of the bed. She pried at the seam with her fingernails, and it moved sideways. Breathing faster, she dislodged a section
of the floor. It was a wooden hatch, perfectly square, with four
linoleum tiles covering it so it looked just like the rest of the floor
around it. Once pushed aside, the hatch opened up to darkness
below.

She scooted feet first down into the darkness, lowering herself as
quickly as possible.

Her feet hit water.

She didn't care. She would rather drown than be cut to pieces.

How deep? She lowered herself another two feet and suddenly
stood belly high in water. Her head protruded from the opening in the
floor, unless she crouched.

She tasted the water. It was fresh water. A cistern under the house!
She guessed it was only five feet from the floor of the cistern to the floor
of the bedroom above.

The cartel men couldn't have known. They'd probably set up their
kill room in someone's empty vacation home and assumed the cistern
was next to the house like on other properties, not underneath the
house.

Aja bent her knees and lowered her head. With trembling hands,
she slid the hatch lid into what seemed like its original position. She
wiggled it until it lowered snuggly into its recessed frame. She hoped it
looked correct from the top side. Maybe the killers would think that she
had escaped by walking out the front door while their backs were
turned ...

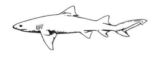

It was pitch black. She carefully hopped sideways and leaned against the concrete wall. If she fell over, it would be tricky getting back to her feet. Drowning was possible.

She paused and drank her fill of fresh water. It might be the only water she'd get for some time.

Terrible screams came muted through the floor. They were sawing the pregnant woman apart right above.

The sounds were soul-grating and bestial, and sickened Aja. She tried to block the horror from her mind and focus on escaping.

Shaking with fear and shock and rising panic, she moved slowly along the wall, feeling her way in the wet darkness. The cistern seemed to have the same square footage as the main floor of the house. After a few minutes, she'd crossed to the far side of the cistern and now stood under the floor of a different room. It was not the kill room, and it was not the room she'd escaped from.

She looked up to see if there might be another access hatch, but everything was black. She raised her hands and pushed up on the ceiling. She ran her fingers along the surface above and felt for a seam. Just solid floor.

She hopped along the wall, searching, stretching her arms out in the darkness. Still nothing but more hard floor above.

Then Aja hopped a little farther, more into the corner. She ran her hands in a circle and suddenly found a break in the flooring.

Another hatch!

She moved quickly. The poor pregnant woman had to be almost dead, and they would be coming to butcher her next and discover she'd escaped.

She pushed the hatch up slowly and slid it quietly backward. She stood up straight and raised her head up. Her face was level with another linoleum floor. The room above was dark, but not pitch dark like down in the cistern.

Aja hoisted herself up, using her hands and elbows—first like a pull-up, then like a push-up—and once she was partway up, jammed her legs straight back and pushed against the wall below with her feet.

She dragged herself soaking wet across the tiled floor. Vaguely, she was aware that the satellite tag was no longer in her pocket. It must have come out in the cistern. She couldn't go back to get it.

Looking up and around, she knew she'd crawled into a second bedroom. The lights were off, and the door into the living room was closed.

Fresh water dripped off her body and pooled on the floor around her. The electric saw and screaming had mercifully stopped.

She could hear their voices talking and the sound of Concha Dores giving them orders. The voices sounded calm, business-like. They didn't know she had escaped.

Not yet.

Aja crawled forward and sat up for a better look at the room. It had a door to the outside.

The men's voices seemed suddenly a little louder.

Aja jumped to her feet and hopped across the room to the door. She made more noise than she wanted to, but she had to get out before they came for her.

She slid the deadbolt and unlocked it.

The door opened inward, and she went outside.

She hopped down the short concrete steps and across the lawn into the night.

As she made her way towards a line of coconut palms, the killers began shouting inside the house—they must have discovered she was gone.

Aja saw a quay and a dock. She couldn't be sure, but it looked like she was on South Bimini island in a residential area. She could see a row of houses, and all the windows were black. Either the occupants were sleeping or these were unoccupied vacation homes.

She had to get into the water and hide. She saw several boats along the dock. Maybe there was a knife in one of the lockers she could use to cut the zip ties off her ankles and wrists.

She paused. The boats probably belonged to the cartel men. In fact, one was a speedboat like the Earless Man had driven. Then she saw a man standing in the speedboat. He was smoking a cigarette and had a gun. A guard.

Aja was going the wrong way, straight into the arms of the cartel. She turned around and hopped into the tall dune grass next to the home. The cartel boats were docked on the leeward side of the island and could enter and exit only through the Alice Town harbor—if she could make it to the windward side of the island, to the ocean, cut the zip ties somehow, then she could swim for her freedom.

Two men suddenly came out of the kill house. They waved flashlights and ran right past Aja, hiding in the dune grass, and down to the dock. They talked to the man guarding the boats—probably asking whether he'd seen anything.

Aja began crawling through the dune grass towards the other side of the island, to the ocean. The brush thickened into bushes and pine trees. She kept crawling and could feel her knees and elbows getting scratched and raw.

Ten minutes went by.

She knew the ocean side of the island was very close (the island at this point was a thin strip of elevated land), perhaps a couple of hundred yards away.

When she looked back, she saw the men with the flashlights searching around the neighboring houses for her. As she crawled, she kept hearing the screams of the pregnant woman in her mind.

She ignored the stinging pain and growing rawness on her knees and elbows. Her wrists and ankles hurt. The zip ties bit into her flesh.

Still, she moved as fast as she could through the brush and pine trees.

Now she could hear the sound of waves hitting the coastline. It grew louder as she moved. *Getting closer to freedom,* she told herself.

Her knees were skinned and bleeding. It felt as if she were crawling over broken glass and thorns.

She crawled under a pine tree and glanced up. An idea popped into her mind. She struggled to her feet and grabbed onto one of the branches. If she could find a dead or weak branch and break it off, maybe she could use a pointed end to break the locking mechanism on the zip ties. She touched three branches and found one that felt dried out and weak. She found a limb thin enough for the job and snapped it off. Luckily, it did not break evenly. One side had a thin, tapered point. She sat down and drew her knees to her chest.

One of the men with a flashlight started her way. The flashlight swung left and right. He moved swiftly like he saw something—perhaps the dune grass that she'd disturbed when she crawled through it.

Aja tugged the zip tie around her ankles until the locking mechanism faced forward. Holding the small plastic locking mechanism steady in her left hand, she carefully stuck the thin, pointed tree branch into it. Then she jammed it in.

The zip tie suddenly unlocked. She kicked it off her ankles.

Aja got painfully to her feet. From a standing position, she could see the night ocean, glistening and shifting, and a line of boulders that reinforced the sea wall. There were piles of giant boulders stacked helter-skelter along the coast of this part of South Bimini—no sand beaches. Half the boulders were submerged in the water.

Sensing motion, she turned her head and looked back the way she'd come. The man with the flashlight started running towards her.

She had no time to unlock the zip tie on her wrists—and it would be harder to accomplish than freeing her ankles had been; because her wrists were bound so close together, getting the angle right would be tricky.

She ran barefoot over the remaining brush and onto the rocks next to the boulder retaining wall. With the small tree branch in her right hand, she began climbing down the boulders to the waves. Her zip-tied wrists made it hard to hold on to the unevenly stacked rock. She almost fell, and clutched at a fissure to hold on.

She dropped the branch and almost swore out loud. The climb would have been a piece of cake but for her zip-tied wrists and the need to rush before the cartel man caught her in the open.

She pressed herself in a space between two slabs of stone, holding the rock with her bound hands as best as she could. She moved her legs from side to side, searching for footholds with her toes.

Once she had climbed down the steep part, roughly ten feet, she dropped to her knees. Groping around, she found the branch and felt a small spark of relief.

She quickly put it sideways in her mouth. Carefully, she bit down with her teeth to hold it firmly without breaking it.

Then she slipped feet first into the waves.

Her body almost shuddered with relief. The ocean, black and deep, with currents and nocturnal predators cruising in from the Gulf Stream, could be dangerous at night—especially for a person with bound hands. But to Aja, it felt like home.

She was now on her turf.

The salt water stung her skinned knees and elbows. She clenched her jaw against the pain. The waves were small but still pushed her against the boulders of the retaining wall and smothered her head under swirling current.

When the fizzing waves receded, she let the water pull her a little deeper so she wouldn't be left exposed on the rocks.

She looked at the land above. The man with the flashlight was walking through the pine trees where she'd crawled—still coming straight towards her. He was pointing the flashlight at the ground like he was tracking animal prints.

The next wave washed over her, and she couldn't see anything. Aja held her breath. She pulled herself sideways along the rocks, butterfly-kicking her legs, and tried to move herself to the right.

Once.

Twice.

Three times. She pulled herself sideways along the underwater boulders in front of her, pumping her legs like her life depended on it. She didn't want to surface in the same vicinity where she'd entered the sea, the place where the man with the flashlight would focus. She felt disabled underwater with her wrists zip-tied, like a sea turtle missing its front flippers, but she could feel herself moving across rocks.

A moment of drifting blackness—the sea alive about her, buffeting her body up to the land, pausing, then reversing back out.

For a terrifying moment, she lost touch with the boulders.

Without anything to hold on to or push off of, she would flounder, out of control. She could tread water with just her legs for only so long before she would drown.

Then a wave swept her sideways, and she felt the hard, coarse surface of the rock with her fingertips once more.

She grabbed on to the rock and pulled herself forward, raising her face carefully and slowly upward from the waves. She needed to breathe but didn't want to get caught.

The wave pulled back from land, and her head and shoulders suddenly emerged from the sea.

Unexpectedly, she lay half exposed on a square stone surface. She fought the urge to panic and make a sudden move. She didn't want to draw attention.

The cartel man was standing with the flashlight pointing at the rocks twenty feet away. Roughly the spot where she'd initially entered the ocean.

Aja quietly breathed through her nose and clenched teeth. She was still holding the small broken tree branch sideways in her mouth. She slowly slid backwards into the sea again.

The cartel man moved his flashlight left and right in a widening search.

Aja scooted lower and lowered her head underwater. Her eyes were open, and it seemed like light flickered above her for a few seconds —as if the man had his flashlight aimed at the water above her face.

Then it went black.

Again, she pulled herself to the right in three separate bursts, gliding underwater, trying to move farther away from the man hunting her. Then she found a good hold on the submerged boulders, angling and clinging with feet and hands, and slowly raised her head out of the water.

The cartel man with the flashlight seemed to be gone. She saw no trace of him in either direction along the rocky shoreline.

But she didn't believe he was gone

A paranoid feeling made her freeze. Slowly, very slowly, she again submerged her head and moved backwards into deeper water to hide.

She moved farther to the right.

Then slowly surfaced again.

On the edge of a half-sunk slab of stone matted with seaweed, she peeked up from the water like a sea otter, with only her forehead, eyes, and nose exposed to air. She clung tightly to a ridge in the giant rock and wedged her feet into a crack she could feel underwater.

Holding herself as still as possible, Aja let the waves bury her, then unbury her in great shuddering blasts of ocean. Fortunately, the sea was mild. Rougher waves could have dashed her to death against the rocks. She continually readjusted to stay hidden and watched the shoreline for any sign of the killers.

Again the waves avalanched over her, water erupting past, sounding in her ears, combing her hair with liquid teeth.

When a wave rushed back out, she was left half out of the water once more. Salt water dripped down her face, and she blinked it from her eyes. She looked up and down the shoreline. Still no sign of the man with the flashlight.

Could he still be watching for her? Maybe standing in the tree line waiting for her to crawl out of the sea?

The next wave hit from the side and sent her raw knees scraping across the rocks.

Aja screamed underwater.

The rushing sea snatched the tree branch from her open mouth, and it was gone before she knew what had happened.

It felt as if her kneecaps had been sheared off.

When the waves receded, she was afraid to touch her knees because they felt so damaged. She let go of the rock and winced as she quickly felt both knees with her fingertips. The skin was scraped away and they were bruised to the bone, but that seemed to be all.

When she surfaced, she noticed a fishing yacht anchored a little farther along the way. There were no lights on inside it. Whoever was on board was sleeping or had gone ashore. It appeared to have a swim platform. It wouldn't be hard to climb into the stern cockpit.

It could be a cartel boat. But there were big-game fishing rods sticking up from rod holders. Maybe it really was just a sport fisherman's yacht.

Aja decided to take the risk and swim for it.

She planned to sneak aboard and cut the zip tie off her wrists. Fishermen often kept knives and other fishing tools in the in-transom fish boxes, lockers, and drawers around the cockpit.

Chapter 49
"Cartel Violence Surges in the Bahamas"
—the Miami Herald

One hour later, Superintendent Poitier walked up to Seabrook's cell. According to the clock on the wall, it was two minutes past nine in the evening.

"Mr. Seabrook, I owe you an apology. We went through all of your belongings and boats. I told my men to be careful and not damage anything. Hopefully, you'll find everything in good order. Please report directly to me if anything is missing or damaged."

"I will. Thank you." Seabrook bit his tongue. He was nearly beside himself. He'd sat in the cell all afternoon and evening waiting to be interrogated. Every second that had ticked by, he wondered whether the cartel was killing Aja. And he was stuck on his ass behind bars unable to do a damn thing about it. His being put behind bars may have cost Aja her life.

Poitier produced a key to the cell door from his pocket. He looked grim and very serious as he turned the key and opened the door. As if something very heavy were weighing on him.

"What has happened?" Seabrook said.

"Mr. Seabrook, we are in the middle of a drug war. And Bimini is being victimized by the violence. Miami police tell me that the Medellín Cartel is trying to take over the Bahamas-Miami route from the Dores Cartel. They stole fifty million dollars from the Dores Cartel, and the violence is escalating. Both sides are killing each other—I sincerely hope both sides succeed and wipe each other out. The drug business is bad for Bimini. You need to be careful. We all need to be careful."

Poitier explained that not only did the Bimini police find nothing implicating Seabrook in Bastareaud's death, but new crimes had been committed while Seabrook was in custody: after the sun went down on the island, the bodies of two decapitated, dismembered people were found by the side of the asphalt on King's Highway in downtown Alice Town, less than one mile from the police station.

Seabrook walked out of his cell.

"I should also tell you that I received a phone call from Mrs. Bastareaud. She and her daughter, Carmelita, are alive."

"In Miami? Bastareaud was telling the truth?"

"No. She is in Nassau. She took her daughter and went in a friend's boat to escape her husband. She called from Princess Margaret Hospital. The little girl is in intensive care. But the boys are missing. They did not go to Nassau. They took one of your boats and are hiding on North Bimini. I have men in a patrol boat searching for them right now. They will find them. She told me exactly where they are hiding. Mrs. Bastareaud said to tell you thank you for trying to help and that she's sorry her boys took your boat. She told them to do it."

"That's good news."

Seabrook walked towards the entrance of the station. Superintendent Poitier told a constable to drive Seabrook back to his house.

"Mr. Seabrook?" Poitier called. "I have one question before you go."

"What's that?" Seabrook stopped and turned.

Poitier stared at him with an expression that was hard to read. Suspicion? Concern? Maybe simple curiosity?

"Where is your fiancée, Aja?"

Seabrook thought for a split second. *What should I say?* He needed to leave immediately and try to find her. If he said the wrong thing, he might get arrested again. Still, the question choked him up unexpectedly—the monsters had taken her. She might well be dead. His face flushed with sudden emotion, and he spoke with a quaver in his voice.

"I don't know. I'm very worried about her ..."

Poitier nodded slightly, but his eyes did not blink.

"And I have a question for you," Seabrook said.

"Yes." Poitier walked slowly towards him.

"Who runs the cartels?"

"You mean who are the kingpins?"

"Yes."

"Pablo Escobar runs the Medellín Cartel. A woman runs the Dores Cartel."

Seabrook thought of the woman with the flickering eyes. "What's her name?"

"Concha Dores. They call her the Queen of Cocaine. Why do you ask?"

"I just want to know who and what we are up against."

"They are bloody terrorists. You don't want anything to do with them."

Seabrook nodded. Then he asked one more question. "Were any of the bodies you found tonight ... my ..."

"What?"

"Were any of the bodies you found tonight ...female?"

Poitier cleared his throat. "The answer is no."

"Thank you."

Poitier nodded. Seabrook turned and left the police station.

One of the young constables who'd arrested him earlier that day drove him down King's Highway to the rental house in Bailey Town. On the way, they drove past a TV news crew that had just arrived by helicopter from Miami to do a story on cartel violence in the Bahamas. They had heard about Bastareaud's shocking death, but the new murders were a surprise bonus.

A young female reporter was standing by the side of the road in front of the spot where the human remains had been found. She was holding a microphone under the glow of lights and talking in front of a TV camera crew.

Chapter 50
Strange Lights and Voices

Earlier that day, Myron and Mookie sat on the big white rock for hours waiting for their mother. They didn't move until the sun made them hot and dizzy. The splashing waves helped cool them for a while, but eventually they had to get out of the direct sun.

Myron led Mookie back into the pinewoods. As they plodded across the sand, he worried that his mother was dead. He worried that they were going to die soon. Mookie seemed half asleep all the time. He didn't even try to speak. It was as if he had started to die already. They slowly crawled under the fallen trunk into their hiding place. Myron pulled the branches into place so that the entrance to their little fort was concealed. They slept on the pine needle floor in the cool shade for hours. When they awoke, it was late at night.

Voices were calling to them on a megaphone, and flashlights were waving down on the beach. There were also strange lights like the police used. The megaphone voice said they were the police and they had a patrol boat to pick up the boys. The voice said that their mother had sent them.

Myron almost went out of their hiding place to see them. The voices had Bahamian accents and sounded friendly. In the dark, Myron couldn't be sure of the truth. The last men that had come looking for them had tried to trick them and wanted to hurt them.

This was probably another trick, a smarter trick. If it was the police, his father was probably with them, just waiting to regain custody of his sons. Then his father would cleanse him and Mookie for hours. Beat the devil out of them. He would lock them in separate crab pens, and Mookie would die terrified and alone. It was better to die together in their nice pine forest hideout.

So Myron decided they should stay in their hiding place. The men claiming to be the police eventually left.

Myron thought they would sit on the white rock for a few hours the next day. If no one rescued them, he would walk miles down the beach and hope someone would help. He didn't think Mookie could walk into town.

He would have to go alone and hope he made it back in time to save his little brother.

As he thought about things, he listened to the sound of his little brother breathing in his sleep. At least Mookie was safe for now.

At least they were together.

Chapter 51
Wolf Eyes

Aja didn't know what time it was, but she had the feeling it was before midnight. The men hunting her had disappeared into the woods. She had to get the zip tie off her wrists so she could use her arms again. The sportfishing yacht moored offshore was a top-of-the-line Hatteras with a flying bridge. It had to have a knife or other tool in one of the compartments in the cockpit.

She pushed off land with her feet and swam into the night ocean, away from the rocky coast of South Bimini. She went straight towards the Hatteras yacht, kicking with her legs and hands extended in front of her. Her bound wrists made it harder but not impossible to swim. Her body position reminded her of drills during practice on the college swim team—except she had no kickboard now. She fanned her hands down and raised her head to the side to breathe. The ocean seemed less rough as she left the shoreline. Still, the waves slapped over her and hit her in the face if she didn't time her breathing right.

In five minutes she came up to the yacht: *Big Dream III*. It had a white fiberglass swim platform at the stern. Aja climbed up. Her knees stung and ached when she knelt with her body weight on her kneecaps. She quickly got to her feet, then climbed over the transom.

Now that she was aboard she could see that, in fact, there were lights on inside the vessel: in the staterooms below deck. *Somebody else was aboard.* All the upper-deck lights were off, though. She felt suddenly very nervous. Was this a cartel boat camouflaged as a fishing yacht? Or was this really someone's pleasure craft?

She glanced around the cockpit and found a long-handled big gaff tucked on the underside of the transom. Two heavy-duty marlin rods were sticking up from rod holsters in the gunwales, one near the starboard-stern corner and the other near the port-stern corner. A fighting chair was mounted to the deck in the middle of the cockpit. An ice chest was packed with beer. The yacht was rigged out like a genuine deep-sea fishing vessel. This was probably not a cartel boat.

She carefully opened the compartments next to the small steps that lead into the salon area of the main cabin. She searched for something sharp to cut the zip tie on her wrist. She moved very quietly, like a thief robbing a house. She suspected the owners were reading in bed or watching TV in their staterooms. The boat rolled with the waves.

One cabinet had fiberglass drawers inside. She opened one and found a set of fillet knives. She picked one up. Even after trying for several minutes, she couldn't angle the tip of the knife into the locking mechanism to pop the zip tie open. But when she turned the blade towards herself, she could saw back and forth and create good upward pressure by pressing up from her wrist. She cut as hard as she could so the blade would bite into the plastic. A minute later the zip tie popped off and fell at her feet.

Someone moved below.

Aja darted over to the gangway leading to the foredeck and lay flat, just out of sight. She didn't know for sure that these were safe people.

Two men came out of the salon and climbed the ladder to the flying bridge. They were sunburned, overweight white men. This was reassuring. They looked like many of the deep-sea fishermen and yacht owners that came to Bimini for the big-game fishing tournaments.

The diesel engines chugged to life soon after. They revved and idled. The anchor was hoisted. The fiberglass deck vibrated against the side of her face.

The running lights came on, and Aja almost dived overboard. In addition to the required red light on the port bow, green light on the starboard bow, and white light at the stern, the yacht was tricked out with blue LED lights on the flying bridge and in its cockpit. Aja felt more exposed, but the lights in her area were dim.

One of the men on the flying bridge looked down over the boat.

He might have seen her, but he didn't show it in any way.

She was ready to dive overboard at the first sign of trouble, but she wanted to stay onboard for now and get away from the men who were searching for her on South Bimini.

The yacht kicked into gear, then high gear, and started to cross the waves on a plane. The Hatteras's twin diesel engines were powerful and propelled the vessel amazingly fast.

Aja felt incredible relief to be getting away from the cartel. She did not move for a time. She thought about how to approach the men driving the boat and ask for their help. She decided she would simply go up to the flying bridge and tell them her story. They could call the U.S. Coast Guard and drop her safely with the authorities. She had been witness to a massacre. This was an international incident.

The yacht continued to race across the sea. After five minutes, she got up from the gangway and moved back towards the ladder to the flying bridge. She noticed they seemed to be heading east across the Great Bahama Bank towards Cat Cay. To the right, under the moonlight, stood the small distant silhouette of the SS *Sapona*. Like a ghost ship.

Aja stepped into the cockpit.

Voices shouted in the salon. Not in English. The salon door slid open, and the voices got louder. Concha Dores shouted orders as she came out on deck.

Fear seized Aja by the heart. She couldn't move for a second. Her limbs felt encased in ice. The moment passed, and she ran across the cockpit to the transom. She felt eyes on her and was going to dive overboard.

"Stop!" Concha yelled.

For some reason, Aja turned to look at her.

Concha smiled with ugliness and shambled towards her. The

moving boat made her unsteady on her feet, and she leaned on the fighting chair to steady herself. Two cartel men were behind her.

"*La linda que se escapó!*" *The pretty one who got away!*

Concha shuffled closer. The blue LED lights shined on her pupils so they glowed like a wolf's at night. "*Tomarla!*" *Take her!*

Aja bent down and took the long gaff hook out from the underside of the transom. She turned and swung it at Concha as hard as she could. The hook tore into the Queen of Cocaine's shoulder. Aja pulled it hard, as if she were sticking a big tuna, and sank the large hook to the hilt. The old woman's eyes bulged, and she screamed. Then dropped to her knees.

The two men ran to grab Aja, but were too late. She hopped over the transom and dived off the swim platform.

Aja disappeared into the dark sea.

Chapter 52
The Crossing

Seabrook ran into the house and went to the box with the new tags. He opened the lid, and sure enough, one was missing.

Each tag had a waterproof casing with a small antenna on it. They were roughly the size of a hot dog and could easily fit in a person's pocket or bathing suit. Seabrook knew in that moment that Aja had taken one of the tags to help him find her. He almost smiled.

Next he went to the lunchbox-shaped case that had the satellite receiver. He took it out and turned it on.

It looked like a large calculator. The small square screen lit up. He selected the first tag from the menu for a data download. A tiny map of the Bimini islands appeared. Then a small red dot appeared on South Bimini island with coordinates.

If it was accurate, Aja was being held on South Bimini in someone's docked boat or in one of the oceanfront houses. He jogged to the shed where he kept the batteries and gas tanks and put a full gas tank in the Whaler. He forced himself to move quickly, but not so quickly that he couldn't think.

Wherever Aja was, he figured she was being guarded by men with guns. Seabrook had no weapons other than his Hawaiian sling spear, a dive knife, and two high-carbon, stainless steel bone knives he used to cut open sharks during necropsies.

Now that it was night, he could sneak up more easily on Aja's location and hide if necessary. He grabbed the satellite tracking receiver, a flashlight, and the weapons he had, and went down the dock. It was his first time on the dock at night since he'd dreamed about the dead man lurking in the sea underneath it. He felt a twinge of fear but ignored it. He started the outboard. Then untied the clove hitch knots and drew in the lines. He drove the Whaler down the channel toward the Alice Town harbor.

Seabrook never drove the Whaler at night—it had no running lights and there had never been a need to do so before. He felt anxious and was drenched in sweat, but he had to stay calm or he'd fail for certain. He forced himself to drive slowly. He couldn't see the channel in the dark and would likely run aground in the shallows if he hit the gas.

He might also collide with one of the channel marker poles protruding three feet above the waterline at high tide. There were four of them, and they were very hard to see at night. Two of them had buoys.

Seabrook waved the flashlight from time to time, searching for the marker poles, but never spotting them. Thankfully, there was no boat traffic at all. The dark water bothered him. He couldn't see what was down in it, and there were occasional small splashes. For a second, he imagined the white face of the corpse under the dock looking up at him.

Fifteen minutes later, he could tell by the shape of the shoreline that he'd safely arrived at the point where the channel started to broaden into the Alice Town harbor. The water was now becoming deeper, and it was safe to go faster.

On the right, docks, quays, and various buildings stood along the waterfront. Some had nightlights that glimmered across the surface of the lagoon.

To the left, the harbor deepened even more, and a handful of sailboats pulled gently on their moorings as the tide flowed past. Halyards clanged against masts like wind chimes. Each vessel was a pleasant oasis of life. Each had interior lights that glowed out its portholes and hatches. Some had music playing. The sweet smell of cooking drifted from the open hatch of one sailboat, where several people were sitting in the cockpit holding beers and talking. Their laughter carried on the water.

Seabrook steered to the left and accelerated as much as possible without causing a big wake. He began to leave North Bimini island behind.

A small ferryboat that routinely shuttled between North and South Bimini came his way. It had bright running lights. A voice shouted at him from the ferryboat, "Where are your running lights, you son of a bitch? You can't cross the harbor without lights!"

Seabrook couldn't see the old man who had shouted at him, and intentionally drove in a wider circle to avoid the ferryboat and several more sailboats.

He motored into even deeper water, past the area where the Chalks seaplanes landed and took off from a wide open stretch of the harbor. The sailboat lights and clanging halyards fell away into darkness. It grew very quiet and pitch black. He trusted he was going in the right direction and drove for another ten minutes.

Up ahead in the offing, silhouetted against the night sky, South Bimini island gradually materialized from the darkness. A nondescript shadowy mass at first. Then, after a few minutes, the features resolved into land. As he got closer, it became more solid. Finally he could see the shoreline and tall coconut palms.

The mouth of Alice Town harbor opened to the right and showed the way to the open ocean.

He motored for another ten minutes, then steered the Whaler into the inlet that was growing increasingly visible as he got closer. The inlet led to the docks, boat ramps, and homes of South Bimini. He'd been to the island before during the daytime and had a basic understanding of its layout. The island was much quieter and less developed than North Bimini. It had a small landing strip for airplanes and numerous vacation homes that sat empty much of the year.

He looked at the satellite tracking console; the little red dot indicated he was getting closer to Aja's tag. *She's probably in one of the empty vacation homes.*

He began looking for any sign of the cartel: speedboats, men on the docks, armed guards. He couldn't see any sign of human activity—but it was dark.

He looked at the console again: he was moving closer to the red dot. He guided the Whaler to a small, empty dock next to a boat ramp. He killed the engine and tied the Whaler to the pilings. Without the noise of the outboard, the night became suddenly very quiet. He would go the rest of the way on foot so the cartel couldn't hear his boat engine. He tucked the sheathed knives in his waistband and got his Hawaiian sling spear ready to shoot. He brought the satellite tracking receiver.

He strode up the dock, crossed over the cement paving of the quay, and slipped into the intense dark under the pine trees and bracken ferns. He walked several yards along the tree line, then checked the console of the satellite receiver to confirm he was moving closer to Aja. He was.

As he walked, he kept scanning the woods and undergrowth for men standing guard in the shadows. He saw nobody. The area was a quiet residential area.

He walked past two houses and started down a gravel path. He had the premonition that it led to the house where Aja was being held captive. The tracking console seemed to confirm it. As he walked past a thicket of bracken ferns, the tree branches parted and a house appeared before him.

The house stood on higher ground, roughly in the middle of the island, equidistant between the lagoon side and the ocean side. This was smart. It meant that the cartel could use both the inlet on the lagoon side and the ocean side to come and go.

Fear and dread wormed into his stomach —he knew what these men were capable of. He expected that the bald man with the scalded-looking skin would be inside, and maybe the old woman with the flickering eyes: real-life monsters. They had cut the man in the bait tub into small pieces, probably alive, and they had probably done it in the house he was about to enter. The reality sickened and frightened him.

Somehow he knew that the old woman had come to Bimini again, that she was close by and behind the evil. Thinking of her eyes brought up the memory of Rudy Defarge in fourth grade. Gimping down the hall, his legs jerking spasmodically, the orbs of his eyes flickering and malefic. His animal stare and little smile seemed to say, *"One day we'll meet again."* The memory made Seabrook's skin crawl.

But to save Aja, he would walk into hell and fight the devil himself. *But there would be more than one of them.*

The cartel would also have guards keeping her prisoner. They would keep her alive until the morning—if he could believe anything Vuelta had said.

He stood still, listening and watching. The whole area seemed closed and quiet. Like everyone had gone to bed or wasn't home.

The house was dark, and the neighboring homes were also dark.

Keeping off the path, Seabrook walked through the brush and among the trees for cover. He moved closer to the house. The satellite tracking console indicated Aja was straight ahead inside. It was a one-story vacation home.

He noticed something on the path, two small things shaped like shell casings. He crouched down and touched one. They were cigarette butts. They were in good shape. As if someone had stood on the path and smoked cigarettes. Whoever it was dropped the butts recently.

He stood up and glanced back, and could see the water of the inlet and an empty dock. Then he looked ahead and scanned the house and the area around it. Dead quiet.

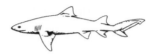

Seabrook approached the front door, careful not to touch anything. He set the satellite tracking receiver down next to the front stoop in order to free up both hands. Next he pulled the Hawaiian sling spear a quarter of the way back, poised to shoot, ready to kill any person standing between him and Aja.

The front door was not locked. Not even shut properly. For a moment he froze. He was standing at the threshold of something terrible. He could feel it. What was inside the house? He remembered the phrase over the gates of hell in Dante's *Inferno*: "Abandon all hope, ye who enter here." If he found Aja dead, it might break him. He might abandon all hope.

He nudged the door open with his knee and stood still, listening for ten seconds. Nothing moved or made a sound.

He stepped halfway inside, spear tip first.

The stench of blood hit him—musty and sickeningly sweet, and mixed with the smell of urine and feces. It overwhelmed his nostrils and sinuses. It smelled a hundred times more powerful than the bait tub full of human meat.

At first, the silence—aside from the faint buzzing of flies—upset him. Then began to devastate him.

The utter stillness, the absence of any human life, and the slaughterhouse reek told him that they had butchered Aja already.

Despair washed over him. His eyes became wet, and he choked. After a couple of seconds, with great effort, he forced the feeling back. *I'm being stupid. I don't know anything for sure yet,* he told himself. He needed to be sure.

There could still be hope. But he felt no conviction in this.

He stepped into the living room. He found the light switch and flicked it up.

He gasped involuntarily. It was the worst sight he'd ever seen. Nothing even came close.

For an instant, it felt as if his heart stopped beating and his lungs stopped breathing.

Dark pools of blood had congealed on the floor. Crimson gouts flecked the furniture and some of the walls. Dismembered bodies. Glutinous tendons. Limbs and pieces were scattered on the floorboards.

Fear crawled like ice in his stomach, and his temples began to throb.

Flies had already found their way into the house. The black insects buzzed around the room, laying their eggs on as many pieces of the dead as possible. They seemed especially attracted to the wet pile of guts in the middle of the room.

Judging by the quantity of remains, he guessed that half a dozen people had been horribly slaughtered. The air itself seemed choked with the terrible energy of unspeakable deeds.

He stared at the pieces of human meat and mush, and felt his body convulse with nausea. It was hard to believe that people could do this to one another. Who was responsible for this sickness? *The bald man with the strange skin and the old woman with the twitching eyes.* And for what? Fifty million dollars?

His eyes searched the carnage for any sign of Aja. There were human hands, fingers, forearms, feet, cut shanks, and torsos that had been halved down the spine like slabs of beef. The glistening mound of viscera and entrails must have come from disemboweled victims. It crawled black with flies. *These had been human beings!*

But the severed limbs looked masculine.

A tiny ember of hope kindled in Seabrook's heart. None of the remains seemed to have come from a woman.

He continued looking for any sign of Aja. There were three battered human heads on the kitchen counter—also all men. The eyes had been hollowed out to black sockets, and the paper-thin skin on the faces was blistered and scorched. The heads glistened like they were perspiring. The mouths were twisted into expressions of agony. These men had been tortured with a blowtorch.

Seabrook looked away in revulsion. An awful numbness crept over him, a kind of shock. He realized he was trying to hold his breath, trying to ingest as little of the polluted environment as possible.

A fly landed on his lower lip. He blew it away in disgust.

He relaxed the tension on the spear and stepped back outside to breathe fresh air and pick up the satellite tracking receiver. He brought it into the living room. It indicated that Aja was here in this building right now.

He didn't want to believe it. Everyone was dead.

If he examined the remains, would he find parts of her?

The idea that Aja might be among the dead hit him like a kick in the solar plexus. A feeling of despair suddenly expanded inside him, sapping his energy, threatening to derail him with overwhelming emotion. But again he forced the feelings back.

He had to keep searching.

He moved around the room, diligently watching the placement of every footstep, careful not to walk in any blood or touch any object.

It vaguely occurred to him that the room must have been set up with equipment. Probably electric saws and cutters that a butcher might use to rend a carcass. He noticed an outlet on one wall where the killers could have plugged in their machines. But everything was gone. The bald man who had dismembered these people had packed up all the equipment and left South Bimini. Probably in the last few hours. If he had murdered Aja, Seabrook vowed to himself that he would hunt the freak down wherever he lived. Killing the bald man would become his life's work.

Again he had to force himself to focus on the here and now. What was in front of him?

The satellite tracking receiver indicated he was standing right on top of the red dot. The tag Aja had grabbed before the cartel abducted her had to be in this house. He didn't want to examine every piece of human flesh to identify Aja, but would if necessary. He hoped the tag lay discarded on the floor.

Maybe hidden under part of a victim? Maybe Aja had dropped it? It could be under the sofa against the wall for all he knew.

Or had they taken her somewhere else?

Before he disturbed the crime scene, he decided to search the other rooms.

The first one looked like a child's bedroom, furnished with a small dresser and chair, and with stuffed animals on the bed. A Raggedy Ann doll sat propped on the pillows. Posters of horses and unicorns decorated the walls.

A grisly human foot with a shoe lay on the floor, next to a four-fingered hand and some other body part. He looked at the hand for a moment and wondered whether it had belonged to the man who had lost his finger to the lemon shark pup.

He checked under the bed and found no sign of Aja.

He went to the next room. It was also a bedroom. His eyes went straight to its door standing ajar. It led to the yard outside.

Then he saw the hatch in the floor in the corner of the room.

He walked over to it and looked down. It was either an access to a crawl space below the house or some kind of cistern. The satellite tracking receiver still indicated he was standing right on the red dot.

Could Aja be down in the darkness below? Perhaps they had dumped some of the bodies in?

He lowered himself into the square entrance hatch in the floor and went underground, below the house. The water wasn't very deep. Maybe four and a half feet. He couldn't see anything. Like a subterranean miner, he groped in the wet darkness.

He called her name several times. "Aja? Aja?"

Maybe she was hiding? There was no response.

He expected to bump into floating corpses. He crouched and began walking and feeling the flat concrete floor of the cistern with his feet. His head was tucked down, and he moved under the flooring of the home. The cistern had the same square footage as the whole first floor combined. He prayed that he wouldn't find Aja's body. He wanted to find her somewhere else. And alive.

He walked back and forth from one side to the other, then back again, trying to cover every inch of the cistern. He didn't know what he would have done if he found Aja dead in the water.

On the fourth pass, he stepped on something hard and cylindrical. He bent down in the water and grabbed the item from under his foot. It was the satellite tag!

Holding it made him feel connected to her. She had been in this space! He almost wept for joy. He kissed it, then stuck it in his pocket.

He felt hope stirring again. With fresh energy, he searched the entire cistern and was relieved and almost even happy—because he did not find Aja dead. There were no bodies at all.

Seabrook tried to imagine what Aja might have done after dropping the satellite tag in the cistern. First, he wondered if she'd dropped the tag on purpose or by accident. He couldn't be sure either way.

He climbed back into the second bedroom and went out the door to the yard. Fresh water poured off his shorts, and his sneakers squished with each step. In one direction, he could walk back to the inlet where he'd docked the Whaler. In the other direction, he could walk to the ocean side of South Bimini. Which way would Aja have gone?

He made his way through pinewoods to the ocean. He could hear its splash and soft roar up ahead. He came out from the trees and walked up to the edge of land. The dark ocean spread out as far as he could see—and far beyond. The waves looked wild and threatening.

A retaining wall of giant boulders protected the coast. He looked down five feet. The waves struck the massive rocks and receded with clawing foam.

If Aja had escaped the cartel, she might have come this way. She might have climbed down the boulders and dived in. Anything to escape the kill house. The more he thought about it, the more he felt that she would go to the ocean, take her chances in the deep, not the shallow inlet, given the chance. But he didn't know for sure.

He gazed at the powerful night-black waves and stirring maelstrom of currents along the shoreline. A gnawing sadness bit into him.

"Oh, Aja," he whispered.

How could he find her?

How could he make her safe?

Was she still alive?

Chapter 53
The Primordial Sea

Aja alternated between swimming and treading water. She tread water because she needed to keep her head up and watch the Hatteras yacht. It was hunting her, and she wanted to make sure it didn't find her. Someone knelt against the guardrail at the prow of the vessel and was holding a powerful light. The yacht circled over the black waves in widening concentric circles. She knew that she'd wounded Concha Dores severely with the gaff and that the evil woman would want to get her revenge. Aja would rather drown than be taken by the cartel again.

When the yacht came her way, she dived under the waves. She swam straight down and hid in the underwater darkness, holding her breath, until the boat passed overhead. That was the only time they came close to finding her. The yacht circled around in the dark for twenty minutes before quitting. Then it headed east.

Aja used the Hatteras yacht's stern lights to set her bearings. She had seen a glimpse of the SS *Sapona* in the moonlight off to the right of the yacht before jumping overboard. She judged it was roughly three miles off.

A spiral cluster of stars glittered in the sky in the direction she was going. It made her think of a double helix made of diamonds, and she set her course by it.

She started to swim towards the old concrete wreck in earnest. When she got to it, she intended to climb out of the water and rest on the upper deck and wait for dawn.

Night currents flowed around her, eternal and primordial. She could not see it, but she knew that an ancient seafloor of compressed limestone coral reefs and Pleistocene fossils, shaped and worn level by multiple ice ages, passed below her kicking feet. Vast meadows of sea grasses grew there, and carbonate sand flats were home to macroalgae, gorgonians, and gastropod mollusks such as queen conches or cone snails evolved from the Paleozoic Era.

Stingrays glided in the darkness and sharks hunted—as they had throughout the world's oceans for 450 million years: a class of fishes from before recorded time, older than the Himalayan Mountains and Mount Everest itself, older than the dinosaurs, older than the first trees, and countless millennia older than the first bipedal primates.

Aja swam for her life through the ancient sea, swept by strange currents that carried even stranger primeval life.

Now that she could use her arms and legs together, she could make good time. She figured it would take around two hours to swim to the *Sapona* wreck.

Although exhausted, battered, and sore, she refused to dwell on it. Instead, she focused on her form and her breathing: flutter-kicking her feet and alternating her arms in a front crawl. She kept her stomach flat and level to streamline her body. The sea felt electric and looked as black as cuttlefish sepia. Within a few minutes she found her rhythm.

Then her mind was free to wander. She did not want to think about what was in the sea with her. So she thought about her fiancé.

Was he searching for her? She felt sure that he was. And woe to any men who crossed him. Seabrook had a paradoxical nature: he was remarkably gentle and good-natured under normal circumstances. Despite his roughneck appearance and busted nose, he was not a true thug. A cold brightness lived in his Celtic blue eyes and in the way he thought and talked about science and life. He could pass for an intellectual. Yet he loved violent sports such as rugby and wrestling, and was physically built for them. He had the skills to seriously hurt people.

The two sides of his personality seemed somehow incompatible. Yet he was truly both. Like a brawling caveman who also understood quantum physics.

The one overlapping constant was that when Seabrook set his mind to a sport or a scholarly goal—or in Aja's case, a person—he was completely committed.

Aja had realized, with a degree of bemusement, that the Bahamian children had a true read on him. They had sussed him out better than most of his colleagues ever would.

She loved that the children loved him—and the more they came to know him, the more they wanted to be around him: playing soccer or Wiffle ball, or helping with morphometric measurements of sharks by the dock. It was fitting, because you couldn't fool children for long. Unlike adults, they could usually see through a phony in a heartbeat.

Their approval was like a stamp of authenticity for "good soul."

More than anyone she'd ever met, Seabrook felt like home to her. He quietly encouraged her, supported her, joked with her, and made her feel adored and respected one hundred percent.

His way of being gave Aja ample space and freedom to be herself. No pretense, no head games, no bullshit.

She was a strong, independent woman who did not need a man to fulfill or balance her life, but still Seabrook was everything to her.

Then a terrible notion came to her. Had Seabrook tracked her satellite tag to the kill house? Had she mistakenly led him to his death?

The thought of it was too much to handle. She pushed it from her mind and kept swimming.

All summer, Seabrook had caught, tagged, and released big tiger, bull, and hammerhead sharks in the Great Bahama Bank—in the very waters she now swam across. Aja also knew very well about the Gorgon Channel, which seemed to be a thoroughfare for large deep-water predators: she remembered the three pregnant sharks Seabrook had followed through the channel.

She knew all too well that it was foolish to swim at night in such water, that it invited unnecessary risk. Ordinarily, she would never do it. That was why, after swimming for more than an hour, she suddenly felt so afraid.

She had the unshakable feeling that something had found her. At first it was just intuition, a feeling that crept up on her.

The feeling intensified when she felt something large swim under her kicking legs. A weird uprising of water and the faintest brush of a tail or dorsal fin across one foot.

This happened again five minutes later.

Whatever it was, was following her in the darkness.

Chapter 54
Last Supper

"You talk of food? I have no taste for food—what I really crave is slaughter and blood and the choking groans of men!" —Homer

In a daze, Seabrook left South Bimini. He drove slowly through the pitch darkness and deep water of the harbor. The loudest noise was the sound of the outboard chugging in low gear. Up ahead he saw the lights of the moored sailboats arrayed across the harbor. They loomed out of the dark like alien ships, and he kept well away, steering the Whaler beyond their lights. Their lanyards clanged like small church bells tolling.

He did not want to be seen and recognized, did not want to be placed in the vicinity of the crime scene on South Bimini island. But more than that, he didn't want to interact with any human beings. The people on the sailboats were part of another world—a casual, comfortable world where people lived on the surface of things: gossiping about acquaintances, discussing what they were going to eat for dinner, talking about their favorite sports teams, or TV shows.

After what he'd seen and felt on this day, he felt stricken and mute. He didn't feel fluent in the language of the trivial or mundane anymore. He couldn't even fake it.

All he could think about was how to save Aja.

He drove the Whaler back to North Bimini, trying to decide what to do next. Images of the mutilated victims swirled into his mind, and also the human meat with which he'd baited the long line. It sickened a place deep in the center of his being.

He'd been arrested once and suspected he'd be arrested again because he was so close to the crimes. But all of that was secondary.

Finding the satellite tag had given him great hope. Consequently, he hadn't searched for Aja among the human remains in the kill house. This was good because he'd left no DNA trace of himself among the dead. The feeling that Aja was still alive had come to him down in the cistern and from the open door to the backyard. The location of the satellite tag on the floor of the cistern made him think that she might have escaped.

As he struggled to come up with any good idea about what to do next, his body seemed to switch to autopilot, because the next thing he knew, he was back at the dock of their rental house in Bailey Town. He didn't remember driving up the channel. Also, unbeknownst to him, he had been weeping and his hands were shaking. He wiped his face dry with trembling fingers.

He tied off the Whaler and jogged up the dock and path to the house. He unlocked the kitchen door and entered their home. Pitch dark.

He switched on the light. He looked to see if Aja had come back. He checked every room, but the place looked the same as it had before he left.

In the bedroom he picked up the photo of Aja kissing Clara. His fingers touched her image and he felt heartsick.

In the living room he looked at the photo of the Sea Cherubs. Where were they? Had the police found them? He hoped so. He thought of Carmelita in intensive care. Again, he felt heartsick but also glad that Reverend Bastareaud was dead.

He glanced at the clock in the kitchen: 10:23 p.m.

Then it hit him.

He suddenly knew what to do.

First Seabrook needed to prepare. He didn't feel hungry, yet he hadn't eaten since very early in the morning—cold cereal.

He opened the refrigerator and saw a nice thick slab of leftover shark steak, from the last casualty on the long line. He'd grilled it for their dinner two days earlier. This was the last piece.

He sat down at the kitchen table with his meal and thought about the day's horrible events. Trying to make some sense of them and maybe find reason in them—if there was any. In the morning, the cartel had abducted Aja and forced him to bait the long line with a dismembered body. Then, in the afternoon, he'd been arrested by the Bimini police on suspicion of murder and forced to waste precious hours sitting in a cell. Then, in the early evening, he'd tracked Aja's satellite tag to South Bimini and found it in the cistern under the kill house. *None of the human remains looked female.* The only good detail of the day.

Why were they in this situation? The cartel wanted money that he and Aja had never even seen, because the Earless Man, under duress of torture, had told the cartel that Seabrook and Aja were the last people he'd seen before the money went missing. So the cartel believed that Seabrook and Aja had stolen it.

What about the evil woman with the flickering eyes? She had been there on the boat with the Earless Man that night. He suddenly remembered Rudy Defarge staggering down the hall in fourth grade, staring at him with animalistic glee—"*I will get you one day.*" The woman with those eyes had to be Concha Dores, Miami's Queen of Cocaine. Something told him she knew where the fifty million dollars was. Something told him *she* was behind this whole nightmare.

Vuelta had said he had twenty-four hours to return the money or they were going to dismember Aja and make him use her for bait. Seabrook calculated he'd already spent twelve hours of his time. Aja had only twelve hours to live. He thought if he could just get Aja back next to him, they could fight their way out of this. Even if they failed, it would be better to be together in the end. Also, it was better to fight.

The cartel clearly expected him to lie down like a victim and accept their terms and demands. Not today, not ever. The best defense is a good offense.

The steak was tough and chewy—cut from a dead tiger shark. An apex predator. A big male. Some sharks were better to eat than others, and tiger sharks were among the worst (bull sharks too). They were extremely fierce animals with high levels of testosterone, and they ate carrion, among other things. Some people believed their nasty diet made their meat bad. Others thought it was wrong to eat them because once in a blue moon they ate a human.

Seabrook didn't care. The meal would be good enough for his purposes. If he turned the steak over, he could still see the dark blotches of the tiger stripes on its rough skin.

He cut big pieces and forked them into his mouth. He chewed and swallowed the cold meat in silence.

He chased the tiger shark with water. A grim thought occurred to him: if his plan failed, this would be his last supper.

Chapter 55
Fifty Million Dollars

Seabrook had to go to the Compleat Angler. That was the only way he could get to Aja. Vuelta had said there would be a man waiting for him in case he "found" the missing fifty million dollars. The quickest way into town was to take the Whaler—he had to hurry if he wanted to be there before last call and closing.

As he went down the dock, he thought he saw something moving in the water underneath. A pale face looking up? Or the moon glaring off the dark water?

Seabrook ignored it, putting it down to nerves. He sat in the boat and started the outboard. He untied the clove hitch knots from the pilings and pulled the lines in. He pushed off the wood post and turned the Whaler, heading south.

This time he needed to get only to the heart of Alice Town. He did not need to cross the harbor.

He used the flashlight as before to see the marker poles in the channel. Time went quickly, and the lights of buildings soon appeared along the shore.

As he motored along, he reviewed his plan. It wasn't very good, but he couldn't think of a better one. Create confusion in your enemy, force a broken play, then be opportunistic and take your chances.

304

In wrestling he used to shoot onto his opponent's legs right off the whistle to put the man immediately on defense. His opening shot was only a setup; he never expected it would work against good athletes. Seabrook was a chain wrestler. He moved from one take-down shot to another, then another, then another, then another, creating a chain of moves until his opponent finally had no answer, no counter. His coach called it flurrying. He'd get into a flurry of moves, and even though it looked uncontrolled to the uneducated spectator, he was always in control, testing and searching for vulnerability, an opportunity to score. It also created chaos on the mat where both wrestlers had to scramble. To think and react in fractions of a second in a high-stakes situation. In this way he forced the fight into unexpected terrain, and that's where he thrived. Seabrook had won the New York State Championship at 195 pounds and been recruited to wrestle in the NCAA Division I for Syracuse because he was a chain wrestler, he loved to flurry, and he was great at scrambling. That's how he won.

When he pulled alongside the concrete quay next to the fueling dock, it was 11:42 at night. The Compleat Angler didn't keep strict hours but was usually open roughly to midnight.

Seabrook tied the Whaler to large cleats on the quay, then ran into town. He raced past storefronts, houses, and other bars, all the way to the stonewall and arch entranceway outside the world-famous bar and hotel where Ernest Hemingway had lived and worked. The Compleat Angler was still open.

The place had started to empty out for the night. The band had finished, and the dance floor was empty. A few power drinkers were perched at the bar drinking shots, talking in whisky voices. A dozen other tourists and fishermen sat at the tables. A woman cackled. Her friend guzzled the last of his beer.

Seabrook's eyes scanned the room and quickly narrowed in on a table against the far wall. Two men were playing cards and seemed out of place. They both had their backs to the wall so they could see everyone who came into the bar. They looked like Colombians and were more sober than the rest of the crowd. They noticed Seabrook immediately and put down their cards.

One reached behind his back—the younger of the two. Seabrook walked up to their table with both of his hands open so that it was obvious that he was unarmed. These were different than the other men Seabrook had met. The one with his hand behind his back looked like a teenager, and the other could have been his older brother. The older one had a long vertical scar straight down the left side of his chin.

"Vuelta told me to come here if I found the money," Seabrook said softly. He didn't want to draw the attention of anyone else at the bar.

"Where is it?" the man with the scarred chin said.

"I hid it in a dangerous place where no one would look for it," Seabrook said. The man studied his face for several seconds.

"You better get it and bring it here."

"I need my partner. The lady."

"No way."

"I put it in waterproof duffel bags and hid it in the sea."

"Where?"

"In a cave where sharks sleep. I thought it would be safe there. It's a lot of money, and I was worried someone would steal it."

The man with the scar snorted, "Only a fool would do that."

"Yes. So I put it in the safest place I could think of. I need my partner to help me handle the sharks and bring up the duffel bags. One man can't do it."

"That's a bullshit story."

"No, it's not. If you want the money, give me back my partner."

The man with the scarred chin stared at Seabrook with a sour expression. He must have heard they were shark scientists, because he didn't fully reject the story.

"I'll be right back," he said. The man got up from his table and walked to the end of the bar. A door led to an office in the back. Seabrook guessed there was a telephone inside.

The younger cartel man stayed seated at the table with his hand still behind his back. He stared at Seabrook with a flat, hard expression. "You should never have fucked with Concha Dores," he said. The guy was a lanky teenager, maybe nineteen at most, with a big attitude. An ectomorph through and through.

Seabrook didn't respond. He wondered how tough the kid would be without the gun behind his back. He looked like he'd break in two with one good shot. Seabrook had destroyed real men, genuine beasts with skills and training, on wrestling mats and rugby fields. With his bare hands.

The teenager seemed to catch the drift of his thoughts. He pulled the handgun from behind his back and rested it on his knee under the table. Just in case.

The man with the scarred chin came back. He sat down in his chair.

"Come back tomorrow at first light," he said. "Meet at the dock where they weigh the giant marlin. Be ready to lead us to the money. You will go into the sea and get it."

"I need my partner. She is a shark expert."

"The boss said yes. Your partner will be here in the morning."

Hope flooded his heart.

Aja was still alive.

Chapter 56
The Hungry Sea

Aja turned to face it. Whatever was following her in the sea had become more aggressive. It had just bumped her feet again. *Please let it be just a dolphin!* But she didn't think so.

Treading water, she turned in a circle—if she could just see it, she could shove the nose to the side as it came in to bite. No chance. She saw nothing but black waves.

After a few seconds, she resumed swimming.

Never in her life had she felt more like a sitting duck. If something wanted to eat her, she couldn't stop it from happening. She couldn't see into the water at all and couldn't anticipate an attack.

She wondered if it was another Gorgon shark—a full-size pregnant bull or tiger shark—that was stalking her. Just the thought made her swim faster.

Five minutes later, she paused swimming to orient herself and make sure she was going in the right direction. She tread water and looked up at the sky, searching for the swirl cluster of stars shaped like a double helix. She found it.

Aja lowered her eyes. Something had changed up ahead. The darkness looked different. Now a faint black structure loomed above the waterline: the SS *Sapona*! Maybe two hundred yards away. She was going to make it.

She took two strokes and started flutter-kicking again when relief suddenly turned into alarm. A powerful current hit her.

A great commotion churned under the sea. The shark was coming to the surface to get her.

Then a sudden flash of light erupted, like underwater lightning. In that instant, Aja saw a dark shadow under her feet.

Then a bigger shadow came out of nowhere and hit it. The light went out, and the sea turned black again.

A great splashing, then a moment of quiet.

Another flash of underwater lightning.

The larger shadow now produced a steady brilliant glow: a jet-black silhouette limned by a brilliant light, a solar eclipse that glided through the water. *Razormouth?*

In the split second before darkness returned, Aja thought she saw a red cloud in the sea. Blood.

Razormouth was feeding on the other shark—the shark that had been following her.

Luckily for Aja, Razormouth had just saved her life.

The sea went black again.

She swam for the SS *Sapona* as fast as her limbs would take her.

Chapter 57
SS Sapona

"It is said that an egg of remarkable size once fell from the sky into the Euphrates River and that the fish pushed it out onto the bank. Doves came and alighted upon the egg, and after it grew warm, it hatched. Out came Venus, who afterward was called the Syrian Goddess. Since she was far more just and upright than the rest of the gods, Jupiter gave her a choice, and she had the fish raised into the stars."—Hyginus

The hulking wreck of the SS *Sapona* still lay ahead. Like a spectral ship risen from the sea, wounded-looking, the grounded concrete cargo ship stood in roughly twenty feet of water with most of its above water structure torn open in many places. The vessel was nearly three hundred feet long. It was a miracle she was still standing upright—instead of being ruined and lost on the ocean floor.

Her top deck was crusted and flaked with rust from decades of exposure to sun and sea. She'd endured a half-century of hurricanes and countless bullets and bombs. The damage had made her incredibly dangerous to walk across—assuming you knew the secret way to climb out of the sea onto the wreck in the first place.

Gaping holes edged by crumbling perimeters waited for intrepid tourists like trapping pits set by hunters. Jagged rebar stabbed out from the structures underneath to impale or maim fallers; or, if you were lucky, a drop straight into the sea twenty feet below would give a last-second reprieve. Thrill-seeking tourists loved to climb up onto the *Sapona* and jump off the bow or snorkel on the reef growing on the submerged lower half of the skeletal vessel.

Aja planned to take shelter on the uppermost forward part of the wreck, or forecastle. But she had to swim inside the wreck first. And she knew the ladder hidden within was dangling by an old hawser rope with its lower rungs in the sea just above the den of Lennie, the resident green moray eel. She wasn't afraid of Lennie. She even had played with him during sunlit afternoons when snorkeling in the area.

But Aja was realistic: morays wandered out of their dens at night to hunt. Perhaps in the dark, Lennie might mistake her moving legs and feet for some kind of fish crossing in front of the entrance to his home. There could be an honest misunderstanding.

If she were lucky, he'd be out hunting spiny lobster or sleeping fish. But either way, she knew it wasn't smart to wave her naked feet about in his front yard at night.

She knew the *Sapona* well enough to walk up its main deck and skirt her way around the crater-like holes—even in the dark.

She wanted to curl up and rest in the forecastle and wait for dawn. The cartel would never find her there. And maybe tourists would stop by in a boat to scuba-dive on the wreck. She could hitch a ride back to land with them.

If they were good people.

But first, she had to swim into the wreck and dangle her feet in front of Lennie's lair.

The *Sapona*'s concrete sides had disintegrated into a weather-beaten row of frame supports. Like the great vertical ribs of a skeletal leviathan, the frame supports stood upright in a row from bow to stern on both sides. The ocean and marine life flowed freely between the ribs that held the deck twenty feet above. The main cargo hold was half submerged in the sea.

Aja swam through one of the gaps and entered the main cargo hold. She immediately felt a little safer. She was no longer in open water.

She turned to the right and headed toward the small compartment next to the engine room.

Inside, she glanced upward in the darkness and saw the old rusted ladder that had been dangling by a thick hawser line for years. She had to climb the ladder to get to the upper deck and out of the water. Was Lennie home? Or was he out hunting sleeping fish and roaming lobsters?

She swam to the ladder and grabbed onto the bottom rung.

The velvety skin of a large moray eel brushed across her shins.

"Lennie! No!" she said.

As she started up the ladder, bicycle-kicking her legs, she accidentally thumped the big eel in the head. In the darkness, this must have confused the serpent-like fish.

Lennie bit her right foot.

Moray eels have two sets of jaws. The large one is obvious to divers and has large fang teeth. Morays use it to grab onto prey. The second set, the pharyngeal jaw, is smaller and hidden in the eel's throat. Once the large jaws have clamped onto prey, the smaller jaws shoot forward and bite onto it and drag the prey into the gullet.

Aja felt only one set of jaws on her foot. She relaxed her leg, hoping the normally friendly eel would let her go.

"Lennie, please let go. It's just me."

The pharyngeal jaws sprang forward and bit off the two small toes on her right foot. Aja screamed.

Lennie let go. He withdrew to deeper water or maybe returned to his den.

Aja quickly pulled herself up the rungs of the ladder, using only her good foot on the rungs.

She climbed to the upper deck and limped her way around the massive holes that pockmarked and punctured the whole ship. Then limped up to the prow and sat down.

She ran her fingers along the toes of her right foot and gently touched the raw stubs. Her two smallest toes had been sheared off right at the nub.

The wounds bled onto her hand.

She was still wearing her T-shirt and shorts, and a bathing suit underneath. She pulled the T-shirt over her head. With her teeth she bit at the edge of the bottom until the cotton shirt ripped. She tore long strips of fabric to use as makeshift bandages. She tied them around her wounded foot, from the heel across the stubs, and made the wraps tight.

Aja lay back on the concrete deck. She crossed her legs and elevated her wounded foot as best as possible. She wanted the stumps to dry and scab over.

Her skin became sticky as the seawater dried. Her missing toes throbbed painfully. She felt tired beyond anything she'd ever experienced, but couldn't fall asleep. She was too worried. Where was Seabrook? Had the cartel killed him? Where were the Sea Cherubs? Would the nightmare ever end?

Several meteors streaked across the sky and distracted her—maybe the Perseid shower. She had briefly studied astronomy at MIT before majoring in biology. It was the right time of summer for the Perseids.

Below, waves splashed softly against the battered wreck and through its jagged ribs. Marine life swarmed around the *Sapona* at night, grazing and exploring her debris field, marine-encrusted engines, boilers, and half-submerged cargo hold.

As Aja dozed on and off, in a half dream state, she gazed up at the firmament. She was not separate and apart from it like an earthbound stargazer. The *Sapona* held her aloft from the salt sea, elevated into the sky, dipping her into the celestial ocean overhead. Constellations, galaxies, and billions of stars streamed around her. Astral light and falling stars swam alongside like companions. While the Caribbean Sea murmured softly in her ears, infinite universes entered her eyes.

She drifted with the Milky Way, the North Pole star, and the V-shaped Pisces constellation.

A sudden loud splash made Aja sit up.

She heard it a second time.

Then she stood up. She limped to the wall at the prow and peered over.

A massive, dark creature was moving slowly in the sea below. Its dorsal fin stuck up, taller than a man. The creature was the size of a small whale. Odd speckles, cuneiform shapes, and strange lines briefly shimmered pearlescent across its wide, long back. As if the deep-sea universe had imprinted its secrets on the creature's iron-hard hide. A heartbeat later the patterns went dark.

Then Razormouth swam in a slow circle right at the surface. The back of its head was raised out of the sea.

Aja saw its peculiar third eye wide open on the back of its head. The shark seemed to be looking at the sky. The Pisces constellation sparkled right above.

What was it doing? A navigational strategy? She had no idea, but the strange shark had saved her life.

Soon the mysterious fish disappeared.

Aja lay down again on the hard concrete deck. She closed her eyes for a spell.

Chapter 58
Late Night

Miles away, in their house on North Bimini, Seabrook was edgy and afraid to close his eyes. If he overslept, the cartel would kill Aja straight out.

He left the house. He carried all the gear he thought he would need down the dock. He lay down in the Whaler to sleep as an insurance policy. This way, when the sky brightened with dawn and the gulls began to caw and cry, he'd be certain to awake.

He lay on his back on the hard fiberglass deck and looked up at the sky. It was lit with stars, but he couldn't appreciate it. The tide was going out and made a satiny seething sound as it flowed under the hull and about the pilings. The boat swayed gently as the sea went by, tugging its lines and restlessly bumping against the dock—as if he were afloat on Queequeg's coffin in *Moby-Dick*. Wood creaked every now and then. His underwater gear sat next to him in a pile: mask, snorkel, swim fins, knives, and Hawaiian sling spear. He'd also brought a gallon jug of fresh water and two Dramamine patches.

He wondered about the dead man in his nightmare and the dark area on the dock. Did they really mean anything? The seabirds and children still avoided the stain on the wood. He couldn't be sure, but he wasn't afraid of anything at the moment. He was in a combat mindset and would take on anything coming his way. He had no choice. If he wasn't ready to rock-and-roll with all cylinders firing, tomorrow would be his and Aja's last day ever.

It was still dark, but the sky had brightened a little. Dawn was near.

After a mostly sleepless few hours, Seabrook drove the Whaler to the meeting place at the weigh-in dock by the Big Game Club and Blue Water Marina.

He couldn't count how many beautiful bluefin and yellowfin tuna, blue marlin, white marlin, swordfish, and sailfish he'd seen dangling by their tails from that scale. The sheer size and extraordinary electric colors of their bodies were unforgettable, as the fish glistened in the late-afternoon light at the end of tournaments. Some were as big as canoes; others the size of kayaks. There was always a whiff of tragedy when seeing such incredible animals ripped out of their environment and dead. The sailfish were the worst. They always looked broken, greatly diminished with crumpled crepe sails. Nothing like their majestic appearance in the sea.

Locals knew that if you went to the weigh-ins, oftentimes you could get the freshest fish in the world gratis. Some of the fishermen only wanted to catch a trophy and pose for a photo. They didn't care about the catch beyond that moment of glory. Or they wanted only enough meat for dinner that night. If they'd caught a five-hundred-pound marlin, that left a lot of meat to waste. It paid to stop by and see if anyone was giving away fresh tuna, marlin, or swordfish steaks. Some-times even mako shark.

Seabrook arrived at the weigh-in dock before sunrise. The place was dark and deserted. The cartel hadn't arrived. Alice Town harbor was sound asleep.

He tied the Whaler to cleats along the quay and walked up to the weighing dock—the scale haunted by the ghosts of many great fish.

He waited.

Chapter 59
The Cave

"The strong do what they can and the weak suffer what they must."
—Thucydides

Right after the sun peeked over the horizon, the cartel arrived. A cigarette speedboat cruised into the harbor. It rumbled past the Big Game Club Marina to the dock where Seabrook was waiting. Vuelta stood in the cockpit. It was the same boat they'd used to deliver the bait tub full of human meat.

Vuelta brought the speedboat alongside. He beckoned, "Come aboard." His voice was loud, to be heard over the thunderous engines.

"Show me the lady," Seabrook said.

"Not now. If you want to see her again, get onboard."

"I need her for this job. There are sharks in the cave. It takes two people at least. Two people who know what they are doing."

"I brought you a partner."

A man walked up behind Seabrook and put a gun in his back, saying "Don't do something stupid."

Seabrook slowly turned and stepped back. He bleakly studied the man. A white guy with bleach blond hair. Medium sized and in good shape. His face was beet red from sun exposure, and his nose was

318

covered with zinc oxide cream. He wore a wetsuit shorty and polarized sunglasses. On the ground next to him, he had a large red dive bag and a spear gun. Two dive tanks stood next to the bag. No sign of Aja. In a way, he wasn't surprised.

"Where's your gear?" Bleach Blond said.

"Where is my partner?"

"You don't get to see her until the money is returned. I'm your dive buddy for this job. I can handle the sharks too. I do a lot of spearfishing." The guy must have come from Miami overnight. He obviously worked for the cartel in some capacity. He held a grave expression, cards close to his chest. He had a military bearing. Maybe ex-Navy.

Seabrook made a split second decision to go. If he didn't, he might get shot on the spot and Aja would be executed shortly. He didn't know whether she was still alive, but he trusted his gut that she was.

"Okay," Seabrook said. "Let me get my gear."

The harbor had stirred to life. One of the sailboats had pulled anchor and started out to the Gulf Stream. Men were loading ice, beer, and bait on a Bertram sportfishing yacht two docks down.

Seabrook walked to the Whaler, and Bleach Blond followed.

"Forget the Hawaiian sling; no knives either." Bleach Blond said, looking at what lay in the Whaler. He let Seabrook bring only his mask, snorkel, and fins. No weapons.

Then the man grew incredulous. His voice was still a normal volume but full of edge. "No dive tanks? Are you fucking crazy? Hey asshole, you better not be wasting my time. You're in a very serious situation here. You expect me to believe that you stashed waterproof duffel bags with fifty million in cash in the sea with just a snorkel?"

"Yes. The cave is thirty-eight feet underwater. I can snorkel and spear-fish to fifty feet no problem."

The man shook his head. "Okay. This better play right. For your sake. I wouldn't want to be you or your bitch if there is no money."

Seabrook stuck a fresh Dramamine patch behind his ear. He carried his snorkel gear and jug of freshwater onto the drug runner's speedboat.

Vuelta held the wheel. He told Seabrook to stand next to him and give directions. Seabrook set his gear on one of the seats in the cockpit. He studied the blond's expression, then Vuelta's.

"What are you looking at?" Vuelta said. He gave a strained smile. Trying to play nice and keep everyone calm.

"Nothing," Seabrook lied. He had the sense they were up to something. Anything was possible. Maybe they planned to kill him once he showed them the money. They certainly would kill him if there was no money; and there was no money in the cave or anywhere else as far as he knew. "Where is my lady? You said I had twenty-four hours."

"After we see the money." Vuelta drove out the harbor and east towards Turtle Rocks.

The sun rose higher. The morning sky turned powder blue. Outside the harbor, the sea was leaping with moderate waves, but Vuelta drove fast. The cigarette boat lunged forward, launching itself from one wave crest to the next. As if the vessel were trying to take flight. Seabrook had never been on a faster boat.

The deep blue water of the Gulf Stream rushed by. He thought of sand draining from an hourglass—when they arrived at the dive site and stopped motoring, the sea would stop flowing past the gunwales. He was about to be out of time. Everything was coming to a brutal defining moment: kill or die. His and Aja's lives would hinge on what he did in the next few minutes.

Bleach Blond threw out the anchor when they arrived at the spot Seabrook had picked. Vuelta killed the engines. They were anchored at the eastern end of Turtle Rocks. Sea birds flew pell-mell over the ridge standing above the waterline. The current pulled the cigarette boat so that it was oriented parallel to the reef line and rocky crest. It drifted a little. Then the anchor set and the anchor line pulled tight.

Vuelta now held a MAC-10 submachine gun.

Seabrook pulled on his fins and spit into his mask. He rubbed the saliva around to help reduce fogging underwater.

Bleach Blond was the cartel's diver—Seabrook figured he retrieved drugs dropped in the sea or salvaged crashed cartel planes. The man screwed his regulator to one of his scuba tanks. He was using Sherwood equipment and had a depth gauge, an air gauge, and an octopus (a backup regulator).

"I have a question," Seabrook said.

"What's that?" Bleach Blond said in a cold voice.

"When we get on bottom, before we enter the cave, can I take a couple of breaths from your octopus?" Seabrook pointed at the backup regulator.

The man looked at Vuelta. Again Seabrook had the sense they were up to something.

"I thought you could free-dive to fifty feet no problem?" Bleach Blond said.

"I can. But we won't know what we are dealing with inside the cave until I go in—a baby nurse shark or an eighteen-foot tiger."

"How did you do it last time?" Bleach Blond said. He smiled contemptuously.

"We checked the cave first and cleared out the sharks. Then we surfaced to breathe. Once the cave was empty, we took the duffel bags down and secured them with lead weight belts. Point is that we surfaced and breathed between clearing out the sharks and dragging the money into the cave."

Bleach Blond's mouth tightened. He wasn't buying it.

"I want to take a breath in case the situation gets out of control, and I burn my air quickly. Otherwise I may have to surface and leave you alone down there."

"Let him take two breaths," Vuelta said. He made eye contact with the man and nodded very slightly.

Bleach Blond lifted his head and responded with his eyes. A hard look that said *I know what to do.*

An order had been given. *They were going to kill him.*

"Sure," Bleach Blond said. "You can take a couple puffs before we go inside." He picked up his spear gun and loaded it. He pulled all three bands down and notched them. The weapon was illegal in the Bahamas because it was too lethal and unsporting—unlike a Hawaiian sling, which required skill and was much more difficult to use.

The spear gun looked like a short rifle with a pistol grip. The spear jutted out from the barrel. All you had to do was pull the trigger, and the spear would fire and impale anything made of flesh. A nylon rope was looped underneath the barrel and would release when the spear launched. The rope was tied to the butt end of the spear at one end and to the spear gun at the other end. This way the gun barrel was attached to the spear and you could pull in what you shot.

Bleach Blond pulled on his BCD (buoyancy control device) vest, snapped on his weight belt, and pulled on his fins. He turned the valve on his scuba tank all the way on. Then he checked his air pressure gauge and made sure he had at least 3000 PSI. He drew a breath from his regulator to make sure everything was in order. With the full scuba tank, he could stay on bottom at a depth of forty feet for almost two hours.

With his snorkel, Seabrook could stay on bottom at forty feet for a little less than three minutes. That's how long he could hold his breath when he was relaxed and had been snorkeling all summer and practicing.

The cartel diver was armed to the teeth. He had a large dive knife strapped to each calf, a third knife in his vest, and his loaded spear gun.

Seabrook had nothing. This was to his advantage. The cartel men didn't see him as a threat.

He was taking a huge gamble because he had to. He didn't know anything about the fifty million dollars or its whereabouts, but he knew that if he did nothing, these cartel men would make him bait the long line with Aja's dismembered body later in the morning. So he had to hit them first, when they didn't expect it. Then maybe, just maybe, he could save Aja. At the very least, he would kill some of the bastards before he and Aja died.

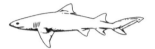

With a little luck, he would kill Bleach Blond inside the cave, take his spear gun and kill Vuelta—after making him tell where Aja was.

Seabrook had been to the cave many times before. He'd discovered it on his first visit to Bimini, the same trip he met Aja, when he was living on the *Colombus Islen,* University of Miami's famous oceano-graphic research vessel.

He'd been snorkeling at Turtle Rocks one afternoon after working on the long line all morning. He swam over the reef and finned down to thirty-eight feet to explore a unique coral formation near bottom. That was when he discovered the opening.

The cave had a narrow entranceway that led to a low-ceilinged chamber. The floor space was about the size of a small living room. In broad daylight, there was just enough light to see inside. A couple of tiny openings in the roof let in shafts of sunlight. Two Caribbean reef sharks (*Carcharhinus perezi*) were resting on the sand and did not react when Seabrook entered the cave. He couldn't believe his good luck. Excited, he surfaced and returned to his boat.

He was conducting an age and growth study, and tagging sharks was part of the process. He figured he could estimate the sleeping sharks' lengths, then tag them. In this way he could add two more tagged sharks to his day's total without the trouble of having to catch them first. It seemed like a great idea. On the boat, he opened his tagging kit. He grabbed two tags and the ice pick-like tool he used to stab the tags in at the base of a shark's dorsal fin.

He reentered the sea and finned down to the cave entrance. He slipped inside and swam up to the first sleeping shark. He prepped the tag for insertion, finned closer, then stabbed the shark at the base of the dorsal fin. He expected the shark to wake up and bolt out of the cave. It did not.

The tagged shark swam in an agitated state in a circle and collided with the second sleeping shark. Now there were two sharks circling inside the cave in an agitated state. Seabrook pressed against the wall to stay out of their way. However, as they raced around, their powerful tails stirred up the fine sand on bottom. A grainy cloud bloomed in the cave, and visibility dropped to almost zero.

Seabrook knew he was in trouble. He could feel the sharks darting around him in the small space but could see nothing. Most important, he could not see the way out. He began to run out of air and searched frantically for the cave entrance. He felt his way around the walls, searching and searching, his lungs burning for air; but no matter which direction he moved in, he could not find the exit. He was trapped.

Just when he felt sure he would drown, he found the opening and raced for the surface. One more second and he would have never left the cave.

Since that first visit, Seabrook found sharks in the cave most of the time. It was a favorite resting place of theirs. However, he'd learned his lesson and never disturbed them again.

Today, he counted on them being in the cave.

He was desperate to see sleeping sharks.

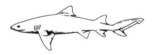

It was time to do it. He and Bleach Blond rolled backwards off the speedboat into the waves. When the bubbles cleared, Seabrook hovered at the surface as the cartel diver began his descent.

He stared down into the sea and gathered himself together. He felt his senses quicken in anticipation. He couldn't afford to be stressed or anxious—it would make him burn through his oxygen faster. He breathed deliberately and in a controlled way, deeply and slowly, through the snorkel. Calming his nerves, getting ready. He watched the cartel diver sink to the seafloor, releasing a swarm of silver bubbles with each exhale from his scuba tank.

After several deep, full breaths and exhales of surface air, Seabrook felt ready. He held the last breath in his full lungs and jackknifed his body for descent to the bottom. He saw the cave down-current, where he knew it would be. It looked like a pile of rubble and coral from his vantage point. The water felt warm near the surface.

He slowly kicked his fins and broke through a thermocline into colder water. He pinched his nose to clear his ears. They equalized with a squeak.

He'd chosen this spot to anchor because he knew there would be a current. He needed to eke out and exploit every advantage. He did as little physical work as possible as he swam deeper, trying to conserve his air and energy. He let the current carry him towards the cave.

Motion to the left. He turned and saw five spotted eagle rays gliding over the white sand. Circles and spots marked their triangular backs, and a long thin tail trailed behind each of them. They swam near the coral growing over the cave, then angled toward deeper water. A parade of rays, each as large as a kitchen table. They slowly flapped their wings and avoided the men.

When Seabrook arrived at the cave entrance, Bleach Blond joined him. Seabrook felt good. He could hold his breath for at least another minute and a half. Nevertheless, he wanted to breathe from his enemy's scuba tank so he could stay down longer. He turned to the cartel diver and pointed to his backup regulator. The cartel diver's white hair flowed above his head like seaweed in a current.

He nodded.

Seabrook reached for the regulator. He spit out his snorkel, stuck the regulator in his mouth, and began to breathe air from the cartel diver's tank. As he did so, the man raised his loaded spear gun and jabbed the tip into the center of Seabrook's chest. Right on the sternum. The man's finger was on the trigger. *You never pointed a loaded spear gun at something you didn't plan to kill.* Was this a warning? A precaution? Because Seabrook was too close? He couldn't be sure.

Seabrook pushed the spear gun to the side and kept breathing. Three exhalations and four deep inhalations.

Then he spit out the regulator and abruptly swam into the cave. It was time to take his shot, time to create chaos.

The entranceway opened up to a dark, low-ceilinged room. There were two sharks sleeping on the sand inside: one Caribbean reef shark (*Carcharhinus perezi*) about five feet long and a bull shark (*Carcharhinus leucas*) roughly eight feet long. *Good! This was very good!*

Seabrook turned to see that the cartel diver was following and made a show of pointing to the back of the cave, implying that the duffel bags full of cash were straight ahead.

The cartel diver stared at him with a blank expression. Seabrook intentionally swam directly in front of the man, blocking his view so that he wouldn't see there was no money until it was too late.

Seabrook swam close over the reef shark and brushed its dorsal fin with his knee to wake it up. He felt it wriggle to life.

As he approached the bull shark, he made a fist and punched it behind the gills. It reacted violently and burst to life with short muscular strokes of its tail. Pissed off.

Seabrook turned and looked back. The cartel diver shouldered past him. The bull shark swam around the perimeter of the cave and right in front of the cartel diver.

Sediment wafted off the seafloor, creating a dark cloud. Visibility turned bad. The sharks were stirring up the sand as planned.

Their bodies looked like shadows in fog, and Seabrook saw the cartel diver pointing his spear gun at the bull shark. The man was deep into the cave now—and was able to see there was no money.

Then, as visibility worsened and dropped to zero, the man turned and shot Seabrook. The spear went through his upper right leg and protruded out the back.

They'd planned to kill him from the beginning.

Seabrook wanted to gasp, but he couldn't without inhaling the sea. His lungs suddenly demanded air. He had to get out of the cave immediately.

The spear made it hard to move, but the pain wasn't crazy yet. He was probably in shock, and it clouded his thinking for a second.

He swam through the cloud toward the cave exit. A shark blasted past and almost knocked his mask off.

Then the cartel diver was pulling him in like a fish, dragging him by the spear and nylon rope away from the exit. The guy yanked the rope hard and dragged him deeper into the cave.

Then everything happened like lightning. Reflex, muscle memory, survival instinct. Time to chain-wrestle, to flurry—or die. His lungs were screaming for air.

He expected that the man was waiting for him with knife in hand.

He would drown soon and didn't have enough air to fight very long.

So he attacked hard. He took advantage of the poor visibility—the cartel diver couldn't see him coming. He went low across the bottom of the cave in the direction the spear gun line was pulling him, and kicked his fins.

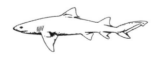

He did everything by feeling and instinct. He could see nothing, not even the sharks. His shoulder collided with the cartel diver's shin and ankle. Seabrook caught his heel in his hand, locked the man's knee straight with his shoulder, stood up on his knees. He lifted up and threw the foot and dive fin hard towards the ceiling. All in one fluid, well-rehearsed motion. Like an ankle-pick move in wrestling. He clambered up the upended diver and turned his falling foe facedown so the cartel man couldn't stab him.

His lungs were suddenly screaming. He started to see white dots.

Now he was on the man's back, grabbing onto the scuba tank.

Everything happened in the blink of an eye.

Breathe or die.

Pain radiated from the spear in his leg, and his lungs burned.

Breathe or die.

He reached around the man's face.

Breathe or die.

He ripped the guy's dive mask off.

Breathe or die.

He jammed his thumb into the man's right eye. Pushing it deep, destroying the orb. A muffled underwater scream.

Breathe or die.

He spit out his snorkel and tore the regulator out of the screaming man's mouth. He shoved the regulator into his own mouth.

He exhaled and nearly blacked out. Then he deeply inhaled and started to breathe from the cartel diver's tank. The first breath brought incredible relief. The little white dots disappeared from his vision.

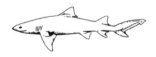

The cartel diver started to drown. He went wild, thrashing and grabbing. If he'd been holding a knife, he must have dropped it during the struggle. The man lost control of himself and panicked out of his mind. He kept trying to turn over and grab hold of his enemy.

Seabrook jammed him flat on his stomach. He chopped his arms when he tried to get up. He expected the man to unsheathe another one of his knives—but he did not. Funny how drowning scrambles a man's mind.

Seabrook kept him face down. When the guy tried to use his back-up regulator, Seabrook ripped it out of his hands.

He broke him down and rode him hard as hell. Like they were in sudden-death overtime in the finals of a national wrestling tournament.

He controlled the guy's hips so he couldn't turn or stand up. He pushed him down by the scuba tank, and the whole time Seabrook kept breathing all the air he needed from the guy's regulator. He grew stronger as the cartel diver grew weaker.

As Bleach Blond began to die, his hands found the spear stuck through Seabrook's leg. He pushed down hard and jerked up even harder on the shaft. It felt like Seabrook's quadriceps muscle would tear off the bone.

Seabrook screamed into the regulator, and bubbles gushed in front of his mask, but he kept the man facedown, maskless in the sand.

The cartel diver cranked on the spear again, but his strength was fading fast now.

Pain radiated through Seabrook's leg, but he did not let go of the cartel diver until the man was completely motionless.

Chapter 60
Poseidon's Altar

The man was dead. Particles of sediment hung suspended in the sea. The inside of the cave looked like an underwater sandstorm. Seabrook couldn't see the body, but he felt it. Heavy and inert.

The sharks must have found their way out. He no longer felt the eddies of their tails sweeping side to side.

He took a minute to think. He breathed deeply and evaluated his situation. He had planned to kill the cartel diver all along, take his spear gun, and use it to kill Vuelta at the surface. He hadn't planned on being speared himself. *Shit!*

In the murkiness of the cave, he couldn't see how bad his wound was. Could he push the spear through? Could he cut it free of his leg? He didn't know; but whatever he was going to do, he'd better do it quickly—before Vuelta became suspicious and took off in the speedboat and had Aja dismembered.

The spear felt like it had gone through the outer layer of his right quadriceps muscle. He was lucky that it wasn't a center shot; it had missed his femoral artery and veins. Still, he needed to look at it and make sure, before he decided how to get it out of his leg. He needed that spear.

330

Razormouth

He was going to reload the spear gun and kill that son of a bitch Vuelta.

A knife. He needed a good knife, and remembered that Bleach Blond had three of them. He ran his hands over the corpse. On one leg he found an empty scabbard strapped to the calf—he'd been right. The cartel diver had drawn his knife after he speared Seabrook.

Seabrook ran his hands across the other leg and found the second knife. He hoped it had a sharp edge and wasn't disappointed. The edge nearly cut his thumb open. He unstrapped the scabbard form the corpse and strapped it to his left leg. He slid the knife in the sheath.

Next he ran his hand down the spear harpooned through his leg and found the nylon rope tied at the end. He pulled it in and dragged the spear gun to him.

He checked the corpse to make sure the man was truly dead. It had turned face up, canted on its right side by the scuba tank underneath. No sign of life.

The body wanted to float off the sand but the scuba tank held it down. Curious. The man must have dumped his weight belt during the fight.

Seabrook turned the corpse over. He undid the Velcro straps clamping the scuba tank to the man's BCD vest—he needed to take the tank if he wanted to keep breathing. He pulled the cylinder free. The body became more buoyant without it.

Holding the scuba tank by its valve in one hand and the spear gun in the other, Seabrook exited the cave. He dragged the tank across the sand and swam in spurts. The spear in his leg tugged painfully against the water.

Once outside the cave, he could see again. He crouched on his knees on the seafloor. He set the scuba tank upright in front of him and the spear gun down in the sand next to him. The glowing blue Caribbean Sea was so bright, it made him feel like he had been nailed into a coffin, buried alive, but had miraculously dug his way out from a suffocating death.

Above, the shadow of the speedboat floated at the surface, waiting for the man he'd just killed to come back to the surface.

The spear in his leg glinted steel gray. It was surprisingly thin.

Yellow wrasses darted around the marine growth above the cave entrance. A large purple and blue parrotfish idled casually towards him. The brilliant fish glanced at him and went back the way it had come.

He didn't know exactly how much time had elapsed, but it couldn't have been more than fifteen minutes. He needed to keep moving. He checked the gauge on the tank: 2,300 PSI—plenty of air for what he needed to do.

As an experiment, he tried to push the spear through his leg. It didn't budge, but the muscle flared with unbelievable pain. It felt like muscle tissue was tearing away from his femur. He couldn't push it through by himself. It was in too tight.

He decided to cut the spear loose. It was roughly two inches deep through the side of his quadriceps muscle. The distance between the entry and exit wound was approximately six inches.

He had to cut it free, but he also had to be careful and gentle with the spear. He needed the weapon straight and intact so he could shoot it from the spear gun. So no bending the shaft or muscling it.

The spear was the most important thing now. It was sacred. He would sacrifice to keep it perfect. *Sacrifice the body.*

When he inhaled from the regulator, he floated upward a little, and when he exhaled he sank, knees into the sand. Bubbles audibly gurgled with each exhale, and the air hissed when he inhaled.

The scuba tank stood in front of him like a small religious altar, and he was attached to it by the regulator hose that was feeding his lungs air. Like an umbilical cord connecting a baby to his mother. He was bent over a little, as if praying to the scuba tank. Worshipping the cylindrical altar. There was truth in the idea—it was keeping him alive. The ancient Greeks had sacrificed at altars to appease the gods. *Sacrifice the body.*

He took the knife from its scabbard on his left leg. He looked at it for a second. It was not a regular dive knife. It looked military grade. The blade was thinner, sharper, and longer: a combat knife of some kind. It also had a wicked tapered point.

He stuck the tip of the knife into the opening of the wound on the front of his leg. Aiming down, he stabbed in next to the spear. His skin bulged up like a small, pitched tent. He cut outward, sawing and slicing through the muscle around the spear shaft. Agony shook him. His eyes flooded, and he feared he might pass out. The knife jumped as he cut through the surface skin. Blood gushed from his leg and became diluted in the slow current.

He put his trembling finger inside the open hole in his leg and found the spear shaft more exposed. Good. If he was lucky, he'd need only two more cuts to finish.

Faster is better.

Wincing, he wiggled the tip of the blade back into his wound, positioning it along the side of the spear. Once it was lined up right, he stabbed hard, cutting maybe three inches in. Again, he could see his skin bulging up like a little tent. Then he sawed back and forth as fast as he could, cutting outward. He bit down on the regulator mouthpiece and screamed underwater.

Faster is better.

He stopped cutting and caught his breath. Both the spear and the knife were protruding from his leg. The blood was coming out darker. He closed his eyes against the pain. He shivered and felt suddenly cold. *My God, it hurts!*

He thought of Aja. She was his goal—and he braced himself for another round of cutting. Then he started again.

Dizziness made the sea swim around him. He sawed his own flesh, back and forth.

The knife cut the surface skin and jumped free. Then everything turned black.

When Seabrook came back to himself, he was bent over on the sand and the regulator was halfway out of his mouth. Seawater was sloshing over his tongue.

He opened his eyes. He was at the bottom of the sea, praying to the scuba tank.

Divine colors—Gothic stained glass disarranged into brilliant fish—moved around him.

The knife lay in the sand in front of him.

He straightened up. He put the rubber regulator firmly back into his mouth and blew the seawater out. Blood billowed up from his leg like smoke from a campfire.

Again, he thought of Aja, and now also of the people who had taken her. He picked the knife up. He bit down on the regulator in anger. If he did this right, it would be the last cut.

He stuck the tip of the knife back into his wound and jammed it as hard as he could along the spear. The blade grated against the shaft. His whole body jumped and shuddered—like when you plunge into ice water and your whole body convulses.

He sawed through his muscle with fury, as if he hated it—telling himself that it stood between him and Aja. Tears streamed down his face and puddled in his mask.

The knife popped through his skin, and he dropped it, twisting to the seafloor. He leaned forward and put his hands in the sand next to the knife.

He breathed and shook, kneeling in front of the steel scuba tank. Trying to recover. The pieces of stained glass swirled closer, bursting with color. Little fins and bright fish eyes. They enshrouded him, luminous and holy in the sea light.

After a few seconds, he angled his head back and looked up. The shadow of the speedboat floated at the surface. Still waiting for the cartel diver to surface.

He ran his finger down the open gash on the side of his quad muscle. It was like a trench with the spear resting in it. His fingertip traced the spear the whole length of his wound. The shaft was free.

Gasping, he carefully pulled the spear sideways and clear of his leg. He looked once at his wound. A flap of skin moved in the current. The leg was gruesome and badly torn open, like he'd been gored by a rampaging swordfish.

He examined the spear and ran his hands down its length, inspecting it.

Dammit! He swore into the regulator with disbelief. The spear wasn't quite straight! After all that, there was a slight bend in the shaft. Would it shoot straight? Would it load properly?

The wound burned as if it had been packed with hot embers, and his leg spasmed like it might cramp.

No time to waste.

No time for regret.

He slid the spear into the spear gun barrel. It wouldn't fit. It wasn't straight enough. *Dammit!* Panic and dismay slapped him.

He tried again and wiggled the shaft as it slid in and, this time, it locked. *Blessed Jesus!* At least he could load the spear; whether it would shoot straight, he couldn't guess.

He stretched the three bands back, one at a time, and latched them onto the spear. Each band was like the string on a hunting bow pulled all the way back, and loaded launch power onto the spear. Three bands superjacked the weapon for a kill shot. He methodically looped the nylon rope around the little hook on the underside of the spear gun and the latch on the trigger guard. The weapon was fully loaded and ready to fire.

He looked up at the shadow of the speedboat waiting above.

He would get only one shot.

He placed the loaded spear gun in the sand. He put the knife in the scabbard strapped to his left leg. He had one more thing to do and would need both hands. He had to leave the corpse dressed in all its scuba gear. Make it look as if his death were a diving accident. Hopefully, by the time anyone found him, the crabs and fish would make it hard to identify him.

He dragged the scuba tank back into the cave. Visibility had improved. Some of the particles of sand stirred up by the sharks and the fight had settled back to the floor of the cave.

The dead man greeted him just inside the entrance. The corpse was floating in the middle of the water column, the air in his chest making his upper torso more buoyant than his legs, so he was upright. He was facing Seabrook and looking at him with a horrible jelly eye and one good eye. The mouth was open like a small cave, and the hair floated straight up. The corpse hovered like it could fly and might embrace him. Begging for air.

Seabrook dragged the scuba tank deeper into the cave, and found the man's weight belt and dive mask in the sand. He buckled the weight belt around the corpse's waist. The lead immediately sank the body to the seafloor.

He put the mask on the face but out of position, so his eyes were only half covered. Then both eyes would be eaten and the gouged eye wouldn't exist as evidence of a violent death.

He put the scuba tank back through the straps of the BCD vest and attached it tightly.

He took a couple of deep breaths for good luck, then dropped the regulator. It fell across the dead man's shoulder. The corpse lay on the floor of the cave as if it were taking a nap. Sleeping at the bottom of the sea for the rest of eternity.

Seabrook put his snorkel in his mouth and finned out of the cave. He picked up the spear gun.

He ignored the burning in his wounded right leg and started for the surface.

Chapter 61
Vuelta

Seabrook ascended slowly to the stern of the speedboat above. He noticed that the rungs of a short ladder had been dropped into the water along the port side of the boat. Vuelta obviously was expecting the cartel diver to surface by the ladder.

Seabrook surfaced at the stern, just behind the propellers and outboard engines. He quietly exhaled and breathed freely. He carefully climbed up onto the mounting bracket supporting five outboard engines. He took the snorkel out of his mouth and the mask off his face. He set them gently on the mounting bracket. Pain shot through his wounded leg as he got into a crouch position. He peeked over the transom.

He saw Vuelta sitting in the cockpit looking at his watch. The cartel man was holding the MAC-10 submachine gun in his right hand. He was too far away for a good shot.

Seabrook crouched down below the transom, spear gun in his right hand.

"We got the money!" he yelled. "Need your help!"

He counted: *one thousand one, one thousand two, one thousand three, one thousand four, one thousand five.*

Seabrook peeked over the transom again. He saw Vuelta standing at the top of the ladder. The man was in range but presenting only his side. He still held the MAC-10.

Seabrook stood up with the spear gun, ready to shoot.

Vuelta turned to look. His face tightened when he saw the spear gun.

Seabrook aimed dead center and pulled the trigger.

He immediately dived into the sea, on the side of the boat with the ladder. He held the spear gun tightly in both hands. He saw the spear hit Vuelta in the middle of his stomach and the nylon rope unloop and straighten between them. Underwater, Seabrook plunged downward with his full weight and momentum, yanking the spear line down with him. Finning as hard as he could, he swam under the speedboat.

Without a mask, everything was fuzzy blue. He could hear the buzzing fire of the MAC-10 while he swam under the hull. He kept holding the spear gun tightly in his hands, and felt the nylon rope grow increasingly taut. Vuelta was jerking like a big fish at the other end.

He felt a rich satisfaction in this. He squeezed the spear gun tightly against his chest and swam even deeper under the speedboat, kicking his fins as hard as he could, trying to drag the son of a bitch overboard.

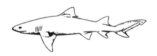

On board the cigarette speedboat, Vuelta spit profanities and emptied the magazine of the MAC-10 into the water. The spear had impaled him clean through the stomach. The point stuck out his lower back. He suddenly couldn't feel his legs, and his knees started to buckle.

The taut nylon rope yanked with great force and jerked him against the gunwale. The latch on the spear opened like the barb of a big hook against his lower back. He leaned forward for support on the fiberglass. *His legs wouldn't work! The scientist had broken his fucking spine!*

The downward pull of the rope was overwhelming and cranked his whole body as if he were a human fulcrum.

Vuelta dropped the MAC-10 overboard and grabbed the spear with both hands, straining for his life. Blood soaked the front of his shirt.

Feet over head, the man flipped into the sea.

Seabrook felt the tension on the nylon rope ease off. He turned towards the surface and finned a little ways upward. He saw the blurry image of Vuelta floundering underwater. He kept his distance to let the man wear himself out.

He swam to the stern and climbed slowly back onto the mounting bracket of the outboard engines. His wounded leg was killing him. He climbed over the transom into the boat. He still had the spear gun in his hand. The line from it disappeared into the water and down to the butt end of the spear stuck through Vuelta's torso.

The cartel man was underwater and no longer moving. Seabrook stood next to the ladder and pulled in the nylon rope. The man was surprisingly heavy, and he didn't seem to be struggling. Then Vuelta emerged at the surface. He was unconscious or dead. His belly and midsection touched air, but the rest of his body—shoulders, face, and legs—drooped underwater. The spear jutted up from his midsection into the air like a harpoon in a whale's back.

Seabrook cursed. The man had died too quickly. He had wanted to question Vuelta. *Where was Aja? Was she still alive?*

Now he couldn't ask the questions. But at least Vuelta couldn't give the order to kill Aja any longer.

A sportfishing boat cruised in the distance, and Seabrook watched it go for a minute. Thinking of his next move.

He had to get rid of the body. He tied the spear's nylon rope to a cleat so Vuelta wouldn't sink. Then he took a mooring line and jumped into the sea. He tied the thick line around Vuelta's chest, under the armpits.

He climbed up the ladder. Then he unwrapped the spear's nylon line, freeing the cleat for the mooring line. With both hands, he pulled Vuelta up by the mooring line and secured the line.

The body hung halfway out of the waves, back against the side of the boat, head lolling forward.

Seabrook pulled the mooring line in again, and raised the corpse higher out of the waves. He cleated the line off once more. Now he could reach the corpse with his hands.

He looked around and made sure there was no boat traffic on the horizon. Not a living soul in sight.

He bent over the gunwale and worked his hands under the wet armpits and underhooked the body. Leaning back and straightening up, he pulled the corpse into the boat. He set Vuelta's dripping body on the deck, resting on its back. The spear jutted grotesquely up from its stomach. The legs were twisted in an unnatural way. Seawater pooled around the body.

A hazy, hallucinatory quality came over Seabrook. His body felt hot, as if he might be getting sick or sunstroke. *I'm probably just dehydrated.*

He looked at the wound in his leg. It wouldn't surprise him if it was already infected. Part of him couldn't believe what he was doing and what he had come through.

Listlessly, he raised anchor and started the engines.

He drove the cartel's cigarette speedboat out into very deep water. He didn't gun the engines. He didn't want to go fast, because he'd never done it before. He wasn't sure if there was a trick to controlling the cigarette boat at high speed. He plodded along at a moderate cruising speed.

He drove until Turtle Rocks disappeared. If he looked towards North Bimini, he could just make out a thin wisp of land. In the middle of nowhere, he throttled down and put the engines in neutral. The vessel started to drift.

Waves lifted and dropped the boat. The position of the sun told him it was late morning. The deep blue waters of the Gulf Stream glittered, and he could see shafts of sunlight piercing into the darker blue depths.

He thought he was close to where he'd thrown the ring of keys and the gun overboard a week earlier. He looked around and was struck by the immense silence and emptiness of the wilderness. Buffeting wind and endless waves in every direction.

He placed Vuelta's corpse over the gunwale. The head hung down towards the water, the lower back rested on the side of the boat, and the legs dangled in the boat. The spear was still jutting up from the stomach, appalling and bloody in the sunlight. He placed the spear gun and line across the waist.

Next, he took the stern anchor from a compartment adjoining the transom. He cut the mooring line that secured the chain of the anchor to the boat. He left five feet of rope above the chain and tied it to Vuelta's ankles. The heavy anchor and chain clanked as he set them on the gunwale.

Seabrook took a minute to make sure everything was tied right. Then he pushed it all overboard. The spear gun and line went into the sea with the impaled body and anchor.

After the splash, he looked down into the ocean. Underwater, the anchor pulled the corpse towards oblivion. Pale hands fluttered and the arms reached upward, streaming tiny bubbles—a final lament to the

world. *Please pick me up. Please remove me from my earthly suffering.*
Almost like a child to a godlike adult.

The body merged into the dark blue.

Then vanished forever.

Chapter 62
Out of the Sky

Three hours earlier, Aja was sleeping soundly on the SS *Sapona's* concrete bow. At dawn sunlight spread in the upper atmosphere, and the brightening sky woke her. Soon the sun began to rise, a fiery orb floating up from the sea.

She stood up and walked, gingerly on her bad foot, to the prow of the wreck. She scanned the ocean in all directions. In the pale morning light, she could see a sportfishing yacht moving in the distance. On the horizon it looked small, like a toy boat heading for the Bimini islands. She glanced at the sea below. No trace of Razormouth or any other big fish.

She sat down and carefully unbandaged her foot. She inspected the small stubs where her toes used to be. They looked clean, and she could see the little white bones in the center of each vestigial toe. She tore off another section of her T-shirt and wrapped her foot tight.

She stood up again and watched over the prow for boaters. No luck. Just empty sea in every direction. On the bright side of things, it looked like it was going to be a beautiful day. Maybe day trippers would come to snorkel or dive on the *Sapona* wreck. She would jump off the bow into the sea and swim to them for help.

She lay back down on the concrete and rested. She listened and waited for the sound of a boat.

Seabrook drove the cartel's speedboat back to Turtle Rocks. He cruised along the underwater shelf, riding the oceanic swells rolling toward the rocks, until he spotted the Gorgon Channel. He steered the ship into the channel and motored through to the shallower turquoise waters of the Great Bahama Bank.

He was going to search for Aja. If his hunch was right, and she had escaped the cartel by fleeing into the ocean from south Bimini, she would likely hide somewhere they both knew well. Where would she go?

She was an excellent swimmer and had been on the varsity team in college, so she could have gone pretty far overnight. Turtle Rocks and the *Sapona* seemed like long shots. His best guess was Round Rock or somewhere along the shoreline of South Bimini.

He planned to cruise along the places where she might be hiding, go really slow, and call out to her. If he couldn't find her at Round Rock or South Bimini's shoreline, he would circle the entire island group. He would drive slowly up North Bimini, around the uninhabited northern tip, check Bonefish Hole, the entrance to the mangroves, and circle all the way out to the *Sapona*. An odd thought popped into his mind: *I might even find the Sea Cherubs.*

He almost set out for Round Rock but had a sudden contrary feeling. On impulse, he decided to check the *Sapona* first. Since the wreck was fairly close, it would be the smarter move.

He steered the cigarette speedboat in a northeasterly direction. The sea glowed aquamarine and seemed to become more luminous as the sun moved closer to its noon position directly above. He hit the gas, and the speedboat lunged over the waves.

The *Sapona* slowly emerged up ahead. Minutes later he slowed the vessel and cruised slowly up to the port stern of the wreck.

"Aja!" he yelled. She could be hiding inside the wreck or maybe on the upper deck.

"Aja!" he called again. He motored slowly along the *Sapona*'s port side.

The vessel stood before him, empty and ragged, like a bombed-out warehouse.

"Aja!" he yelled, trying hard to be louder than the five outboard engines.

He idled forward along the main cargo hold of the wreck.

"Aja!" he yelled again. He was almost up to the bow, the place where tourists liked to jump thirty-five feet down into the sea. He killed the engines.

Now it was quiet except for the sea splashing and rinsing quietly along the *Sapona*'s great support beams.

"Aja!" he yelled as loudly as he could.

"Seabrook!" Aja cried from above.

He looked up and saw Aja standing on the bow of the wreck.

"Seabrook!" She waved.

"Aja!" he yelled with joy in his voice.

She jumped.

Aja dropped out of the sky and back into his life.

The Caribbean Sea caught her in its wet embrace. She swam up to the speedboat, and Seabrook helped her aboard. They hugged and kissed, and their faces were wet with tears of disbelief and the sea.

They were happier, more relieved, and more in love than they'd ever been in their lives.

Chapter 63
On the White Rock

Seabrook gave Aja the jug of fresh water he'd brought that morning. She drank, tipping the jug to her mouth several times. They briefly looked at each other's wounds and decided that they were not immediately life-threatening. They didn't want to talk about their experiences yet—that they were both alive was enough, and there wasn't time for a proper talk. More pressing than catching up or getting medical attention was where to abandon the cartel's speedboat. They didn't want to be caught with it, and they didn't want to be caught by the cartel again. Where should they go? And where should they ditch the speedboat?

They briefly considered crossing the Florida Straits and heading to Miami, where it would be much easier to hide from the cartel, but the gas tank indicated a quarter tank.

After a brief discussion, they decided to go north, around the headland on the northern tip of the island. That part of the North Bimini was uninhabited, and there was a good chance that they could abandon the vessel without being observed by anyone. Then they could walk down the empty beaches to Bailey Town.

Seabrook raced across the Great Bahama Bank. As they drove near the vicinity of the long line, he wondered whether he'd caught any sharks with the human bait. He was tempted to veer near the line for a quick look, but he didn't. They had to get away from the cartel boat as fast as possible.

They drove past Bonefish Hole, the entranceway into the mangroves that formed a protective barrier that shielded the lagoon from the open ocean.

A little farther north, they rounded the headland and started south down the western shoreline. The deep blue water of the Gulf Stream opened and stretched to the right. They left the shallow Great Bahama Bank and were now hitting rougher waves.

Up ahead on the left, a massive white rock stood half submerged in the surf along an empty beach. It caught their attention because it looked as if something was sitting on it. Maybe driftwood? Or sargassum weed had piled up?

Then there was movement. As they got closer, they realized that children were lying on the rock like seals sunning themselves: two young Bahamian boys.

At the sound of the approaching boat, one of them sat up and pulled at the other. They seemed panicked. They stepped off the rock into the sea and started wading, in the thigh-deep waves for shore.

"It's Myron and Mookie!" Aja shouted.

Seabrook drove the speedboat closer in to shore, and Aja took the wheel. He jumped into the water and swam towards land.

The two boys were heading for the woods, staggering and stumbling. Myron was pulling Mookie by the hand, but his little brother fell twice.

Seabrook ran up to them, limping on his bad right leg.

The boys finally recognized him and suddenly sat down. Gaunt, exhausted, and dehydrated.

Seabrook picked them up, one in each arm, and they hugged him. He carried them down to the water's edge. He set Myron gently in the sand.

"Just wait here," Seabrook said. Myron nodded.

Seabrook swam out with Mookie first, and Aja helped pull the boy into the boat. Then he brought Myron out to the speedboat. After Myron was safely aboard, Seabrook climbed into the boat.

Aja gave him the wheel and began doctoring the boys. She gave fresh water to Mookie first, then to Myron. She made sure they drank in small sips so they wouldn't shock their systems.

They were in dangerously bad shape, especially Mookie. He was delirious.

Aja told Seabrook they needed to take the boys to the medical clinic straight away. They would have to risk being seen. He immediately drove the vessel down to the ocean side of Alice Town.

She took the boys onto the beach closest to the medical clinic. Limping on her eel-bitten foot, she carried Mookie. It felt as if he weighed no more than forty pounds. Myron walked next to her, carrying the jug and taking sips. They walked up the dune towards town.

Seabrook drove the speedboat out two hundred yards from the white sand. He killed the engines. He put on his mask, snorkel, and fins.

He dived into the sea, ditching the boat, and swam to shore.

Part Three

"So now you may call me a monster, if you wish. A Scylla housed in the caves of the Tuscan sea. I too, as I had to, have taken hold of your heart."—Euripides

Chapter 64
Lazaro Dores, Part One

Two years earlier, Concha Dores's husband and business partner in the cocaine empire, had become very sick. Lazaro Dores had worked with Concha from the very beginning, starting back in the Colombia days. Together, over two decades, they built the Dores Cartel into a billion-dollar juggernaut.

Lazaro's illness was severe, and he needed medical help badly. He was pissing blood, and the pain in his stomach and chest had brought him to his knees. That is when he met a doctor who changed his outlook on life. He felt safe going to Mercy Hospital in Miami, because he hadn't been shot or wounded during the commission of a crime. Therefore, whatever was wrong with him could be treated as a normal civilian matter. Nobody would need to notify the police.

The doctor surprised him with his boldness. The man walked into the examination room and seemed to know exactly who Lazaro was. Yet he was not scared of him and delivered bad news without fear.

The doctor wore a white lab coat, had thin white hair combed left to right, and had a pink face. His appearance was truly remarkable and unnerved Lazaro. The squint of his eyes, the shape of his head, his high forehead, and the line of his mouth made him look almost exactly like Pope John Paul II.

Lazaro immediately wondered if the doctor could use his X-ray machine and ultrasound machine to see into his soul, like he imagined the Pope might be able to do with just his eyes.

The holy man doctor sternly warned him, "Mr. Dores, before we proceed with your diagnosis, I need to be absolutely straight with you." He paused and stared into Lazaro's eyes.

"It is clear you've been poisoning yourself a long time. And unless you stop immediately, you will die soon. That is a *fact*," the doctor said. He cleared his throat and continued, "If you don't stop . . . drinking and using drugs . . . I won't accept you as a patient. I don't care how much money you can pay. I have too many patients already and don't have time to waste on people who are going to die soon. I only accept patients who want to live and follow instructions to the letter. Is that clear?"

Lazaro nodded yes. He couldn't believe doctors were allowed to talk like this. The guy had incredible balls—Lazaro had killed men for less. Still, he respected the man's directness and strength.

"If you won't follow instructions, we have nothing more to discuss and you need to leave this room now and never come back."

"I'm still here."

"Do you want to live or die?"

"Live."

"So you will stop the alcohol and cocaine?"

"Yes."

Then the doctor showed him the ultra sound images. Lazaro had gall stones and kidney stones too.

He was initially stunned. The gall stones probably were not a problem, but the kidney stones had to be removed. He was treated with a new procedure that the doctor called a lithotripsy, which broke up his kidney stones with shock waves so the broken stones could pass in his urine.

He felt much better after the lithotripsy, but while he was in the hospital, the doctors gave him the first physical examination he'd had in many years. His examination included extensive blood panel work to check how well his organs were functioning. That is how he discovered his insides were rotten. They did more tests. He had severe liver and kidney damage. He was confused by this and found it hard to believe.

If he looked in a mirror, he could see that he was still handsome, tan, and strong. But that was only his outside. How could he still look good but be nearly dead inside? He asked the doctor this very question.

"Sometimes the outer appearance is the last thing to go. Have you ever been to a funeral with an open casket, and the embalmed corpse looked pretty good?"

"Yes, I have seen that once. A beautiful young woman," Lazaro said, remembering a sad moment years ago.

"Well, you have been embalming yourself. Turning yourself into a corpse from the inside out. You must have good genes, or you wouldn't have lasted this long." Then the doctor smiled and said the human body sometimes had an amazing ability to heal itself, that Lazaro might have a chance if he truly quit everything. He mentioned a drug-addiction treatment program that also might help. Lazaro waved off the suggestion.

The diagnosis actually had been unsurprising. You can't drink oceans of Chivas Regal and snort or smoke mountains of high-grade cocaine every day for decades without getting sick. Even the King of Cocaine knew this.

The problem was that he had lived every day and every night as if it were his last. He had always expected to be assassinated, that his life would end in mere days, maybe weeks at most. He had more enemies than he could count. But nobody had killed him, so the joke was on him. Now the doctor told him he was going to die unless he stopped his partying immediately.

Nonetheless, just eight hours later, Lazaro disregarded the doctor's stern warning and relapsed into the only life he'd ever really known. He just couldn't help himself.

But the doctor's warning did cause him to dramatically change his life before it was too late. He divorced his wife and longtime business partner, Concha Dores, Miami's Queen of Cocaine. He also fell in love with a beautiful young woman who worked at his nightclub. She was eighteen, pure and innocent, raised in Wyoming far from the drug world. She represented everything that his life had been missing.

It was a very bold move on his part. At first, he thought Concha would get viciously jealous and try to kill him and his fiancée—but after several days of heinous insults and threats (relayed by surrogates), she finally agreed to the divorce. She said that a divorce didn't matter, that he should get the fuck out of her life. This was a great surprise. His lawyer had been communicating with her lawyer while he was secretly out of harm's way on vacation in Costa Rica with his new wife. He felt immense relief that the divorce wasn't going to start a small war.

Concha's personality had changed so much that he could no longer predict what she would do anymore. And their marriage had become a total sham. They were never together—one was in Colombia while the other was in Miami, or vice versa. And Concha had many young lovers. The only thing that kept them connected was their only living son, Salvatore, who'd had his ears cut off by the Medellín Cartel, and Salvatore's young daughter, whom Concha doted on. They had raised three other boys, but they had all been murdered in the drug war while still young children. Salvatore and his five-year-old daughter were the only good that had survived from his life with Concha.

Concha had changed dramatically over time—become warped and degraded in bizarre and monstrous ways—so much so, that during their last years together, it was hard to believe that they had been married so long. She had always been cunning and ruthless, but after all the years of cocaine, her mind seemed to work differently, and not for the better. In the old days she had been pretty, in a rough way, and she knew how to laugh. They had built an empire together. They had lived through many great and wild times. But that person no longer existed.

Instead, he sometimes saw something etched in her face and posture—especially when he was high—that frightened him deeply. Her body hunched forward a little bit, and she walked differently, as if her legs had grown uneven. But her face had changed the most. This alarmed him so much that he secretly talked to a doctor in Colombia about it. He wondered whether she'd had a stroke. The doctor said it was most likely just the normal aging process and too much hard living.

Then he talked to a learned priest, and the man used big words. He said, "For the first half of life, people have the countenance that God has bestowed upon them." Then he added, "For the second half of life, people develop the lineaments, spiritually and physically, that they have earned with their conduct." The priest said it was a tricky art to interpret people's physiognomies, but that people's faces did reveal their inner natures to an experienced and educated eye. A small number of people could read others naturally because they had been born with the knack for it, but most misread their fellow man. He wouldn't comment any further when asked for his evaluation of Concha's altered appearance. But he seemed unnerved by the question, and absentmindedly touched the crucifix on his necklace.

But there was no secret about it. Lazaro knew her best and could attest to the changes: no sparkle in her eyes anymore, or real laughter in her throat, or true smile on her lips. Instead, her face was now always puffy and bloated, and her heavy make-up made her look disgusting—like a fat whore grandmother still turning tricks.

The changes went even deeper than that: her laugh had turned hollow and spiteful, and sounded like a cross between a bark and a cough. But her eyes were the worst. The pupils were always unnaturally dilated from drugs, and flickered rapidly as if tiny tremors shook the eyes inside. If she looked at you without sunglasses, you always wanted to look away. They used to be normal!

The Concha he had known in the old days had been replaced or burned up. What remained was something almost inhuman; a shadow now lived inside her, and it looked at him through her twitching eyes and smiled with secret knowledge—reminding him, every now and then, with a terrifying little grin that they had been partners in unspeakable crimes, that they were bonded together in this life, and maybe for all eternity, by their ugly history.

As if the divorce papers didn't matter.

As if she owned him somehow.

He saw the shadow most clearly in the strange, gleeful expression that came over her face when she was watching Pelon, the Hairless One, cut people apart in their chophouses.

Lazaro had killed plenty of people himself and was not squeamish or cowardly, but he did not like doing it anymore. For some reason, it increasingly made him feel sick to torture people, so he avoided it. He wondered if he was going soft. And, as he'd grown older, some of the people he'd killed had started coming back and haunting him, especially the ones that had been religious. For the first time in his life, he sometimes saw ghosts.

But Concha got excited and horny when she killed. It was no longer just business to her. It was the highlight of her existence.

More and more, she loved to watch people scream as they were cut to pieces. When the victims were innocent and good, such as small children, she loved it even more. Especially if they were beautiful or gentle toddlers. She studied their tear-streaked faces and talked to them— telling them lies, such as their parents didn't love them and had asked for them to be killed, or that they were going to suffer in hell for eternity —even as she had them chopped apart. Sometimes, with a blowtorch in hand, she demanded that they say they hated their mother and father. And that they hated God too.

When they said those words, her terrible laugh would fill the room.

This, followed by cocaine cigarettes and naked boys, was all that made her happy anymore.

Chapter 65
Lazaro Dores, Part Two

Now, two years later, his holy man doctor told him he was actually dying of stage-four liver cancer and renal failure. The man also made good on his promise and said he would no longer accept Lazaro as a patient. Then he referred him to another doctor. The damned *gringo* seemed too smug and too comfortable rejecting him.

Lazaro thought briefly about stabbing him in the neck with his pen for failing him—the man should have done a better job convincing him to change his ways—but decided against it. The doctor's resemblance to Pope John Paul II saved him. Besides, Lazaro needed to plan his last days, not get arrested.

He was a very rich man, but his money couldn't save him. He was only forty-nine years old, had quit the cartel, and had invested in legitimate businesses where he could launder his money: a nightclub, a restaurant, and even a flower shop. He had genuinely begun to change his life and become an honest businessman. But he had been partying since he was a teenager, and that was the one thing he couldn't change. His addiction, as it turned out, was killing him. According to the doctor, he was basically already dead. He would last no more than three months, and much less, if he didn't come in for kidney dialysis three times a week.

Lazaro laughed bitterly as he thought about it. He'd been nearly killed so many times while trafficking drugs—shot, burned, poisoned, stabbed, in plane crashes, in car crashes, hit on the head with a baseball bat, strangled, and car-bombed—it was crazy to believe that he was going to die because of fucking whiskey and cocaine. What a pussy way to go.

Still, it was all the more reason he needed to do something for his young wife. He had to leave something behind for her and their unborn child.

They were the only things precious to him anymore: his sun and moon. They were his legacy. They had nothing to do with his violent, ugly past.

In his mind he had drawn a line, an impassable boundary, between his old life and his new life. Sometimes he liked to deny his old life and pretend he'd always been a legitimate businessman, a good man, who'd made his fortune honestly. A man that helped his community and his loved ones. But now his life was about to end, and he'd barely tasted its true sweetness. He suspected his impending death was a kind of judgment against him—and he begrudgingly accepted it as penance. Who was he to complain? If God had truly watched his every deed, he was getting off lightly. With his remaining hours and days, if he couldn't live a good life, at least he could make some gestures and move in that direction.

He wanted to help his son, Salvatore, quit the business and live a better life. He knew that Salvatore or someone close to him had stolen fifty million of the cartel's money and that Concha had sent men to find him. She would kill her own son over money—this he knew for certain. Lazaro was willing to pay the fifty million to get his son out of trouble, but he wanted to talk to him first. To set him as straight as possible, tell him that he loved him one last time, and say goodbye.

His wife and children were his last and only chance to do something good in the world and maybe earn a tiny piece of redemption before he died and faced God.

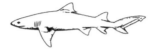

Lazaro talked to an old friend and associate in Miami, the lead smuggler for the Dores Cartel, about delivering fifty million to Concha in exchange for Salvatore's life. He asked him to tell Concha immediately so she didn't kill Salvatore before he had a chance to pay the debt. Hours later, the man contacted him and reported that the exchange could be made the following weekend in the Bahamas. His old friend told him that Salvatore was still alive and Concha had agreed to the deal. The Dores Cartel bosses were planning a celebratory banquet because they'd made more than half a billion dollars in one month—a new record for them. The American consumers couldn't get enough cocaine, and business was skyrocketing.

Lazaro had hosted these banquets many times. Concha handed out bonuses and gifts to her best people. The gifts were usually top-of-the-line luxury cars or sports cars like Lamborghinis. One year they were Aston Martins with trunks full of cash. She'd give the men the keys at dinner, and they'd find the cars parked in front of their house when they returned home. The best food and wine were flown in from around the world and elite chefs prepared the meals. No expense was too much. Usually family and children attended as well. It was normally a great party and usually without any of the ugly side of the business.

The exact location of the banquet was always kept secret until the last possible moment so the authorities and other enemies couldn't crash the party. All Lazaro knew was that the event would be held on one of the islands near Florida. He would receive a call Thursday morning and be told where to go. The banquet was being held that same day. He was assured that the island would have a landing strip long enough for a small private plane. He had to be ready to fly with just a few hours' notice.

Lazaro made the necessary preparations and arrangements. He called his pilot, a man he'd used for such work many times over the years. He told him to fuel the plane and be on standby, ready to go all day, on Thursday.

Early Thursday morning, he loaded fifty million dollars in cash into four large Samsonite cases. He completely depleted his cash reserves. Forty million had been hidden behind a false wall in his closet, and ten million had come out of a secret compartment in the ceiling of his garage. If Salvatore had stolen more than that, he couldn't have bailed him out. It seemed a lucky coincidence that the missing money was exactly equal to his hidden cash reserves.

He and his bodyguard took the suitcases to the private landing strip and loaded them onto the single-engine plane: a Cessna 182. His bodyguard stayed with the money on the plane.

Lazaro drove back to his Miami home by himself.

Chapter 66
The Call

Lazaro could tell that he was dying by how awful he felt. Exhaustion was crushing him. His skin had turned a grayish green, and he'd lost twenty pounds. His liver cancer had metastasized, and all of his organs were shot. Sometimes he just wanted to lie down and close his eyes for good. He toyed with the idea of not seeing the doctors anymore and skipping dialysis treatments—but he'd been warned that doing so would cut his remaining days even shorter. The doctors originally had told him that he had three months to live. Ten weeks had already passed. The end was very near.

He was relieved and glad that his young wife had gone to stay with her family in Wyoming. He didn't want her to see him this way. She'd been gone a week. Her family didn't approve of their marriage, and whenever she visited them, after she called to let him know that she'd arrived safely, she usually didn't call again until she was coming home. He was more than twice her age, and her parents had refused to attend the wedding.

She was coming back home in two days, and he had a lot to tell her. She was going to be shocked by how ugly he'd suddenly become.

She didn't know that he was dying. He needed to go over the will with her and explain that he had deposited a million dollars into their joint bank account. He'd met with lawyers and transferred all of his assets into her name—the houses, the businesses, the cars. Everything was hers. He'd even made his own funeral arrangements.

He wished he had enough time to see a dentist. He'd chipped the ridge of a lower-right molar, so now food got stuck between his back two teeth every time he ate meat. He had to dig it out with a toothpick or dental floss after every meal. Maybe he would see a dentist after he got back home with Salvatore.

The phone rang. He picked up the receiver and pressed it to his ear.

He was to fly to Sawfish Cay, a small privately owned island near the Bimini islands.

Chapter 67
Sawfish Cay

"It well behooves him take a lengthy spoon who eats with devils."
—Geoffrey Chaucer

Armed cartel men greeted Lazaro on the tarmac of the small landing strip of Sawfish Cay. They took the suitcases of cash off the plane and loaded them into the back of a jeep.

Lazaro didn't mind. He'd expected Concha would want the money before releasing Salvatore.

His bodyguard and pilot stayed with the Cessna. Lazaro expected to be returning to Miami with his son in a matter of hours. He would eat, pay his respects, then leave before the sun went down.

He rode with the cartel men to the clubhouse—he didn't know any of them. The Dores Cartel had rented the Sawfish Cay Yacht Club and half a dozen luxury beachfront homes exclusively for two days. The main banquet was being held in the club's dining room on a veranda overlooking the sea. Some people brought their families, and others brought their mistresses. Everyone looked sunburnt from fishing and sitting on the beaches too long. He walked out among the tables, and several old friends greeted him.

Lazaro recognized most of the senior cartel members, but there were some new young faces. Most were friendly towards him but couldn't hide their surprise at how horrible he looked.

"I have liver cancer," he said matter-of-factly. "But I'm here for one last party!"

He took a seat.

Before he could get comfortable, Concha Dores walked out onto the terrace. She looked beaten up. Her arm was in a sling, and she had a bandage under her shirt. Her neck was bruised.

She was dressed in black slacks, a black blouse, and her favorite seashell necklace. Her face was puffy and covered in a thick mask of makeup. He could tell that she'd already been smoking cocaine cigarettes. Saliva moistened the lipsticked corners of her mouth.

"Lazaro," she called in a deep, smoky voice. "Come sit here." She pointed to a table next to the head table where she was going to sit. "You are the guest of honor."

"Where is Salvatore?" he asked.

"He'll be coming out after we count the money. He's in the guesthouse with the whores."

She studied him and smiled strangely. "You are dying, aren't you?"

"I have cancer. What happened to you?"

"A woman I will kill hooked me with a fishing gaff," Concha said. Her smile disappeared.

These banquets always started in the midafternoon, and the food never stopped coming. Waiters brought out Scottish smoked salmon, Beluga caviar, bottles of Dom Pérignon, and foie gras eggs Benedict as the tables began to fill up.

Concha sent two very young and very beautiful prostitutes to sit with Lazaro.

One of them said, "We are a gift from Concha." She pulled her bikini top down and showed him her breasts. The other girl put her hand on his leg.

"Not today."

"*Whenever* and *whatever* you want . . . *we are yours.*" She covered her breasts.

Lazaro didn't feel good and didn't want sex. He barely wanted to eat. The prostitutes fussed over him and tried to feed him. He skipped the appetizers and bleakly wondered if Concha was going to kill him. Something didn't feel right. He knew it was a great risk coming to the banquet, but it was worth it if he could save Salvatore.

Soon all the tables were full, and Concha started awarding car keys to the best earners. She called out their names, and each man came forward to get the keys to the new Rolls-Royce Corniche parked in the driveway of his mansion back in Miami. People were already drunk and high. They cheered like mad for each name called.

The prostitutes snorted lines of cocaine off the table.

"Vuelta!" Concha called. The crowd started to applaud, but the man did not stand up. She called the name twice more. Still the man did not come forward. The crowd grew restless. Then Pelon, the Hairless One, went up to her and said something.

Concha grew visibly enraged. Something had happened. Lazaro overheard the next table saying that Vuelta was missing and so was the *gringo* diver that worked for the cartel in Miami. They hadn't come back from a job.

Concha whispered orders to Pelon. The bald man nodded.

The main dishes started coming out: roast rack of lamb with mint sauce, spicy Argentinian chorizo, grilled sweetbreads, locally caught red snapper, and beef fillet prepared with chimichurri marinade. Like a traditional Argentinian *assado*.

A waiter brought him a plate and told him the chorizo had been made specially by the chefs. Lazaro politely tasted a little of everything. The prostitutes insisted on feeding him. They cut little morsels for him to eat, but he could finish nothing.

He felt Concha watching him eat and began to wonder whether she was trying to poison him. She smiled as he chewed a piece of chorizo. He put the fork down and sipped some water. *Damn!* A piece of meat had lodged in the crack between his molars. He poked at it with his tongue.

The way Concha was watching him made everything clear. She was going to kill him for sure. He knew that look on her face. She was on the hunt. That was okay. He knew the risks in coming here and had prepared for this possibility. His young pregnant wife was set up for life. She was safe in Wyoming. That was an absolute good. Also, he'd paid the money for Salvatore. His son would be free. If accomplishing these things cost him his life, so be it.

He pushed his plate forward. He was done. He told the pretty prostitutes to leave him.

"Where is Salvatore?" he called to Concha.

"He's coming now," she said. The Queen of Cocaine stood up and walked over to his table. Her legs seemed more uneven than ever. She shuffled and hunched forward. A tiny bit of drool came out of one corner of her mouth—too much cocaine. A *sicario* he didn't recognize walked next to her with a MAC-11 machine gun. A bad sign.

A waiter brought a covered platter across the room and placed it on the table in front of Lazaro.

"Here is Salvatore! Here is your young wife! And here is your unborn baby! You have had them for dinner!" Concha said.

She lifted the cover off the platter. The heads and hands of Lazaro's loved ones were arranged in a row on a bed of greens.

Lazaro's mind spun. He stood up and fell over onto the ground, stunned. As if he'd been struck by lightning. The piece of meat stuck in his teeth made him want to vomit. He wretched but nothing would come out. He couldn't breathe for a few seconds and nearly blacked out.

As he lay on the veranda, Concha walked over and looked down at him. In that instant, he knew Concha's secret. There had never been any missing money. Nobody knew the truth but her and maybe the accountant. The evil bitch had pushed the lie, blamed Salvatore, and sent her killers to the Bahamas to get it back because she knew it would draw him out. She knew that Lazaro had fifty million in cash. She knew he would try to save his boy. Concha had set up her own son and had him tortured to death: Salvatore, the Earless Man.

She had done everything just for this moment: to rip out Lazaro's heart, to take everything from him, to hurt him as deeply as possible. This was not about business at all.

"Do you really think you could ever leave me?" Concha hissed.

Her eyes flickered, and Lazaro could see the shadow smiling inside her.

"We are bonded together for eternity," Concha said. She turned to her *sicario*. "Don't let him die. I want him to live as long as possible. Take him to his plane and send him home."

Chapter 68
Bimini Medical Clinic

Fortunately, business was slow. The clinic was nearly empty when Seabrook, Aja, and the boys walked in. One elderly man had just finished his appointment and slowly teetered out as they went in. The secretary at the front desk took Myron and Mookie straight back into one of the examination rooms. Seabrook and Aja sat waiting for their turn to see the doctor.

The doctor and nurse put Mookie in a hospital bed and hooked him up to an IV for intravenous rehydration. Myron sat in the next bed drinking Gatorade and eating cherry-flavored Jell-O with a plastic spoon.

The secretary called the Bimini Police Station at Seabrook's urging and reported the safe recovery of the missing boys.

The medical clinic was a small building in Alice Town made of cinder block walls painted white on the inside and outside. Panoramic photos of beaches and tropical birds decorated the walls. In one corner was a play area for children with a box full of toys. Steel airport chairs with padded vinyl cushions formed two seating areas: one for families with children and another for adults only.

The medical care was very good. The Bahamian doctor took Aja next. He unwrapped her makeshift bandages and examined the stubs of her toes. He cleaned her wounds with iodine and asked what had happened. She told him about Lennie, the moray eel.

"These will not heal properly if the bones protrude above the flesh," the doctor said. "I need to trim the bone."

"Okay," Aja said.

The doctor injected a numbing solution near her wounds. Blinding pain flared briefly in her foot, then she felt nothing. He pulled the flesh down on each toe stub and cut the little bones flush with her skin. Then he pulled the flesh back up over the bones and sutured the skin closed. He cleaned the wounds with saline, applied antiseptic, and bandaged them. He told her she would feel phantom pain. Her toes would hurt, even though they were gone.

Next the doctor examined Seabrook's leg. It was caked in blood, and the gash looked deep and ugly. He carefully bathed and opened the laceration. The doctor asked how he'd gotten injured. Seabrook said he'd fallen through one of the holes on the *Sapona*'s deck and scraped the sharp edge of the wreck in the fall.

"This is deep," the doctor said. "Are you up to date with your tetanus shots?"

"Yes."

The doctor gave him a local anesthetic. The man thoroughly debrided and cleaned the wound. First he stitched the deepest part. He used dissolvable sutures to join the damaged muscle tissue. He stitched the whole length. Then he treated the surface flesh. He closed the opening over the sutured muscle, aligned the sides, and stapled it closed. He wiped the blood away with saline, applied antiseptic, and wrapped the leg in gauze.

He gave them both ibuprofen pills to manage the pain, and he gave Seabrook antibiotic pills. He told them to watch for redness and swelling and follow up with doctors in Miami in a few days for a reevaluation.

Superintendent Poitier stopped by the clinic to talk with Myron and Mookie. The boys told him about their father and about the cartel men who had tried to catch them. They also told him about Seabrook and Aja's rescuing them. He asked them for details about everything.

At the end, the boys wanted to talk with their mother. The clinic allowed Superintendent Poitier to place a call to her in Nassau. The call was put on speaker, and Seabrook and Aja could hear the conversation from their rooms.

Their mother wanted to know how they were, and they wanted to know how she and Carmelita were. When the stories ended, Myron and Mookie asked their mother for permission to stay with Seabrook and Aja until their flight in two days. They were joining their mother and sister in Nassau. She said yes.

"Are you sure that is acceptable?" Poitier said.

Their mother said yes again.

"We waited on the white rock for you," Mookie said.

"I know you did. You are a very good boy."

"Uh-huh," Mookie said softly. "I was afraid."

"You are a very brave little boy."

"Uh-huh," Mookie said.

"Things will get better now. Nobody will hurt us anymore."

"They say that our father is dead," Myron said. "Someone killed him, and we can't go back in our house."

"I know, Myron. We will get a new house. We will make a better life."

"I want that."

"I love you both."

At the end of the call, it was arranged that the boys would remain at the clinic for observation until closing. One of the nurses agreed to drop them afterward at Seabrook and Aja's house.

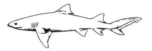

Superintendent Poitier stood in the doorway of the room where Aja and Seabrook were sitting on cots with their bandaged injuries. They were drinking fluids and waiting for the ibuprofen to kick in.

"Is there anywhere safe for us to stay for a couple of days?" Seabrook asked Superintendent Poitier. "It's not safe for us to stay in Bastareaud's rental house. The cartel is looking for the boys, and they may come for us in the middle of the night." Also, Aja had gaffed Concha Dores and Seabrook had killed two of her men, but Seabrook wasn't going to tell the police that.

Poitier nodded. "There is a rental apartment across the street on the second floor. I know the landlord. I don't think it's occupied. Let me check."

He went out to his cruiser and used the radio. When he came back inside the clinic he said, "The landlord did me a favor. You can stay there for a couple of nights. It's on the second floor, and you can see your house and the lagoon from the window. He's going to unlock the door and leave the keys on the kitchen table. I told him I was putting you in witness protection." Poitier smiled. "You are witnesses, aren't you?"

Seabrook nodded. "I guess."

"Tell me how you found the boys," he said suddenly.

Aja described how they'd found the boys on the white rock. Poitier looked at their injuries. "What happened to you two?"

They began to tell the same version of events they'd told the doctor.

"I know what you said to the doctor. And I don't believe it. I think you know a lot more than you're saying. The boys just told me you picked them up in a red cigarette speedboat. Help me understand how *that* happened."

"Can we do this later?" Seabrook said. "Or are we under arrest?"

"Do we need a lawyer?" Aja said. "We can get someone from Miami to come tomorrow."

Superintendent Poitier sighed.

"There is nothing to charge you with. I know you're not the killers," he said. "But I need to know everything if I'm going to catch these people."

"We need to eat something and rest a bit," Seabrook said.

"We will answer your questions tomorrow," Aja said.

Superintendent Poitier looked angry. "Don't leave the island."

Seabrook and Aja went down to the quay, walking slowly, and drove the Whaler back to their dock in Bailey Town.

Chapter 69
The Return

T hey entered the rental house to get food for dinner from the cupboard: boxes of spaghetti and jars of marinara sauce. They were going to make enough to feed Myron and Mookie as well. They hadn't eaten all day, and made peanut butter sandwiches to hold them until supper.

They didn't mind being in the house a short time, but they didn't want to stay there. Seabrook thought about the dark bloodstain on the dock. The grade-school memory of Rudy Defarge's glaring eyes as he limped down the hall swirled into his mind—and the story of him killing his baby brother.

"How fast can you run?"

While in the house, they quickly changed the water in both of the hundred-gallon aquariums in the living room. Afterward, the cone snails in both tanks emerged from the sand, invigorated by the fresh seawater. One of the nonlethal Caribbean snails moved slowly across the rubble of the miniature reef in its tank. One of the deadly Indo-Pacific snails crawled up the glass of its aquarium. Its shell was five inches long and with beautiful markings, like an artfully stirred cup of cappuccino: swirls of dark coffee and steamed milk scalloped into bright pearls. The cone snails hadn't been fed in a couple of days and were hungry. Aja felt too tired to catch silversides and feed them. The snails would have to wait one more day to eat.

They gathered their toiletries and a change of clothes. They locked up the house and took their belongings and the makings for dinner across the street to the safe-house apartment. Then went up the stairs to the landing.

From the second-story balcony walkway and the living room window they had a clear view of their rental house across the street and, over the roof and beyond, one could see the dock and the lagoon.

Aja looked at the rental house for a moment. The bright halide lights of the reef tanks made the kitchen window glow as if someone were inside using the place.

They went inside the apartment. It had two bedrooms. They took the one with the queen-size bed and turned on the air conditioner. The other room had two single beds and would be good for the boys. Seabrook and Aja lay down on the bed for a nap. They were exhausted and quickly fell asleep.

A little after five p.m., one of the nurses at the clinic drove an old Volkswagen to the rental house and dropped Myron and Mookie off. The sound of the car and its door slamming shut made Seabrook get up. Aja was still asleep. He went outside and down the stairs to meet the boys. The nurse waved at him as she drove away.

"Can we see Clara?" Myron said enthusiastically. He'd told the doctor at the clinic about the baby nurse shark, and the conversation had made the boys keen to see her. They wondered if she looked bigger yet.

"Can we feed her?" Mookie said.

"Good idea. I'll bet she is hungry," Seabrook said. He patted his shorts and found the key to the rental house still in his right pocket. They would have to get a piece of mackerel from the freezer inside.

Up in the safe house, Aja woke up with a bad feeling. She got up and walked to the living room window. She saw Seabrook and the boys standing outside looking at the rental house. Then they walked towards it, and Seabrook began to unlock the kitchen door to go inside.

Seabrook and the boys disappeared into the house.

Aja raised her eyes and looked over the roof at the lagoon. She flinched with alarm.

A black cigarette speedboat was parked at their dock.

The cartel was on the property—probably inside the house waiting.

Aja ran down the stairs to a neighbor that lived just next door. She ignored the throbbing pain of her missing toes—at least they were protected inside running shoes. She'd occasionally crossed paths with the neighbor over the summer: a large Bahamian woman who usually wore brightly colored clothes. They'd never spoken to each other but had made eye contact on several occasions and acknowledged each other as good-natured strangers sometimes do.

Aja knocked loudly on her door, and a small dog started barking inside. The door opened and the woman looked surprised.

"Hi, I'm sorry to bother you," Aja said, trying to tamp down the panic she felt. "We are having an emergency! The drug cartel men who killed Bastareaud are in our house right now. Can you please call the police? Tell them the cartel has a speedboat at our dock. They have Myron and Mookie. They are going to kill them."

The woman's eyes widened. "Yes! I will call on the radio." She disappeared into her living room.

"Thank you!" Aja called. "Do you have a gun or any kind of weapon?"

"No. I have nothing like that," the neighbor said from inside her home.

"I'm going to the house!" Aja said.

"May God bless you and keep you!" the Bahamian woman called.

Chapter 70
Conus geographus

Aja ran to the kitchen door of the rental house. The only weapon she had was the knowledge that the police would soon be on their way. She wanted to stall the killers but had to be careful. If they panicked, they might shoot everyone and run. She paused and listened for any sound inside. Voices were talking on the other side of the door. She slowly turned the knob, opened the door, and stepped into the kitchen. A man quickly shut the door behind her and locked it. He pointed a machine gun at her.

A sick feeling flooded her heart. She flashed back to the kill house for an instant—saw the dismembered bodies and the blood, and heard the terrible screams—but then came back to the present. There were four men, and two of them were holding MAC-10 submachine guns. One man was holding Myron and Mookie by their necks, and another *sicario* was pointing his gun at Seabrook. They'd smashed him in the face and made him sit down. Blood was seeping down his cheek from a cut on his head. Their eyes met, and she could tell he was ready to go down fighting.

Pelon, the Hairless One, had his large case with "Jarvis Products" embossed on the side. He opened the case to take his tools out, getting ready to do his horrible work. One man pulled zip ties from his pocket and started to bind Myron's ankles together. Aja swore to herself she would not let herself be bound. She'd rather be shot than dismembered.

Everyone moved slowly and seemed to be waiting for orders. The energy in the room was palpable and menacing. It emanated from the cartel's leader.

In the center of the room stood Concha Dores. Her right arm was hanging in a sling, and her neck was bruised—near the place where Aja had gaffed her shoulder. The woman hardly looked at Aja when she walked into the kitchen.

Instead, the Queen of Cocaine stared at the aquariums full of cone snails—especially at the tank with the deadly venomous Indo-Pacific species. The square boxes of light seemed to have cast a spell on her. She stared at the beautiful shimmering mini reefs and was especially transfixed by a large *Conus geographus* with a strikingly beautiful shell.

The man pointing the submachine gun at Aja pushed her across the room until she stood next to Myron and Mookie. The boys looked at her. Tears filled Mookie's eyes.

Pelon, the Hairless One, looked impatient. "*Empezamos a matar ahora?*" We start killing now?

"You kill nobody until I give the order," Concha said. Then she turned and looked at Seabrook, then at Aja. "What are they?" she said, gesturing to the cone snail crawling up the inside of the glass.

"Sea snails," Aja said.

Concha stared at the beautiful shell. "Give me that one," she said, pointing to the large *Conus geographus* on the glass.

"I'll get it," Seabrook said quickly.

"They are mine," Aja said. "Let me do it."

Concha turned from the aquarium and looked at her captives for a long moment. As if she'd detected something in their voices—why did it matter who took the creature out of the tank? For a heartbeat Seabrook saw Rudy Defarge looking back at him—the saturnine face, the twitching eyes, malefic and watchful. Concha's shoulders hunched as she stepped forward and pointed at Aja with her good arm. "Youuuu ... get it."

The man guarding Aja let her walk across the room to the tank.

She reached into the water. Her arm looked pale under the bright halide lights, and tiny bubbles stuck to her skin. She carefully grasped the big cone snail by the back of its shell. She pulled it gently off the glass, trying not to hurt it.

She wanted the deadly creature to be in perfect condition.

She raised the cone snail out of the water. Salt water dripped off Aja's forearm and the snail in her hand. Concha watched carefully.

One of the *sicarios* said something in Spanish.

"*Es venenoso?*" Concha asked. *Is it poisonous?*

"No. I wouldn't touch it if it was dangerous. It's perfectly harmless. It lives in the sea around here." She held it out, offering it to Concha.

Aja wore her best poker face. Seabrook sat quiet.

Concha studied Aja's face, then her hand, and the careful way she handled the snail. An expression of animal cunning and suspicion wriggled across her features.

"Put it against your face," Concha rasped.

"I'll do it," Seabrook said, sitting up straighter, as if he might spring to his feet. He spoke in as bored a tone as he could muster. "They're from the local area."

"You killed two of my men. You will die last."

Pelon put a blowtorch on the kitchen table. The boys stared at him, their frightened eyes darting from the blowtorch to the shark jaw tattooed around his eye, then back to the torch.

Aja locked eyes with Seabrook and raised the cone snail towards her face. She could see the snail moving its foot and rostrum. It was trying to find a surface to latch onto. The moment seemed to stretch in time.

Then, before Aja could press the snail to her cheek, a child's voice spoke.

"I'll do it," Myron said. "I like to play with the snails. This one is my pet," he lied. He'd never handled the cone snails.

"I want to show her!" Mookie whined, lying as well. "I take care of it too. It sings to me. I know him best. Let me have a turn."

The Sea Cherubs were volunteering despite knowing full well the danger.

"It sings?" Concha said.

"It makes a funny sound," Mookie said. As an eight-year-old boy, he was the smallest and meekest person in the room—her favorite kind of victim. And he already had tears in eyes. The thought of torturing the child excited Concha.

"The boy will do it," she said.

Mookie confidently walked up and took the cone snail from Aja. Before anyone could say anything, he pressed the opening of the shell against his deaf ear.

"It's singing!" He giggled.

Seabrook could feel his heart beating in his chest. Cone snails didn't sting every time they were touched, but their sting was fatal.

Mookie held it to his ear for what seemed an eternity. He smiled as if he was having fun. That seemed to anger Concha.

"Give it to me!" she barked, and snatched the cone snail from Mookie. She pressed it to the side of her ear and made a quizzical expression.

From Seabrook's vantage point, he saw the cone snail's proboscis suddenly extend from the base of the shell. The venomous harpoon fired into her cheek.

"I hear nothi—" Concha's face froze mid-sentence. She suddenly couldn't move or talk.

A small sound like an inner scream escaped her throat.

She abruptly collapsed onto the floor, and the cone snail rolled across the living room. With one hand she pulled her gold-plated .45 from her waistband and spastically waved it around.

Her body shook and stiffened. Her neck and the side of her face started to swell monstrously. The small screaming sound from her throat repeated again and again.

The muscles of her face started to spasm, and her jaw muscles contracted involuntarily so that her mouth opened and closed like a gasping fish.

Then the spasms grew more violent, and her teeth snapped together with terrible force.

She bit off part of her lower lip.

She bit her tongue in half.

Blood dripped from the corner of her mouth. Her eyes widened as if she saw something terrifying yet invisible to everyone else in the room.

Her finger pulled the trigger of her pistol, and the bullet went harmlessly into the sofa.

Gradually she grew more still and seemed to be dying.

The *sicarios* pointed their MAC-10s at Seabrook and Aja.

"*Tenemos que irnos ahora,*" Pelon said. *We need to leave now.*

A police siren started in the distance.

"*Los matamos?!*" one *sicario* said. *Do we kill them?*

"*Ella no dio la orden,*" Pelon said, shaking his head no. *She did not give the order.*

The cartel men immediately went out the sliding glass door in the living room. Seabrook stood up and watched them run down the dock to the cigarette speedboat.

They left Concha on the floor, and Pelon left his case and customized hock cutters and blowtorch on the kitchen table.

Seabrook cut the zip tie from Myron's ankles with kitchen scissors. Then he picked up the cone snail and dropped it back into the tank.

Aja went to Mookie and looked at the side of his head and ear.

"Are you okay?"

"Yes I am," Mookie said.

The police siren grew louder and louder. A few moments later, Superintendent Poitier came into the house with two constables.

"That's Concha Dores," Aja said. She pointed to the body on the floor.

"The rest took off to the dock," Seabrook said. "But look what they left behind." He pointed to the portable hock cutters and blowtorch.

Superintendent Poitier told his men to go down to the dock and warned them to be careful. He said more men were coming in the police patrol boat. He looked at the cutters and said, "I'll bet that is the murder weapon they used on Bastareaud."

Concha suddenly hissed. She was paralyzed but still faintly alive. She looked at them with bulging frog eyes. A piece of her lower lip dangled like a little slug on her chin. Half her tongue lay loose in her open mouth. She moved the arm that held the gun as if she wanted to kill Aja.

Poitier pulled his pistol and shot her in the side of the head.

Chapter 71
Gunfight

The cartel men detoured their cigarette speedboat out of the channel to escape the police patrol boat coming up the channel to intercept them. They ran aground on the flats.

The *sicarios* were stuck like sitting ducks in the shallows. Even though they had only pistols and MAC-10 machine guns, which weren't accurate long-range weapons, they refused to surrender. During the standoff, one of Bimini's constables used a Winchester sniper rifle to pick off cartel soldiers from the shoreline. He killed three and wounded a fourth.

In the weeks that followed, Bimini's police force made international headlines for bringing down the leaders of one of the biggest and most violent drug cartels in the world.

Superintendent Poitier was singled out for special recognition for killing the drug lord and narco-terrorist Concha Dores. He received the Queen's Police Medal for services to policing and the community.

The morning after the gunfight and death of Concha Dores, Seabrook checked the long line. He drove across the glowing blue water of the Great Bahama Bank and worried about what he would find on the hooks. He quickly spotted one of the marker buoys and steered towards it. As on most days, he was alone out on an empty sea.

He lifted the giant orange buoy and raised the horizontal line than ran across the seafloor. He gaffed onto it and began slowly driving down the half-mile line.

He checked every single one of the thirty hooks and, by the end, felt immense relief. There were no sharks on the hooks, and all the human flesh had completely vanished—consumed by the myriad denizens of the sea.

Chapter 72
Afterward

Seabrook gave Aja the good news about the long line and set about fixing breakfast. The kitchen smelled like brewing coffee and the diced onions and butter sizzling in the frying pan. He mixed in scrambled eggs and made enough for four people.

After breakfast, they all went down the dock to feed Clara for the last time. It was low tide, and the water was pale green and very shallow. The algae-covered pilings were exposed to the air and smelled like drying seaweed. They could see the shark resting in the sand near the dock.

Myron and Mookie called to her and waved their arms, trying to get her attention. She must have anticipated getting fed, because she came splashing to the surface. Myron threw a mackerel into the water. The small nurse shark went straight for it. She had fully healed and grown more robust. She was now big enough that she swallowed the whole mackerel in one gulp. She swam around the pen searching for more food.

Seabrook and Aja decided it was time to free her. The boys helped Seabrook take down the chicken wire walls of the enclosure. Aja watched from the dock, because she didn't want to get her wounds wet.

Once the chicken wire walls were gone, Clara swam into the channel, and they never saw her again. She left so quickly that it was anticlimactic and made them all feel a little sad—but she was a wild animal after all.

They looked at the smooth green stillness of the lagoon for a moment, wondering where she'd gone.

While the boys stared across the water, looking for Clara, Seabrook glanced at the dock.

"Look," he said to Aja.

Aja turned and studied the wooden planks. "It's gone," she said.

It was true. The bloodstain of the dead man had disappeared. All the planks looked the same color now.

Later that afternoon two seagulls landed on the pilings. One glided down to the walkway and cavorted across the planks, pecking at where the stain used to be.

Chapter 73
Leaving Bimini

On the next Saturday morning, Seabrook and Aja drove the boys to the Bimini airport station in the Whaler. They rode down the channel and past the moored sailboats in silence. When it was time to board the seaplane, the boys, especially Mookie, started to cry and promised not to forget them.

Aja gave them a piece of paper with her and Seabrook's home phone number and physical address, and also the address and phone number of their offices at Rosenstiel.

"You can call or write us for help," Seabrook said.

"Anytime," Aja said. "And you must come and see us if you come to Miami."

"I would like that," Myron said.

"Me too," Mookie said.

Both boys grew very emotional as their departure became imminent.

"I will miss you both," Myron said in shaky voice.

"I will too." Mookie began to sob, and tears streaked his face.

Seabrook and Aja gave them big hugs. "We will never forget you," Aja said. "You are so brave."

"You are good-hearted, intelligent boys, and you will make fine men one day," Seabrook said. "Keep reading books. Get a good education."

The boys smiled and nodded.

Myron and Mookie went up the ladder stairs to the open passenger door of the seaplane. They stood briefly on the small landing at the top and waved goodbye.

Seabrook and Aja waved back. Then the boys went inside. Ten minutes later, the plane left.

They flew to Nassau and reunited with their mother and sister, Carmelita, who was soon released from Princess Margaret Hospital.

The Sea Cherubs were starting a new and better life.

On Monday, Seabrook and Aja returned to Miami for a ten-day convalescence. They rested and healed and visited doctors. Going to the mall and movie theater gave them culture shock—so many people walking about aimlessly. So many giant, soft people endlessly eating and buying unnecessary junk, apparently without a care in the world.

Seabrook contacted the manufacturer of the tracking equipment and managed to replace the ultrasonic receivers that Bastareaud had destroyed.

After the new receivers arrived, Dr. Nixon drove them and the new equipment back across the Gulf Stream to Bimini in the Aquasport speedboat to finish their field research.

Chapter 74
The Missing Prisoner

The events of what became known as the Bimini Lagoon Gunfight grew into a major news story and continued to unfold for months. Reporters followed the fate of the only cartel member to survive that day, a notorious assassin they called Pelon, the Hairless One, or the Shark Eye Killer. The newspapers and TV news described how he had been shot through the neck and taken to a hospital. He was wanted in the Bahamas and the U.S. as well as in Colombia, where he was believed to have killed hundreds of men, women, and children. After several months of legal maneuvering, it was determined that the cases against Pelon weren't strong enough in the Bahamas or the U.S. to guarantee a conviction.

In the end, international authorities agreed to extradite Pelon back to Colombia to stand trial for his many crimes. Somehow the local Colombian police "bungled" the transfer of the prisoner from one location to another and Pelon "escaped."

Unverified reports indicated that he was given to the Medellín Cartel, the Dores Cartel's arch rivals. Pelon was believed to have tortured and killed many members of the Medellín Cartel. Officially, he was listed as a missing person, and one report speculated that he'd escaped to Brazil.

However, rumors abounded that he was tortured for a week by his enemies, kept conscious the whole time by a doctor, then put in a barrel of acid while still alive.

Chapter 75
Sea Goddess

When Seabrook and Aja came back to Bimini from Miami, their days returned to the idyllic, honeymoon-like time they'd experienced before the Earless Man and the Reverend Bastareaud had turned everything upside down. Their daily routine went back to normal—except, of course, their provisional family had been broken up: the Sea Cherubs and Clara were gone. Still, it almost seemed as if they'd woken from a horrible nightmare and had resumed their real lives once more.

After spending most of the first day back in the sea, they showered together and examined each other's wounds. The warm water sprayed over their naked bodies. It relaxed them and loosened their muscles. It was a needed tonic, and they indulged themselves by having a longer soak than usual—using more fresh water than they normally would. They didn't mind, not this time.

Aja shampooed Seabrook's hair, and then bent down on one knee in front of him. She gently washed the stapled wound on his leg, then kissed it for good luck. As she stood up, she ran her fingers delicately up his thigh, then took him in her hand. She looked him in the eyes, one eyebrow raised in fun, and gave him a nice squeeze and a slow, flirtatious tug. Instantly, he was crazy for her, but he reined it back—for the moment.

Seabrook washed her hair, gently kneading her scalp with his fingertips. Then he got down on bended knee to soap her poor foot where her little toes had been bitten off. After rinsing the suds away, he lifted her foot by the heel and kissed her wounds for good luck. He set her foot down and looked up at her glistening naked body. A sea goddess! And she was smiling at him!

Then he slowly kissed his way up her naked legs, left and right, left and right, climbing from her scraped knees to the miracle place between her thighs, making her crazy like he was.

She stood still as long as she could stand it.

Then she grabbed his head with both hands, and they made love right there in the bathroom ... then in the bedroom. Afterward, they lay tangled together on damp sheets and almost fell asleep.

For dinner they ate bowls of hot conch chowder seasoned with Tabasco from their favorite restaurant. On the side they had thick pieces of sweet Bahamian bread toasted and buttered. The spicy chowder and sweet bread together tasted like heaven. Later, they relaxed and sipped rum with wedges of lime and read a good novel out loud to each other. The sea air swept in through the open glass door. It blowed the curtains and caressed their skin with invisible feathers.

They took turns listening to each other read. There were no sounds other than their own voices, save the occasional distant cry of a seabird settling down for the night. In this way they absorbed the story and gazed meditatively out at the lagoon, watching the brassy light slowly drain from the sky and the color of the blue water and distant green mangroves darken to twilight.

At the very end of the evening, they lay down side by side on their bed. They slipped under the sheet and rested, heads on soft pillows. Aja's hair, like threads of black silk, lay across the white linen next to Seabrook's Celtic red. They kissed and shut their eyes. Her missing toes throbbed with phantom pain, and his leg still ached from the spear and knife. While they sank slowly into sleep, and breathed more deeply, the sea came seeping into their dreams for its nightly visit.

The ocean rolled through their nocturnal minds once more. Knowledge older than language and beyond language ... scales and gills and mermaid tails ... schools of baby sharks, blue rainbow depths, and trumpetfish.

Even Lennie, the green moray eel with filmy eyes, was there, gliding half blind on the eternal currents. Swimming deep to the secret vaults where Razormouth and other unknown species lived invisible to human eyes.

In the sun-sparkled surf, the Sea Cherubs played and laughed. They were safe.

The air conditioner rattled and creaked cold air into the bedroom but could not wake them. Or separate them. Any of them.

They drifted deeper.

Sound asleep, Aja pulled the extra blanket over herself and pressed close against Seabrook.

Sound asleep, Seabrook stretched his arm across her body and murmured with affection and sweet recognition ... "*Amphitrite.*"

Epilogue

"Not only is the Universe stranger than we think, it is stranger than we can think."—Heisenberg

At the end of August, it was time to take in the long line. The calm sea stretched its immense turquoise surface in all directions and touched the encircling horizon. The sky had just one cloud drifting across its vaulted blue arch.

Seabrook and Aja started at the south end and unsnapped one hook rig after another and laid them out on the deck of the Whaler, nice and neat. The steel hooks glinted wet in the sunlight.

They also pulled in and coiled the long line in a separate pile.

After three hours, they were nearly done. They had taken in twenty-eight hooks, and there were only two more in the sea.

Something small and heavy was on the second-to-last hook. It was also an extremely powerful swimmer for its size. The mystery fish tried to swim away as they pulled it to the surface. It jerked hard against the line.

When they hoisted it up to the waves, they immediately recognized the creature as a small Razormouth shark, just four feet long—a newborn?

Its hide was thundercloud gray and dotted with strange markings like an alien alphabet. The shark seemed able to make the patterns appear or disappear at will.

Seabrook and Aja were incredibly excited. This was the type specimen they had hoped for all summer. Capturing this animal would change their lives!

Fortunately, Aja always brought her Nikonos underwater camera to the long line. They wanted to get photos of the living fish in its natural habitat—before collection.

They roped Razormouth's tail and tied the fish alongside the Whaler by the hook in its mouth and the rope tied at the caudal peduncle, or base of its tail.

Aja jumped in the sea and photographed the shark from every angle. It had a disproportionately large head and mouth. It also seemed to have the anatomy of a male. They would have to confirm it during the necropsy.

Seabrook measured the shark as best he could—the measurements would be more accurate once it was dead and no longer moving.

This was the first time in their lives that they were going to intentionally kill a shark. To establish a new species, a type specimen had to be captured and stuck in a museum.

But every time they tried to raise the shark out of the water, it spun and thrashed wildly. Once they nearly raised it over the side, and it closed its mouth and clamped onto the Whaler in a fearsome display of power. Razormouth bit clean through a chunk of the fiberglass gunwale with its incredible jaws.

They dropped it back into the sea. No shark had ever bitten through the thick fiberglass wall of the boat before.

They tried to lift the shark into the boat again. This time it blinded them with a brilliant flash of light like a lightening blast from its body. Afterward, glittering small dots floated in the air like golden snowflakes until their eyes could return to normal.

"That came from its body," Aja said, blinking.

"What an amazing creature." Seabrook sat back, waiting for his eyes to recover. "He absolutely blinded us."

"A brand-new species," she said. "Wait till Dr. Nixon sees this."

Gradually their eyesight returned to normal. The fiberglass chunk of the gunwale floated across the waves.

Seabrook pulled the shark's nose up out of the sea so its mouth opened, revealing teeth from another world: two-inch gray blades unlike any teeth they'd ever seen—especially on a juvenile. The giant mouth reminded Seabrook of a bear trap. He wondered if they would find pieces of coral in its stomach.

"How are we going to get it in the boat?" he said.

"Wait until the world sees it," she said.

"Feel the skin."

"That is crazy." It felt like steel but with electricity in it. "It would be real hard to tag him if you wanted to. The skin is so tough."

"My God, what a beautiful creature."

The small cloud in the sky crossed in front of the sun. The light from above diminished, then came back full strength. The universe seemed to blink. And just like that, an unsettling feeling came over both of them—as surprising as it was powerful. It changed their mood from ecstatic jubilation to distress and worry. An explanation would have been impossible to put into words: maybe because an adult Razormouth had saved Aja's life, or maybe because they'd seen so much horror and death that summer, or maybe something even deeper was happening; but what they were doing suddenly felt terribly wrong.

They looked at each other, then at the strange fish: how many existed in the world? As far as they knew there were only two. Maybe a mother and one juvenile?

A moment passed.

"Let's let him go," Seabrook said.

"Yes."

They carefully extracted the hook from the corner of its mouth and untied the tail rope. Then they stuck the shark at the base of the dorsal fin with one of the prototype satellite tracking tags. This way, if the technology worked properly and could handle the extreme pressures and temperatures of the deep, they could track the shark in the future.

The fish sank to the bottom and lay in the sand. They could see it from the boat. Seabrook and Aja put on their snorkel gear and went into the sea. They finned down to the bottom and picked the fish up. They took turns swimming with the shark to make seawater flow through its gills. The whole time they touched the animal's skin they felt a mild electric current—like static electricity underwater.

As the shark revived, its tail serpentined from side to side. They took photographs of each other swimming with the otherworldly fish.

Once they felt him take over and start swimming independently, they let him go.

The Razormouth pup seemed lost at first and circled around them aimlessly for several minutes.

Then he found his way. His tail swept from side to side as he disappeared into the distance, taking all of his secrets with him, into the veiling deep.

They climbed back into the Whaler.

They took off their snorkel gear and sat still, resting and stunned for a moment by all that had happened. They drank fresh water from the gallon jug they always brought. Now that the excitement of catching and swimming with Razormouth was beginning to subside, a soft weariness came over them. It had been a full day's work.

The sun had coppered and reddened their faces, arms, and legs, despite layers of sunscreen. Their wrists were tired and felt swollen, and their hands were chafed from pulling in a half mile of line.

It was time to go home. The scorching heat of midday had passed and the wind had increased so that the sea began to roll more noticeably.

The Whaler, laden with the coiled line, giant buoys, and hook rigs, was heavier and more difficult to maneuver. It plowed its way through the troughs and waves. Seawater occasionally splashed through the hole that Razormouth had bitten in the gunwale.

Seabrook held the tiller and Aja stood at the bow holding the anchor line as they cut a fleeting wake across the Caribbean Sea toward the blue horizon.

If you enjoyed Razormouth

Please consider leaving a short review at Amazon.com or other online site; reader reviews are extremely important for the life of a book or series. Your support is deeply appreciated. Thank you.

Razormouth is the second book in the **Wild Ocean** series of sea thrillers. For more information or if you'd like to be notified when the next volume is released, please follow Howard Butcher on Amazon.com, BookBub, or use the contact link at the following site to leave a note and email address:

www.howardbutcher.com

www.facebook.com/HowardButcherAuthor

About the Author

HOWARD BUTCHER has worked as a shark researcher in the Caribbean Sea, apprentice commercial diver in the Gulf of Mexico, and as the manager of a horse farm in the San Juan Mountains. Today he teaches high school English and lives in Colorado with his wife Sue and their children. His other works include the sea thriller **Jonah, A Novel of Men and the Sea** and the children's book **The Dancing Pumpkin**—also the animated show **The Dancing Pumpkin and the Ogre's Plot**.

Lightning Source UK Ltd.
Milton Keynes UK
UKHW040953190122
397370UK00008B/332/J